MERCER GIRLS

OTHER BOOKS BY LIBBIE HAWKER

MERCER GIRLS

LIBBIE HAWKER

LAKE UNION
PUBLISHING

F
HAW

Text copyright © 2016 Libbie Hawker

Published by Lake Union Publishing, Seattle
www.apub.com

ISBN-13: 9781503951976
ISBN-10: 1503951979

Cover design by Laura Klynstra

Printed in the United States of America

*For the toughest, smartest, truest women in all of
Seattle: Emily, Devin, and Kelsey.
And for Paul, who introduced me to Seattle's
vibrant history.*

PART 1
MARCH–MAY 1864

CHAPTER ONE
DESPERATE MEASURES

The thaw had come early to Massachusetts. That was one piece of good news and cause enough for gladness, even if the war still lumbered on. The great rebellion was, by now, a fact—a truth sinking grim and cold into the nation's bones. War rolled across the hearts of every woman and man in the States: towering, dark, inescapable as a thunderhead. It cast a shadow black enough to dim the brightest light and left a chill on the skin that neither fires nor furs could entirely chase away.

But in spite of the rebellion's stoic onward march, the first touch of spring was kindly to the town of Lowell. The early warmth had nearly cleared the gray-brown patches of snow from the shoulders of wide streets. Winter's bleakness was melting off, running in tiny rivers between the cracks of the cobblestones. Noon light glimmered among the cobbles, netting the street in silver. The bright sky reflected from the roadway with an energetic bounce, a dancing flash—with something close to cheer.

That stir of silver light seemed a good omen to Josephine. Or at least, it seemed as if it *ought* to represent some intentional good, some deliberate act of kindness from the Lord. As she rounded the corner of one of the great redbrick millhouses and headed toward the river, she made up her mind to take the morning's delicate beauty as a sign from God—or from one of His lesser angels, at least—that all would be well. *Her* luck would soon change, even if Lowell and the war dragged on forever in their present courses, grinding toward some dim, ignominious fate.

The lace of sunlight along the cobbles might have been enough to make Josephine smile—truly smile, with no determination necessary—if she hadn't been so twisted up inside with anxiety. Even if the sparkle and flash of light and thaw were indisputable signs from God, Josephine felt ill at ease. Just being in that place made her shiver. Amid the long, drab avenues of the industrial district, with the silent, soot-darkened facades of the textile mills rearing above, she was insignificant and weak—a small, furtive thing. She was a mouse picking its way along the floor of a vast canyon that still echoed with the whispers of ghosts. Josephine had had her fill of being a mouse—of being silent and small. Yet even now, as she reached out to grasp her future—her last frayed shred of hope—she couldn't help but cringe and wish for a safe place to hide. The eerie stillness of the mill district was enough by itself to give anyone the whim-whams. But Josephine's predicament was worse than mere jitters. If anyone recognized her—if she were spotted here, wearing her best dress (such as it was), making her way over the cobblestones toward Merrimack Street, where she certainly had no good excuse to be . . . A cascade of images tumbled through her head, all the possible consequences that might result from this mad, desperate folly. None of them were pretty.

"Make way, Miss, if you please!" Josephine gave a jump at the gruff shout from the road behind her. The man's tone was thick and harsh— just the kind that always made her fearful—but she yielded the street at once, swinging aside with a natural, businesslike efficiency, as if walking through the great, stifling ravines of Lowell's shuttered textile mills was all in a day's routine. She pressed against a long redbrick building to let the wagon pass, and the driver raised his hat in thanks. He was ruddy-faced, and the hard, deep lines of his skin were darkened by Lowell's soot. His horses were haggard and down-headed, but they pulled their burden with apparent ease, and although Josephine couldn't see into the wagon's bed as it trundled by, its loud, loose-jointed rattle told her plainly enough that it was empty.

The rough brick of the building seemed to press right back against her. It leaned its cold, hard weight into her flesh, willing her to feel its hollowness and stillness—the vast, echoing fact of its inutility. It was, like virtually all the silent hulks along this avenue, a textile mill. Almost every large building in Lowell housed a mill, where raw cotton was spun into thread, and thread was woven and dyed into uncountable yards of fabric—broadcloth and calico; poplin and lawn; gingham and muslin and fine, light organdy. Lowell was an empire of cotton mills, and the Good Lord knew there were not a few of them. But since the rebellion, most mills, like most wagons, were empty.

When the wagon had passed, Josephine breathed as deeply as her stays would allow and stepped gratefully away from the building's palpable barrenness. She peered up at the sky—a wash of pale, wintery blue running in a straight line between two high rows of unrelieved brick, an avenue of well-shined silver stretching all the way down to the river. The day's brightness made her squint and tickled her nose with the threat of a sneeze. The sky was without its customary haze of coal smoke, the ever-present, grimy, orange-brown fog that Lowell wore as proudly as a lady wears a flower-trimmed hat. Of late there were far more clear days than hazy; more than half the mills in Lowell had closed, for the South kept a firm grip on its cotton, and no one could say when the factories might return to life—or if they ever would.

This dismal place is making me grim, Josephine reflected. *It won't do to greet Mr. Mercer with a scowl on my face. The sooner I'm away, the better.*

She lifted the hem of her skirt with care and hurried across the cobblestones. The crinoline beneath her skirt was old—a cast-off from an elderly aunt—and had to be handled just so, or it would buckle on one side and bang against her thigh. It was far too stiff for current fashions, thanks to the real horsehair worked into its weave. But Josephine had never troubled herself much over keeping current with her dress. She had long since decided that she simply didn't care if she were outmoded. An old crinoline could do its job just as well as a fancy new one, with boning and flounces and soft, machine-made fabric. And besides, who ever laid eyes on a crinoline, save for the woman who wore it? Ruffles and pin tucks were superfluities, and nothing to which an honest undergarment ought to aspire. Josephine bolstered herself with a scornful sniff as she made her way toward the river. Her stiff underskirt swung, bell-like, around quick-stepping feet. If the stylish ladies of Lowell only knew what dwelt beneath Josephine's petticoats, the scandal of it all might actually transport a few straight into their graves. The horsehair crinoline was nothing beside her dreadfully dated drawers. *Those* would certainly send the fashion-plate brigade into fits!

But what did it matter, after all? Unless they left the dying textile town for cities with broader prospects—Boston, New York, or the capital—the most persnickety dressers in Lowell would soon be wearing horsehair and Grandmama's woolen drawers, too. The war against the southern states showed no signs of ending. The supply of cotton had dwindled to a trickle and would further slow to a desultory drip. Even in Lowell, a city built by spinning jennies and the flying shuttles of industrial looms—a town where spindles of milled yarn outnumbered even the smokestacks in the sky—current fashion was a luxury not many women could afford. Not for much longer, at any rate.

At last, Josephine left the eerie stillness of the avenue and turned onto Merrimack Street. The city came to life around her with a vigorous bustle, a bold, deliberate defiance of the disused mills and the empty riverside wharves where ships once waited, their holds laden with great cream-white, sun-scented bales of cotton. Wagons plodded along the road, and here and there smart carriages with teams of four went darting between the slower conveyances, their drivers shouting to make way. The rumble of wheels and the clatter of hooves on stone rang out in a ceaseless din. The noise echoed from the high walls of the great brick buildings, a boisterous redoubling of sound. The sheer *noise* of the town made Josephine's head ache and her heart pound. Here on Merrimack Street, she felt more hopelessly exposed than she had in Lowell's silent canyons, as if all the eyes of the city would turn to her at any moment—as if the entirety of Lowell would know at a glance exactly what she was up to.

Two women paused to greet one another outside the shoemaker's shop, each carrying a pair of button boots in need of resoling. They nodded to Josephine as she made her way past. She scarcely returned the courtesy but kept her eyes fixed on the road at her feet, fearful that she would recognize the women from church society and that she would soon become the subject of their gossip. She passed a carpenter's workshop, which emitted the pungent, burnt-hair odor of hot glue, and somewhere in the shop's interior a mallet thumped hard and fast, mirroring the racing of her heart. A newspaper boy made his way up the street, shouting over the hubbub, "Ulys'z Grant now Lieutenant General! 'Spected to take command of all forces! Read it here first, read it *here*!" The boy eyed Josephine eagerly, hoping for two pennies for his paper. But she shook her head curtly, and with a sullen shrug, he moved on.

As she crossed in front of a long, narrow alley, a commotion of thrashing and snarls erupted at her feet. Josephine stifled a shriek as two small dogs burst from the alley, tangled in a fight, so intent in their fury that they nearly threw themselves beneath a wagon's wheels. The surprise left an unpleasant, tingling sensation racing along her limbs and a coppery taste on her tongue.

To calm herself, she reached into the pocket of her dress and pulled out a folded bit of newsprint. She had torn it carefully from a recent edition of the *New York Times*. The scrap featured a letter—a rebuttal to a rather critical and insinuating article, which the *Times* had printed a week before, questioning the motives and morals of one Mr. A. S. Mercer, who had recently arrived in Lowell from the far West on what was, Josephine had to admit, a rather peculiar errand. As she walked, she read the letter—not for the first time. She took in Mercer's elegant phrases with mingled hope and excitement, though in truth she knew it so well by now that she could have recited its contents by heart.

> In accordance with your request and to sat-
> isfy many inquiring minds, I make a statement
> of the reasons why I have spent so much
> time and money in the endeavor to introduce
> a female migration into Washington Territory.

The territory, so the letter explained, had been settled by young men from the eastern states—educated and principled, men of great quality who had found small prospects for either home or fortune in the crowded, war-ravaged East. And so those enterprising men had ventured west, carving a new land of promise from the richly forested hills where the frontier met the sea.

> Churches and schoolhouses there are, but
> the great elevating, refining, and moralizing
> element—true women—are wanting. Not that
> the ladies of Washington Territory are less
> pure or high minded than those of any other
> land, but the limited number of them leave
> the good work greater than they can perform.

Josephine skimmed down to Mercer's final lines, though even before she had found them, the memorized words were already ringing in her head, a hopeful echo that straightened her spine and injected a lively spring into her step.

> **Those who accompany me must not expect to occupy a flower garden, or live upon sweet perfume, but must calculate that they are going into the vineyard to labor, and that their labor will be rewarded. Hoping that this rough sketch may answer to satisfy those who would know my motive, I am, very truly, your obedient servant.**

A. S. MERCER

Beside the name, Josephine had marked down an address in pencil—an address that she had carefully ferreted out through feigned casual conversation with her neighbors and the ladies of her church society. Uncovering the whereabouts of A. S. Mercer had been a long and delicate task. Some women had flatly refused to speak of the man, believing his intentions to be *questionable* at the very best. Those who would discuss him did so behind fluttering hands, their eyes popping over the delightful scandal of it all. *Imagine,* they had said, *a stranger from Washington Territory—or so he claims as his origin, if you can believe him—standing up at a podium in the square and exhorting young ladies to leave their homes, their fathers, their beaus, and travel with him—actually travel with him—out into the West! Oh, he says he wants teachers, but let us be frank. Any man who proposes to traipse off with unaccompanied ladies in tow can only be after a particular sort of lady. Teachers, indeed! Josephine, you should have seen it!*

Never before had Lowell soared to such happy heights of turpitude. Mr. Mercer was both devil and saint, for even as he proposed to spirit the city's young ladies off to the far West like some villain from a fairy story, he *had* provided Lowell with a distraction. In these dark times, with so many men off to war, an equal number already killed, and half of those left in the city unemployed, cooling their heels in bars and gutters, there was nothing Lowell needed more than a distraction. And so Josephine had pried with a delicate touch, sifting through the ample gossip to discern the exact location of Mr. A. S. Mercer, without—she hoped and prayed—arousing the slightest bit of suspicion.

She checked the address once more. Many small offices and shops lined Merrimack Street, and each had numbers stenciled on their door-frames. Josephine noted the addresses as she walked. Narrow, dusty windows crowded beside heavy doors, and in the shadows of the brick mill buildings, the glass of each window looked as dark green and murky as pond water, concealing rather than revealing whatever lay within. This was not a well-to-do avenue. It hadn't been, even during Lowell's best days. If Josephine had indeed discovered the correct address, then Mr. Mercer—in fact, all of Washington Territory—must have exceedingly tight purse strings. This dingy avenue made for a dubious base of operations.

It doesn't matter, Josephine told herself. *Even if I consign myself to life in a hovel, with wolves howling around my door, it will be preferable to my present situation.*

To keep her spirits up as she searched for Mercer's office, Josephine recited her favorite lines from his letter to the *New York Times.* These, of all his elegant words, filled her with the greatest hope. In fact, she admitted with some surprise, they seemed to have imprinted themselves upon her soul. These words were the very same that had inspired Josephine to this fit of reckless and uncharacteristic bravery.

"'I appeal to high-minded women,'" she quoted quietly, so as not to draw attention, "'to go out into the West to cultivate the higher and purer facilities of man by casting about him those refining influences that true women always carry with them; to build happy homes and let true sunlight shine round the hearthstone.'"

True sunlight. How long had it been since she had felt that warmth and brightness? She had lived without happiness for so long. *Lived?* Josephine choked back a scornful laugh. The shadow under which she dwelt couldn't rightly be labeled a life. A mere *existence* was all anyone might call it. Josephine was getting old—she had recently turned thirty-five—but still she prayed that it wasn't too late to find happiness, to actually *live*. Since her first perusal of Mr. Mercer's letter, Josephine had felt her shroud of shadows lift. Bright, warm light spilled down on inner vistas, and her future looked as vast, as emerald green and rich, as she imagined Washington Territory to be.

Josephine's mind was quite made up. It had been many years since she had last worked as a teacher, but all the same, she was resolved to apply for the position. She, unlike the flap jaws of her church society, would take this A. S. Mercer at his word; she would not assume wickedness where none had yet been demonstrated. And even if he proved to be a wicked man . . . well, still she would manage, if the Lord was willing. She would go to any length—and travel any distance—to find the peace she longed for.

Josephine slowed. She had drawn very near the Merrimack River, swollen from the rapid thaw. Its crisp, earthy scent filled the street, driving back the everyday odors of pipe smoke, horse dung, and the bitter, chemical bluntness of industry. She found office number 108 and peered at its small window. Affixed to the inside of the glass was a sign—and though it was neatly written in a clear, steady hand, Josephine could see that it was made from nothing more elegant than plain brown butcher's paper. It read:

**ASA SHINN MERCER
OF SEATTLE, WASH. TERR.
INQUIRIES WELCOME**

"This is it," Josephine said briskly, though she spoke to nobody but herself. The moment had come. Now she would reach out with a strong, steady hand and seize a new life. Now she would make herself anew—shape herself into a woman who could hold her head up high. She felt rather tempted to get the jitters, but she breathed deeply as she folded up the scrap of newspaper and returned it to her pocket. This was not an advantageous time for flying all to pieces. Washington Territory was waiting for her. All she had to do now was keep her wits about her, and inquire.

Josephine entered the small office without knocking. She stopped short just over the threshold, blinking as her eyes adjusted from the brightness of a clear March day to the dim, cramped interior, lit by the sallow glow of a single, old-fashioned gaslight. A large desk dominated the space. Its surface was nicked and pitted, and here and there, in the chips along its edges, the warm, honey hue of freshly exposed oak showed against the lustrous, dark patina of age. Several neat stacks of paper stood to one side, of equal height and spaced precisely. A man rose from a squealing chair with prompt grace; he bowed over that broad desk with a fluidity that took Josephine aback. She stood speechless, still holding the open door with one hand.

"Good afternoon," the man said. He was dressed smartly in a dark velvet coat with wide lapels, with a waistcoat and bow tie of matching green. His curly black hair was fixed in three elaborate waves—one over each ear, and one arching high at the crown of his head, giving him an altogether dandy appearance. His eyes were a bold, demanding shade of blue, and one had the smallest suggestion of a cast—a feature which only added to his considerable presence, rather than diminishing his charm. Though his beard was thick and full, Josephine could see that his cheeks were smooth, the corners of his eyes unlined. He couldn't have been older than twenty-four or -five.

"Good afternoon," Josephine replied. She glanced around the small office. Its walls were unadorned, and their exposed red brick gave off a faint odor of mildew. A file cabinet stood in one corner, topped by a dusty, copper-lusterware vase that held nothing, not even a few twigs of winter greenery. A John Bull hat, banded with silver ribbon, lay beside it.

"I am looking for Mr. A. S. Mercer," Josephine said after a pause.

"You have found him. Please, come in."

Josephine turned away from him as she shut the door, the better to master the surprise that had, she felt certain, blanked and paled her face. The gossip mills of Lowell had painted Mr. Mercer as a rake; Josephine had envisioned him an old, leering man, with grasping, claw-fingered hands, an accompanying reek of tobacco, and an unpleasant laugh— perhaps even drooling a little. Even with this unpleasant expectation, she had been thoroughly prepared to make her escape to Washington Territory. If she had to suffer long-distance travel in the company of a profligate, she was ready to withstand that trial. To be confronted instead by *this* vision of A. S. Mercer, fresh as a schoolboy and smart as a lord, left Josephine fairly dumbfounded.

Mercer gestured toward a narrow bench that stood opposite his desk. Josephine edged her hem and crinoline up with her heel, moving as warily as if she confronted a viper, then sank down on the bench. The horsehair crackled against her petticoats, and she was conscious for the first time in years of her shabby appearance. She had donned her very best dress—a soft, lavender-and-brown muslin that she had tamboured herself many years ago. But now, faced with Mercer's high style and obvious youth, Josephine realized just how dated and moth-eaten she must look. *It's a wonder the women of Lowell haven't dropped dead at the sight of me already!* She didn't even have a snood to gather up her hair—she had rolled it into a bun, which pulled back her rather thin, plain brown hair severely. She had searched for her snood that morning as she'd hastily made ready for her trip to Merrimack Street. But it had vanished without a trace. A good many of her personal items had disappeared of late—especially if they had any valuable embellishment, like the tiny seed pearls that had adorned her snood.

Josephine arranged her embroidered skirt along the bench as Mr. Mercer resumed his seat.

He said, "How may I be of service, Miss . . . ?"

"Carey," she supplied quickly, glancing out the window. "Josephine Carey."

"Miss Carey."

"I've heard you are looking for women to move west, to Washington Territory. I've heard it's teachers you want."

"Yes," he said. But a flash of doubt moved across his face, drawing down his dark brows for an instant and shadowing his eyes before he could replace that hesitation with studied calm. "You are a teacher?"

"I was. Until very recently," she hastened to add. In truth, it had been more than ten years since Josephine had taught. But, she reasoned, whether an event was recent or in the distant past was all a matter of perspective. "I am ready to go west. I was most inspired by your rebuttal in the *Times*, and shame on them for slandering you so!"

Mercer's smile lit his blue eyes with an impish twinkle. "If I'd been an old man, I think the newspapers—and even the rumor circles of Lowell—would have passed me by with very little comment. But young as I am, I believe they suspect that I plan to steal women away for my own gratification. Perhaps they assume I'm setting up a Turkish harem."

"But it is teachers you want?"

"Indeed. We've plenty of young men in Seattle, all of them high-minded and thirsty for knowledge. I founded a university there some years ago, but I'm sorry to report that the current administrators lack the faculty to staff it well."

A university! The mere thought fairly took Josephine's breath away. She had loved teaching little children, back in the days of her youth, when she had still felt hope for a bright future. She had often dreamed of loftier goals, too—of founding a preparatory academy or tutoring college scholars. But she had never allowed herself to hope for an opportunity to teach at a university.

Mercer noted her sudden eagerness. "Have you any experience with college students, Miss Carey?"

"No," she admitted, "but I have plenty with younger students, including those studying for entrance examinations. And I'm certain I could be useful to you, Mr. Mercer. If you'll only give me the chance—"

His quiet, rather bashful laugh brought Josephine up short.

"I appreciate your interest," Mercer said, "but I'm not certain you're quite right . . . that is, that you are entirely suited . . . to the, er . . ." He dropped his eyes and gave a helpless little shrug. His cheeks flushed a surprisingly bright shade.

"But I am an excellent teacher, sir," Josephine said quickly. "That is what you're looking for, isn't it? Women to educate all those young men, to impart knowledge, to influence them toward good acts and higher ideals."

"Yes, yes," said Mercer rather dismissively. He drew a deep breath, and Josephine had the impression that he was steadying his nerves. "Teachers—yes. There will be work for any woman who comes west with me, if that is what she desires. Well-paid work, too. Seventy-five dollars a month—that's what we've settled on for a teacher's salary."

Josephine folded her hands in her lap, pinched the skin between thumb and finger to keep her eyes from popping, and prayed fervently that Mr. Mercer did not see. *Seventy-five a month!* It was nearly twice what a man with a trade could earn in Lowell. Only the mill owners made more—back when the mills had been running at full capacity. Josephine had only sought a way out of Massachusetts, some distance between an old life and a new. But with seventy-five a month, why—she could found an academy after all!

"That is very generous," she said calmly. "I'd be happy to take a position as a teacher in Washington Territory, if you'll have me."

Mercer's lips compressed within the thicket of his beard.

"What's the matter?" Josephine smiled as she spoke, struggling to fend off her rising desperation—a prickling, goading force that was, moment by moment, issuing ever stronger commands to leap up from the bench and shriek in wordless panic and helpless desire. "Have you already found all the teachers you need?"

He gave a short, self-deprecating laugh. "No—indeed, no! It's only that . . . well, Miss Carey, I'm afraid it's a rather indelicate subject, and I know you ladies of Lowell are virtuous. How can I say it gently? I don't wish to offend you, please understand—"

"Better out with it," she said, more brusquely than intended. She had expected far more enthusiasm from this western stranger, who, after all, faced a rather onerous task. Public opinion was not in Mercer's favor. He had not found Lowell bursting with eager teachers, leaping at the opportunity to be carted off by a stranger to the very edge of the frontier. Josephine's dream of a better life, so newly kindled, was already guttering and smoking, on the verge of being snuffed out for good.

"What I am truly seeking," said Mercer with slow, deliberate care, "is brides."

Josephine leaned back on her bench, startled to silence. Suddenly the delicate meaning, so carefully stitched into Mercer's rebuttal to the *Times*, became mortifyingly clear. All that talk of hearth and home— why hadn't she perceived it at once? She had always considered herself as a sensible, clear-thinking woman, capable of reading between the lines. But just like that, she had allowed her own enthusiasm—her desperation—to blind her to the truth.

"Brides," she said, when she had recovered command of her tongue. "I see."

"And while I have no doubt that you are quite a capable instructor, Miss Carey, I question whether the men of Seattle will . . . that is to say, whether *you* will—"

"I am not as old as I look." Josephine sat up straighter.

"I see. You are . . . er . . . if I may ask . . . ?"

"Thirty-five." The moment the admission was out of her mouth, Josephine bunched her fists in her skirt. She was gripped by the urge to tear the bun from her own head. Why hadn't she given a younger age? She could pass for twenty-nine. Or thirty-one, at worst. Desperation clawed at her chest, thrashing in a frenzy as she felt her last hope for happiness slipping beyond her grasp. She blurted, "I am still capable of . . ." She cleared her throat, looking away from Mercer's intense, blue stare. "Of *bearing*. Pardon my indelicacy, but let us speak of the real business at hand."

Mercer's face flushed again—Josephine felt a reciprocal flame on her own cheeks—but his smile was relieved. "Let us, indeed," he said. "You are unattached, then, I take it? That is to say, if you were to receive a proposal . . . if you found a man of your liking . . ."

Mentally, she amended his words. *If your greatly advanced age doesn't send all the Territory's bachelors running for the hills.* But she nodded with instant acceptance. "I would be very pleased to marry, if I were to find a man of my liking in Seattle."

She hoped Mercer took her renewed blush for a virtuous woman's embarrassment at such open discussion of marital matters.

"In that case, Miss Carey, I shall be glad to have you."

Relief and joy surged in Josephine's middle, so suddenly and with such force that she could only stare at the man in awe.

"There are two conditions," Mercer said cautiously. "First, we must leave tomorrow morning—quite early, I'm afraid. It gives you little time to prepare, I know, but I have already made arrangements for our transportation. If you have any business you must see to before you can go—"

"None," she interrupted, shaking her head vigorously. She blinked a mist of grateful tears from her eyes. "I shall be ready whenever you are."

"Very good. The second condition is . . . well, I'm afraid it's rather an expensive trip. We must travel first to New York, and from there we'll take a ship south to Aspinwall, in Panama. From Aspinwall, we travel by rail to Panama City, and by sea once more up the Pacific coast."

"I understand. What is the cost?" Whatever it was, she was resolved to pay it, one way or another. No obstacle would prevent her from leaving Lowell with this man.

"Two hundred and fifty dollars," said Mercer.

A chill crept up Josephine's spine. It was a heavy price. But the money was accessible to her—she knew just where she might obtain it. "Very well." A cool calm settled in her gut. "I will have my fare in hand by tomorrow."

Mercer jotted a few lines on one of his papers—a list of suggested items for Josephine to pack. Then he added the time and place where the party would assemble, at the train depot on the southwest edge of town.

"Please see that you arrive on time," he told her. "If you are not present at this precise hour, I will have no choice but to assume you've changed your mind."

"I understand." Josephine folded the paper neatly, then tucked it in her pocket with the clipping from the *New York Times*.

Don't worry, A. S. Mercer, she told him silently. *I'll keep a vigil by the tracks all night long, if need be. I will not miss that train for any inducement the Devil may dream up.*

Mercer rose as Josephine did, and he extended his warm, youthful hand across the desk. Josephine grasped it tightly—her lifeline, her rescue—and smiled into his vivid blue eyes.

"Best wishes for a good journey," Mercer said. "And my best wishes to Seattle's future bride."

Josephine made her way back up Merrimack Street, striding with invigorated purpose. The two papers in her pocket crinkled faintly with the swing of her skirt, and she could still feel the shape of Mercer's palm against her own. The sensation burned and itched on her skin—an uncomfortable reminder of the falsehoods she had told.

But she had no time for guilt. The afternoon was fast fading; she had only a few hours to prepare. She was resolved to be ready, cash in hand, when Mercer called for her. Josephine would be waiting on the train platform in the early morning light, ready to leave this life far behind.

CHAPTER TWO
A WORKING GIRL

Dovey stood beside the great parlor window, watching the sun sink toward the broken, hard-edged silhouette of Lowell's quiet skyline. The bright afternoon had faded into a dejected evening, dimming the late-winter sun behind a gathering veil of violet-gray clouds. Lowell was eerie in its peace—ominously unproductive. Only a few of the tall, narrow smokestacks released their plumes into the sky. In the weak light of the brief winter sunset, Lowell's haze of industry mingled with a gathering drift of clouds. It looked, to Dovey's eyes, like a ragged shawl draped around a widow's shoulders—or like the tarnish on a long-forgotten silver ornament, once sparkling and fine, now worn, dull, and dark.

She shifted on her feet, wiggling numb toes inside her stiff, pointed boots. Her legs were sore from tramping up and down the long rows of the millhouses. She had inquired at every business still in operation whether there was any work for a girl of sixteen. But each foreman had turned her away with short, impatient words. Lowell's streets were packed with mill girls, drifting at loose ends, all of whom had lost their places when their employers folded. And even the rawest, youngest mill girls moping in Lowell's alleys had far more experience than Dovey.

It was hopeless, and she knew it. She would not find work. She had searched for more than a week now, and each day her luck was more rotten than the last. Even if a position came open—and who was mad enough to give up steady work?—the job would certainly go to someone who already knew how to mind the spinning jennies, not to a neophyte like Dovey. She would only waste an overseer's time with tedious training.

She stared down at her hands. They were soft and white, nothing at all like the calloused, work-chapped paws of the girls she had met on the streets. The sight of her idle hands filled Dovey's stomach with a thick, bubbling shame. For the first time in her young life, she was embarrassed by her former wealth and comfort, and she realized with a prickle of tears that she was almost relieved those times of ease had come to an end—*almost*. She clasped her untroubled hands behind her back, where she didn't have to see them—where she would not be confronted by her own maddening uselessness.

If she could only find a job! Then she'd show the world what she was made of—then everyone would know her mettle, her spirit, the broad, strong force of her worth. If only she had the chance, she would prove that Dovey Mason could work as hard as any girl. She'd show them all that she could earn her keep, and then some. She could make her own way in the world—if only someone out there would give her the opportunity.

The ache from her long day's fruitless search crept from her legs up into her back. Dovey would have sunk into a parlor chair with a sigh, but there were no chairs in the parlor—not anymore. Her father had sold the last of the fancy seating three days ago, along with the beautiful carved-oak bureau, the one that had stood beside the parlor window ever since Dovey was a little girl. *Just as well,* she told herself. Lately the bureau had only infuriated her with its empty top. It used to hold two lovely, slender candleholders—silver, fashioned like the trunks of birch trees—and a long silk runner with tasseled ends. The candleholders and the runner had been among the first items sacrificed and were followed by the parlor's ornate Persian rug.

As in the parlor, so in the rest of the Mason house. Once the finest home in all of Lowell, now it was grand on the outside alone. The only sticks of furniture that remained inside were Dovey's bed and her father's, and a small, plain table with two chairs where they took their skimpy meals. Father had even begun prizing the plaster molding from the edges of the ceilings. The plaster would bring in some money—not much, but every penny was a fortune in these dark days.

Dovey swallowed the hard lump in her throat. *It's a good thing after all that Mother fell ill,* she told herself stoutly. If Mother hadn't gone off to Boston last May, to live under the care of her second cousin—a nurse who had done plenty of work with consumptives and knew just how to bring them back to health—then her heart would surely break now, to see her once-fine home reduced to bare planks and lathing. *It would be the death of her, to watch her world torn up and sold off, piece by piece.* The war ground on and showed no signs of ending. Dovey could bear the sight of this carnage—of the Mason family being crushed first to rubble and then to dust. But Mother would never have been able to bear it, and Dovey thanked God for sparing her the terrible sight.

It was, however, a cruel enough prank on God's part that all three of Dovey's brothers had been sent off to fight the Confederates. From there, divine malice had only escalated. Last spring, when they'd received word that John, the eldest, had been killed at Chancellorsville, the news was enough to drop Mother into a faint. She never had recovered from that shock.

In fact, she had grown paler and weaker by the day, and when Father finally sent word to the Boston cousin and hustled Mother away, Dovey had her doubts whether the move had been for Mother's good, or for Father's. Everyone knew that consumption was an illness of the poor. If word got around Lowell that Mary Mason had gone consumptive, well—that would be all the proof anyone needed that John Mason Sr. was no longer the lord of the factories. To Father, Mother's illness seemed a presentiment—or a judgment from God. It was a portent of the fall to come, of his long, slow, unremitting slide into poverty.

Of course, John Mason had not forestalled the inevitable by sending his wife away. In fact, Dovey rather suspected he might have hastened his own downfall. Dovey was only sixteen, but she was wise enough to perceive that a mere man—even a very rich one—couldn't hornswoggle the Almighty with a trick as simple as stashing his consumptive wife away. God was a mite too clever to fall for such a trick.

The sunset's glow sent a pallid flush creeping over the windowsill, lighting the skirt of Dovey's green dress as if to emphasize its expensive fabric, the uselessness of her finery. She refused to look around the parlor, refused to see the warm light playing upon the unadorned walls. As the house's walls grew barer, Dovey felt them closing in around her, squeezing with a terrible pressure that fuddled her up so badly, she didn't know from one minute to the next whether she wanted to cry or scream. She had hoped that if she could find work, she might contribute to the family's needs—ease some of the burden from her father's shoulders and slow the disassembly and sale of the only life she had ever known. But what work could Lowell offer a girl of sixteen? None but the mills. And the mills, as Father knew all too well, were rapidly closing.

Dovey turned her head sharply at the slow, dejected tread of footsteps on the stairs. She adjusted the high lace collar of her dress and smoothed the pleats of her green woolen skirt, then fixed a bright smile to her face as Father entered the parlor. His coat was carelessly unbuttoned, and the fringe of dark hair that ringed his bald pate was flattened and disheveled, as if he'd been napping and had only just rolled from his bed. His heavy mustache drooped from the corners of his mouth.

"Doreen—where have you been? I looked for you this morning, but you were nowhere in the house."

"I . . . I went out, sir." She clutched her hands more tightly behind her back. All that inquiring had amounted to dirty work. She hadn't had time yet to wash the grime from her hands or to soothe knuckles scraped from knocking at countless mill doors. She had a sudden childish fear that Father would disapprove of her scuffed, sooty appearance, and that he would chide her for it.

"Whatever were you doing *out*?" he asked mildly, shaking his head in amazement. "I do hope you weren't spending money. We haven't anything to spend."

Dovey sighed. "Give me more credit than that, Father. I'm not a simpleton."

"What, then?" He stepped toward her, and his eyes narrowed in a suspicious squint. "Were you consorting with a young man? I've told you—"

"I wasn't visiting with any young men, so you needn't think—"

"I've told you how important it is, Doreen, for our family to maintain appearances. My mills may have closed, but this is only a temporary situation. The Masons are still a family of good breeding and high class. You cannot comport yourself like a doxy! You risk your future by—"

Dovey's hands unclasped and balled themselves into fists. Before she quite knew what she was doing, she was shaking both of them in the air before her—almost threatening her father, who stared at her quivering, raw-knuckled fists with an air of genteel surprise.

"How dare you call me such a name!" Dovey cried. "I'm no strumpet! I've done nothing to sully the family name."

In the weak glow of the sunset, Father stroked his mustache, watching Dovey in expectant silence, his stare both wary and knowing.

"But I was out looking for work," she admitted in a rush. "Good, honest work, so you needn't worry."

Father's hand stilled, then fell. A frown like a thunderhead creased his brow, dark and intimidating. "Work?"

"In the mills," Dovey explained. "I thought if I could find a job on the jennies, or—"

"No daughter of mine will work," Father said. His voice was fiercely low, his hand clenched and motionless at his side. "No woman in my family need ever take a job."

Dovey's shoulders sagged; she cast a helpless sigh up to the few imprinted tin ceiling tiles that still adorned the parlor. "Father, there's no shame in it. A good many girls work in the mills."

"You are not 'a good many girls.' You're a Mason—my own daughter, my *only* daughter. If I can't care for you, then what use am I?"

Dovey shook her head mutely. In the face of his buckling pride, his wounded masculinity, she felt helpless to assert herself. He was at the end of his wits and his resources—and she was able-bodied and clever, and more than willing to earn her keep. Couldn't he see the sense in that? Didn't he welcome an easing of his burdens? What did it matter if relief came from his sixteen-year-old daughter? A hand was a hand, and Dovey would give Father hers, gladly—if only he would humble himself enough to take it.

"I will not stand for this." Father's voice rose with every word. "I'll not be humiliated; I'll not have all of Lowell knowing that I sent my only girl out to the mills to work like some unfortunate immigrant!"

"You didn't send me out," Dovey protested. "I went of my own accord!"

Her words could not reach him; he seemed deafened by the force of his anger—by the hopelessness of their circumstances. "And your mother already beyond my reach," he ranted on, "in Boston, where—"

"In Boston, where *you* sent her!" Dovey shouted. "Don't play the martyr where Mother's concerned. I simply won't hear it, Father! You sent her away."

"For her own good," he insisted. "With my prayers that she will recover her health. I am not coldhearted, Doreen."

"Aren't you? I wonder! Did you send Mother away for *her* health, or for your own?"

He took one slow step toward her, towering in his superior height, the air crackling between them with the tension of a fierce winter storm. His familiar smell—pipe tobacco, cedar, and warm, soft wool—was undercut by a faint, sourish reek, an odor that reminded Dovey of restless sleep, of sickness, of despair. "Whatever are you talking about, girl?"

"You didn't pack Mother off to Boston for her good. You did it so no one would know consumption had fallen on our house. Consumption—the poor man's plague!"

Father flinched; his face seemed to crumple for an instant, and vulnerability gleamed through the hard lines of his glower like raw, painful flesh showing through the cracks of a crusted wound.

Dovey pressed her advantage. "But we *are* poor now, Father. Just look around you! Our house is bare, your mills have failed, and our prospects are gone. There's more dignity in accepting what the Lord has dealt us than in trying to carry on as if nothing in our lives has changed."

Father's face softened—smoothed into a mask of well-controlled calm. He even managed a smile. It was thin-lipped and pinched, but still his satisfaction seemed genuine to Dovey. Grim but genuine. "My prospects may be gone—for now. But yours are not."

A wary chill settled into her stomach. She resisted the urge to press her hands there, to drive the creeping sensation away. "What do you mean?"

Father's expression grew stern, and his shoulders squared—a sudden turn of temper that Dovey knew well. He had put on his businessman's facade, the stiff, unyielding aspect that had earned John Mason his reputation as the hardest driver of deals in all of Lowell—in all of Massachusetts, in fact. "Just this morning, Norris Stilton approached me to inquire about your temperament and skills. It seems his son, Marion, has taken notice of you. Only a few hours ago, I thought you not yet mature enough to take on the responsibilities of marriage and motherhood. But after all, if you are out traipsing the streets, looking for work—"

Dovey gasped. "Father!"

"You're sixteen. Early to wed, perhaps, but if *I* cannot care for you properly, as you were so quick to point out, then perhaps Marion Stilton will do a better job of it."

"An arranged marriage? After all, Father, this isn't the Orient!"

Father huffed. "Don't put on dramatics. You know an arrangement is perfectly commonplace."

It certainly was *not* commonplace, except in very old-fashioned families—or among immigrants. Dovey had always thought of her upbringing as quite stylishly progressive. She did not relish the idea of being shoved in the direction of some dolt of a husband, as if she were a sheep prodded along by a drover. That sort of thing was for the Catholic girls—the daughters of the Irishmen who had dug the canals that served Lowell's factories. Imagine—John Mason's only daughter, traded off like some Irish chit! What *was* Father thinking?

Then the rest of his odious proclamation caught up to her speeding thoughts, and Dovey goggled at her father, rendered speechless by the terrible possibility. Marion Stilton—speaking of dolts! He was the most perfect specimen of a dullard the Lord had ever made! And he was vain in the bargain, always fussing over his suit and his oiled hair at parties. And that was to say nothing of his selfish nature, which was enough all by itself to turn Dovey's stomach. Marion was twenty-two now—more than old enough to fight in the war. Yet he had commuted instead—paid a fee of three hundred dollars to dodge the mandatory enrollment. It wasn't fair, nor right, that all three of Dovey's brothers had gone off to service—and poor John Jr. dead in his grave!—while Marion Stilton skipped carefree down the lane, tossing dollar bills out casually in his wake. Dovey would never marry a man like him—*never*!

She rounded on her father with a scornful laugh. "Aha! Marion Stilton—because *his* father's mills are still running. I suppose that's your reason for choosing that coward as my husband—to get a share of his family's business."

It was a cruel thing to say, and Dovey knew it. Father's brows knitted up and he turned his face away, as if Dovey had struck him across the cheek. For an instant she regretted her words. She knew how the closing of all his factories ate at Father's soul. He was so possessed by the desire to revive his business that he had little attention for anything else—he would not even speak of Ewing and Bart, his two living sons who were out there somewhere, toiling in the trenches, still wearing the blue and fighting on—or so Dovey prayed, night and day. She doubted whether Father even spared a thought for the boys—whether he was capable of considering anyone other than himself. He had thrown everything he had into trying to restore his business—money, connections, and every waking moment he could spare.

And now he's thrown me in, too, Dovey realized. *I'm his last possession of any value—his final gambling chip. And he'd gladly sell me to the Stiltons to gain a share of their mills.*

All her guilt evaporated, leaving her conscience as dry as her throat. She turned a look of perfect contempt on her father, her chin held high and her nostrils flaring with rage. "I will *not* wed Marion Stilton."

Father's face darkened. His mustache bent steeply along the curve of his frown. "You will."

"Just wait and see!"

"Listen to me, Doreen. The war has been hard on us all—"

Dovey snorted—most unladylike, she knew, but she could find no verbal expression for her disgust at Father's audacity. Father—who wouldn't even *speak* of Ewing and Bart!

"—but I fear its longest-reaching effects aren't truly felt yet." Father took Dovey's hand, making a bid for sincerity. She pulled her fingers from his grasp. "There are so few young men," he went on. "And virtually none of them are as well positioned as Marion Stilton. When the war finally ends and all the young ladies of Lowell find themselves without suitors, Marion will have his choice of any girl he pleases."

"So I should lock him in now, is that it?" Dovey tossed her head, sending her dark curls flying. "Get him into a contract where he can't budge and pin him up against the wall? Turn the whole deal to my advantage?" It was businessmen's talk. Dovey had heard her father sling such phrases often, back when he was still the Lord of Lowell.

"You don't know what's best for you!" Father's voice was rising by the moment, increasing again to an angry bellow that echoed from the parlor's blank, cold walls. "I am your father, and I only have your interests in mind!"

"I *do* know what's best!" Dovey shouted back. Tears stung her eyes, and she cursed herself for going weak and soft. She knew there was nothing Father despised more in negotiations than a weak opponent. She balled her fists; the bite of her nails against her palms drove the tears away and helped to focus her speeding thoughts.

"I don't care if there are no husbands left when the war is over," she said, cool and composed now. "I'll be an old maid. I'd far rather *never* marry than spend my life strapped to Marion Stilton."

"You won't feel the same way when your anger settles. You've always been headstrong, Doreen, but you're not a fool. Once you've calmed yourself, you'll see the sense in what I propose."

"Oh? Is that what you think?"

"It is."

Father reached out before Dovey could twist away from him. He seized her by the upper arm, and his grip was steely—painful. She tried to jerk out of his grasp, but his hand only tightened until she gave a hiss of pain. He marched her out of the parlor, their shoes clattering on the naked floorboards, and pointed her toward the stairs.

"Go up to your room until you've calmed yourself," he said.

Dovey wrenched her arm again, and this time she managed to break Father's grip. She pulled her sleeve straight with an indignant glare. "I will not be ordered off into confinement like a child."

"You *are* a child, and an unruly one at that."

"If you think I'm old enough to parcel out in marriage, then I am not a child." Sensing that she had gained the upper hand of logic, Dovey folded her arms pertly. "I wonder what Mother would say to this idea. I'll write her, and then we'll just see what she says! Fixing me up a marriage like I'm some Irish filly—!"

Father's slap caught her on the cheekbone with a breathtaking sting. She clamped her hand against her face, staring at him through the blur of shocked tears. She didn't know whether he'd struck her because she had mentioned Mother, or because she'd compared him to the Irishmen—who made up by far the greater population of the poorhouses. Either way, the hot throb of her cheek was proof that she'd done it this time, and *good*. She turned away from him, running up the stairs as fast as her heavy skirts would allow, hating every tear that spilled down her cheeks and every sob that strangled in her chest.

"I only want to care for you properly," Father called up the stairs. His voice was heavy with regret, thick with exhaustion and despair. "You will be far happier with a husband to care for you, Doreen, than you ever could be out there in the mills, working for a few meager pennies per day. What are fathers for, if not to give their daughters the best lives possible?"

"I can give *myself* the best life possible!" Dovey turned at the head of the stairs and glared down at him, the tears of her futile defiance burning her eyes. "I should have the chance, at least—a chance to prove I can!"

Father shook his head slowly, his brows drawn down in disgust. "I will tell Norris Stilton that you'll be glad to marry his son. And the sooner it's done, the better—for your own sake, before you do something so rash your reputation cannot be saved. You'll wed Marion Stilton next Sunday, and I'll hear no more about it!"

Dovey screamed her defiance at her father—screamed until her throat felt red and raw. "I'll *leave* you first! I'll run away! You'll never see me again, do you hear? *Never, never!*"

When the reverberation of her shrieking voice died away, Dovey heard the slow tread of Father's feet ascending the stairs. She clutched again at her swollen cheek, her heart pounding in sudden fear. But when Father reached the upper floor, his face was as blank and smooth as the naked walls of the parlor. He reached for her, and Dovey quailed. But he only laid his palm on her shoulder and pushed her gently backward into her bedroom.

The door closed, shutting Father from her sight. Dovey heard a faint, metallic jingle, and then, with a cold clutch of horror, the grating of a key in the lock. The lock's tumbler seemed to clang as loud as a church bell as it turned. Then the key withdrew, and Father's footsteps receded, slow and deliberate, down the staircase.

CHAPTER THREE
TRUE WOMEN ONLY

After a quarter of an hour, the tears had dried on Dovey's cheeks, leaving behind a prickle of salt that itched ferociously and irritated the tender skin where Father's blow had landed. The discomfort of it made her angry—at herself, not at Father. How could she have lain on her bed, caterwauling into her pillow like the useless, spoiled girl she was? Weeping had gained her nothing. Even her heart felt no better; it was sick and hollow and sad, and if anything, it beat with a rhythm more desperate than before.

Dovey scrubbed the memory of tears from her cheeks with the cuff of her sleeve. *A mill girl wouldn't sit around whining, or weeping her eyes to blindness. A mill girl would face her troubles head-on . . . do what needs must.* If ever there was a time for Dovey to prove that she was the equal of any girl in Lowell, this was the hour.

She sat up on her bed, folded her hands in her lap, and tried her best to take stock of her situation. But no matter how she admonished herself to stay calm, to think through this mess clearly, her heart pounded with anger toward Father, and her arms and legs shivered at the injustice of her predicament. Finally, unable to sit still and remain rational, she sprang to her feet and paced the length of her dim, empty bedroom.

A thick tallow candle stood on a bare shelf; she took up a little packet of matches and lit it on one of her circuits around the room, for twilight had gathered and shadows crowded in through the curtainless window, reaching for her with a promise of dark despair. Dovey wouldn't give in to tears—not again. Tears wouldn't make a way out of this mess. She would allow herself to feel all the rage she could muster—but not one stitch of despair.

The candle's light opened around Dovey, blossoming like a golden flower, and she stood at the very center of its unfolding, watched the flame's energetic flicker. Its ring of light was like a shield—it pushed the night, and Father's demands, far away. Within that golden circle, in a tiny world of private possibilities, Dovey stood alone. She looked down at her hands again. In the ever-shifting candlelight, patches of shadow and bursts of golden brightness flowed across her fingers, her wrists, the places on her palms where she could still make out the faint impression of her nails. Her hands did not look soft or weak now. In this changing light, she thought she could hold any future at all—any life she chose—and it would fit just so between her palms. She could carry any burden with ease.

But where would she go, and what would she do? There was no work for her in the mills—that much was plain, after a week of searching. Besides, anywhere she went in Lowell, Father would surely find her. She would never be free of his scorn, or the pressure to wed Marion Stilton, until she left Lowell entirely.

I could go to Mother in Boston. For a moment, the decision crystalized, then hardened, in her heart. *Yes—that's exactly what I'll do.*

But she knew that word of her whereabouts would soon get back to Father, and Mother wasn't strong enough to prevent the marriage. In fact, Mother might even approve of the idea, if indeed a marriage with the Stiltons could bring Father's mills back to life.

No, not Boston. As Dovey stared into the flame, she saw the way it must be. She had no choice but to remove herself from the reach of both Father and Mother. New York, then. Or somewhere else entirely. But someplace far off, where neither of her parents could find her.

And then, with a sudden jolt of inspiration, Dovey knew exactly where she would go.

Days past—on the first day of her search for work—she had happened upon the town square, where a man stood at a podium, holding court to a crowd of men and women who murmured behind their hands at the odd things he said. At first, Dovey had kept well to the back of the crowd, far more amused by the racy comments the men of Lowell had made—and the shocked giggles of the women—than by the speaker's words.

But soon enough she had grown bored with the gossip and turned an ear toward the stranger. The man's speech began to pluck at her, word by word, phrase by phrase, until she felt compelled to push her way through the crowd to stand at its very front. There she remained, watching Asa Mercer in captivated silence. He was dressed as sharply as any businessman, and his hands lifted from the podium, emphasizing his words with elegant precision as he spoke rapturously of the rugged beauty of the frontier—of the great and honorable work that needed doing there. And Dovey recalled now with a significant stillness in her middle, Asa Mercer had said that only *women* could do that particular work.

When the dapper man's speech was concluded and the muttering crowd dispersed, Dovey noted the litter of leaflets, printed on creamy yellow paper, discarded on the cobbles. She snatched one up and stuffed it in her skirt's pocket without reading the thing. She had paid no mind to the leaflet from that moment on, but now she flew to her closet and rummaged through the few dresses that remained to her until she found the one she'd been wearing that day—the light-blue wool with the laced pagoda sleeves. She clawed at the voluminous skirt, biting her lip, fighting to quell the panic that flared in her stomach. Perhaps she had taken the paper out and tossed it into the kitchen stove—the thing had seemed so insignificant that she might have gotten rid of it without thinking. She bit back a sob of mounting fear.

Then she heard the leaflet crinkle.

Dovey yanked the paper from the dress pocket, clutched it close to her heart, and crowded close to the candle. The block print stood proud and dark on its field of wrinkled, torn paper, and as Dovey read the words, she heard them ringing in her head like a clarion.

SEEKING

Unmarried Women of TRUE and QUALITY Character

to venture into

WASHINGTON TERRITORY

and there Aid in the Settlement and Civilization of

the City of SEATTLE

High-Minded TRUE WOMEN Only need apply!

seeking Teachers Especially for the schooling of
Children & University men

SALARY to all TEACHERS $75.00 per month

apply to A. S. MERCER at 108 Merrimack Street no
later than 12 March

departing Lowell, Mass. 13 March from rail depot

Travel fare $250.00

Dovey's breath caught in her throat. The pounding of her heart in her own ears muted the rumble of carriage wheels outside, and the desultory chirrups of the crickets who had been lured from hibernation by the early thaw. Her fingers had gone numb. This was the night of March twelfth. It was surely too late to apply. She bit her lip as she estimated the time: half past six—more likely, it was nearly seven. Even if Father hadn't locked her in her room, Dovey knew she couldn't make it all the way down to Merrimack Street in time to catch Asa Mercer.

With a helpless sob, she crumpled the leaflet in her fist. But the candlelight still danced with an optimistic glow, and Dovey still stood within its cheery circle. The calm resolve of absolute determination stole upon her, settled on her soul like a warm cloak in winter, soothing and plush. She breathed deep, then smoothed the wrinkled paper against her thigh and studied its words again.

Washington Territory. It was certainly far away. Clear on the other side of the continent, in fact. There would be precious little danger of Father tracking her down. Mr. Mercer's party of women would leave tomorrow. Dovey had no way of knowing when they would depart Lowell, but she knew from where. And she was sharply determined to be waiting at the train depot when A. S. Mercer arrived, even if she had to stand all day in the cold and the mud.

The travel fare, though . . . two hundred and fifty dollars! Once, the Mason family could have managed the sum with ease, but now it was certainly beyond Dovey's reach.

Unless . . .

Dovey's gaze unfocused against her bedroom wall, then traveled reluctantly down to the dark, bare boards of her floor. She crept from the candle's protective light and dropped to her knees near the wall, her skirt and petticoats pillowing around her. She found the loose floorboard and pried it up carefully with her nails. Below, in the space just above the parlor ceiling, lay her little cache of treasures—memories—the things she had salvaged from Father's desperate greed.

When he'd sold off the silver candlesticks, Dovey had known at once that Mother's jewelry would follow. She couldn't bear the thought of Mother losing all the baubles she loved, and so Dovey had sorted through her jewel boxes, picking out the pieces she knew to be Mother's favorites and leaving the rest for Father to ravage. Dovey had always intended to give the jewelry back to Mother, a welcome-home gift when she returned from her convalescence. On that grand day, Dovey imagined, Mother would be healthy, glowing a rosy pink once more, and all the pallor of consumption would be as distant a memory as Father's loss of the mills.

Dovey examined each treasure in turn as she pulled it from the gap in the floor. The emerald teardrop earrings; the bracelet of small, starry diamonds; bits of filigreed silver; and a long, delicate chain of buttery gold. She stroked the soft, coral-colored cameo pendant she had so loved to see her mother wearing ever since her childhood days. The cameo featured the profile of a woman in white stone, but the face did not look as fine and dreamy as Dovey had remembered. Now it seemed icy—scornful—and Dovey closed her fingers around the pendant so she could not see the little carved woman's face, nor feel her mother's disapproval at the desperate act she was considering.

I have to do this, Mother, she said silently. *Please understand.*

Shaking with shock at her own audacity, Dovey clambered to her feet, the last of her mother's keepsakes clutched in her hands. She spread them on her rumpled bed, then tore off a corner of her sheet and tied the jewelry in a small, compact bundle, which she shoved deep into her skirt's pocket. She pulled her pillow from its linen case, and felt the sharp quills of the pillow's feathers pricking her hands, insistent little stabs, as if from a devil's pitchfork. She tossed the pillow aside.

There's so little time. Dovey had never before packed her bags for a journey of any length, let alone for a cross-continental abscondment. She forced herself to take slow, calming breaths, and tried to imagine all the goods and particulars she might require. But in truth, Dovey had no idea how long the journey to Seattle might take, nor what challenges it might entail. Would she be exposed to weather? Had she to walk any great distance? Would she be expected to present herself well, as a young woman of good breeding—or would plain and even shabby clothing suffice?

She reasoned it was better to be safe than sorry, and so she pulled the blue, pagoda-sleeved dress from her closet—the finest she still owned. Folding it neatly would have taken nigh on an hour, it had so many pleats and frills. Instead, Dovey wadded the dress into the bottom of her pillowcase and mashed it hard with her fist. Its generous skirt took up half the available space, even when she tamped the blue wool down firmly with her foot.

An extra chemise and two fresh drawers followed the blue dress into the bag. The rest of her clothing she would have to leave behind, save for the green dress she still wore.

She dropped to her knees inside her closet, and threw open the lid of her little wooden hygiene box. There she found the muslin belt she used for her monthlies. She wrapped it around a handful of her old cotton pads and the packet of pins that secured them to the belt. She wedged the bundle deep into the pillowcase, then tossed in her comb, a plain netted snood, and a few simple ribbons and hairpins. Last of all, she packed her straw hat with the long blue streamers. She could just hold the ends of her pillowcase closed around the fat, heavy bundle.

Her impromptu travel bag packed, Dovey sat back on her heels and eyed her bedroom door. *How to get out?* She might shout for her father, and then when he unlocked the door, bull past him . . . but no. Despite his advancing years, John Mason was a large man, and far stronger than Dovey. She realized that she would have only one chance to get away, and could risk neither capture nor the discovery of her plan. If Father puzzled out what Dovey intended, he might drag her off to the church that very night and shackle her to Marion Stilton for all eternity.

She turned to consider her bedroom's tall, narrow window instead. Outside, the fullness of night had arrived, heavy and thick as a velvet cape, banishing the last smoke-gray tones of twilight. Beyond the house's stone wall, through the bare limbs of the two gnarled old oaks that guarded the gate, Dovey could see the street, long and level, gleaming dully like a sheet of beaten copper in the glow of gas streetlights on their tall iron posts. Night had fallen indeed, but the hour was still early enough, she prayed, that she might make her escape. But she knew she must act quickly.

Dovey pulled her skirt and petticoats up, wrestling them over one shoulder. She worked frantically at the ties of her crinoline, cursing each time the knots slipped from her grasp, for her fingers were stiff and clumsy from the chill of anxiety. Finally, though, the heavy, bell-shaped cage of steel and muslin dropped from her hips, landing on the bare floor with a resounding clank. Dovey held her breath, hoping the sound hadn't alerted Father. But after a few moments, when the hall outside her room remained still, she stepped out of the crinoline and let skirt and petticoats fall. Walking without the crinoline was a cumbersome chore; the heavy folds of her skirt and underthings draped against her legs, pressing her knees and shins with their layers of ruffled lace. And without the crinoline to flare her garments outward, both skirt and petticoat were too long by several inches, and dragged beneath her boots.

Dovey issued an indelicate curse, but she saw at once what she must do. She pulled a pin from her hair and stabbed at the edge of her green wool skirt, six inches above its hem, then worked the pin back and forth until she could fit her fingers into the hole. The wool ripped with a tremendous hiss; Dovey pulled the entire hem away, ignoring the ragged threads that hung down from her skirt's ruined edge. She attacked both petticoats next, leaving a heap of ribboned lace on the floor beside her crinoline.

Then, biting her lip against rising panic—time was already so short—Dovey set to work on her bedsheets, jabbing holes with her pin and tearing the linen sheets into long strips. These she knotted well into a series of hand- and footholds, then she wound one end of her makeshift ladder into a large, messy tangle and tied it as securely as she could.

Dovey wrestled the sash of her window upward. The night was calm and quiet, but the air bit with a reminder of the winter's chill. She tossed her embroidered cape around her shoulders, then placed her stuffed and straining pillowcase carefully outside the window, on the projection of shingles that roofed the front porch below. The pitch of the roof was not steep, and after giving one alarming tip toward the street, the pillowcase came to rest and sat waiting for Dovey to follow it out into the night.

She took a final look around her bedroom. It was empty of everything now, except her sorrow. The candle still burned, its circle of light dancing and flitting over the bare slats of the floor, the featureless walls. Dovey crossed to the shelf and blew out the flame. The room was plunged into darkness.

She bent, and, working by feel alone beneath the concealing edge of her torn petticoats, she tied the unknotted end of her sheets around one ankle. The moment had come. She was on her way to Washington Territory—and by God, she would get there, one way or another. Her heart began to pound again, and with each insistent beat of her pulse, the place on her cheek where her father had slapped her burned hot and red.

"Good-bye, Father," Dovey said to the darkness. Then, as she braced her hands on the windowsill, she thought, *We'll see who slaps the hardest.*

The bedroom window wasn't much wider than Dovey's shoulders. She worked her slow way over the sill, squeezing her body through inches at a time, feeling the scrape of hard wood through the layers of her bodice and underthings. Her weight pressed down against the sill, causing the whalebone stays to bite hard into her flesh. She resisted the urge to cry out in her pain, and resisted, too, the temptation to move faster, to kick her feet and flail her arms. It would do her no good to catch Father's attention with careless thumping about or thrashing on the rooftop. Dovey gasped and panted until she was light-headed, for her corset would not allow her to breathe as deeply as the work demanded. Many times she found herself tangled in the folds of cape or skirt, and she was obliged to wiggle and squirm until she could move freely again. But at last she spilled through the window, and crouched on the porch roof beside her bundled pillowcase while the ache from her hard stays dissipated.

When she felt somewhat recovered, Dovey untied the sheet from her ankle, then pulled it slowly through the window until the large knot at its other end rested just inside the sill. She eased the sash down quietly, closing it just at the knot's edge. The makeshift ladder of torn sheets draped over the edge of the roof, silvery-blue and obvious as sin against the uniform dark of night. The sheets did not quite reach to the ground below, but Dovey figured it was close enough. She pulled the open end of her pillowcase snugly closed, gripped the fabric in her teeth, and crept on hands and feet to the roof's edge. Then she turned carefully in her mass of pleats and ragged-edged ruffles, and prepared to descend over the edge.

Her body shook violently, with exertion as much as fear, and the air was fiercely cold against her sweat-beaded brow. But she could still feel the burn of her father's palm against her cheek, and her mind was good and made up. She would go down the sheets, or straight to Hell— anywhere but back inside that sad, empty home. She pulled hard on the ladder, throwing as much of her weight against it as she could. The window frame creaked, but the knots held. With one frantic prayer for mercy, Dovey lowered herself over the edge.

Almost at once, gravity seized her, dragging with a ferocious weight. The heavy pillowcase tore from her teeth and fell into the dark yard below. Dovey clung to the highest knot, a foot or more below the edge of the roof, paralyzed, squeaking like a kitten on a thin, wind-whipped bough. Her arms burned until she thought they might snap clean away from her body; it was all she could do to hold still, stiff and wide-eyed, rotating slowly on her slapdash rope.

I can't do it, she thought frantically. *I'll let go in a moment and fall! I'll break both my legs—or my neck!* She told herself she ought to clamber back up onto the roof—but when she looked up at its black edge, it seemed higher above than the vaults of Heaven, and she knew she couldn't haul herself up to safety any more than she could lower herself down.

The windowsill creaked again—much louder than before. The knot she clung to gave an alarming lurch, dropping Dovey a fraction of an inch before it caught and held again.

"Oh, Lord of mercy, spare me!" Dovey whispered.

She forced her white-knuckled fists to loosen, and her groping feet found another knot some inches below. Her hands skittered frantically down the sheet as she eased her feet lower down still. Linen slid through her fists, burning her skin, and Dovey nearly hollered in pain and fear—but her hands clenched reflexively around another knot, and she lowered herself again, faster this time, and faster still as she learned the trick and rhythm of it.

Her hard-soled boots clamped around the last knot. The ground was still some four feet below—and might as well have been a mile down, for all Dovey felt able to reach it. She sent out another prayer in a rapid, breathless mutter, then willed her hands to open. She fell through darkness into the yard. The impact of her body against the earth was so sudden and hard that she couldn't tell which part of her had struck the ground first—feet, knees, bottom, or shoulder. She pressed her face into the wet, muddy grass to smother a cry of pain. After a long moment, when the shock of her fall ebbed, leaving a fit of trembling in its wake, Dovey stood with care, testing her weight on her ankles. All her parts seemed to be in good working order, thank God, even if she was as quivery as an aspic, all fumbles and nerves.

She located her pillowcase bundle in the darkness, hiked up her torn skirt and petticoats, and hurried toward the street. At first, corset and fear conspired to restrict Dovey to a fast but unsteady walk. When she reached the empty sidewalk, however, Dovey ran as fast as her shallow breaths would allow, impelled by a fantastic rush of hot, prickling energy that whipped along her veins like the white bolts of a lightning storm.

She knew where she must go, and only prayed she was not too late. She darted down one street, then another, closing on the shopping district as quickly as she could manage. Sweat soaked her chemise, and the hard edges of her corset chafed the tender skin below her armpits, but she did not slow. Nor did she slow when the backs of her heels began to blister inside her boots. Time was running out—it may have expired already. She couldn't coddle her sore feet when her future might slip away at any moment.

Finally, Dovey rounded the corner of the great clock tower and looked out over the avenue of high-class shops—the ones she and Mother used to frequent, before everything in life had turned sour. The sidewalks here were empty, too, and most of the shops' windows were already dark, though a few lamps still burned through the painted panes of display windows.

Dovey's chest heaved as she struggled to catch her breath. She glanced around desperately, trying to recall whether the jeweler's shop was north of here, or south . . . and then she saw it, half a block away. Mr. Fredericks, the shop's suave, quietly assessing keeper, stood with his back to the street, his head bowed over the door handle—locking up for the night.

"Wait!" Dovey cried.

Mr. Fredericks looked up. The orange glow of a nearby streetlight glinted off his spectacles, and for a moment, the reflected light danced like the candle flame in Dovey's bedroom. She hurried toward him, letting her skirts fall so she could wave to him in frantic appeal. "Wait! Please! Don't close yet!"

The jeweler watched, curious and still, as Dovey rushed toward him. By the time she reached the shop front, she was so faint from her panting and exertion that she could only lean against the brick of the building, patting her damp forehead with a trembling hand.

"Miss?" Mr. Fredericks took her gently by the elbow. "Are you well? Do you need some assistance?" Then he recognized her face, though it had been nearly a year since her family had last patronized his business. "I declare—you're Doreen Mason!"

Breathless, Dovey could only nod.

"Has something happened, Miss Doreen? Tell me—should I call for the police?"

Dovey shook her head violently. "No!" she gasped. "No, please."

Mr. Fredericks eyed her mud-stained dress, the heavy pillowcase dangling from her hand, and the ripped hem of her skirt. His thin, rather prim mouth tightened in worry. "Miss Doreen—"

"I'm all right," she insisted. Recovered enough to speak on, she reached into her pocket and withdrew the knotted square of linen. "I have jewelry to sell."

"I'm sorry, Miss Doreen, but I've closed for the evening."

"Please," she said, her voice going thick with fear, almost strangling on the word. She had come so close! Could fate be so cruel, to snatch her future away when she stood on the raw edge of freedom?

Mr. Fredericks hesitated, struck by her frantic state, and Dovey took advantage of the moment. She dropped her pillowcase on the damp sidewalk and picked apart the knot in her little bundle. It opened in her palm. The lamplight raised a flicker of fire from the diamond bracelet, and the jeweler's mouth worked in a soundless exclamation. He reached tentatively for one emerald earring, then held it up to the brassy glow of the streetlight, squinting at the glittering teardrop with one sharp, assessing eye. Then he turned to Dovey with a searching look.

"Two hundred and fifty," she said, her insides cold with fear. "Please—can you give me two hundred and fifty for the whole lot?"

Mr. Fredericks stroked his chin as he pondered the gems in Dovey's hands. Then he reached into his pocket and withdrew the shop's key. "You'd better come inside," he said, "and we'll see what we can do."

CHAPTER FOUR
A FRIEND IN NEED

The weak winter sun could scarcely assert itself through the gray-shrouded sky. Dawn spilled low and halfhearted along the horizon, a smear of pale light like thin cream slopped from the edge of a bowl. Even as Josephine's hired carriage rolled nearer to the rail depot, the pallor of early-morning light made the little wood-sided building seem cool and distant, a destination she might never reach. But at last, the carriage came to a rather lurching stop beside the curb.

Josephine glanced nervously over her shoulder before she left the confines of the cab. Lowell still slept. Only a few sounds of early industry carried through the morning mist—men's voices drifting faintly from the piers; the rumbling of a laden wagon; the snorting of its horses; and far off, from the direction of Merrimack Street, a repetitive, heavy clanging, the waking of some great, cold piece of machinery, the noise dampened by distance.

There was a time, not many months ago, when the morning would already be cacophonous, and the streets bustling with the vigor of early

risers and hopeful men. Those days were past—forever, Josephine suspected. She drew a deep breath, tasting one last time the coal-smoke
bitterness, the river-damp taste of Lowell.

She was glad to leave—grateful the Lord had provided an egress.
Lowell's expiration by degrees—the quiet, hopeless moan of its fading—left Josephine feeling confined and depressed. She could scarcely
bear the sensation of watching a city die slowly. She would much rather
watch a city being born. Births, at least, were as full and flush with hope
as they were pain, mess, and uncertainty. Seattle was Josephine's hope
now—her future, her bright new dawn.

The driver of the hired carriage gave a tremendous yawn—an
unsubtle hint, Josephine assumed, that she ought to be on her way.
She climbed down quickly without waiting for the driver to secure
his reins and offer a hand. Unused to the particulars of hiring cabs,
Josephine feared that if she accepted the driver's help, she would be
bound by some obscure point of etiquette to tip him above the fare she
had already paid—and every cent was precious to her now. She stamped
her feet against the cold, surreptitiously patting her pocket to be sure
the worn leather purse was still there.

Even through the thick wool of her navy-blue dress, the purse
felt fat and heavy. Its weight simultaneously reassured Josephine and
increased the tension in her gut, that fast, tight thrum of anxiety that
had not left her since she'd first made her way to A. S. Mercer's office.
She hadn't realized how much money two hundred and fifty dollars was
until she'd acquired the necessary fare—and a few paltry dollars more
to see to unexpected needs—and spread the banknotes and coins across
her bed. The sight of so much money had astonished her, and made her
deeds and misdirections seem all the more terrible. The money was an
accounting of her failures, her wrongdoings—a tally of all the risks she
ran, the gambles on which her life depended. The weight of her purse
dragged at her like the weight of sin. She only hoped her conscience

would lighten when she handed the fare over to Asa Mercer and left Lowell behind forever.

Josephine reached for the long, low travel trunk she had placed on the floor of the cab. The driver attempted—slowly—to clamber down from his seat and assist her with it, but she seized its nearest handle and dragged it out of the carriage before he could stir himself too far. The trunk wasn't especially large or laden, but it was heavier than she'd thought, and as she lifted the modest cedar chest to her hip, Josephine grunted in surprise at its weight. How could it be so difficult to carry? She had packed only one change of clothing, her sewing kit for practical purposes, and the provisions Mr. Mercer had suggested.

"Won't you let me carry that trunk for you, missus?" the driver asked.

Josephine shook her head. "Thank you, no. It's no difficulty."

She made her way to the curb slowly, hoping her deliberate steps masked her stagger. She set the thing on the sidewalk and straightened, stifling the urge to puff from the effort. Josephine pulled the agreed-upon sum from her purse and counted it into the driver's palm. With one more narrow-eyed glance at her trunk, the man straightened in his seat, clucked to his horse, and was gone in a rattle of wheels.

Josephine watched the carriage until it rounded a turn and vanished into the soft blue shadows of early morning. Then she scowled down at her trunk and sourly eyed the distance to the depot.

A few women were already gathered on the faded wood of the platform, milling and chatting in the pale wash of morning light. Even from the curb, Josephine could tell the other women were fresh and full of pluck, their youth evident in their slender figures and sprightly, eager movements. They laughed gaily together, or embraced their loved ones in farewell, and their buoyant, optimistic energy sent a stab of uneasiness through Josephine's chest. *I am nothing like them,* she thought bitterly. *Life has worn me down, cowed and silenced me.* She watched the young women gather on their perch above the black lines of the train tracks. The colors of their traveling dresses, muted yet still cheerful, seemed to Josephine like the plumage of birds—flocking together, all of a kind—and a species to which she did not belong.

Despite her sense of otherness—the bleak certainty that she would be an outsider among these bright, cheerful girls, so hopeful of becoming brides—Josephine knew she must go on. Seattle was her salvation, her sanctuary. No other hope existed for her between Lowell and Washington Territory.

There's nothing for it, she told herself stoutly. With a sharp inhalation to steady her nerves, Josephine squatted awkwardly and hoisted the trunk onto her hip. She crossed the depot's yard and climbed the steps to the train platform, then picked her way carefully through the assembled women. Somehow it seemed wrong—almost sacrilegious—to brush the hems of their skirts with her own, and each time Josephine made inadvertent contact with one of Mercer's volunteer brides, a little shiver of guilt raced up her spine, and she feared her very nearness might corrupt that woman's joy or tarnish her happy future with the soil of Josephine's long-borne sorrows.

She was relieved when she made it through the crowd of women without speaking to anyone. Weariness was already pressing down upon her, and not only from the weight of the trunk. She had slept little the night before, caught between her need to prepare for the journey and fear that somehow she would be stopped before she could steal away. Her back ached with the need to sit, to rest. A few wooden freight boxes stood beside an unoccupied bench, and Josephine made her way to the bench as quickly as she could, then thumped her travel trunk down onto the crate with a sigh of deep relief. She fell onto the bench, panting and dabbing at her brow with an old patched kerchief.

Josephine glanced around the platform, taking in each of the younger women in turn—their smartly tailored but practical dresses; their glossy, upswept hair crowned by hats of felt or straw, modest enough for travel yet still of the latest style; their air of lively expectation.

All of them were so very young—none older than her middle twenties, Josephine guessed, and most closer to eighteen or nineteen. Their eager smiles and straight-backed confidence seemed a mockery to Josephine. Inadequacy rose once more in her gut like a bubble of thick black tar. She worked to swallow it down. *Teacher or bride, every one of them will find an easier time in Seattle than I. Youth is always so resilient, so hopeful. And I have no hope left—only desperation.*

She sighed and turned her face away from the chipper crowd. It was only then that Josephine noticed one woman alone, seated on a splintery crate at the far edge of the platform, dressed in parrot-green wool with a skirt that lay limp across her thighs. The woman's very stillness and isolation amid the bustling excitement on the platform made her so conspicuous that Josephine blinked in surprise and wondered how she hadn't taken note of this woman right away.

Josephine squinted, analyzing the woman in green with a more pointed air. A thick tumble of natural coffee-brown curls framed a rather sweet, heart-shaped face, with cheeks as round and smooth as a girl's. Josephine assessed her clothing. The green skirt lay so flat, it seemed, because it was devoid of its crinoline, and the hem was rough and frayed—perhaps torn. The young woman's dirty boots swung gently, rhythmically—kicking against the crate in a rather childish gesture that added to her youthful air. There was something curious about her posture—a straightness of the spine that was just a mite too straight, a lift of the chin that was too ostentatious—that spoke of insecurity and fear. Josephine tapped her chin, wondering why the girl in green, alone of all the assembled save Josephine herself, was without a sister or a friend to bid her farewell.

The puzzle of it made a welcome distraction from Josephine's fears, and so she resolved to find out. Something about the young woman's unusual appearance—her obvious lack of a crinoline, her mussed hair—drew Josephine in like a moth to a candle. And, Josephine reasoned practically, if she and the lone woman in green spoke to one another, neither of them would seem so conspicuous amid the happy chatter and well-wishing of the rest of Mercer's girls. She left her trunk sitting on the freight boxes and picked her way once more across the platform.

As Josephine approached, the girl in green seemed to shake off a clinging haze of distraction or exhaustion. She perked up like a spaniel, charming and alert, and flashed an impish smile at Josephine, all rosy cheeks and deep, beguiling dimples. Josephine couldn't help smiling back, but her brows jumped in surprise. The stranger didn't simply have a girlish face—she *was* a girl in truth.

"Hello," the girl said. She stifled a yawn as she spoke, but Josephine could tell that her voice was melodious and sweet. At close range, she could see how red and puffy the girl's eyes were, and that many of her rich, brown curls had worked free of her hairpins. A faint suggestion of mud grayed the front of her dress, as if she had been wet and stained hours before but had brushed the dirt away. The hem of her skirt and petticoats, Josephine could now see, were ragged and ripped away.

"Have you come to travel with Mr. Mercer?" Josephine asked.

Surely not, she told herself sensibly. The girl was pretty as a picture in spite of her dirt and disarray, but even so, she looked more beggar than would-be bride.

"Yes," the girl said eagerly. She gestured to an overstuffed pillowcase leaning against the freight box. "I'm all packed . . . I think."

Josephine looked down at the pillowcase in some surprise. The girl couldn't be older than sixteen, if even that. She yawned again, and gave a slow, heavy blink, and Josephine frowned at her red-rimmed eyes. Had she waited at the depot all the night through? Her mud-stained, ragged appearance now gave the impression not of a beggar but of a runaway—which the bulging, hastily packed pillowcase seemed to confirm.

Somebody ought to march this wayward child back to her parents' home, Josephine thought grimly. But she recalled with a shiver her own troubles, the dense, dark shadow of despair that hovered over Lowell. *Somebody ought to take this girl home, but that somebody won't be me.*

Besides, the poor thing must have her reasons for escaping this town. The Lord knows I have reasons of my own.

"I'm Josephine Carey," she finally said.

"Dovey."

The girl offered her hand to clasp, but did not offer a surname. *Fair and well,* Josephine thought as she squeezed Dovey's warm fingers. *I have no room to begrudge any woman her secrets—not at present.*

"You're to travel with Mr. Mercer, too, then?" Dovey asked. She eyed Josephine rather skeptically—doubting, Josephine assumed, whether a woman of her advanced age could make a suitable bride.

"Yes. I mean to take up a position as a teacher in Seattle. Whatever other plans the Lord may have for me in Washington Territory, I leave up to Him to dictate."

Josephine glanced around the platform again, counting the assembled women. They were thirteen in all, including Dovey and Josephine herself. *And what a pair we make, we two castoffs. The eldest and the youngest, the bookends of Mercer's cargo.*

Dovey's plaintive voice broke into Josephine's thoughts. "You aren't going to tell my father that I'm here, are you?"

The girl sounded so dejected—so defeated—that Josephine turned back to her abruptly, wide-eyed and nearly laughing. "Dear laws, Dovey, I don't even know who your father is!"

Dovey's swollen eyes narrowed, and she watched Josephine's face for a moment in suspicious silence.

"Even if I knew your father, I wouldn't tell. You have your reasons for leaving Lowell. So do I."

The girl's display of misgiving—that peek through her chipper, ready exterior to the vulnerability Josephine had glanced before—sent warmth surging through Josephine. She felt rather protective of the girl, quite suddenly and with a fierce insistence that took her aback. Was it merely their mutual status as outcasts that drew Josephine to Dovey? Was it the girl's natural charm—amply evident, even through her exhaustion and bedragglement? Perhaps it was only the fact that Josephine needed a friend so sorely—an ally who might stand beside her, or a distraction from the fears that would not relent even as she stood on the very brink of freedom.

She looked down at Dovey's pillowcase. "I have some room in my trunk—that one over there, on the crates opposite. Why don't you come along and add your things to mine?"

"Oh—may I? It's ever so kind of you!"

"You may, but you'll have to help me carry the thing. It's a bit too heavy to manage on my own. I think we can handle it together, though."

Dovey eased herself down from her perch and stood gingerly. But though she moved with deliberate care, still her face crumpled in distress and she uttered a little, choked cry of pain.

"What is it?" Josephine took her arm.

"My feet. They're terribly sore. I ran all night to get here, and when I couldn't run any longer, I walked. I'm afraid I can't go another step now."

"Come over to the bench, at least, and let me have a look."

Dovey leaned on Josephine's arm, hobbling and hissing softly with the pain. When they reached the bench, Josephine eased her down. She reached beneath Dovey's ripped, muddy hems and pried the boots from her feet—then stifled a gasp at their state. Dovey's winter-wool stockings were crusted with the fluid of blisters, and stained here and there with spots of blood.

"Lord," Josephine muttered. "You look like you've been chewed by a dog."

She pulled the stockings away as gently as she could manage. Angry red splotches covered the girl's feet from toes to heels. In many places the white bubbles of unruptured blisters stood boldly above the tender flesh, and on the knobs of her delicate ankles the skin had worn down into raw, half-scabbed abrasions.

"It hurts," Dovey admitted quietly, as if fearful the other women might hear and judge some weakness in her.

"I'll just bet it does."

Josephine retrieved her sewing kit and set to work with her embroidery scissors, gently releasing the fluid from the remaining blisters. Dovey flinched each time the scissors approached. Exhaustion and fear had left Josephine rather shaky, and she feared she might pierce more than just a blister if she couldn't keep Dovey still. She cast about for something to distract the girl from the sad plight of her own two feet.

"You're young, to venture west in search of a husband," Josephine said. "What inspired you to join Mr. Mercer's party, if I may ask?"

Dovey's pretty, rose-pink lips compressed for a moment, and she searched Josephine's face with a wary flick of her eyes. Finally, though, she huffed a little sigh of surrender. "Oh, Jo, it was awful. My father locked me up in my room and planned to marry me off to the worst man I know. Marion Stilton is a boor—and a bore. And he's vain and dim-witted. If I'm compelled to be charitable, I can admit that he's good-looking—though there isn't much else I can say in his favor. But I don't want a good-looking husband; I want a *respectable* one."

Josephine lanced another blister. "Mr. Stilton is not respectable?"

The girl snorted. "I should say *not*. He dodged the draft! Paid the exemption, and he's off scot-free, while all three of my brothers went to fight the Confederates. My eldest brother is dead now, and I have no idea how the other two fare."

"I'm sorry." Josephine looked up from her work, and was touched to see tears welling in the girl's red-rimmed eyes. Beneath Dovey's bold, brash exterior there beat a soft and gentle heart; despite the girl's bluster, and her alarming air of wildness, Josephine felt herself warming yet more to her company. "I wouldn't want to marry a dodger, either," Josephine said.

"My feelings on the subject were of no interest to Father." Dovey's voice was dark and low, and Josephine could practically smell the resentment simmering inside her—acrid and oily, a dish long stewed. "His only care is for his business—his wealth. Only, there's no business left, and no wealth, either."

"A mill man?"

Josephine was not surprised when the girl nodded. Dovey's father was hardly the only man in Lowell to have plunged from wealth to poverty, and it seemed each one who made that precipitous drop had the same sad tale to tell.

"I'm sure he thinks," Dovey said loftily, "to revive his business by hitching his wagon to the Stiltons. *I'm* his wagon now, his last good asset—but I won't be hitched. Not against my will. I'd rather go clear to Seattle and choose a man of my own, if I must have a man, at any rate."

"That seems reasonable enough."

"Then you won't tell my father?"

"Of course not."

Josephine had a few spare handkerchiefs in her trunk—they didn't take up much room—and she sacrificed these for Dovey's sake, cutting them into strips and binding her battered feet tightly.

"Thank you, Jo." Dovey's lip quivered with emotion as she gazed at Josephine. "I can call you Jo, can't I? I think I'd like to be your friend. You seem—well, sensible and fair."

Despite the worry that still shrouded her—she could almost feel hard, possessive hands reaching for her from the cold depths of the city—Josephine smiled. No one had ever called her Jo—nor any other nickname. Pet names didn't seem to suit her plain, sober face or her high-collar, old-fashioned style. But somehow, on the tongue of this sad, bedraggled little imp, the handle fit just fine.

"Your stockings won't do until you can wash them. Pack them away in my trunk, and your other things, too."

Josephine ventured back across the crowded platform to retrieve Dovey's heavy pillowcase. When she returned to their shared bench, she found Dovey staring at the provisions Josephine had packed with a morose air.

"Food." The girl's tone suggested she was about to administer a smart slap to her own forehead.

"You didn't pack any food for the trip?"

Dovey shook her head. "It was all so sudden, you see—my decision to join the Mercer party. I'm afraid I didn't think it through."

"You can share mine," Josephine said at once.

No charitable Christian could leave a waif like Dovey without crumb or crust to eat, but even so, Josephine wondered how on Earth she would make her provisions stretch now. She had packed everything she could scare up from her own pantry: a few hard sausages, a packet of ground coffee, a wheel of cheese no wider than her two hands, dried apples wrapped in oilcloth, and several oat biscuits, which would be stale long before they reached Aspinwall. It was poor fare, and if it were to sustain Josephine all the way to Seattle, then Jesus Christ himself must make an appearance on the voyage to repeat His miracle of the loaves and fishes. How the paltry store of food could possibly feed two women was beyond Josephine's comprehension.

We'll find a way, the told herself stoutly. *Perhaps I can patch and mend for the other women to earn a few more bites, a few little pennies.* She watched Dovey ease back into her boots. The girl stood and tested her weight on her feet, and grinned broadly at Josephine when she found herself able to walk. *Or perhaps I can lance the other women's blisters, too.*

"You're a saint, Jo." Dovey transferred her few goods into the trunk, including a lovely dress of fine blue wool, which made an indecorous rumple in the cedar box. Dovey closed the lid and brushed her hands together. "Sakes alive, but I feel awfully better now. I could run another night without stopping!"

"Don't try it," Josephine advised. "You'll have to coddle your feet, I'm afraid. As soon as we're settled on the train, take your boots off again and let your toes breathe. Your blisters will never heal properly if you keep your feet shut up all the time."

A hollow clatter rose above the platform's murmur of conversation—the sound of many hooves ringing against the cobbles. Dovey and Josephine stared at the noise. A fine carriage, pulled by six dappled grays, rolled to a smooth stop at the curb. The clarence was as lustrous and dark as black satin, and curtains of red velvet hid the occupants from view. A footman stepped down from the carriage's rear to swing the door open.

Josephine felt her brows rise of their own accord; the figures that emerged from the depths of the clarence were intriguing, to say the least.

A short, plump, older woman, with white hair streaking her dark-golden temples, was the first to descend from the carriage. Arrayed in a wine-red jacket and matching skirt, the black plumes of her extravagant, wide-brimmed hat nodding in the morning breeze, she stood with one hand on her hip, surveying the depot and the women gathered on its platform with a frankly dismissive air. Two girls followed, each younger than Dovey, both with curls of soft, butter-yellow hair falling to their shoulders in precise, orderly rows.

Next came a tall, slim woman of about twenty years. Even across the crowded platform, Josephine was struck by her beauty—her features were as sharp and delicate as flakes of ice, and her coloring was milk-glass pale, with hardly a blush to warm her angular cheeks. The young woman's hair, swirled into a thick bun at her nape and secured with a comb of glinting sapphires, was so light a shade of blonde that it seemed touched by frost. She held herself with a proud, erect bearing, and eyed the depot and the assembled women with the grim resolve of a soldier preparing to march into battle.

Last, a small, portly man with a shiny pate clambered gracelessly from the carriage. The women gathered about him, and, lifting his hands in a gesture reminiscent of a minister at the pulpit, he struck up an oration. The words of his speech did not reach Josephine across the platform, but she could hear the rising and falling intonations of his voice clearly enough. That bold, ringing tone cut through the open air and the murmur of the gathered women as smoothly as a spoon through cream. Josephine and Dovey watched as the man raised his hands to the stately, pale young woman's head. She bowed her head, accepting his blessing.

"What a show," Dovey muttered. "How did they all fit inside that carriage? Do you suppose the girls sat on each other's laps? Is this spectacle for our benefit, do you think? Or do they honk and flap like a flock of geese all the time?"

"I can't say," Josephine muttered, eyeing the young woman in sapphire blue with a twinge of wariness. Her staunchly upright bearing and the proud carriage of her fine, pointed chin gave her a particularly haughty air.

She seems just the kind of woman who'll be quick to judge someone like me, Josephine thought. *Just the sort who might expose me.*

If that vision of imperious pride was to join the Mercer party, Josephine knew she must guard her secret with even greater vigilance. Otherwise she might not make it to Seattle after all—and what hope could she cling to then?

CHAPTER FIVE
SECRETS AND INCITEMENTS

When Sophronia's father closed his blessing with a hearty and resonant "Amen!", her mother burst out with a theatrical cry. Her black plumes shivered as she dabbed at her cheeks with a kerchief. Sophronia dutifully pulled her mother against her breast in a farewell embrace, inwardly sighing at the dark spots left on her sapphire bodice—the traces of Mother's tears.

Sophronia turned to kiss her sisters on their cheeks, with more feeling than she'd embraced her mother.

"Mind your manners at all times," she told Elspeth, patting the girl's yellow curls—how she wished she could snip off a lock of those beloved tresses, and another from Augusta's head, and carry those precious mementos of her sisters with her across the wide, unfriendly continent. "Both of you must always be mindful of your reputation. Promise me you won't harm your chances at a good match. A respectable, righteous husband is your hope for a life well lived."

"We promise, Sister," Elspeth said, sniffling and wiping at her nose with the back of her hand.

Sophronia tutted and handed the girl a kerchief embroidered with her initials in a florid script. "There's no sense in crying."

"But we can't help it," Augusta moaned, clinging to Elspeth's arm. "We may never see you again!"

"Such histrionics," Sophronia gently scolded, and not without a note of fondness in her voice. "Our separation is but another trial from the Lord. And if we are faithful, all trials may be overcome."

Elspeth's fine features crumpled and reddened. "I despise trials from the Lord!"

Sophronia's back stiffened in shock. "Don't say such things. Nothing that proceeds from God's word or hand is to be despised."

But Elspeth went on weeping, and Augusta joined in, her small, slender form shuddering with hiccups and sobs.

Tears burned in Sophronia's eyes; she blinked them away mercilessly. "Come now," she said, taking each of her sisters' hands. "'Count it all joy when ye fall into diverse temptations, knowing this: that the trying of your faith worketh patience. But let patience have her perfect work, that ye may be perfect and entire, wanting nothing.'"

Sophronia paused expectantly. Elspeth blew her nose into the kerchief with an unladylike honk.

"James, chapter one," Sophronia prompted. "Verses?"

"Two through five," Augusta muttered sullenly.

"Two through four," Sophronia corrected.

Then, before her own treacherous tears could return, she swept her little sisters into a tight embrace. They clung to her, pressing their wet cheeks against her sleeves, whimpering in what, Sophronia knew, would likely be their final embrace in this life.

"You are two very fine girls," she said, willing her voice to remain steady and unshaken. "In a few years, you will have suitors—and then, the Lord willing, families of your own. Bear yourselves always with good grace, and in all things be worthy of your future husbands, your future children."

And may God grant you better prospects than I had, she told them silently as she kissed their flushed brows.

"It's time we were off," Father said, a trifle reluctantly. He took Sophronia's hand—a restrained display of affection, but all the more precious to Sophronia for its rarity.

She gave her father a trembling smile, gazing at his solemn face, his stout, sturdy shape, the neat precision of his coat and tie. "I will do you proud in Seattle," she told him. "I'll carry the Lord's word faithfully."

"I am certain you will, my girl." His throat seemed to constrict on that last word, and he turned abruptly away to climb into the carriage.

"Do write," Mother said faintly, holding Sophronia against her plump bosom again. Then she, too, was turning away, hurrying back into the safety of the carriage with a flurry of dark plumes and rustling silks.

Sophronia turned away from her family, gave a few curt instructions to the footmen who handled her baggage, and strode across the train's crowded platform, refusing to turn back, unwilling to watch Elspeth and Augusta depart. The murmurs of the women waiting for the train—the rest of the pilgrims in Mercer's party, Sophronia assumed—rose mercifully around her as she made her way into the crowd, and the chatter of their high, excited voices nearly drowned out the horses' hooves as the carriage rolled away.

Sophronia peered at the other women as she wended through the crowd. Most of them smiled politely, but none offered an introduction, and Sophronia kept moving. A few even shrank from her a little, as if intimidated by her presence. *Imagine, being intimidated by a mere woman!* She handled her deep-blue skirt deftly, careful not to lift the hem too high, as she brushed past groups of girls who conversed in the pale morning light with flushed faces and sparkling eyes, all of them intent on adventure.

"I'm Kate Clement Stevens," said one—the only young lady among them to offer her hand when Sophronia passed.

Kate had merry eyes and broad, high cheekbones that gave her face an aristocratic appeal. Her smile was friendly and eager, but Sophronia's chest tightened as she spoke to the girl, managing a few rote lines of courtesy through the sudden, sick welling in her gut.

Clement. The very sound of that name was a shock and an ambush—and Sophronia felt assaulted from all sides by bitter memories of her most recent beau.

Where was Clement now? Sophronia wondered as she nodded and smiled blankly at Kate's enthusiastic prattling. Was he off wooing again? Had he set his sights on another girl already? Was Clement even now winning the heart of some girl just like this Kate—blithe and convivial, untroubled by any care—and pretty as a picture into the bargain?

Clement would like you, Sophronia thought grimly as she listened to Kate's chatter. *He was forever telling me I ought to be more cheerful.* As if a rollicksome disposition were anything a proper woman should cultivate!

Clement hadn't approved of Sophronia's high principles, either. He was forever hoping to "melt the ice," as he so coarsely put it, seeking to tempt Sophronia into questionable behavior. On one occasion he'd even expected to plant a kiss on her cheek! She had shut that presumption down quickly, with a freezing stare and a handy Scriptural quote or two about chastity. When Clement had finally called off his suit, not so many weeks ago, Sophronia almost felt relieved—almost. In spite of all his urging to be more carefree and gay, Sophronia was firm in her resolve. Moral purity was the only reliable compass for any young woman's life. She would not give up the guidance of righteousness for anything in all the world—not even for a handsome face like Clement's.

A pair of younger women—sisters, by the look of them—distracted Kate from her chatter, and the girl turned away to engage with her friends. Sophronia slipped off into the crowd with some relief.

Clement, indeed! Sophronia had hoped to get through this journey without recalling her most recent beau—or any of the others. She was leaving behind her a long string of failed courtships, a trail of redacted proposals. Lowell was a wasteland to her now, as was Boston, where her father often preached, and the countryside where the Brandt family summered. Every eligible bachelor who had not been swept up by the war had set his heart against Sophronia, citing her good morals and righteous bearing as *flaws*—of all astonishing outrages. Clement had been her last sensible prospect for a good marriage, and when he had withdrawn his interest, Sophronia had searched for some escape from Massachusetts and the certainty of spinsterhood. In this expedition to Seattle, she fervently prayed, she had found the fresh start she needed.

As she made her way off through the crowd, moving as quickly as the press of bodies and scatter of baggage would allow, two women in particular piqued her curiosity. They sat together on a bench near a pile of shipping crates, conspicuously separated from the gaggle of women on the platform, and they stared at Sophronia with a stillness that could only mean they'd recently been talking about her.

Persiflage, no doubt. Sophronia narrowed her eyes at them. *Gossip all you please, ladies. I have heard it all before, and I know by now that loose tongues cannot hurt me.*

She had just made up her mind to turn pointedly away from their stares, but the state of one in particular caught Sophronia up short. The younger of the two was dressed in dirty green wool with a ripped hem, and her limp skirt seemed to have no crinoline beneath it. She had an especially youthful, almost childlike face. *Why, she seems entirely too young to be here.* Sophronia strode toward the pair on the bench, strafing them both with her eyes.

The elder of the two—a woman somewhere in her middle thirties, with a properly modest, if rather strained and tired appearance—offered Sophronia a mild nod. "Good morning."

"How old are you?" Sophronia asked the younger. She hadn't intended to ignore the mature woman's greeting, but at close range the girl in green seemed even more youthful. She certainly could have no sensible business with Mercer's party.

The girl did not answer right away, evidently taken aback by Sophronia's brusque query. Finally she tipped her pert little face up to meet Sophronia's stare and said, "Old enough."

"I doubt that. I doubt that *very* much. Are you fourteen? Fifteen? You cannot be fit for this role."

"Role?" The girl sputtered and lurched up from the bench—then immediately stifled a cry of pain and swayed as if her feet pained her. The older woman took the girl's hand, a soothing gesture.

Sophronia's mouth tightened in disapproval. She eyed the shabby green dress with its ragged hem. "You aren't even properly dressed. Where is your crinoline?"

"I don't like crinolines," she retorted. "Who does?"

The mature woman rose from the bench and held the girl's elbow in subtle restraint. "If you're part of Mr. Mercer's party," she said to Sophronia, "then we'll be traveling together. Let's try to get along, since we'll be so often in one another's company. I'm Josephine Carey, and this is Dovey . . ." She trailed off uncertainly, as if she didn't know the girl's surname.

"Dovey Douglas," the girl said. She gave an evasive bat of her lashes, and Sophronia felt sure the name was a lie.

"I am Sophronia Brandt." She, at least, would not prevaricate. A moral woman like herself had nothing to hide. "My father is William Brandt—you know, the Presbyterian minister at Lowell's largest church."

Dovey raised her brows. "You are traveling with Mr. Mercer, then? To Seattle . . . to marry a Washington man?"

Sophronia sniffed. "I do not look on the voyage to Seattle as an opportunity for marriage, but rather as a mission."

"A mission?" Dovey squinted at her in confusion.

"Seattle," Sophronia said grimly. "I have heard *much* about that frontier town—much about its *women*. A viler, more sinful place has hardly been seen since the Lord sent His judgment down on Sodom and Gomorrah." *And besides,* she added silently, *I've learned better than to encourage my own hopes where marriage is concerned.*

"Whatever do you mean?" said Josephine. "Mr. Mercer spoke very highly to me of Seattle and all its citizens."

"No doubt he did. One cannot lure flies with vinegar." Sophronia leaned toward the women and lowered her voice, speaking with quiet emphasis. "But mark my words, Miss Carey, Seattle is all vinegar. The place is a kettle of sin on the verge of boiling over. Mr. Mercer, I believe, hopes that brides will civilize the men of his town—and perhaps they will. But look around you: there aren't many of us gathered, are there? For every man Asa Mercer tames with a wife, ten more— *twenty* more—will still be free to wade deep into dreadful filth and wickedness!"

Dovey rolled her eyes and made no attempt to hide her scoff.

"Laugh all you like," Sophronia said loftily. "You'll not be laughing when God brings His judgment on Washington Territory. Remember Sodom and Gomorrah, young lady. Remember the words of the Lord's angels to Lot: 'For we will destroy this place, because the cry of them is waxen great before the face of the Lord.'"

"Careful you don't turn into a pillar of salt," Dovey muttered.

Sophronia lifted her chin. This was not the first time she'd faced mockery. No, not by any stretch of reckoning. *All they that see me laugh me to scorn,* she quoted within her heart, and the familiar Psalm restored her composure. "I shall be obedient to the Lord's will, as ever. I am not crossing the continent to hunt for a man, like these other women—but rather to bring what is sorely needed to the wayward women of Seattle: influence, an example of true virtue—and salvation of their eternal souls."

Dovey sputtered with laughter. "How grand of you!"

"If the Lord is willing, I will help make the frontier a pure and worthy place. With the help of my sisters and brothers in this great work, I will snatch Seattle back from condemnation before the Lord can rain down His righteous fire."

Dovey wound a dark curl around her finger, casting a mischievous smile at Sophronia. "That's an awful lot of work for one girl, don't you think? After all—the salvation of an entire city!"

Sophronia raked Dovey with another assessing frown. "I'm match enough for the work. And I can see that Seattle isn't the only place where women lack virtue. I suppose my mission must begin before I leave Lowell!"

"What on Earth do you mean?" The girl squared her thin shoulders, striving to look poised and grand in her tattered dress.

"*You're* a proper shame," Sophronia said. "I would never allow my young sisters to behave or to speak as you do! And I'd wager that you aren't even old enough to undertake this journey. When Mr. Mercer appears, I shall alert him at once, and see that you're sent back to your parents where you belong, young lady."

Dovey balled her fists and advanced, all the wobble gone from her step. "Oh, you will not! Just try it!"

Sophronia ignored the girl's protest and turned away. She craned her neck as if searching the crowd of women for Asa Mercer. Then she began to drift away, still looking about as if searching for a man of authority—someone to whom she might report Dovey's dubious presence. Such theatrics always brought her sisters into line. But this was no idle threat. Dovey Douglas, if that really was her name, was clearly unsuited to a voyage to the frontier. For her own good, Sophronia would see that she was restored to her senses and to her guardians.

Sophronia watched from the corner of her eye as the girl clutched Josephine's hand, wide-eyed with horror, but Josephine only shook her head in helpless confusion. Then, apparently realizing that she would get no aid from her friend, Dovey dropped Josephine's hand and took a few short strides after Sophronia.

"I'll show you Sodom and Gomorrah!" She spat the words like a cat squaring up for a fight. "Careful I don't rain my own judgment down on you, Little Goody Two-Shoes!"

Josephine cried, "Dovey, no!"—but too late. The girl rushed across the platform faster than Sophronia could countenance. She gaped in surprise as Dovey advanced, a blur of mud-stained green wool and fury, then spun away from that scowling whirlwind. But Sophronia hadn't moved quickly enough. Dovey planted her hands between Sophronia's shoulders and shoved, hard enough to make her stumble. Sophronia vented an undignified shriek as her boots clattered helplessly across the platform, and found herself tumbling into Kate's arms.

"Land sakes," Kate said, righting Sophronia and steadying her on her feet. "Are you all right?"

"Step away and let me at her!" Dovey bawled over the shocked murmurs of the crowd.

"Now, now! Ladies, this isn't becoming." Josephine stepped quickly between them, holding Dovey back with a hand on the girl's shoulder. "Let Dovey alone," she added coolly to Sophronia. "She's old enough to make the voyage, and if what you say of Seattle is true, then Mr. Mercer can't spare a single woman of good quality—not even the youngest."

"Of good quality?" Sophronia said dubiously, patting her hat to be sure it still rested straight atop her bun.

"At any rate," Josephine said, undaunted, "I've taken Dovey under my wing."

Sophronia's brows drew down and she opened her mouth to reply—but in that moment, the high, hoarse whistle of an approaching train sounded. Every woman on the platform turned eagerly toward the long grid of the railway tracks. The train came in from the west, the round, sooty face of its engine growing larger by the moment, a great plume of black smoke rising and trailing along its length, darkening the pearl-gray sky.

The girls of Mercer's party stirred in a renewed bustle, flitting about their trunks and bags, checking their hair and tugging the sleeves and tails of jackets straight.

Asa Mercer emerged from the depot building. He paused to shake the hand of a gray-haired man in a smart brown suit—some official of the railway, Sophronia assumed. Mercer looked toward the train with a weary, almost sad smile, but Sophronia did not trouble herself to wonder at his strange mood. Somehow Mercer's presence—his youthful face, crowned with its three high, distinctive waves of black hair—seemed a token of reassurance from the Almighty—a promise that all would be well.

The train crept on, slowing, sending a gout of dirty steam out from beneath its soot-darkened skirts. As it approached the depot's platform, its rust-red wheels let out a piercing scream. Sophronia winced at the sound and fidgeted on her feet. Her heart leaped in her chest.

Soon—I'll be away soon. I'll leave Lowell behind, with all its disappointments, all its shattered hopes. My life will start anew.

At last, the train ground to a halt. Sophronia would have leapt aboard and tucked herself at once into its interior, but the man in the brown suit summoned a stream of workers from the depot, and soon his men swarmed over the platform, collecting and loading the women's baggage. The girls, their faces alight with hope, clapped their hands and hugged one another in joyous anticipation. Sophronia might have joined in their glee, had she been able to call anyone among them a friend.

Mercer stepped atop a freight box and held his hands aloft. The assembled women settled politely, turning their beaming faces up to their leader. Josephine, standing beside Sophronia, bit her lip and paled. She alone among all the women seemed devoid of delightful anticipation. In fact, she seemed to be restraining herself with great effort—keeping back a shriek of impatience, perhaps, or some other expression of desperate, jaw-chattering fear.

Whatever has affected her so? Sophronia wondered. She cut a surreptitious stare at Josephine as Mercer began to speak, addressing the crowd in his smooth, even tenor.

"Ladies—you brave and true women of Massachusetts. I welcome you all to this expedition—this voyage of courage and love. And I thank you, most sincerely, for undertaking it. Seattle is waiting to welcome you all with gratitude and good will.

"We shall travel by rail to New York City, and from New York by ship to Panama."

Central America. It was such a terribly long way from home. Sophronia could still feel the warmth of her sisters as they'd clung to her, crying. *Now it is all real,* she told herself stoically. *Now my mission begins. Now I must sacrifice for the Lord's sake, and if I am righteous and faithful, surely He will reward me. Surely He will break my long loneliness, and grant me the husband and children—the* life *I long for.* She added a hasty amendment to her prayer: *If it be His will.*

Mercer concluded his speech as the last of the women's bags were carried aboard. His words were pleasant enough, and Sophronia did feel braced up by their brave, triumphant sound. But she could feel her past falling away already, before she had even boarded the train. *It's all for the best,* she told herself, *to leave the old life behind—all the disappointments, the heartbreak.* But despite Mercer's inspirational words, Sophronia knew Seattle to be a mire of sin. Even a warrior for the Lord's cause couldn't help feeling daunted at the prospect of leaving the staid, civilized society of Massachusetts behind for the unknown terrors of the frontier.

When at last Mercer had talked himself out, Sophronia pressed toward the front of the platform, determined to be among the first women on the train—to go boldly toward her new life, in spite of her misgivings. Never mind the bedraggled waif with the saucy tongue; if

Josephine wanted the girl under her wing, that was her own business. Sophronia had her own future to think of now.

At close range, the train's metal flank was warm with the fire of its engine, and the air around it stank of coal and heat. The women's excitement—the joy of a new beginning—tinged the air as heavily as the odors of the rail yard.

Mr. Mercer stepped down from his crate and came to stand beside Josephine at the platform's edge. Sophronia, still musing over Josephine's strained demeanor, turned one ear toward their conversation. Despite her eagerness to board the train, the line of girls streamed past her as she stood listening.

"Good morning, Miss Carey," Mercer said. "I see you made it on time."

"Of course." The older woman sounded tense and distracted, but when she saw how the smile faded from Mercer's face, she turned to him with more attention. "Is everything well? All is according to plan, is it not?"

Mercer tugged distractedly at his neat little beard. "According to plan—not precisely. It's a good thing you came after all, Miss Carey. It seems I need all the women I can get."

"But there are fourteen of us here," she said. "A very respectable number."

"Respectable—that is true. But I had hoped to—er—recruit rather more."

"More? How many brides were you after, Mr. Mercer?"

"I had hoped to find two hundred women ready to settle our city."

Sophronia forgot to be surreptitious. One hand flew to her mouth, and she gasped loudly. "Two hundred!"

Mercer smiled at her and offered a self-deprecating shrug. "I could have made do with half that number."

Josephine shook her head in wonderment, so startled that she was deaf to the engineer's call of "All aboard!" Sophronia, too, remained on the platform, staring at Asa Mercer in shock. What kind of strange land were they traveling to, where a hundred brides would have been a meager disappointment? *And if Seattle's need for women is truly so great—with barely more than a dozen of us, what kind of future awaits?* A flurry of terrible images crashed through Sophronia's head—a Seattle that was far worse than her wildest imaginings—the dark haunt of rapacious, wild men, with tangled, beastly beards and manners like bears. For a moment, Sophronia considered withdrawing from the voyage and remaining in Lowell. But there was nothing left for her here. Her final hope had departed when Clement had withdrawn his suit. There was no possible direction for her to go but west.

I am *going to Seattle, even if it is a jungle of desperate, grasping, frightful men.*

Sophronia ducked through the narrow portal of the train car, her neck and shoulders tense with resolve. The car's interior was arched and pale between its ribs of well-oiled wood. She slipped down the aisle, holding her skirts close. The women of the expedition, so happy in their hope, chattered and laughed as they found their seats and settled in for the ride to New York.

Sophronia and Josephine were the last to file aboard, and they found their seats at the rear of the car. Josephine sank onto the red-cushioned bench and peered out the narrow window. Sophronia followed her gaze. Men trudged up and down the sidewalk, paying no heed to the train or its passengers. A carriage rolled by, and Sophronia saw one of the little newspaper boys take up a post outside the depot, his mouth opening wide and round to call out the morning's headline. A perfectly innocent scene, placid and benign. Yet Josephine stared through the window with obvious trepidation. When Dovey reached across the aisle and took Josephine's hand, the older woman jumped and stifled a cry of alarm.

"Mercy," Dovey said, "what's come over you?"

Josephine gave a shaky laugh. "Travel nerves, I suppose. Don't worry about me; I'll be fine."

Dovey tilted her head to consider Josephine's washed-out complexion and trembling hands. "Jo, are you sure you're well?"

"I'm perfectly positive." Josephine tried a reassuring laugh, but Sophronia pursed her lips at its unconvincing sound. "I'm not terribly fond of trains—that's all."

"Get sick, do you?"

"Sometimes."

"You do look very pale," Sophronia told Josephine. "Do you have any gingersnaps in that trunk of yours? They'd cure your stomach."

Josephine made no reply but pressed herself into the bench's back as if she hoped her navy-blue wool might blend into the train's interior and hide her from view.

Whose view? Sophronia peered sharply out the window. *Did she see someone out there—someone she recognized? Somebody she's fleeing?* What other motive could explain Josephine's sudden, strange turn of behavior?

"Josephine," Sophronia began, "who—"

But in that moment, the engineer called the last boarding, and the train's whistle shrieked again. The sound of it vibrated down the length of the car, rattling Sophronia's bones until her head felt ready to split.

Then the train began to move, ponderous, slow as molasses dripping from a spoon, and all the while, Josephine remained pressed into the bench's cushions. It wasn't until the train found its speed that Josephine began to relax. Its rocking, swaying rhythm seemed to smooth the rough edges from her fear.

Whatever ails her, it's not travel sickness, Sophronia decided. She glanced out the window again and saw the town of Lowell falling away, its smokestacks dwindling, the long, empty rows of cotton mills vanishing behind the screen of the train's coal-black breath.

"We're really on our way," Sophronia said quietly. "We're truly leaving Lowell behind."

Josephine breathed a reply, so softly Sophronia was sure she wasn't meant to hear. "Thank God."

You're keeping a secret, Josephine Carey, Sophronia thought as the city vanished on the horizon. In Sophronia's experience, secrets were born of shame, and shame had its origin in sin. *I'll find out what you're hiding, for sin endangers us all.*

CHAPTER SIX
CHRISTIAN DUTY

Sophronia stood silent and resolute on the curb outside the boarding-house, watching the streets of New York City fill, moment by moment, as the morning grew later. Men in square-topped hats shouted to one another—greetings or threats, Sophronia could not tell. All the shouts sounded alike from her perspective, harsh and sharp and booming, like the barking of agitated dogs. Horses tossed their heads as they pulled jouncing carriages to and fro, dodging one another, swerving around the men who scurried between gray buildings with sides as smooth as glass.

That focused, tight bustle of industry was a sight she had not wit-nessed often in recent days, as Lowell sagged ever further into depres-sion. Although she had never been interested in business, she watched New York's awakening with keen attention, as if by focusing on the city's pother she could blot out her own predicament so completely that it might vanish altogether.

She had been the first woman to rise from her bed that morning. She was always early to rise, but the urge to be up and decently pulled together before any of the other women stirred was especially strong. There was no privacy to be found in a boardinghouse. Especially not one of this type, crowded and close, where the party of fourteen women and their lone guide were obliged to wait out the days until their ship, the *Illinois*, arrived to bear them south to the Central American railroad town of Aspinwall.

Sophronia endured those long hours of confinement with the best grace she could muster, guarding her modesty with a keen eye and an iron will. Oh yes—the first to rise in the morning. She would rise and dress *hours* before dawn if necessary, having no wish for any of the other women to look upon her bare skin. Sophronia abhorred the very thought of vulnerability, of exposing any part of herself to scrutiny or observation. She would not allow herself to be seen—not in the company of women she did not know.

And so she was the first to pack her things, the first to exit the boardinghouse and stand, expectant, in the chilly air outside. She was glad to leave the hard bed in that stuffy, rented room. The room itself was almost as narrow as the bed, and sepia shadows clung damply in every corner. The women had spent two nights and one day confined in the boardinghouse, and with each passing hour, as Sophronia had stared at the age-yellowed paper on the room's walls, as her eyes had roved over the buckles in its surface where moisture had collected beneath, her concerns and suspicions had only grown.

Two hundred and fifty dollars, indeed! Surely better accommodations could be had for such a princely sum. Since arriving in the shabby boardinghouse, Sophronia had begun to wonder whether the rumors in Lowell were true. Perhaps Asa Mercer's professional, efficient, well-dressed exterior was only a disguise. Perhaps, like a wolf in sheep's clothing, he had fooled them all, and was spiriting these women off—Sophronia herself!—not as respectable brides, but rather to force them into the coarse toil of ladies of ill repute!

This—the surprise she found waiting for her on the curb—the *thing* she could not bring herself to look at—only seemed to drive home that grim possibility with the force of a sledgehammer's blow. Sophronia sniffed and kept her eyes on the fine carriages whizzing by on the cobbled street, and refused to look at the—

"Wagons!" Dovey's delighted shout came from the boardinghouse's porch steps. "What fun!"

Wagons. Oh yes. That's what her two hundred and fifty dollars had purchased: the hire of a pair of flat-bedded, open-sided wagons, painted a bright, vulgar blue. It was a remarkably inelegant way to travel to the docks where their ship waited.

"Yes, indeed!" Sarah Gallagher, a pretty young woman with a pert, pointed nose, answered Dovey gaily. "And I, for one, will be glad to toss my travel box up into a wagon's bed, and from there into a ship's hold. I can't stand to carry it about any longer."

Sarah drifted over the sidewalk and hooked her arm through Sophronia's in an overfamiliar sort of way. "We'll be ten days sailing to Aspinwall, Sophie. Imagine it—ten whole days without having to lift a trunk once!"

Sophronia could think of no reply. She gaped at Sarah in astonishment. The girl couldn't have feigned the rosy flush of her cheeks nor the sparkle in her eye. Apparently she truly did relish this adventure, untroubled by the prospect of seasickness—or of being set on display before all the male eyes of New York City in the back of some blasted wagon!

"Be careful what you wish for," Sophronia finally managed. "Sea travel is not as romantic as you might imagine."

She was no stranger to travel by boat, and the promise of a queasy, wave-tossed voyage was nearly as bad as the certainty of yet more cramped, dingy quarters. And if they were to proceed to the waterfront packed into buckboards like so many bushels of turnips—well! Sophronia could not expect the *Illinois* to offer much in the way of accommodation. Or basic comfort. *Two hundred and fifty dollars, indeed!*

Sarah tutted good-naturedly at Sophronia's dark mood, then flitted off to join her friends in excited chatter. Sophronia smoothed the front of her skirt, begging the Lord to grant her forbearance.

I had best reconcile myself to this unrefinement, this coarse, hard new world. Mercer's rough accommodations could only be a foreglimpse of the trial to come. Seattle was sure to be ten times worse than any half-rate ship, and a hundred times more difficult to bear than the narrowest, dampest room in the shabbiest boardinghouse. But Sophronia's course was clear, and even if her road ran through Hell itself, she would walk it without complaint. Seattle—and her mission to save the fallen women of the frontier—was her last chance for earthly happiness.

What I must endure, I shall. God will lend me the strength to face all trials.

When the last of the travelers emerged from their brownstone boardinghouse, and all the women of Mercer's party stood arrayed on the sidewalk, the last of Mercer's hired wagons appeared. There were three of them in total, flat-bedded and with low, open sides. The drays were pulled by stout horses whose muddy legs and weary, patient heads looked better suited to toiling at the docks than to driving through the streets of New York. Sophronia eyed the nearest wagon carefully as its driver sprang down from the seat and began loading the women's trunks aboard. Beneath its coat of ostentatious blue paint, she could see the faint outline of letters: BOXLEITNER'S BEER.

Even if my road runs through Hell itself, she vowed, *I shall walk it without complaint.* But she sighed. A sigh did not count as a complaint.

Sophronia climbed aboard her beer dray with Mr. Mercer's help and sat on her trunk, as straight and placid as if she were riding in her family's fine clarence carriage. Several other women settled around her, including Josephine and, rotten luck, Dovey. That gamine little beast seemed *amused* by their situation, carted off to the docks in beer wagons for the whole of New York to gawk at. The girl grinned as the wagons began to roll, and fidgeted like a restless child where she sat on Josephine's trunk. Once, Sophronia caught Dovey waving at staring passersby, and the audacity of the gesture so mortified Sophronia that she could not even summon the composure to correct the girl.

Oh, there were not a few passersby who stared. Sophronia donned a mask of perfect calm, and kept it fixed in place all the long ride to the pier. But she felt every man's eye upon her back, her face—her *body*. Yet, she told herself sensibly, trying to quell the flume of outrage that rose up in her breast, it was only natural to stare at a train of liquor drays carting off a cargo of women. She would stare, too, if she witnessed such a spectacle.

What must they all think of us—of me? She felt exactly as tawdry as the men of New York deemed her to be. Her fair complexion always announced a blush most readily; she might sit regally still on her traveling box, as cool and composed as a queen, but she could not disguise her flaming mortification as the wagons rolled along. *I will most definitely speak to Mr. Mercer as soon as the opportunity presents itself,* she decided. *And I will not bridle my words!*

Josephine noted Sophronia's discomfiture. "Are you well?" she asked, leaning across the bed of the wagon to take her hand.

Sophronia could only nod in response—her voice would certainly come out as an undignified squeak, if she could manage any sound at all. But her mind worked furiously, churning over this bleak dilemma, seeking some recourse and finding none.

Have I gone and sold myself into filthy affairs? If she had, she would get out of this mess on her own. She did not need Josephine's inquiries into her health, nor her sympathy, nor her help. She would not—*could* not rely on the aid of any of these women—who, for all Sophronia knew, were only too happy to become tarts. Dovey's dimpled glee at their present circumstance was proof enough of that. The girl was completely at her ease, displayed before all the men of the city like a frosted cake rolling to and fro on a dessert cart.

After half an hour, when Sophronia's composure was strained to its absolute limits and she felt herself on the verge of standing up in the wagon bed to scream hysterically, the beer wagons reached the waterfront. The salty stink of wharves surrounded her, and that sharp, familiar odor of brine, rot, and bitter coal tar came as a relief. If a long journey into the unknown still waited ahead, at least their mortifying exposure to stares and speculation was ended.

Sophronia was the first to scramble down from her wagon, only too happy to distance herself from that ignominious conveyance. She brushed the wrinkles from her skirt and stood staring up at the *Illinois*, moored at the nearest dock. Its hull was as black and glossy as a beetle's shell. A needle-thin bowsprit thrust out from its forward deck, and the lines that ran from that long, sharp beak to the first of three great masts hummed lightly in the wind. The dark cylinders of two high, even stacks rose amidships, releasing gentle puffs of black smoke. At port and starboard, two huge paddle wheels reared above the decks, encased in white-painted wooden cages, reaching almost as high as the smokestacks.

"What do you think of the boat?" Josephine had alighted on the cobbles beside her, and stood gazing up at the *Illinois* with a vague, uncertain smile.

"It looks capable," Sophronia said. "To be honest, it's better than I'd hoped to find, after our stuffy little boardinghouse and these . . . *wagons* we rode in."

"You have an eye for ships," Josephine observed.

"I've sailed often with my family."

That was true. The Lord knew the Brandts were well traveled, but plenty of seasonal jaunts up and down the Atlantic coast hadn't been enough to inspire Sophronia to learn about ships and seafaring. Only

James Gooding had sparked her interest in the sea. James—her second suitor, and the only prospective husband with whom Sophronia had felt herself truly in love. The loss of his suit had hurt her more than all the rest combined. When James finally tired of Sophronia's rigid ways, he had withdrawn his interest and returned to the sea.

For all she knew, he was a bachelor still, married only to his ship and the sigh of the waves. Sophronia often wondered whether James recalled their days together, their sailing trips when he had shown her how to harness the wind and breast the swells. Did he think of her fondly now and then, or were all his memories of Sophronia ruined by the last bitter days of their quarrels?

It's just as well, she told herself ruthlessly, to quell the tears that threatened. *Sailors are all fornicators at heart.* Everyone knew that sailors kept loose women in business. Why else did fallen women love port towns and piers so well? *If I had married James Gooding, it would have been but a matter of time until he took up with whores.* Not even love could eradicate the filthy habits of seafaring from a man's soul.

Asa Mercer led the women aboard the *Illinois*. They were granted an hour to settle in and acquaint themselves with the ship, for the *Illinois* was primarily a mail carrier, and its cargo of letters and packages was still to be loaded. Sophronia was pleased to find that although the passenger cabins were narrow and rather dark, they were not as dismally uncomfortable as she had feared. The bunks were tolerably soft, and there was ample storage for her trunk and all her bags.

But Sophronia refused to be lulled into complacency. She left her baggage sitting on her bunk and returned to the ship's deck to seek out Asa Mercer. She found him without much trouble—a lone figure at the ship's prow, distinctive in his dark, well-tailored coat. Mercer leaned his forearms on the *Illinois*'s rail, his hat dangling in one hand as he brooded down on the pier and city below. He looked up with a tentative smile as Sophronia made her way briskly toward him.

"Miss Brandt," he said. He reached up as if to tip his John Bull hat at her, and then, realizing it was clutched in the other hand, his flat cheeks colored.

"Mr. Mercer." She gave him a tight nod. "I have come to express my displeasure."

"Displeasure?" He seemed truly startled by this, and straightened gamely. "With what, may I ask? Only tell me, and I'll put it to rights at once."

"I . . ." Sophronia hesitated. Mercer's readiness to see to her comforts took her aback. She had spent so long musing darkly over his hidden motives that she had come to suspect the worst of him. She had been prepared for some other response—an evil cackle, perhaps, and a villainous rubbing together of his hands—not this eagerness to please, this genuine concern lighting his handsome features. She cleared her throat. "I'm afraid there's nothing to be done about it now. But what were you thinking, sir, driving us about in *beer wagons?*"

"Ah, that. Yes." He scratched the back of his neck, in obvious abashment. "I hired the things without seeing them firsthand. I didn't expect them to be quite so . . . exposed. I hope you were not too much offended."

"Now, it's neither here nor there. The moment is gone and past. But really, Mr. Mercer, certain of your decisions have led me to wonder . . ." She trailed off, shifting her weight from one foot to the other, suddenly reluctant to breach the terrible topic.

"Yes, Miss Brandt?" He gazed at Sophronia, attentive and patient.

"I have been led to wonder about your motives, sir."

"I see." A certain darkness passed across his face—not anger at Sophronia, but rather a strain of self-doubt. He turned the John Bull hat in his hands, traversing its rim with distracted fingers.

"Have we been led astray, Mr. Mercer? Are your intentions as pure as we were made to believe?"

"I assure you, Miss Brandt, they are. It is my preference, like yours, to travel in greater style and comfort. But I truly thought I would find more women in Lowell who were eager to make the journey to Seattle. After all, Lowell has fallen on such hard times, with the cotton trade in dramatic decline and so many young men off to fight the rebels. I had assumed—falsely, I now see—that Lowell would be bursting with young ladies eager for better prospects. I'd thought to have dozens more to share the cost of travel. As it is, we must tighten our belts. We are not quite as poorly off as church mice, but I'm afraid we must cut close to the bone."

"Two hundred women," Sophronia said, louder and more sharply than she'd intended. "I overheard your words to Josephine Carey at the train station. Land sakes, Mr. Mercer, what *can* you be planning for two hundred women? The figure itself is obscene; I can only hope your intentions are not."

"I intend nothing but marriages, Miss Brandt—happy, fruitful marriages. You cannot know how sorely the men of Seattle need the influence of good women—ladies of upstanding character, like yourself."

Sophronia subsided with an effort. "I have heard much about your city. It is rough around the edges, I understand."

"Around the edges, and straight to its core. My family was among the first to settle there, when it was nothing more than a muddy hillside and a few lean-tos built from cedar branches. I've watched Seattle grow, and I've only feared for its future as it has expanded.

"You fear I've come east looking for women of ill repute—you needn't look surprised, nor try to deny it, Miss Brandt. I've heard every accusation and assumption already. But believe me when I tell you, there is no need to look outside Seattle for sin. There are ten men for every woman in Seattle, and nearly every woman is a working lady . . . if you understand my meaning. The few women of real character are married already—most of them came to the city already wedded to their husbands. With no prospects for courtship, no hope for respectable futures, the men of my town are content to descend ever further into vice. Drinking and gambling will soon turn the place into a sinkhole of immorality, I fear—one from which it will never recover. Unless the men of Seattle have reason to hope for something more."

"And we are to be that hope."

A thrill of confirmation raced along Sophronia's limbs. Indeed, this was why the Lord had denied her love, withheld the companionship and security she so longed for. She *was* being preserved for a great mission—set apart for this important task. The very morality that had so isolated her in Massachusetts was to be her standard, her banner. She would march into Seattle and bring righteousness to that untamed land.

"I pray that you and the rest of the women will bring the influence Seattle so desperately needs," Mr. Mercer replied.

"And how are we to find husbands? Have arrangements already been made?"

Mercer chuckled. "No, no—God preserve me, no! There are so many men hungry for a good wife, I never could have found enough women to meet that demand. As it is, I'm woefully short of my most conservative estimate. It will be up to you ladies to sort through the men Seattle has to offer, to consider their suits and entertain their courtships, just as you would do at home. It's my hope that each one of you will find love and happiness with some lucky man of my city—for despite the grim picture I painted, Seattle has more than its fair share of good men, willing to give up sin and vice for the sake of a good woman."

"I wonder that *some* of these ladies had to leave Lowell at all to find love and happiness." Sophronia gazed out at the city, carefully arranging her features to hide her anxiety. Well did she know that she was likely the only woman in Mercer's expedition who had exhausted all possibility for love in Massachusetts. "It makes a person suspicious of their motives, their characters . . ."

"I won't bring you to the West against your will, Miss Brandt. If you have any misgivings, about Seattle or your fellow travelers, or about me, now is the time to act, before the ship sails. It's not too late to go back to Lowell. Life in Seattle is not easy, and the work will be hard—but rewarding in the end, I pray."

Sophronia lifted her chin in a display of courage—but her mind was already made up. Seattle offered a great work in the name of the Lord, and she would be true to her purpose. At last, all the disappointment and pain of her failed courtships made a kind of divine sense. No force in Heaven or on Earth could dissuade her from going now.

The ship sounded its loud, hollow cry—so sudden and close it made Sophronia and Mr. Mercer both start in surprise. The engine in the *Illinois*'s heart boomed to life. With a loud creak and a slow, rhythmic slap, the paddle wheels began their ponderous turning.

"Last chance to return to Massachusetts," Mr. Mercer said.

But Sophronia only smiled in reply as the ship pulled slowly away from New York.

The *Illinois* was not long out of the harbor before the journey grew rough. March was not the friendliest month for sea travel; the waves were hard and relentless, the ship's deck pitched unmercifully, and the constant, rhythmic thrum of the engine—the numbing slap-slap-slap of the paddle wheels—sent an endless vibration through the ship's bones that made rest next to impossible. Before the first day of the voyage was through, even Sarah Gallagher had lost the optimistic bloom of her cheeks. Not one of the women had bargained for an adventure quite like this.

Sophronia, who was the most experienced with sailing, fared well enough, though her patience was thin and frayed. But several of the travelers grew quite ill. Hardly an hour passed without one or another of Mercer's women wobbling from her cabin across the cold, spray-covered deck to empty her porcelain pot over the ship's rail. Most of the girls adapted to the constant sway and lurch of the waves within a day or two, and the plague of vomiting eased. But a few remained bedridden, moaning and heaving, trapped in disoriented misery.

To Sophronia's surprise, it was Dovey—plucky and hardy though she seemed—who fell sickest of them all. She didn't see the girl emerge from her cabin once, and the other women of Mercer's party took turns seeing to Dovey's needs.

On the fifth day of the sailing, as Sophronia lay reading her Bible on her bunk, an urgent tap sounded on the cabin door. She found Josephine outside, her face drawn and pale—with the strain of sea travel, Sophronia wondered, or with fear?

"Dovey is terribly ill," Josephine said, her voice cracking with weariness. "We've all done everything for her that we know to do, but . . . nothing seems to help her."

"I can't imagine what I might do to help," Sophronia replied.

"You know ships, don't you? You know the sea. You said your family sailed. And you know how to treat sickness of the stomach. I remember—back at the train station, you told me—"

"But I'm not a doctor, Josephine."

"You're the only one of Mercer's party who hasn't fallen ill. You've more experience with this boat business than any of us. Please, Sophronia—come and help Dovey."

Josephine's worry was so plain that Sophronia relented, just for the sake of Josephine's nerves. She followed the older woman down the narrow, inner hall between cabin doors and squeezed with her into Dovey's crowded quarters. Catherine Stickney, slender and rather nervous by nature, perched on a small, rickety stool beside Dovey's bunk, holding the girl's limp hand. She looked up as Sophronia entered, and her pleading eyes were dark-ringed with the remnants of her own recent bout with seasickness.

"Oh, Sophronia," Catherine said, "is there anything you can do for her—anything at all? The poor girl—so young and frail!"

Frail was the one thing Dovey was not. Sophronia had expected to find Dovey sitting up in her bunk, rolling her eyes at her friends and dishing out her typical sauce. But to her surprise, Dovey lay flat and insensate, her dark curls plastered to her forehead by sweat. She was clad only in a stained chemise, and through its grimy folds her body looked too small and thin. Her eyes were sunken, the lids an alarming shade of violet-blue; her lips were cracked and raw. She shivered faintly.

Sophronia felt a pinch of fear. Was this something more than a bad case of seasickness? Fever, perhaps? *Lord preserve us! It will spread like wildfire on a ship.*

Sophronia mustered her calm. The stench of vomit—and worse— was thick inside the cabin. The girl was dehydrated—severely so, after days of vomiting—but it was surely nothing more dire than that.

"Brace up, girls." Sophronia gave Catherine and Josephine a reassuring smile. "She's worn herself out with all the heaving, but if we can get her to keep down a few sips of water, she'll be all right."

"We can't," Catherine nearly wailed. "We've been trying to keep her watered for days, but she heaves up anything she swallows down. Oh, I'm terribly afraid she'll die!"

Josephine clutched Sophronia's elbow; she could feel the other woman's hand trembling. "I don't know what to do, Sophronia. I'm afraid that if we can't get her to drink—and to keep it down . . ."

Tears shone in Catherine's eyes. She lifted Dovey's pale hand to press it against her cheek. Dovey gave a weak moan and her dry lips twitched, but she said nothing.

She very well may die, if she cannot drink. A hard lump rose in Sophronia's throat, and she swallowed it down before it could turn to tears. Dovey might be unpleasant, and Sophronia's dislike for such a wicked, amoral creature was as natural as breathing, but she could not call herself a Christian if she weren't moved by the sight of suffering. *Perhaps it's not only my mission to Seattle that will atone for whatever wrongs I've done—that will earn me the love I so crave. Perhaps the Lord wants me to humble myself and care for this hardheaded girl, too.*

She nodded, ready to minister to this wretched child if God required it. "Josephine, come with me. Catherine, you must stay here with Dovey until we return."

Sophronia had packed plenty of dried ginger for her own use—a must-have for sea travel—but even with the rough seas of early spring, she had found little need for the stuff. One could never predict whether seasickness would strike; Sophronia had learned the truth of that long before James Gooding had carried her heart away. Back in her own cabin, with Josephine looking on, Sophronia rummaged through her trunk until she found the packet of ginger amid her ample stores. She opened the packet and poured a few of the small golden nuggets into her hand.

"Brew a dozen or so of these into a strong tea," she told Josephine. "I've a few porcelain cups in here somewhere; I'll give you one. You'll need to hold the cup over a candle flame, I'm afraid—there's no reliable way to keep it brewing in these rough seas, so you must monitor the process yourself. But once the cup begins to steam, the ginger should do its work."

"It will stop her vomiting?"

"If God is willing. It acts quickly, and should put a stop straightaway to her nausea. We'll know after the first cup whether it will work or not."

In the dim confines of the cabin, Josephine looked at once more stoic and more afraid than Sophronia had ever seen her before. Her hazel eyes darted down to Sophronia's open trunk, and at the sight of all the goods on display—plump sausages in their waxy white casings, six rounds of hearty bread still soft beneath their crackled crusts, and even little pots of strawberry preserves and honey, their lids clamped shut by metal springs—Josephine's lips thinned in a worried frown.

"How well was Dovey eating?" Sophronia asked cautiously. "Before the sickness, I mean."

Josephine's eyes welled, and she shook her head in defeat. "Not well. The poor girl brought no provisions of her own, and she has been sharing mine. I . . . I brought what I could from Lowell, but it was barely enough to keep my belly full, let alone hers, too."

Sophronia clicked her tongue. "Josephine, you cannot deprive yourself of food. You'll fall ill, too."

"I already have."

"It's a wonder you recovered, then, and didn't end up like Dovey."

"But I couldn't let her go hungry, Sophronia. She's only a girl."

"Exactly." Sophronia drew herself up and folded her arms tight below her bosom. "I told you both back in Lowell that she was too young for this journey. But you insisted she was under your care! The poor child should be back home with her parents, not withering away on a ship."

"The one place Dovey should *not* be is back home with her parents. Each of us left Lowell for good reasons of our own. We all hope to find a better life in Seattle. That's as true for Dovey as it is for me—and for you, despite all your talk of this mission from the Lord."

Sophronia sniffed at Josephine's outrageous assumption. "My mission to save the wayward souls of Seattle is all the motivation I need."

Josephine folded the packet of ginger carefully. "Thank you for the medicine," she said evenly. "I know you'll pray as hard as the rest of us that Dovey will pull through."

Josephine turned for the cabin door, but before she could open it, words tumbled from Sophronia's mouth. "Wait. You need food—you and Dovey both."

The older woman glanced back in surprise, and Sophronia could feel her own startlement writ large across her face. She hadn't intended to say any of this, and her sensible side still muttered that Dovey would be better off sailing north to New York, not south toward Central America.

But her heart was moved to pity—for Josephine and for Dovey—and Sophronia knew that no matter how she might try to armor it with righteous ideals and rigorous morals, that soft and gentle heart would always rule her spirit.

"Take some of my food," she said, still hugging her body with her slender arms. "Share it with Dovey. Once she's sipped on the ginger tea for a few hours, the poor girl will be ravenous."

"It's very generous . . ." Josephine shook her head, wide-eyed and dazed. "But Sophronia, I can't."

"You certainly can, and you shall."

"*I* took responsibility for Dovey—I took her under my wing. I can't ask you to—"

"You aren't asking. Yet I am insisting. You're in need, Josephine—both of you. We must never be too proud to accept help when we are in need."

"But I can't take what you offer on . . . on charity." There was a sudden hardness to Josephine's voice so entirely at odds with the deep, fearful vulnerability in her eyes that Sophronia stepped closer to the other woman, drawn by a desire to examine her. Josephine pressed her lips together and stared back, a display of strength—and Sophronia saw that for all her coddling of the hoyden Dovey, Josephine was, in her own way, as idealistic as she. *And as proud,* she admitted to herself, though she knew well that pride was a sin.

We're more alike than we are different, she wanted to say. *That makes us sisters of a sort. There is no charity between sisters—only love, only giving.*

But the lump had returned to her throat, and those sentimental words refused to come. Instead, Sophronia offered, "If it makes you feel better, I'll allow you to sew for me in exchange for the food." She reached out and brushed the tamboured linen of Josephine's dress. "This is very fine embroidery. Can you do the same for me?"

Josephine's self-deprecatory chuckle filled the cabin. "It may be fine, but it's terribly outdated. This type of needlework fell out of style years ago, I'm afraid."

"It ought to come back into style, then." Sophronia smiled, and Josephine's answering grin was wide and warm.

"You have a sweet, kindly smile," Josephine said. "You ought to let it show more often."

Sophronia tossed her head. *What nonsense.* Even stuck on a ship, she had no time or patience for sentimental talk. She led Josephine back to Dovey's cabin, then sent Catherine Stickey off to fetch a bucket of water. It was time Dovey's soiled clothes were washed. Sophronia helped Josephine peel the dingy chemise from the girl's body, then, together, they tucked her beneath a wool blanket.

"Bring that candle here," Sophronia said. "I'll show you how to brew the ginger tea."

"I'm so glad of your help, Sophronia."

"It's only my Christian duty, to ease the wretchedness of the world."

"All the same, I'm glad to have you beside me."

Sophronia patted Josephine's hand, then guided it to the candle flame, showing her how to hold the cup just so, how to move with the rolling of the waves so that the heat never left the cup, until its steam released the soft, subtle perfume of ginger into Dovey's cabin.

"Together," Sophronia said, "we'll bring this girl around."

And may the Lord grand that we can *bring her around,* Sophronia prayed soberly. *Her salvation as well as my own may depend on it.*

CHAPTER SEVEN
ASPINWALL

The coast of Panama appeared as slowly, as softly, a dream through a low, humid mist. Dovey watched from the rail of the *Illinois* as the horizon turned from the blue-gray of the sea to a brilliant streak of emerald green. Even on the open water, far outside of harbor or mooring, she could sense a change in the air—a certain thickening, a palpable density, as the canopy of trees on the shore held the moisture low in the air. She closed her eyes and breathed deeply in relief. The shore was far off yet, but Dovey could smell it—or perhaps she only imagined she could—the warm-green, soothing spice of damp leaves and rich, firm ground.

It would be a blessing to set foot on land again, and no mistake. This voyage had already amounted to more than Dovey had bargained for, and it was only half done. She was clearly not cut out for sea travel, but she would rather be here, on the rolling deck of the *Illinois*, still shaky and weak from her days of illness, than standing at the altar with Marion Stilton.

She breathed in another deep lungful of thick, warm sea air. *Now that I'm gone,* she wondered lightly, *how will Father get along? What will he do about his closed mills—his dead business?*

He would manage well enough, Dovey felt sure. He had always been a resourceful man, and though he seemed to attach great importance to shepherding Dovey through life—enough to threaten her with marriage—she felt sure he wouldn't dwell on her going. Not once he found some way to revive his business.

Mother was far more troubling to Dovey—Mother and the boys, still off at war. She could write to her mother, Dovey knew, once she was settled in Seattle and her days of travel were behind her. *But it's likely I'll never see her again—never set eyes on her, or hear her voice, or hold her hand.*

She'd been a fool to run off so impulsively. And to sell Mother's jewels for the travel fare—that gnawed at Dovey's conscience, stabbing her heart with a pang that never quite abated.

I should have stayed and reasoned with Father. I could have found some way to calm him, to make him give up his mad plan of packing me off to the altar.

Even as she thought it, Dovey knew it wasn't true. John Mason was the most single-minded, bull-headed specimen of blustering masculinity the Lord had ever created. Once he'd set his mind to marry Dovey off, he'd have seen the deed through to its end. Dovey had had little choice, and she knew it. But was her mother's love the price for her freedom and self-respect? She feared her mother's reaction, once she learned what her only daughter had done. *Mother is a kind soul, but she's so terribly proper. She won't understand why I've run away—the pain it would have brought me, to marry the Stilton boy.* Her dismay might even be great enough that she would disown Dovey. That threat carried a powerful sting.

Josephine stepped out from the long, covered hall that sheltered the *Illinois*'s passenger cabins. Dovey, glad for the distraction from her dark thoughts, waved a greeting, and Josephine stared beyond her, to the lush, green glow on the horizon. A smile of pure awe lit her face, animating her otherwise severe features.

She really is a pretty lady, Dovey thought, *and could be prettier, if she'd only allow herself to be.* Through the days of Dovey's recovery, she had puzzled over Jo, who had hardly left her bedside. The older woman's show of mousy humility seemed contrary to her true nature. Dovey always felt as if Jo wore her studied plainness like a disguise. But what need did she have of any disguising? What secret was Jo keeping—what was she hiding from?

More of Mercer's girls made their way out into the fresh morning air, and the deck filled with exclamations of joy at the sight of Panama— of blessed, solid, unmoving *land*. Dovey watched them all, more curious than ever before as to their motives, their stories—the secrets they, too, must keep. Each woman had her own reason for embarking on this mad journey. Surely some among them simply wanted a change—Lowell and the entire war-torn East Coast had become a tiresome, depressing place. But it was such a *drastic* change—terrible, even—to leave one's whole life behind and start over anew, to bet on a future that lay shrouded beyond a misty horizon.

Terrible—that was exactly the word for the upheaval Dovey had wrought in her own life. True, she had little choice in the matter, but still the fact of her circumstances gnawed at her. It was most unlikely, she knew, that she would ever see her brothers again—if Bart and Ewing survived the war. *And Mother . . .* Would she ever again set eyes on her beloved face, or feel her warm, gentle touch?

Sarah, the pretty, blue-eyed songbird, had begun to sing a hymn of thanksgiving, while a few of the girls, unable to maintain their dignity in the sight of land, swung one another about by the hands, laughing. Dovey watched them from the rail, chewing pensively at her cracked lip. Were some of these women glad to leave their old lives behind—as relieved to be rid of the past as they were to reach this tropic shore? If they had left Massachusetts reluctantly, did they mourn what they'd left behind? What greater hope motivated them to cast off the comfort and familiarity of their old lives? What hope did Seattle hold for them? What longings could the West fulfill that home could not?

Sophronia was the last woman to step out into the morning light. She stood beside Jo, considering the coast of Aspinwall with cool, distant eyes. The collar of Sophronia's jacket had been delicately stitched with pale-pink thread, an intricate embroidery of vines and flowers. It looked rather old-fashioned, Dovey thought, yet it had a charm all its own. The twisting pattern of the little pink vines was much like the embroidery on Jo's old lavender dress.

Jo must have embroidered Sophronia's collar. So those two are friends now?

Dovey felt a surge of envy, and knew at once that it was a foolish reaction. Jo and Sophronia had worked together to nurse Dovey through her illness, and she owed them both a debt of gratitude.

Jo and Sophronia joined Dovey at the rail. Despite the days they had spent in close quarters, with Sophronia helping tend to some of Dovey's most personal needs, the icy blonde carefully placed herself on Jo's other side.

Too good to stand near me—is that it?

"You're looking much better," Jo said. "I'm glad to see you up out of bed."

"And just in time to see Aspinwall, too." Dovey resolved to shake off Sophronia's chill. She had much to be thankful for today, and she wouldn't let that self-righteous cat with a ramrod for a spine cast a shadow over her joy. "I still feel awful quivery, but I guess I'll make it."

Dovey peered at Sophronia from the corner of her eye, watching that calm, regal profile as Sophronia studied the emerald horizon. Even though the pale woman ignored her most strenuously, Dovey said, "Sophronia, I owe you my thanks. You nursed me through that illness, and I'm grateful to you."

"We *all* nursed you," Sophronia said, as if saving a life were nothing.

"But it was your ministrations that brought me through the worst of it. I was pretty ill, wasn't I?"

Sophronia shrugged, still watching the horizon. "You were dehydrated from all the vomiting. Another day or two and you might have been in real danger, but seasickness is easy to treat, once you know the knack of it."

"How did you learn the knack?"

At last Sophronia turned her pale, piercing eyes to Dovey. Pain and regret flashed in their depths, so forceful that Dovey stepped backward. But in another moment, Sophronia's expression smoothed. "I've traveled often by boat, ever since I was a little girl. Have you never been on a ship before, Dovey?"

"I suppose I have," she said. "When I was very small my parents took me with them on a pleasure trip down the Atlantic coast. But I don't remember much of it, except that it was cold on the deck of the ship. And I remember the seabirds calling and floating in the air beside the rail. I never got sick—or if I did, it wasn't so severe."

Sophronia raised one silver-white brow in her maddening, appraising fashion. "Your parents have some means, then. Your father is a wealthy man?"

Dovey gripped the rail hard and glanced at Jo, seeking some guidance from the older, wiser woman. But Jo turned to her with a gaze as curious, if not as frosty, as Sophronia's.

"My family does well enough," Dovey finally said.

Sophronia wordlessly considered Dovey's mended hem and scuffed boots.

"*Did* well," Dovey amended. "His business has suffered from the rebellion—but that's no surprise. Who in Lowell hasn't fallen on hard times, with the cotton trade ailing?"

"Your father was a mill owner, then?" Sophronia asked.

Dovey didn't like her tone—its slick, ferrety persistence. In a great rush of ire, she made up her mind to drop all pretense of hiding and out herself to the whole expedition. Let Sophronia do her worst; they had practically made it to Central America, anyhow, and there was little anyone could do to impinge Dovey now.

She drew herself up and faced Sophronia's level, judgmental stare. "Yes, my father was a mill owner. John Mason is his name. Perhaps you've heard of him—the Lord of Lowell, they used to call him, before every one of his factories closed."

Sophronia's eyes widened, and Jo let out a little gasp.

"I'm Doreen Mason—his only daughter. And if the Rebels have their way, I might end up his only living child."

"My goodness," Jo muttered. "The Mason family! Oh, but Dovey . . . if your poor brothers are killed—and I pray they are not—you would inherit a fortune! Whyever did you decide to run off to Seattle?"

"Because I *won't* inherit a fortune," Dovey snapped. "My family is all but destitute now. Mother's terribly ill and is in Boston under the care of a relative. I left Lowell with the only possessions I still had: the dress on my back and a sack full of a few necessities. And those few necessities weren't nearly enough." She wrinkled her nose, recalling with chagrin that Sophronia had donated half her food stores to the effort of nursing Dovey back from the brink of death. "Still and all, I got away not a moment too soon. Jo knows the rest of the story."

"But I had no idea you were a Mason," Jo said. "How did you come up with the money for the fare? Two hundred and fifty is steep enough for anyone to manage, but for a family fallen on such difficult times . . ."

Heat—and a slow worm of anxiety—crept up from Dovey's middle, flushing her chest and neck, and finally painting her shame bright and undeniable on her cheeks. But she held her head up high, and looked boldly into Sophronia's eyes as she said, "I sold my mother's jewels to raise the fare."

Sophronia gasped. One hand flew to her mouth and trembled ostentatiously. "Oh, your poor mother! I *never* could have done such a thing. Why, if your mother is as ill as you say—if the Lord takes her—then her jewelry might have been the only memories you had left of her!"

The same bleak thought had plagued Dovey as she'd tossed and turned in the tight, fierce grip of her own illness. To hear her fears repeated on Sophronia's sharp tongue only made her angrier—at herself, and no one else. Still, she tossed her curls and said, "I don't care! I did what needed doing. And I'm sure I'm not the only woman on this voyage who did what needed doing!" She cut a quick glance at Jo, wondering again about that mousy disguise, that veil of mystery. But Jo would not meet Dovey's eye.

"Don't be so hard on the girl," Jo said to Sophronia. "Dovey is right: we're all here for reasons of our own, and no woman is making this journey as a holiday. We've all sacrificed something precious to us. We've all faced our share of hard choices. And all of us chose to start anew in the West. We ought to support one another—be sisters and friends. We cannot snipe at one another all the way to Seattle."

Sophronia folded her arms tightly and arched her brows, a perfect picture of an ice queen. "And what are *your* reasons for making the journey, Josephine? How are you starting anew in the West?"

"I . . ." Jo faltered. Dovey noted how her throat tightened for a moment as she swallowed down her sudden anxiety. "I'm a widow," Jo finally said. "It makes sense, doesn't it, that I'd want to get out of Lowell? Wouldn't you, if your husband died and you had no family left in the world?"

Sophronia said nothing but held the older woman's gaze. Jo's brow furrowed and she turned away, fidgeting with the sleeves of her jacket, and made no further attempt to explain.

Dovey shared a knowing glance with Sophronia. Jo was *definitely* hiding something. Widow she might be, but there was more to her past than a dead husband. She was fleeing Lowell—trying to leave something far behind.

When the *Illinois* pulled into port an hour later, Dovey forgot the mystery of Josephine's past, and even the nagging worry about her mother left her in peace for a few blessed moments. She leaned over the rail of the ship, drinking in the thick air, tasting its spice of lush green land, of the coal smoke of industry and the sharp, the exotic tang of delights yet to be discovered. She had never been so far from home before—and doubted whether any of the Masons had, either. Even Father couldn't have gone so far in all his life.

Aspinwall spread out from the sleek black flank of the *Illinois*, a map unrolled under Dovey's feet, ready to guide her on to new adventures. Cream-white sand carpeted a great, smooth curve of beach that stretched beyond the wharves into a blue, hazy distance. Ahead, where the waterfront gave way to cobblestone and packed-earth streets, curious homes stood among lush, palm-fringed gardens—each house painted in candy-bright shades, each crowned by a flat-topped, red-tile roof. A flock of children scurried down a sidewalk, toting schoolbooks in their arms; Dovey raised a hand to them in greeting, and a few leaped and shouted when they saw her wave.

When Mr. Mercer welcomed the travelers to disembark, Dovey helped Jo carry their shared trunk down the ramp to the cart waiting below. Their boardinghouse was only a few blocks away; the women walked the distance, glad for the chance to stretch her legs and delighted by the fresh air. As they strolled along in the cart's wake, Dovey peered eagerly at the faces of her fellow travelers, noting which women's eyes lit up at the novelty of Aspinwall, its warmth and dense, vibrant greenery—and noting, too, whose eyes dimmed with worry at the strangeness of their surroundings.

The Aspinwall boardinghouse was a good deal better than the New York house had been. Its windows were high and breezy, and from their vantage on the second story they could just make out, between the flat, red roofs of the town, the white curve of the beach and the gray-green sea beyond. Dovey claimed a narrow bed with a simple metal frame between Jo's and Sophronia's bunks, then returned to the window, gazing out at the ocean.

"Can you believe it, Jo?" Dovey said. "We came all across that great, wide distance."

"If you squint hard enough, you can see New York," Jo said drily. "Lord, but I'm glad that leg of our journey's over. Just one more sea voyage to endure, and we'll never have to set foot on a ship's deck again."

The spring wind rushed over Aspinwall's tile roofs, and Dovey gave a shiver. She slid the window closed. Another sea voyage lay ahead—she hadn't considered it until now. The joy of seeing land again, and the vivid colors and carefree bustle of Aspinwall—or Colón, as the locals called it—had driven the memory of her illness from her mind. But now she recalled that desperate sickness with shuddering force—the days of feverish tossing, the weakness, the dreams of Lowell and her family that had drifted with her in and out of sleep.

She tossed her head to shoo away her fears. "We have two days until the train takes us to Panama," she said to the room at large. Half the expedition's girls were tucking away their trunks or splashing water on their faces from the basin beside the door. "Who wants to go out there with me and have a look around Aspinwall?"

"Stay put," Sophronia warned. "You don't know your way in this city, nor do you know what dangers might be out there waiting for you."

Dovey scoffed. "Dangers! This is a town like any other. I'd wager it's no more dangerous than Lowell."

"Lowell had plenty of hazards, believe me," Jo said quietly. "Sophronia's right, Dovey. It's better for us all if we stick together. Besides, the mistress of this house will soon be serving dinner. You don't want to miss that, do you?"

Boardinghouse stew, Dovey thought sourly. The rich, peppery scent of local cooking still lingered around the window. *That* was what she craved: the new, the unknown, the adventuresome. Beyond the walls of their boardinghouse, the world was opening wide, revealing its hidden delights, like a gift box with its lid tossed aside. She wanted nothing more than to plunge both hands into that box and draw out its contents in one great, overspilling armful—to learn every nuance, every taste and texture of the miraculous new life she had been granted.

"Jo," she whispered chidingly. But Jo peered out the window with a suspicious air. She seemed torn between the enticing mystery of Aspinwall and Sophronia's warning about unknown dangers.

But Dovey's mind was made up. Never again would she have the chance to experience Central America—never in her life. And by God, she was determined to make the most of the one opportunity she had. She took up her loose skirt in both hands—she still had no crinoline to her name, but she was beginning to enjoy the sensation of going without it—and strode toward the long room's door.

"Where do you think you're going?" Sophronia shrilled. "Catherine, Sarah—stop her!"

Dovey growled as Catherine made a grab for her wrist, and the timid woman shied away, exclaiming, "Oh!" as if Dovey had bitten her.

"Don't be a fool!" Sophronia marched after Dovey, but before the icy woman could lay one cold hand on Dovey, she sped to the door and slipped through, slamming it hard in Sophronia's face.

It opened again at once, and Sophronia called, "I'll tell Mr. Mercer!"

But Dovey was already halfway down the stairs, plowing on toward the boardinghouse's outer door—and freedom.

CHAPTER EIGHT
THE GOOD WORK

Dovey wandered the streets of Aspinwall for hours, exploring narrow alleys that jagged crookedly between the high-walled gardens, walking the length of a marketplace where sellers called out their wares in both Spanish and English—and tormenting herself with the intoxicating, heady scents that drifted from bakeries, beer shops, and teahouses. She would have given almost anything for a few pennies in her purse—just enough coin to buy a spiced biscuit or a cup of hot chili soup. It wasn't so much hunger that gnawed at her—that was a sensation sharp enough, but she had grown used to its presence since leaving New York, while she shared Jo's meager stores.

It was a deeper pain that afflicted her now—a low, hollow regret that she could not enjoy all the exotic delights that Aspinwall had to offer. After all, in two days' time she would never see this colorful town again—never walk amid its clamor of tongues, nor take in the dizzying swirl of its fiercely bright colors. She reveled in the town's strange, wild beauty, and the knowledge that this taste of Aspinwall was fleeting made her hours of strolling and staring all the more precious. Her heart ached already with nostalgia for the place, even as she walked along its narrow streets.

Eventually, Dovey's peregrination brought her back to the waterfront. She found a small, rickety bench outside a blue-painted warehouse and sat, sighing with relief. She now suspected that some of her blisters had not quite healed, and a moment of rest was welcome. The *Illinois* was still moored at its dock; Dovey watched the crew haul bags of mail up the ship's ramp, busy as ants on a sandy hill as they made ready for the return trip to New York.

I survived you, she told the *Illinois* silently. *I'm tougher than you— tougher than the sea, and my father, too.* She remembered her first journey by boat, when she had been only a little girl clinging to her mother's hand. She recalled the white backs of the seabirds, their high cries, the long, strong span of their wings as they glided easily on the wind. Dovey stared north, over the endless stretch of the ocean. Her future seemed as wide and boundless as the sea; never in her life had she felt herself so light, so unfettered by duty or care. She could spring up and glide on the wind, just like a bird herself. All she lacked were the wings to spread, the feathers to catch the breeze.

Dovey flung out her arms and closed her eyes, breathing deep the warm, salty air. She heard a musical giggle nearby, and froze, opening her eyes slowly.

At a warehouse's corner stood a girl close to Dovey's own age. She leaned one hip against the bright-blue wall, toying with something in her hands, smiling broadly at Dovey. The girl was brown-skinned, like so many people in Aspinwall, and dressed rather gaudily in a pink skirt with a proliferation of bows and ruffles. Her corset was laced in such a way that her small breasts pushed up like two round islands rising from the seafoam of her lace trim. Even with her dark complexion, Dovey could see that the girl's cheeks were thoroughly rouged. She was pretty—her face was exquisitely carved, her shining black hair curled and arranged just so. But her beauty was somehow overt—forceful, asserting itself in a way that intrigued Dovey even as it sent a thread of anxiety through her veins.

The girl lifted the object she held. It was a piece of bread, flat and dark, smeared with some pale substance. Dovey's stomach rumbled as the girl bit into it. But Dovey smiled and beckoned, and soon the girl in pink approached, and lowered herself onto the bench at Dovey's side.

"Where do you come from?" the girl asked. She spoke English well, though her accent was thick. "I have not seen you here before."

"Massachusetts," Dovey replied, and the girl giggled again, unwilling to try the tangly word.

"I'm called Orquídea," she said.

"Dovey." She shook the girl's hand, and couldn't help gazing at the bread lying in Orquídea's lap. The rich scent of roasted garlic filled the air, and Dovey's mouth watered.

"Have you come to work?" Orquídea asked politely.

Dovey tore her eyes from the bread and stared at her quizzically. "Work?"

"You know . . ." She gestured toward the docks with a conspiratorial half smile.

Dovey was on the point of asking whether Orquídea hauled mail bags up the ships' ramps, when at last she realized just what the girl mean by *work*. She chided herself. *You dolt. Are you so hungry that your head has turned to dough?*

"*That* work—no," Dovey said. "I've come looking for a husband."

Orquídea threw back her head and laughed, exposing teeth as small and white as pearls. "Good joke," she said. "I've come looking for a husband, too. Just for one night," she added, choking on her giggles, "then a new husband the next day!"

Dovey grinned in response. She knew she ought to go all stiff and offended—propriety demanded it, and she was a member of the Mason family, after all—but she realized with a flutter of amusement that she didn't mind if the girl thought she was a prostitute. No doubt Sophronia would have asphyxiated on her own outrage if anyone suspected *her* of dallying for money. But as Dovey sat beside her new friend, she saw no shame in the profession. The world was a hard, unfriendly place for a woman. Either a girl allowed herself to be traded away like a fattened heifer, or she made her own way through life. Every woman Dovey knew was making her way, whether she worked the piers like Orquídea, or tied all her hopes to a mad gamble in Seattle. Even Sophronia was doing what she had to in order to get by. The way Dovey saw it, there was no difference between Sophronia and this pretty little dockside whore—no difference that truly mattered.

Orquídea lifted the half-eaten crust of bread from her lap. She extended it to Dovey, an offering of fellowship.

"Truly—may I?" Dovey took the bread as if it were a sacrament, and sat staring in awe before she bit into the thick slice. The roasted-garlic spread sent a tingle of satisfaction along the roof of her mouth, and she closed her eyes in bliss as she chewed.

When she had finished the bread, Dovey leaned back on the bench and sighed. Orquídea turned her face up toward the sun, soaking in the warmth of the afternoon.

"I meant what I said, you know," Dovey told her. "I *am* on my way to find a husband. I'm going all the way to Washington Territory, to be wedded."

"Ah!" Orquídea gestured toward the *Illinois*. The crew still hauled their bags of letters and wrapped parcels up the ramp to the ship's deck. Orquídea muttered a Spanish word, then tapped her chin, searching for the correct translation. "Delivery," she said. "Mail."

Is that what I am? Dovey wondered. *A bride by order—like a parcel picked out of a catalog?*

If she was, then so be it. It seemed a damn sight better to become the wife of a man she didn't know at all than to agree to marry a draft dodger whom she knew to be a pudding-headed sap.

She rose from the bench and pulled Orquídea up with her. "Come on. I don't have much time in this place; I want to see all the sights before the sun goes down."

Orquídea strolled with her along the waterfront, pointing out the ships that glided into the harbor, calling greetings to the sailors she knew—and her acquaintance with Aspinwall's sailors seemed legendary, though she couldn't have been more than seventeen years old.

At first, Dovey found herself tensing and blushing every time Orquídea waved to a man or stopped to offer a few words and her charming, pearly grin. Despite Dovey's growing conviction that a prostitute and a prospective bride were not so very different when all was said and done, a lady of the Mason family simply wasn't so free with her attentions. But after a time, as the sailors and dockside merchants began to cast their smiles and little compliments at Dovey, too, she began to find Orquídea and her wharfside domain more intriguing than mortifying.

It seemed right enough to Dovey that a girl ought to be free to cast solicitous glances toward any man she pleased. As she watched Orquídea lift the hem of her rosy skirt just a little too high, batting her eyes at a butcher, she thought, *Why, after all, shouldn't a girl be open in her intentions?*

The longer she walked the streets of Aspinwall, drifting on its slow, heady currents of spice and heat, the less Dovey cared for the prim, proper world of American society, with its rigid strictures and pointless conventions. Let Sophronia dwell within the small, stuffy confines of propriety. The world was a broad, varied place—as vast and airy as the sky—and Dovey would find her own place to dwell. She would set her own borders, make her own conventions. What had she left Lowell for, if not to set herself free?

As the sun lowered in a petal-pink sky, Orquídea was just showing Dovey how to lean against a wall or a lamppost in a more appealing manner—shoulder shrugged up coyly, hair falling down to half conceal her face—when a shout rang across the docks. The cry was wordless, but there was no mistaking its shrill, mortally offended note.

Dovey gritted her teeth. "Lord," she breathed, and stepped away from the lamppost, braced for the coming storm.

Orquídea glanced around at the shout, then uttered a quick exclamation in her native tongue. Sophronia swept past the girl, a streak of pale gold, and seized Dovey by the arm. She dragged her several paces away from Orquídea, as if fearing the merry little prostitute might combust at any moment and set Dovey's skirts ablaze.

"Let go," Dovey said, jerking out of Sophronia's grip.

But it was no use—Sophronia released her upper arm only to clamp her hand around Dovey's wrist with a painful, biting grip. Jo came hurrying along in Sophronia's wake, and Dovey turned to the older woman, pleading.

"Get her off me, Jo! She's ferocious!"

"I'll *show* you ferocious," Sophronia promised, hissing her threats into Dovey's ear. She never took her eyes from Orquídea, and made a shooing gesture with her free hand, as if the young prostitute were a stray dog begging for a bone. "Get away from this creature, Dovey! What on Earth were you thinking?"

"She's not a *creature*, you mean, coldhearted louse! She's my friend!"

Sophronia's shock was so monumental that she loosed her hold on Dovey. She stood still for a moment, wide-eyed and dazed. "Friend? Dovey—you *cannot* mean it. A . . . a *fallen* woman!"

Dovey jerked down the sleeve of her parrot-green jacket; Sophronia's grip had twisted it awry. "I certainly do mean it. She's been good to me—better than you have!"

"Dovey!" Jo exclaimed. "After Sophronia nursed you through your illness—"

But Dovey's feathers were too ruffled to feel any remorse for her unkind words. "And anyway, I don't think she's so far fallen."

Sophronia, gaping, as glassy-eyed as a landed cod, turned to Jo in speechless horror.

"Her line of work seems perfectly fine to me," Dovey added with vicious deliberation. "I just might take it up myself."

Sophronia finally managed one high, warbling exclamation: "Oh!" She clutched Dovey by the arm again and began marching her up the nearest street, toward the little rise where the boardinghouse stood.

"Good-bye," Dovey called to Orquídea. But the girl had already turned away, shaking her head and laughing.

Dovey scowled at Sophronia as the pale woman propelled her through Aspinwall's narrow lanes. "You really are rotten, do you know that?"

Jo trotted along beside them, panting and wrangling her stiff skirt with both hands. "Dovey, it's late. The sun is nearly set. We were worried about you—all of us. You mustn't run off that way. We *must* stick together!"

"Stick together, indeed," Sophronia barked. "This ill-tempered little beast doesn't belong in civilized company. She isn't one of us, Josephine."

"Come now, Sophronia—"

"I'll hear nothing more about it. When we get back to the boardinghouse, you must keep her in the room with the rest of the girls, and I shall go straight to Mr. Mercer. He needs to know."

"Know what?" Dovey spat, jerking against Sophronia's iron grip.

"He needs to know that you are not the high-minded woman he thought you to be—not the sort of girl Seattle needs."

"I'm just the sort of girl Seattle needs—wait and see!"

"Oh no," Sophronia said darkly. "Seattle has more than its fair share of girls like *you*, Dovey. You're going straight back to Lowell, if I have to pay your passage myself. You can leave the good work in Seattle to worthy girls—women with high ideals and pure hearts."

"The good work!" Dovey hooted with laughter, which only made Sophronia's grip bite all the harder. "Don't you understand what Mercer is about? We're nothing but mail-order brides, Sophronia. That's the only work he has in mind for us—to go meekly into the homes and beds of those men waiting in Seattle."

"You make it sound tawdry," she objected.

"It *is*! We're goods to be traded, Sophie!"

"We're more than that, you little fool. We're companions—"

"So is that girl you called a creature—"

"We're to start families in Washington, to bring a settling influence—"

"To breed, just like livestock. Who's a creature now?"

"Raising up a good, moral family is a world away from *breeding like stock*. And it's the *only* work that need concern a woman," Sophronia added.

"It's not the only work that concerns *me*. There's a whole world out here to see, and I've only got one life to live. What if I don't want to spend my life tied down to one man?"

"What other choice do you have?"

For answer, Dovey cast a glance back toward the docks. In the violet-gray of approaching twilight, she could see nothing of Orquídea's bright-pink dress, but Sophronia read Dovey's meaning clearly enough. The pale woman strode all the faster toward the safety of the boardinghouse.

"*That* is no kind of life for a girl of your background."

"My background—fiddlesticks! Girls like Orquídea have freedom—adventure! Can't you see it, Sophronia? That's the kind of life any woman ought to desire."

Jo cut in smoothly. "That kind of life is *danger*, Dovey. It's not freedom or adventure—not for long, anyway. Soon enough it all turns to illness, insecurity—and men who might hurt you just as soon as pay you."

It was more than Dovey could bear, for Jo—her only true friend since leaving Lowell—to speak out against her. Anger surged up inside, making her head throb and her neck ache with tension. *Men—men who might hurt me, men who must pay me.* It seemed no matter where she turned, men would forever control her freedom, her life. Father back at home, plotting to cart her off to the Stiltons, all meek and tame, bundled up in a bridal gown. Mr. Mercer here in Aspinwall, to decide whether she was worthy of Seattle. And if she did make it to Seattle, she would be in the thrall of another man still: a husband she didn't know, who would care not a whit for Dovey's ambitions or desires.

With one final, furious effort, Dovey wrenched out of Sophronia's grip. She could feel the impression of each of Sophronia's hard fingers; the bruised places throbbed with the speed of Dovey's pulse. "This is *my* life, Sophronia—not yours. Not my father's, and not some dullard husband's! I'll make my own way in the world. You run off and tell Mr. Mercer anything you like. I'll leave his expedition if I please, or stay with it if I choose. Neither you nor Asa Mercer can tell me what to do!"

She spun away and stormed off into the dusk. Her tears veiled the town in a blur of color—but as night approached, even Aspinwall's brightness faded.

CHAPTER NINE
TROUBLED WATERS

The train rocked and swayed, rattling through a long green tunnel of foliage. Josephine sat silent and alone, watching the fields and dense, broad-leafed forests glide past her window. The glass reflected her image like a vision of a ghost in a mirror. Whenever the train crossed open country where sunlight glowed on farmers' fields or vast, burned clearings, Josephine's reflection faded into nothing. But when the train passed again into shadow, she looked into her own face with sudden force—her features so sharp and exactly carved, she seemed a woman made of alabaster—of unfeeling stone. But always, even as sunlight warmed outside the train and her image began to fade, her eyes glittered with anxiety.

The train rattled past a field full of cows, standing belly deep in lush spring grasses. The beasts raised their heads to stare as the train rolled by, and beyond, where their pasture fringed into bright, glowing woodland, a flock of black birds took to the sky. Josephine watched the birds fly for a long moment, allowing the simple, rustic quiet of the landscape to soothe her troubled soul to peace. Then she turned and glanced along the train's interior.

The other women of Mercer's expedition had, by now, found good company with one another, and shared their stories and hopes freely. They sat in twos and threes, conversing happily or simply enjoying one another's presence as they read or stitched at their needlework. Josephine had, during those dark days on the *Illinois* when she and Sophronia had tended to the ailing Dovey, come to think herself Sophronia's friend. And she certainly cared for Dovey, brooding over the hot-tempered girl like a mother hen.

But she could not trust either one of them—not entirely. Not with the secret she kept. She could share her story with none of the women on this voyage. And as for hopes, Josephine had only one: that she might get to Seattle with the truth of her circumstances undetected.

She cast an uneasy glance at Dovey and Sophronia. The two young women were sharing a bench seat a few rows away—not by choice— stiff and silent, with as much space between their bodies as the bench would allow. The other seats in the car had all been claimed by the time Dovey scrambled aboard, tailed by the disapproving, watchful shadow of Sophronia. Now the girl practically hackled like an ornery terrier, indignant at her self-appointed guardian's proximity but refusing to speak, while Sophronia held her chin high with an air of bearing with good fortitude the misfortunes that must be borne.

Dovey still had not forgiven Sophronia for hauling her away from that dockside harlot two nights before. The girl truly did not know what was best for her—Josephine conceded that much, even if she thought Sophronia a mite harsh.

Dovey had vowed to forge her own way in life, to make up her own mind—and so she had, it seemed. After storming away from Sophronia and into the uncharted wilds of Aspinwall, the girl had crept back to the boardinghouse at midnight, slipping quietly into her bed beside Josephine's. Moonlight had spilled through the window, dim and gray, and in that dull-pewter glimmer, Josephine had reached out her hand to Dovey. The two of them had lain that way for some time, hands clasped in the space between their beds, and Josephine had ached with loneliness. She'd nearly told Dovey everything, then. Thank God better sense had prevailed. For all her rough charms, Dovey really was a fool sometimes—weren't all girls of sixteen?—and the secret could have flown between the women's bunks before the sun was up. It would have spelled an end to Josephine's hopes for certain.

If I can only keep silent for a few more weeks—until we reach Seattle. Then all will be well.

She could endure until then. Josephine knew she could. She had endured much already—more than most women or men could stand. What were a few more weeks of guarded silence?

In another hour, the train reached Panama City. The depot was near enough the wharves that as Josephine stepped from the rail car to the platform, she could see a forest of masts and the smokestacks of steamships rising clear and straight above the tile roofs of the city. Bright flags lifted on the masts, rippling in a steady, salt-scented wind. The sky was as soft and blue as hope itself, yet she felt a pinch of foreboding in her stomach.

It's only my sour mood—the dark thoughts that have followed me from Massachusetts. I must shake off this bleakness. The final leg of the journey was about to begin—the last gate through which she must pass before she attained her freedom.

The women of the expedition hoisted their trunks and bags, then followed Asa Mercer's dark head and velvet jacket through the streets. Panama was much like Aspinwall—a clamor of bold colors, the air thick with the warm, furry breath of the tropics. A scent of smoke and spice hung above the streets, and from the high red rooftops, unknown birds cried out in harsh, scolding tones.

They made the docks just as Josephine's stays were beginning to chafe in the heat.

"There she is," Mercer proclaimed, gesturing grandly up at the nearest vessel.

A paddle-wheel steamer like the *Illinois*, the *America* seemed to strain eagerly at its lines, thrusting its pert bow high above the pier. The sun sparkled on its clean, wind-polished hull, and a remnant gust of smoke swirled up from its stacks, dancing gaily on the breeze. It seemed a very sound and capable vessel to Josephine, although she had no experience with seafaring. She felt her spirits rise in its presence.

As the women assembled on the pier, checking over their bags and fussing with one another's heat-wilted curls, Mr. Mercer approached a pair of men who made their way down the *America*'s ramp. They seemed to be the final passengers to disembark the ship. Josephine peered at them curiously as Mercer raised his hand in greeting. Something about the passengers' haggard faces gave her pause. Their footsteps along the dock were dragging and heavy, and they stared about them with a kind of hungry disbelief, as if they couldn't quite believe they had made land.

Josephine lifted her hem and edged behind Mr. Mercer, stepping as quietly along the sun-bleached planks of the dock as the hard soles of her boots would allow. She leaned her hip casually against a pyramid of barrels and stood with folded arms, gazing out across the harbor, never looking at Mercer or the *America*'s two passengers. But her ears strained to catch every word.

Mercer called out to the men in his smooth-polished tenor. "Good afternoon, sirs! You've come from San Francisco?"

The men paused and shared a weary, cautious gaze. Finally one, a gentleman with a dark mustache, said, "We have. And made it safe to Panama at last, thank God."

"Was the passage troubled?" Mercer asked the question lightly, but Josephine could detect the smallest quaver of concern—or perhaps of defeat—in his voice. His shoulders slumped a little, and his feet shifted anxiously, scraping against the dock.

"I should say so," said the man with the dark mustache. "The sailing took five days longer than intended. It seemed the boilers leaked—or so we heard—but engine troubles weren't half the woes we faced, my good man."

"No, indeed," the other gentleman supplied. His lined face spoke of middle age. "There were two deaths aboard—two burials at sea."

"Deaths?" Mercer exclaimed.

"Fever," said the older man. "That's why we were obliged to consign them to the deep. A crewman and a passenger, they were. I can't imagine a worse fate than to die of fever while at sea. It's no good keeping a corpse around if he's expired of the fever, you know. The illness will only spread."

The other passenger said, "May God have mercy on their souls. When Gabriel blows his trump, the poor fellows will have a difficult time resurrecting, trapped as they are now in the bellies of the fishes."

Josephine had heard all she needed. Quickly, she slipped back to her trunk before Asa Mercer could spot her loitering on the dock.

Fever—and a passenger dead of it! Fear coiled tight in her gut. Was the illness lurking even now in the dim, cold quarters where she and the other women must dwell for sixteen long days, confined in the close, laden air of the cabins? A bead of sweat trickled down her spine, and she twitched her shoulders in irritation.

"What's the matter, Josephine?" Sophronia, resting on the lid of her trunk, looked up at her with concern. "You seem rather shaken."

Josephine gazed up at the *America*. The ship moved slowly, leaning away from the pier, and its mooring lines issued a tight, high moan.

Dovey had been closer to death than Josephine cared to admit, those long, terrible days on the *Illinois*. Who would be next to fall ill? And with fever lurking in the *America*'s hold—an illness far worse than mere dehydration—could anyone hope to survive?

I can still go back, she thought frantically. The rush of her heartbeat filled her ears. *I can turn around now, go back to Massachusetts . . .*

Go back to Lowell, and face what she had left behind. Go back in defeat, and look despair in the face, and know that it would be hers forever.

Josephine shook her head, driving away the impulse to flee back the way she had come. *I can never go back. I cannot. And I never will.* She would only move ahead from now on—forward, toward what was, she prayed, a brighter future.

And her only way forward lay to the west.

She turned back to Sophronia with the most unconcerned smile she could affect. "All is well. How could anything be amiss? We're halfway to Washington Territory already!"

All too soon, as Josephine sat fretting and staring up at the towering smokestacks of the *America*, the steamer's captain approached Mr. Mercer to welcome him aboard. She rose reluctantly from her trunk and took one final look around. Panama was ablaze with color in the afternoon light, so garish that its cheer seemed forced, a trap laid to lure the unwitting to a grim, sad fate.

But whatever the voyage held in store for Josephine—tossing waves, raging fever, or the cold embrace of death itself—it was sure to be better than what she'd left behind.

"Forward," she muttered as she lifted her trunk and carried it resolutely toward the *America*. "Forward, and west, to whatever fate God has planned for me."

A slash of white light appeared, cleaving the dark as the cabin door creaked open. Sophronia looked up from Annie's bunk, blinking against the sudden brightness. Annie Adams moaned in her restless sleep, turning her face away from the intrusive light. The sweat shimmered on her brow.

"Close that door," Sophronia snapped. "You'll wake her, and she needs rest."

A silhouette darkened the entry, then the door softly closed. Sophronia blinked into the dimness. Josephine stood with her back to the cabin door, her limp, light-brown hair tousled and tumbling out of her bun. "How is Annie doing?"

"The fever broke at last," Sophronia said. She stood from her small, three-legged stool and stretched her back, swaying with the unceasing movement of the ship. "She'll pull through, thank God."

"Our work isn't done yet," Josephine said. "Now it's Sarah Gallagher who's taken to her bed."

Sophronia sighed, weary to her bones. The *America* had left Panama City five days before, and almost at once, the fever struck its first blow. One by one, the girls fell ill, sweating and moaning, helpless in the grip of the disease. It struck each girl in a different manner, rattling some with violent shakes, making others vomit into their pots until they were weak and mewling like day-old kittens. Sophronia's supply of ginger tea vanished all too soon; she and the women who remained healthy were left to combat the fearful plague with only the medicines the *America* and God could provide: cool, damp cloths on the forehead; soothing words; and fresh air, when the chill could be tolerated. They were poor weapons with which to fight, but Sophronia and Josephine soldiered on.

The fact that no woman had yet perished—nor Mr. Mercer, who had also been afflicted with the shakes and sweats—was nothing short of a miracle. This fever was as bad as any Sophronia had seen, and seemed to spread quickly.

It was little wonder, though, that the illness had taken root aboard the *America*. Despite the ship's fine, polished exterior, the accommodations left much to be desired. The cabin walls leaked, allowing constant dampness to invade, along with an odor of mildew so strong that Sophronia was almost glad when the stench of sickness overcame it. Wind whistled unceasingly through the cracks in the wood, affording no restful silence, night or day. And the seas were rough and heaving, so that even when one lay down, one was jostled to and fro, and tired out by the mere act of sleeping.

Every woman who was fit to stand tended to the ill, under the direction of Josephine and Sophronia. Neither had much experience nursing the sick, but all the same, the other women seemed to look to them for guidance. Perhaps that was natural, in Josephine's case—her age and maternal impulses toward Dovey, as well as her old-fashioned style and soft-spoken manners, made her a figure of comfort.

But Sophronia could not understand why the women of the expedition seemed to place their trust—perhaps their very lives—in her hands. She certainly did not consider herself a match for this fever, and she tended the ill with a level head and calm demeanor only because it seemed the only dignified thing to do. During her few hours of rest, when another girl would take her place at the side of a sickbed, Sophronia would fall onto her hard, heaving bunk, shaking from exhaustion, squeezing her eyes tightly shut to drive away hopeless tears.

In those hours, with the wind screaming through her dark cabin, when she tried and failed to sleep, she entertained bleak thoughts of the future. *What kind of Hell am I sailing into?* she asked herself wearily. And she wondered with a dull, fatalistic acceptance how Seattle would be worse than the *America*. For she perceived somehow, through some obscure, clouded instinct, that what awaited her when the ship finally made landfall was far worse than her present torment. She knew, with a shiver of dread, that she had already been judged by God and found lacking—that her eternal punishment had only just begun.

When the fever finally struck Sophronia, eight days into the voyage, she felt the fires of Hell roaring all around her. Through those terrible hours the faces of all her regrets stared down upon her, flickering like candle flames, warped and distorted by the heat—James Gooding, Martin Steele—all the young men who had professed their love and then withdrew it. Shuddering with cold and doused in sweat, she tried to struggle from her bed, tried to hide from the pain of her past. But cool, gentle hands pushed her down, and soothed her brow with water.

Voices mocked her from the fire; demons wearing Clement's mask shouted scorn and roared with laughter, while James's distorted face wept tears of fire. Sophronia clung tightly to the hands that held her own—and always their touch was loving, forgiving. Always the presence that never left her bedside was female.

Now and then she would remember her own cries, her sobs in the night when, again and again, more times than any woman could bear, her heart broke in the wake of an angry, departing suitor.

Worse still was the memory of Elizabeth Steele—Elizabeth, whom she had loved so well, as much as she loved her little sisters. She was the sister of one of her earliest suitors, Martin Steele. Elizabeth was of an age with Sophronia, but they were opposites in every way; Sophronia's pale-golden coloring made Elizabeth's lustrous, black hair and olive complexion all the more striking when they walked side by side, and where Sophronia was proper and restrained, Elizabeth was fond of mischief and had a laugh that could be heard from miles away. Sophronia loved her even more for all their differences. She was the first—the *only* friend Sophronia had ever known.

Martin Steele made no impression on Sophronia; he was kind enough but unremarkable and lacking in ambition. She never would have considered his suit were it not for his sister. The prospect of gaining Elizabeth as a true sister had filled Sophronia with hope and longing. And when Sophronia's rigid ideals finally chased Martin from her side, it was Elizabeth's wooden, offended departure that had cut Sophronia to her heart. It was the loss of her friend, not the loss of her suitor, that had taught her how deeply pain could cut.

In the grips of her fever, she heard Elizabeth's laughter—then her voice calling, fading. And then, distant and soft, mingling with the never-ending moan of the wind over the waves, Elizabeth weeping. Sophronia tried to call out to her, to ask her forgiveness, to beg to start their friendship anew. But she heard no reply, save for those distant sobs.

Then the sobs came from somewhere closer to hand—not from memory or the fancies of the fever, but from her own chest. The force of her grief wracked her body, wringing the frail strength from her limbs.

Whenever she cried out, a woman's voice answered. Sometimes it was Josephine, murmuring below the howl of the wind. Sometimes it was Sarah Gallagher, or Annie Adams, or either of the two Catherines. Now and then it was even Dovey who nursed her, stroking her hand, her round, pretty face gazing down at Sophronia like an angel of mercy.

Sophronia clung to those threads of friendship with all the force of her soul. Even if she sailed through Hell itself, she sensed that these girls, at least—the women of Mercer's expedition—would not judge her, even if God already had. Their voices were a balm to her, their hands one soft, collective blessing.

When at last Sophronia rose from her sickbed, with San Francisco only a day away, she felt renewed—washed clean, as if by baptism, even if her limbs shook with a terrible tremor. She knew the Lord had shown her mercy, not only in delivering her from the fever, but by placing her in the care of this band of thirteen sisters. Even Dovey was her sister, Sophronia now knew, and would be good to her if only she could only make herself mend the needless rent between them.

Sophronia leaned on Dovey's arm as she stepped through her cabin door into the fresh air of the *America's* open deck. *I have come through a trial of tribulation,* she thought, holding tight to Dovey as she had once done to Elizabeth, *and found my family, and my true heart, at last.*

She gazed north and east, where a heavy white mist obscured the horizon. But somewhere beyond that blur of misted light lay San Francisco—and farther north, tucked in the green fold of the earth's velvet robe, Seattle. *My future, my salvation. My fresh start.*

The future would be kind to her, Sophronia knew, if only she could withdraw her defenses, her barbs and spines. If she could find it in her wounded heart to join this sisterhood, she would have her reward at last.

"I'll try, Lord," she whispered as San Francisco drew nearer. "You know I'll try."

CHAPTER TEN
DOCKSIDE TRYST

Rain beat against the boardinghouse windows, tracing crooked lines down the panes, obscuring the hills of San Francisco behind a veil of low-hanging clouds. Dovey pressed close to the sill. A chill crept inside the room, brushing her cheeks and eyelids with the rain's damp touch. But the girls gathered close beside her pushed back the dismal cold. They clustered together, warm and comforting in their solid presence, arms around one another's shoulders or waists, the room filled with the sweet mélange of their powders and perfumes.

Annie sighed. "Another city, another boardinghouse. They're all starting to look the same to me."

"Nonsense," Sophronia replied. "This one is clean and bright, and everything in it is so fresh and new. That place in New York . . ." She shuddered.

"It was miserable, wasn't it?" Georgianna Pearson, a dark-eyed beauty with a face as regal as a Roman statue, gazed out at the gray layers of San Francisco. "I hate being cooped up here, like a bunch of hens in a shed—but we can at least be thankful that the wallpaper isn't peeling away. And the beds aren't so hard or narrow as in New York."

"That's some consolation," Catherine Stickney agreed. "I've slept better these past six days than I have since leaving home."

Six days, Dovey thought morosely. *An awfully long and dull spell to stay put in one boardinghouse, no matter how wide the beds are.*

The *America*'s voyage from Panama had been one long, cold, heaving torment, fraught with bleak anxiety and shrouded by a pervasive stench of illness. Dovey recalled the dark passage on the *Illinois*, when she had lain trapped, weak and helpless, on her tossing, rolling bunk. She had been certain she'd fall hopelessly ill on the *America*, too—certain that this time she would meet her fate, out there on the cold, gray peaks of the Pacific waves.

When Dovey reached San Francisco without contracting that terrible fever, she had nearly fallen to her knees on the dock to kiss its pale, salt-roughened planks. When they'd arrived at the boardinghouse, its homey comfort had been more than a relief: it had seemed to Dovey an omen of good tidings, like Noah's rainbow—a promise that she had been delivered safe from destruction, that the worst was forever behind her now and she need never fear a cold, watery death again.

But six days of confinement had ground comfort into monotony, and what had once felt like a home now seemed more like a prison. Asa Mercer had not intended this delay. The women were to while away two nights at most in San Francisco before boarding a new steamer that would carry them up the coast to Seattle. But the *America*, with its leaking boilers and its plague of fever, had limped into the great, blue curve of the harbor too late. All the steamships had gone, and no one could say just when another, northward bound, might arrive. Mercer had spent every day since their arrival, even the Sabbath, scouring the city for news of a suitable vessel. But if he had found one yet, none of the women of his expedition had heard of it.

And so the girls remained gathered at their windows, watching San Francisco through its mist of springtime clouds. They were not forbidden to leave the boardinghouse—no, of course not! They could venture out as often they pleased, and the well-off women did so, nearly every day—for San Francisco beckoned with a raw, ceaseless energy that could scarcely be denied, pounding with a rapid heartbeat—gold, gold, *gold*!

Gold. That was just the trouble. The only women who could fancy themselves up and take off to the shops and shows were those who had plenty of coin to spend. Most of the girls were obliged to live frugally, to experience San Francisco from the inside of the rainy windowpanes—Dovey most especially, who was already indebted to Jo and Sophronia for their generosity. Whenever one of the girls would declare that she'd had enough of this dull waiting, and would someone please help her on with her best dress, for she was going *out there*, Dovey would sigh and swallow her envy and then watch from the window as the lucky adventurer disappeared up the hilly streets, her bright parasol bobbing on her shoulder.

Jo left the pack of girls pressing around the window and sank down onto her bed. The springs gave a squeal. "What I wouldn't give to go out exploring," she said dreamily. "Who knows how many more days we have in San Francisco. Mr. Mercer could find a boat to Seattle this very hour, and we'd be off."

"I wish he *would* find a boat this very hour," Sophronia muttered. "I don't like this city. It's a pit of avarice."

"It's not so bad, Sophronia," Georgianna replied. She and her sister, Josie, had been among the lucky few to go exploring, and they had brought back popcorn and taffy to share with the girls who had remained behind. "The people do seem very nice, and not avaricious in the least. Everyone we met had perfectly lovely manners, didn't they, Josie?"

"But the whole town lusts after gold," Sophronia said. "You can feel the hunger for it pressing in through the walls of this very house. You know your Scriptures, Georgianna: 'The love of money is the root of all evil.' I shudder to think what evils may stir in the streets and homes of San Francisco."

"It's not an evil place," young Josie said. "Really, Sophronia, it's not."

Sophronia sniffed. "God may judge otherwise. Be careful, you girls who go out strolling. Beware of fire from the sky."

Silence fell over the room as all the girls turned to stare at Sophronia. There was an unaccustomed twinkle in the pale woman's eye, and it took Dovey a moment to realize that Sophronia, in her crabbed, chilly way, was making a joke—or *trying* to make one. It was a rather grim attempt at humor, but all the more amusing for its flatness and grit. Dovey laughed aloud, and Sophronia's prim, emotionless mask cracked with a hesitant smile.

"Doom, doom," Catherine said, throwing one arm around Sophronia's shoulders. "Our own golden-haired Cassandra!"

Georgianna joined them. "Come on, girls. This rain is too depressing. If we all get out our sewing kits, I think Jo will teach us how to embroider, and that will cheer us—even Sophronia."

Dovey had no sewing kit of her own. She lay on her bed, watching the other women work their stitches and listening to their chatter, but always, through the low, pleasant murmur of their words, she heard the rain drumming on the glass. It pattered and pinged, a constant reminder of what lay outside—what new adventures the city promised, what secrets lay waiting for Dovey's exploration. She tried to remain still, but her feet kicked restlessly of their own accord, and she shifted this way and that on her mattress, making the bed frame rattle and bump against the wall.

The song of the rain filled Dovey's head. Finally she sat up, then stood slowly, surrendering to curiosity's insistent pull.

"Where are you going?" Jo looked up from her embroidery as Dovey made her way down the length of the room.

"Just to the washroom. Don't fret."

But as soon as she was safely in the hall, Dovey hiked her skirt and hurried through the boardinghouse to its front door. The proprietress, a plump, graying woman of half-Spanish descent, was nowhere to be seen; the parlor and cozy little library stood empty.

Perfect, Dovey thought, taking a heavy shawl from a hook beside the door. *I'll just be gone half an hour, and then I'll return. No one will miss me, and no one need worry on my account.*

But she hesitated in the dimness of the hall with one hand on the cold brass doorknob. Sophronia's voice chose that very moment to ring in Dovey's head. *I shudder to think what evils may stir in the streets of San Francisco.*

A chill of foreboding prickled up Dovey's spine. But she shook her head, resisting it. "Don't be silly," she muttered to herself—to Sophronia—and slipped out into the rain.

Dovey walked for a quarter of an hour at least, descending the steep hill where the boardinghouse perched above rows of bright-colored, peak-roofed homes. She drifted with the clouds, allowing the broad, brick-lined streets of San Francisco to carry her where they would. The road leveled out into a wide avenue running with a dull-brown sluice of rainwater. To either side of the broad brick street, magnificent buildings stretched into the lowering sky. Their facades were smooth, palely new, and cast with a luminous sheen of dampness.

Here the city's many new businesses thrived—mercantiles and shoemakers, tailors, butchers, and lawyers. She peered into every window, her heart racing over the goods on rich, abundant display, the colorful signs with their fancy notched-and-scrolled lettering shouting their messages bright and clear through the rain. CALVERT'S CARBOLIC PRICKLY HEAT & BATH SOAP. MURATTI'S HIGH-CLASS CIGARETTES, GOLD-TIPPED FOR LADIES. BEST OF ALL SHOES ARE STANDARD SCREW FASTENED! BURNETT'S COCAINE RINSE—CURES DANDRUFF, MAKES THE HAIR GROW!

Once Dovey passed a chocolate shop just as a fine lady entered, tapping her umbrella against the green-painted doorframe to shake the raindrops from its lace-trimmed edge. Someone inside the shop was singing—a slow, wistful tune in a language Dovey did not know. The melancholy of the song's refrain drifted out on a warm current of air, mingling so sweetly with the low, earthy scent of chocolate that her eyes filled with tears even as her mouth watered. A bell on the shop's door chimed as it closed, shutting away the song and the deep, soothing perfume of chocolate. Dovey, her heart surging with a clamor of emotion—nostalgia, ambition, and joy—walked on.

The business districts of San Francisco were as full and flush as Lowell ever was before the cotton trade had faltered. As she watched the shoppers coming and going down the sidewalk, the well-dressed women and dapper gentlemen going briskly about, even in the rain, with wrapped packages tucked beneath their arms, Dovey's chest welled with a great, steadily beating confidence. Vividly, she recalled Orquídea, the pretty young working girl leaning so artfully against the blue corner of the Aspinwall warehouse. She pictured the swing of Orquídea's rose-pink skirt, envisioned that bawdy flush of pink drifting down the San Francisco sidewalk, dodging and swaying through this flock of wealthy men.

This city was so new, so *alive*. And so was Dovey—young and fresh and bursting with an energetic, determined drive. *Let Asa Mercer take all the time he likes to find a new ship*, she thought with dry satisfaction. Dovey was in no hurry to flit up to Seattle and hand herself over to some log-splitting lout as his bride. As she watched San Francisco thriving around her, she suspected that a girl might make a better way in the world than *that*. Oh, not as a prostitute. Dovey could see no good reason to turn up her nose at that particular profession, but business was in her blood—she was John Mason's daughter, after all—and she suspected there were wiser, far easier ways to earn a dollar than to do it on her back.

San Francisco seemed as good a place as any to set up a bordello—in fact, it seemed the very best place Dovey could imagine. The grand, glittering capital of the frontier empire, San Francisco surely had gold enough to nurture yet another establishment—and men with heavy pockets willing to patronize the place. *A place like our boardinghouse,* Dovey thought, her cheeks flushing as the sun of her grand idea rose. *Comfortable, pretty—not extravagant, but a place that makes a fellow feel welcome, with soft, wide beds and private rooms. A man would pay a cut above to be entertained in a clean, cozy spot.* And Dovey, as proprietress, could pocket that cut above—tuck it away for her own use, and with it, make her own way in the world. *Make my own way—and answer to no man at all, not even a husband.*

Dovey mused over the plan as she crossed the wide avenue and headed down toward the harbor, her eyes turned thoughtfully down to the slick, wet brick of the street. *If I'm to have any hope of starting an establishment, I must befriend some of the local working girls.* The docks seemed the wisest place to observe San Francisco's night flowers in action. Docks ever were their most profitable places of business.

Dovey found the waterfront easily enough, following the downward slope of the streets and the smell of salt and sea grass through the rain. She was surprised to see the *America* still in port. Its black hull glistened, rain-washed and cold. From the pier, Dovey could make out the shadowy figures of men working around its smokestacks—repairing the tricky boilers that had plagued its last two voyages, she assumed.

She stood gazing up through the veils of rain, watching the workers scramble about the paddle wheel, listening to the desultory clanking of their tools against steel.

That ship carried me a long way from home. I'm on the other side of the continent now. Oh, Mother—will I ever see you again?

"Now why should a girl as pretty as you look so pensive and sad?"

Dovey whirled in surprise. A tall, broad-shouldered man stood beside her on the pier, dressed against the weather in a long dark duster coat. He swept off his bowler hat and offered a courteous bow, exposing thick hair of a sandy-brown color, so tousled that it gave him a beguilingly roguish appearance. He replaced his hat and smiled down at Dovey. His face was somewhat lined, and the chilly weather had brought out a ruddy flush to his features, but his blue eyes shone with a confidence that intrigued Dovey, and his strong jaw and well-trimmed mustache quickened the beat of her heart.

"Oh," she said. "I'm sorry; I . . . I was only thinking about that boat there."

The man glanced up at its soaring black hull. "The *America*. Came from Panama a few days ago, so I hear."

Dovey nodded eagerly. "Yes. I came with it."

"All the way from Panama?" He laughed warmly. His voice was low and rich and seemed to vibrate out from his broad chest with the deep resonance of a church bell. The sound of him made Dovey feel queer and warm and kept her rooted to the spot with fascination as he spoke. "That's quite a journey. But you're from Massachusetts, aren't you? Or else I've mistaken your accent."

She blinked at him. "Yes, I am—and say, you are, too!" She had grown so used to speaking to her fellow travelers that she hadn't realized how a Massachusetts accent stood out here in the streets of San Francisco. "Are you from Boston, sir?"

Instead of answering, he responded with a question of his own, but his smile and demeanor were so charming, his bearing so warm and instantly familiar, that Dovey forgave his lapse in manners.

"Are *you* from Boston, pretty miss? Or are you from some other town?"

"I'm from Lowell," she said at once, laughing a little, delighted at the prospect of speaking of home once more.

"Where are my manners?" The man reached into his duster and produced a black umbrella. He unfolded it with a flick of his wrist and held it over Dovey's head. The rain drummed against it cheerily; she smiled up at him in gratitude.

"Lowell." His smile was broad and winsome. "And yet you say you sailed here from Panama on this very ship."

"Yes, indeed, sir!"

"How was the voyage?"

Dovey shook her wet curls. "Simply terrible. Just about all of us fell terribly ill. It's a wonder the *America* had enough crew members well enough to sail into port!"

"All of you fell ill, you say?"

"All the other women."

"A ship full of women, sailing together. How strange!" His eyes shone with warmth as he gazed down at her. The hand that held the umbrella trembled a little, as if he struggled to restrain his admiration. "And yet I am sure none of the other women are as lovely or as charming as you."

Dovey laughed. "Me? I must look a perfect mess, all wet through!"

"No, my darling. Even soaked in rain, you are enchanting as a seraph. I was taken with you at first glance. What strange luck, that we met here on this dock in San Francisco, so far away from home." His other hand reached for her, then fell back to his side. He gave a deep sigh, as if the strictures of propriety pained him to his very core. He spoke on in that rich, intoxicating voice. "Don't you think it's very strange—fated, perhaps, that we should meet this way?"

Dovey's cheeks burned. She gazed up at him through lashes that she could not keep from batting. The umbrella shadowed his face, but she could still read the warmth in his eyes. "I—I don't know," she stammered. *Lord, but he's terribly charming!*

"Two lonely hearts brought together by chance. Fortune smiles on me today! But come—tell me of your voyage from Panama. You say you traveled with other women. Sisters? Aunts?"

Dovey laughed uncertainly. "No, no—just fellow travelers. We're all coming from Lowell to the West, you see—"

One corner of his mouth turned up in a slow smile, and in the umbrella's gray-black shadow, Dovey could not quite be sure the expression was as warm and doting as it had seemed moments before. She paused.

"How exciting," the man said. His voice was still as soothing, as captivating, as ever. "Ah, now I recall some fuss in the Massachusetts papers about some fellow called Mercer."

"Yes," Dovey said. "We've all come with Mercer's expedition. We're going to—"

"And is there," the man said hastily, a hard edge crowding into his low, smooth tones, "a woman with you called Josephine?"

Dovey bit her lip and said nothing.

He gave an amiable laugh. "I only ask because I have a cousin—a fine woman who'd expressed some interest in this Mercer expedition. My letter back home has not yet been answered, so I don't know whether she joined Mercer's party . . ."

He trailed off and cast a hopeful look down at Dovey, brows raised beneath the brim of his bowler hat. His smile was lulling; his proximity and strong, handsome features made her skin prickle with a pleasant kind of heat. She opened her mouth to answer, but a rapid flicker of—*something* in his eyes halted her. It was there and gone in an instant, and Dovey could not name the emotion that burned so briefly in the stranger's face. Triumph? Anger? Perhaps it was hatred. Whatever spell passed over him, it pulled a creep of caution up Dovey's spine.

"It's no matter," the man said at once. "I'd much rather talk about you. I know it's forward of me to ask, but we have no mutual acquaintance to make introductions. So I must be appallingly direct: May I know your name, Miss?"

"D-Diana," she stammered. He was all charm once more, but that momentary revelation of some darker emotion haunted Dovey. Instinct told her she was better keeping some details to herself—at least until she knew more about the handsome stranger. "Diana Smith. I was a mill girl in Lowell. I don't know much about anybody else in Mercer's expedition. I'm afraid we all keep very much to ourselves, and that's all I can tell you, sir."

"Never mind the other women. I'm so taken with you, you might as well be the only lady in the world."

"You're very charming, but—"

"My name is Bradford. And this rain is falling harder than ever. May I escort you home?"

The thrill of caution redoubled itself and burned in her bones with a cold flame. Dovey stepped away from him, out from under the umbrella. The rain beat against her head and shoulders with sudden force. "I think not, sir. That would hardly be appropriate."

"But the rain—"

"A little rain is nothing to a mill girl. I'll be quite all right; you needn't worry."

She turned to hurry away, but Bradford caught her by the hand. Dovey whirled on him, wide-eyed, sucking in a breath to tell him off— and he stooped, pressing his lips to her own.

His kiss was long and melting. Dovey's initial shock and indignation quickly gave way to fascination, then to trembling desire as his tongue moved deftly against her lips, then, when she opened her mouth to gasp in surprise, entered with gentle confidence. After a moment—or an eternity, for all Dovey could tell—he pulled away, gazing down at her with an expression of great tenderness.

No man had ever kissed Dovey before. Not in that way. Speechless, she brushed her lips with trembling fingers.

"I must see you again, Diana," he whispered.

"You *are* very forward," Dovey managed at last.

"Please, for the sake of my aching heart, tell me you'll see me again. Meet me here again, in this very place where I first set eyes on your beauty, tomorrow evening, just before nightfall."

"I won't," Dovey gasped.

But she felt her cheeks flush a traitorous shade, and she could tell by Bradford's slow, satisfied smile that he knew she would meet him after all.

CHAPTER ELEVEN
THINK OF THE DEVIL

As she ran, speeding through the rain toward the crowded sidewalks of the shopping district, Dovey turned now and then to look behind her. Bradford did not follow her up from the docks, but still, Dovey kept moving. She craved desperately for the company of her friends, their good sense and familiar presence, and the peace and seclusion of the boardinghouse's stout walls. But even as she hurried up the streets of San Francisco, she felt the fire in her middle burn hotter every moment with the memory of Bradford's kiss.

Her legs ached as she pushed up the long, high hill toward the boardinghouse, and the shawl clung to her body, filling her head with the pinched, sour smell of soaking-wet wool. She was out of breath and sick with agitation by the time she reached the boardinghouse steps.

Dovey stood panting beside the porch, eyeing the slope of the hill behind her. The first purple tinge of dusk cast its shadows across the cobblestones, dulling the bright, cheery colors of the neighborhood's houses to cautious shades of gray. Evening had arrived; Dovey had strayed through the city far longer than she'd intended.

She left the shawl dripping on its hook beside the door. In the parlor, she could hear the tense voices of several women raised in a fearful jumble.

Dovey poked her head around the parlor door. Georgianna was the first to spot her; she leaped up from a tapestry stool beside the fireplace and rushed to embrace her.

"Dovey! Oh, thank the Lord, you're all right!"

The other girls of Mercer's party, and even the boardinghouse's plump mistress, crowded around. Each cooed her relief, and each one pulled Dovey into an embrace until she felt like a ball of dough on the kneading board.

"Yes, yes, I'm in one piece," she finally said rather crossly. "Is Mr. Mercer here? I suppose he's really angry with me."

"He hasn't returned yet; he's still out looking for a ship to Seattle," Sophronia said.

Dovey exhaled in relief. "Good. My skin is saved, then."

"I don't know about that," Sophronia fired back. "You've done it this time, Dovey—gave us all the holy terrors. What *were* you thinking? Mercer ought to send you back to Lowell, and this time I mean it!"

Jo laid a hand on Sophronia's arm to still her. "Wait, Sophronia. Something's happened to her. Look at her face—she's so pale."

"I am not," Dovey said. And then, because she suspected she was, in fact, as white as a sheet, she pinched her cheeks to bring up their color. "So there!"

"What happened out there, Dovey?" Jo took her by the shoulders, gazing into her face with such concern and sympathy that Dovey choked back a sob. She pressed both hands over her face, never knowing if she wanted to drive away the memory of the kiss or savor it, reliving the moment over and over.

"Jo, I need to speak to you privately."

Jo glanced around the room, meeting each woman's eye with a nervous blink. Then she took Dovey by the hand. "All right, girls. I'm going up to our room with Dovey. All of you, please wait here."

They climbed the staircase to the largest boarding room, hand in hand. Dovey couldn't quite make herself release her grip on Jo. She clung to the older woman's hand with a startling ferocity. When they let themselves into the empty room, Dovey turned to Jo with a desperate cry, throwing her arms around her shoulders, almost weeping against her collar as the welter of her emotions overwhelmed her.

"Dovey—get ahold of yourself! What happened to you out there? Were you hurt—attacked? Are you in some danger?"

Dovey pulled away, dabbing at her eyes. "I'm in no danger—I don't think. But, oh, Jo! The man I met!"

Jo's lips thinned. "A man? Dovey, tell me what happened."

"He was terribly handsome, Jo, and ever so charming. And he said it was just like fate that we'd met."

Jo sighed and closed her eyes. "You silly girl. So this is what's stirred you up?"

"And . . . and . . ." Dovey trailed off, biting her lip. Ought she to tell Jo the man had asked after a woman named Josephine? She felt the warm intoxication of the kiss again, felt the quivering fire spreading through her belly, and decided against it. She wanted to keep Bradford all to herself—to keep his smile, his resonant voice, his accent that spoke of home, as her own gift to savor.

"And he held your hand, is that it?" Jo asked brusquely. "Or kissed you?"

Dovey's widening eyes and indrawn breath gave away the secret.

"Lord, Dovey, you can't go around kissing strange men! Such behavior is dangerous, as well as scandalous."

Dovey folded her arms tightly; her rain-soaked dress pinched at her elbows. "Scandalous? You sound as bad as Sophronia."

The door opened suddenly. Sophronia's pale head popped into the room, thrust past the doorframe like a jack-o'-lantern on a stick. "Josephine, what's the matter?" Sophronia narrowed her eyes at Dovey, then slipped past the door and shut it firmly behind her.

"Think of the Devil, and he shall appear," Dovey quoted acidly. "Shoo; I said I'd talk to Jo alone. Don't stick your nose in where you have no business!"

Dovey glanced to Jo for reinforcement, but Jo only pulled Sophronia closer.

"Dovey, get out of those wet clothes, put on a nightgown, and go dry your hair by the fire. You can't sleep with wet hair; you'll catch your death. And put all thought of this man out of your head. You didn't join Mercer's party to flounce off with some cad in San Francisco. You're going to Seattle to meet a good, decent man—the kind who doesn't kiss girls he finds on the streets."

"Kiss?" Sophronia gaped at Dovey in astonishment. "You did *not* kiss a man out there. Tell me you didn't!"

"Fiddlesticks," Dovey spat. "People kiss all the time, and the sky doesn't fall down because of it. Nor does the earth swallow them up. You're riled up over nothing."

Sophronia folded her arms under her small breasts, raising her downy-white brows, an expression of infinite orneriness. "You truly are incorrigible, Doreen Mason. Mr. Mercer wanted *true* women for this expedition, not . . ." Her lips worked soundlessly for a moment as she wrestled with every possible descriptor of shame and iniquity. "Not *hussies* like you!"

"Hussy! I'll hussy *you*, and then we'll see!"

Dovey swiped at Sophronia, her fingers flexed like claws, nails flashing in the candlelight. Sophronia darted back with a tiny shriek that sounded like the squeaking of an indignant rat.

Jo stepped between them and caught Dovey by the shoulders. "Enough of this, now! Fighting won't do you any good. Sophronia's right; you haven't behaved properly, Dovey—not for a young lady bound for marriage in Seattle."

Sophronia sniffed. "I tell you, Josephine, we *must* inform Mr. Mercer. He has a right to know that a woman of his party has misrepresented herself and isn't what she pretends to be!"

Jo's face paled, and her gaze slid from Sophronia's face to the floor. "I don't . . . I don't think that's strictly necessary. We needn't tell Mercer anything, so long as Dovey promises—*solemnly*," she emphasized, turning to Dovey with a fierce stare, "to mind her behavior from now on, and to comport herself like a proper young lady."

"She'll spoil the whole lot of us with her influence," Sophronia said. "'A little leaven leaveneth the whole lump.'"

Dovey rolled her eyes.

"First Corinthians, chapter five, verse six," Sophronia added, with a triumphant air that said her point was well proven.

Dovey raised her fist. "I'll give you a lump to leaven!"

"Enough, Dovey!" Jo rounded on her, and her stern face put paid to the girl's rising temper. "Neither of us will inform Mr. Mercer, if you swear to behave yourself from now on. It's for your own good that we say this, and believe me, you'll thank me one day for looking out for you."

Dovey's stomach twisted sourly. Jo's words were so like her father's, that day when she'd locked her in her bedroom with plans to cart her off to the chapel. *For my own good.* Dovey knew exactly what was good for her own body and soul, and she was sick, from the tip of her toes to the crown of her head, of being told otherwise.

But she only nodded. "All right. I promise."

"Good," Jo said, threading her arm through Sophronia's and leading the other woman toward the door. "Now change into something dry and come downstairs. It's time we all settled in for the night. We've had more than enough excitement to go around."

CHAPTER TWELVE
A PERILOUS REUNION

"Jo," Catherine Stickney called from the boardinghouse's hallway, "where has Dovey got to? Do you know?"

Josephine lurched up from her bed. Her embroidery hoop spilled from her lap—she had hardly lifted her needle anyway over the past hour, lost as she was in a tangle of dark memory. Her back and legs, grown used to sitting still, cramped with sudden pain, and her head went dizzy from a terrible alertness. "What do you mean, Catherine? Dovey isn't here?"

"No. I just asked some of the other girls downstairs, and they thought perhaps she'd told you where she'd gone, since you're so close with her."

Josephine looked desperately around the long room with its rows of neatly made beds, as if Dovey might roll out from beneath one of them or step from behind the heavy, velvet drapes that framed the room's single window. But of course the girl was nowhere to be seen. Dovey hadn't approached Josephine all the long day. In fact, she had kept most definitely to herself, Jo now realized, ever since her reappearance, soaking wet and with cheeks aflame, the night before. That was unusual for the girl.

"The blasted fool has gone out again," Josephine said. "I'm sure of it. That brash child! She'll land herself in more trouble than she can imagine if somebody doesn't shake some common sense into her curly head!"

Josephine helped the other women search the boardinghouse from attic to foundation, but the whole while she knew the effort was futile. They would find no hint of Dovey in the house, she was sure, and no clue as to where she might have gone. The girl might lack caution, but she wasn't entirely witless. She left no note behind, no hint of her whereabouts or plans. The only consolation to Josephine was the sight of Dovey's few belongings, still tucked into the trunk they shared.

"She's planning to return, then," Catherine said sensibly.

"She must be," Josephine agreed.

But God only knew who this strange man was. If his intentions were honorable, the best Dovey could hope for was a rapid marriage to a perfect stranger. If his intentions were less than kind . . . Josephine shuddered at the thought.

I can't simply leave her to wander the streets alone, Josephine thought miserably, pressing her aching eyes with the heels of her hands. *Perhaps there is some hope that I might catch her before she does something she'll regret. Or something dangerous.*

The other women were mollified by the sight of Dovey's blue pagoda dress folded neatly in the trunk. Certain that their friend would return, their fear evaporated and they settled into their evening routines of reading or sewing. But Josephine could feel no such surety of Dovey's safety. As night fell, raising a thin banner of moonlight to shine weakly through the clouds, Josephine pulled Sophronia into the dark corner by the bedroom window.

"Dovey is missing," she said.

Sophronia gave no answer but a sigh.

"I assume she has run off to meet that handsome man of hers again." Josephine drew a deep breath, trying to steady the cold quiver in her middle. "She could be in terrible danger, Sophronia. I'm going out to find her."

"Josephine! At night? You *can't*! Wait until Mr. Mercer returns. We can send *him* out to search. It's safer for a man."

"Mercer has been so preoccupied with looking for a new ship to carry us to Seattle. We don't know when we might see him again. Not for several more hours, perhaps—and by then, Dovey could be . . ." She trailed off as the grim possibilities raced through her mind, speeding her pulse and raising a sweat on her brow. *Married. Assaulted. Killed!* She had to find the girl, and soon.

Sophronia glanced around the room, at the other girls bent over their stitches or paging through their leather-bound novels. She lowered her voice. "But, Josephine, it's dark out. Imagine how it will look, for a woman to go out into the streets alone, at night. Anyone who sees you will think you're—"

"I know." Josephine smoothed her skirt in a businesslike way and set her shoulders straight and square. She hoped the effort made her seem both calm and capable. "But I don't care, Sophronia. You remember the things Dovey said back in Aspinwall—all that talk of managing her own life. Well, my fear is that the girl has finally made up her mind to go and do just that."

"You don't mean—"

"What if she's run off to marry this stranger who swept her off her feet? Or worse, what if she's decided to take up the oldest profession?" Josephine gave an uncomfortable shrug at the indelicacy of the subject. "What if she's *setting up business* right here in San Francisco?"

Sophronia shuddered. "I can just see Dovey doing something as disgraceful as that! That child has no sense of decency."

"We must stop her, Sophronia. We must find her and turn her from whatever mad path she's taken tonight, before she ruins her life!"

"But we'll look just like a pair of fallen women, walking the streets after dark!"

"We have no choice, Sophronia. Dovey needs us."

Sophronia's blue eyes sparked with bitter insistence. "We *do* have a choice—and Dovey has a choice, as well. She has made her decision, but you and I needn't follow suit. Or even give the appearance of following suit."

"You're quite right," Josephine said coolly. "You and I needn't go."

Sophronia's single curt nod spoke volumes of self-satisfaction.

Josephine bent quickly and lifted her fringed, woolen cape from the trunk. "I'll go alone."

"What? Josephine, no!"

Sophronia clung to her arm all the way down the stairs, squalling over propriety until Josephine had hauled her clear out onto the boardinghouse's front porch. There, in the flickering, orange light of a streetlamp, Josephine turned to her friend with a frown of stern expectation. "Your last opportunity: will you come with me and help me bring Dovey home?"

"I . . ." Sophronia peered past Josephine, down the steep angle of the hill to the night-darkened city beyond. "I can't," she finally said, and Josephine was startled to see tears in Sophronia's eyes. "It's wrong for a woman to walk alone at night—*wrong*! And I simply can't do it."

Josephine turned away coldly. The night seemed to beckon, quiet and amused, patiently drawing her to the snare. She would have been glad of Sophronia's help, just so she would not feel so alone—so helpless and frail, so doomed. *But if the Lord wills it, I'll do this on my own.* She hurried down the porch steps before she could change her mind.

Josephine moved carefully through the streets. Whenever she could, she edged around the pools of yellow lamplight, clinging to the shadows that hung over the roofs of buildings or eddied in the stone alcoves of windows and doors. She hadn't ventured out into the city since their first day in San Francisco, and then she had spent only an hour taking in the sights with several of Mercer's girls. The lay of the city would have been unfamiliar even in daylight. Now, cloaked and clouded by night, made featureless by the wash of a weak moon, the streets seemed to twist and shift like the track of a labyrinth.

Josephine did not know where exactly she might find Dovey. But she had recognized the girl's strange and shocking ambition that afternoon in Aspinwall, when Sophronia had found Dovey loitering with the prostitute. If she was to have any hope of finding the wayward girl, Josephine knew she must find the city's night flowers—the *fallen women*, as Sophronia would say. And Josephine had seen enough of the world to know that when a woman fell, more often than not she landed at the waterfront.

Even for one who knew nothing of the city, it was simple enough to find the docks. San Francisco sloped ever down toward the water; Josephine followed each street's decline until it leveled out in a swath of cobbles and lamplight. Then she scurried along the block until she found another lane with a downward slope. She worked her way on in this haphazard manner, until at last the thick, briny scent of seawater pushed away the city odors of coal smoke and horse dung.

Josephine pressed herself against a warehouse and peered out into the night. The docks stretched in countless rows to either side, the masts of innumerable ships rising against the dark sky like a forest of pale, winter-bare trees. From somewhere in that vast, shadowed thicket a dog barked once, twice, the sound echoing and thin. Closer to hand, from the deck of a nearby boat, a man whistled a few notes and fell silent.

Josephine shivered. The cold of the early spring was dampening her skin, seeping into her bones, and she felt that she might never feel warm again. The waterfront was too large, the docks too many for one woman alone to search. She would never find Dovey here—never! A sob of desperation threatened to rise in her throat, but Josephine strangled it with resolute calm.

Any search, no matter how hopeless, must begin somehow.

Josephine stepped away from the wall and turned to the right. Any direction would do, she reasoned, as she walked steadily along the waterfront. Dark, menacing shapes seemed to rear up out of the night, revealing themselves as stacks of empty crates and abandoned barrels as Josephine drew nearer. Now and then small, sinister things scuttled in the darkness around her feet, and once a large cat sprang across her path, its lithe body arching as it ran. A rat dangled from its jaws, kicking and twisting in futile rage.

Josephine had walked for twenty minutes or more with no sign of her missing friend. She halted on the edge of a sallow puddle of lamplight and peered uncertainly around. Should she go back the way she had come, search in the opposite direction—or press on?

She had just made up her mind to retrace her steps when the sound of a woman's voice caught and held her. Josephine shrank back against a stack of crates, watching the night. Slowly, from the curtains of shadows that hung raggedly beyond the lamp's glare, the unmistakable shape of two people standing close together materialized out of the darkness. They faced one another—a towering man with a broad, strong frame and the small, slender form of a girl. In one warm rush of relief and joy, Josephine recognized the parrot green of the girl's dress, though its bright color was subdued by the dimness of night. There was, however, no mistaking the strange flatness of the skirt without the aid of its crinoline.

"Dovey!"

Perhaps the girl didn't recognize Josephine's voice. Or perhaps she *did*. Whatever the cause of her fright, Dovey uttered a tiny squeak and spun away from her suitor. Josephine caught one quick sight of Dovey's ruffled petticoats as the girl hiked them high—then Dovey scuttled away from the docks, vanishing into the darkness of a nearby alley before Josephine could blink.

Josephine breathed a curse and hurried after the girl, never sparing a glance for the man who stood still and surprised in the shadows. She could make out little of Dovey in the blue-dark confines of the alley, save for an occasional flash of pale petticoats bobbing through the corridor ahead. The clatter of Dovey's running feet drew Josephine on, past a heap of refuse and a pile of old, discarded palings. The alley was thick with the smell of rot and human waste; Josephine choked and coughed as she ran, unable to call out again, to persuade Dovey to stop—or at least to slow.

The alley ended in a seven-foot wall of dark, slime-dampened planks—the rear fence of some adjoining storage yard, Josephine assumed. A halo of lamplight arced over the fence, casting Dovey's face in planes of sharp shadow and yellow glow. The girl's eyes were wide and strained with panic.

"Dovey—it's only me!" Josephine reached for her, but Dovey pressed back against the foul wooden fence.

"Land sakes! Why did you follow me here?" Her brow furrowed. "You'd better go back to the boardinghouse, Jo. I'm not coming back with you."

"Of course you are, Dovey. Don't be foolish."

"I'm not. I'm staying put. San Francisco suits me just fine. I've made up my mind: I don't want to go on to Seattle."

"But what will you do? How will you support yourself?" Josephine bit her lip; perhaps she didn't want to hear Dovey's answer after all. "Is it that fellow you met on the street? That man back there, lurking in the darkness? Really, Dovey, a tryst at the docks—it's hardly a hopeful start to a good marriage."

Dovey braced one hand on her hip. She indicated the waterfront with a jerk of her head that tossed her curls wildly. "He's a good enough man, I reckon. And it's my choice to make, not yours. Not anybody's choice but mine!"

Josephine's stomach went hollow and cold. "You're making a grave mistake, Dovey."

"You just let me alone to run my own life. I can take care of myself."

"Dovey, I . . . I *can't*. I can't just let you alone. After all we've been through together—Lowell, and your sickness, and the terrible passage on the *America*—I can't let you come to any harm. Don't you see? I'm your friend, and I'd be failing you if I left you to throw your life away on a stranger. Now be a sensible girl and come with me to Seattle."

"All the men in Seattle are strangers, too. I like San Francisco, and I intend to stay here."

"You're every bit as much a fool as Sophronia thinks you are!" Josephine stepped forward and took Dovey by the hand, but she pulled roughly away.

"Well, well. What have we here?"

Josephine's breath caught in her throat. She recognized that voice, low and smooth, thick with amusement. Oh yes, she recognized it— with a chill of terror that froze her heart in her chest.

Dovey turned toward the man's voice eagerly. "Bradford, there you are. I'm sorry I ran, but—"

"His name isn't Bradford," Josephine said. Her voice was frail and thin, barely more than a whisper.

She turned slowly—not wanting to see him standing there, but determined, now that her final fate had come, to face it bravely. Even in silhouette, she recognized Clifford's hulking size and half-hunched shoulders. Her knees shook so hard she swayed, and her eyes prickled with tears.

The slow, cold snake of Clifford's laughter twisted down the alley toward them. "So I found you at last, you bitch."

Dovey gasped. "Bradford!"

He glided toward them where they cowered at the alley's dead end, moving with the same confident grace of any feral predator. Dovey, finally laying claim to sense, realized the man was not who she thought him to be. She breathed a quiet whimper and grabbed Josephine's arm, clinging so hard that her fingers bit into the flesh.

Perhaps it was the girl's fear that spurred Josephine on. She did not know where the sudden, solid well of courage came from, but she stepped toward Clifford with her head high, moving fearlessly to meet him.

"Get out of our way, Clifford. Leave us be. I'm none of your business anymore."

"Oh, you are my business. You *are*." He drew so close that she could smell the whiskey on his breath. The old, instinctive fear of him—of his wild, drunken fury—rushed in a tingle along her limbs. But courage won out, and Josephine stood firm.

"Get back," Dovey said over Josephine's shoulder. "I don't know who you are, but—"

"Who am I?" Clifford asked Josephine. The clouds overhead parted for a moment, and a spill of silvery starlight lit his face. He was as handsome as ever—firm-jawed, bright-eyed. And the old, familiar brutality glittered in his eyes. "Tell the girl who I am, Josephine."

She swallowed hard. So she wouldn't make it to Seattle with her secret intact. In fact, she wouldn't make it to Seattle at all. She had ended, after all her efforts, after all her hopes and desperate prayers, back in Clifford's hands.

"He's my husband," Josephine said. Her voice was firm, unshaken.

"Your . . . husband?" Dovey stammered. "Jo!"

"And *you* are a thief," Clifford said. "I've come for the money you stole, Josephine. Two hundred and fifty dollars. I'll have every penny of it back—with interest."

"Interest?" Josephine snorted. "You're not a bank, Clifford."

The taunt only riled him further. Quick as a bolt of lightning, his hand shot out. He caught her by the high, old-fashioned collar of her dress and pulled her tight against his body. She could feel the muscles of his chest and stomach, as hard as hewn stone, pressing against her until she felt as small and bruised, as utterly helpless as a baby bird fallen from the nest. Josephine turned her face away from his reek of whiskey, stifling the scream she knew Clifford wanted to hear.

Dovey obliged with a wild shriek instead. Her high, wordless wail rebounded from the brick walls of the warehouses, mingling with Clifford's cruel laughter.

"I'll be bringing my money back home with me," he promised, his voice hoarse and grating. "My money—and my runaway wife."

Dovey's scream cut off abruptly. The girl fell on Clifford like a whirlwind, slapping and kicking, hollering threats and foul curses that would have burned a blush into Josephine's cheek, had she heard those words under less dire circumstances.

Clifford, still chuckling, knocked Dovey aside with a casual blow. The girl slammed into the nearest brick wall like a rag doll tossed by a child, and nearly fell to the ground. Josephine gritted her teeth, watching as Dovey steadied herself with her palms flat against the brick, gasping and shaken.

A fist full of brutal promise rose over Josephine's face, and the world was eclipsed by the dark, hate-filled curve of her husband's smile.

"Let her go!" Dovey shrieked in desperation.

Josephine braced herself for the impact of his fist, but Clifford paused. He eyed Dovey again, his eyes lazy with amusement.

"When I'm done teaching this good-for-nothing bitch a lesson, I'll give you what you've looking for. Oh yes, I know what little toms like you are after. Kissing me last night like a common whore, and out walking the street in the dark—don't tell me you don't want it."

Even in the dimness of the alley, Josephine could see Dovey's face go pale.

He'll do it, too. I know he will. He'll hurt her, unless I can stop him.

Josephine brought her knee up hard, aiming for the fork of Clifford's legs. But held tight as she was, her blow went awry, thumping against his thigh.

Clifford laughed softly. "That will only earn you another lesson." He raised his fist again, and Josephine held her breath, waiting for the pain, the burst of stars across her vision.

But in that moment, a figure as pale and forbidding as a ghost stepped from the shadows behind Clifford's shoulder. A high, fast whistle cut the sound of Clifford's laughter, and something long, white, and flat arced through the air. There was a tremendous crack that made Dovey gasp and Clifford's body jerk; a piece of splintered wood flew past Jo's face, sailing into the depths of the alley.

Clifford bellowed like a whipped bull and released Josephine's collar. He reeled, clutching his head—then wheezed out one long grunt and collapsed in a heap on the cobbles.

Josephine danced back, pulling at her skewed collar, heaving for breath. She peered at the newcomer—and, when recognition dawned, shook her head in astonishment.

"Sophronia!"

The pale, elegant woman stared back at Josephine with unruffled coolness. Her war club—a piece of paling, now broken at one end—dangled easily from her hand.

Clifford stirred and moaned. Sophronia raised one brow and then the splintered paling. She cracked it down on Clifford's head, no more concerned than if she'd batted a shuttlecock with a racquet.

Clifford went silent and still.

Dovey leaped away from the brick wall. "Bully," she shouted. "I've never seen anything so sharp! You knocked him right out cold!"

"Hush," Sophronia told the girl calmly. "You're coming back to the boardinghouse with us—and from there to Seattle. No more arguments."

Dovey glanced down at Clifford. His chest stirred with uneven breaths, and Dovey edged away from him. "I will," she promised. "I'll stick with you. What he said, you know . . . about giving me what he thought I wanted . . . it gave me a chill."

"So the life of a fallen woman is not for you after all?" Sophronia said loftily.

"All right." Josephine stepped around Clifford and headed briskly for the alley's mouth. Her hands trembled violently as she raised her hem, and her legs felt as solid as bathwater. But she marched on—away from Clifford, away from her fear. "Stop arguing, you two! Let's get back where we're safe. *Now.*"

Dovey and Sophronia caught up to Josephine in a matter of moments. They hurried up dark streets together, arms linked, desperate for the comfort of one another's proximity. Hardly a moment passed when one of the women didn't glance back to be sure the monster from the shadows had not revived. When they crossed the broad avenue of the business district, Josephine turned to Sophronia. "You came to help me after all. I thought you never would. You said—"

"I know what I said," Sophronia interjected smoothly. "But I was wrong. I shouldn't have let you go out alone—and I shouldn't have left Dovey to her fate."

"I'm glad to have a friend like you," Josephine said.

She cast a glance at the paling Sophronia still clutched in one fist; Sophronia gave the thing a long, assessing look, then hurled it off into the street. "We're something more than friends, after what we've been through—all of us," she added with a sharp nod at Dovey. "I couldn't abandon either one of you to that sort of danger. To let either of you come to harm, while I sat back and waited for help—well, that would have been a sin even worse than traipsing around the streets like a night flower."

They pressed on in silence. The warmth of her friends' bodies was a shield against the night's fears, but soon a new chill curled along the base of Josephine's spine. *What must Sophronia think of me now,* she thought miserably, *now that she knows my secret?*

"A sin," Josephine mused aloud. Her mouth was dry, her eyes stinging with fresh tears. But she had to know what Sophronia thought of her shame—and Dovey, too. "Would it have been as grievous a sin as leaving one's husband?"

Sophronia did not answer the question. The hill sloped up steeper beneath their feet, and though Josephine's body warmed with the effort of the climb, her heart felt clumsy and cold. Of course Sophronia thought it a greater sin. How could she not? For there was nothing Sophronia disliked more than a fallen woman—and in a sense, Josephine was just that. She had failed to live up to Sophronia's lofty ideals—and to the expectations of so many other women and men.

Is it worse to abandon a marriage or to remain with a brutal man? Josephine didn't know the answer to her own question, and not knowing filled her with a sick quiver of guilt.

Sophronia broke her silence. "Your predicament does present a problem, Josephine. We are meant to be brides. Marriage is our purpose, not only in life, but also—especially—in this business with Mr. Mercer. But you cannot marry a Seattle man if you're already wed."

"You might end up a widow, though," Dovey interjected with obvious glee. "Sophie gave that brute a real crack to the nut."

"He'll recover," Sophronia said. "I'm not so terribly strong that I can break a man's skull."

Josephine gave a sharp huff—part sob, part sigh. "I lied to Mr. Mercer so I could come on this expedition," she confessed. "I feel terrible about deceiving him, and the rest of you, too—but you saw what Clifford is like! You understand why I had to do it . . . don't you? It was the only chance I had to get free!"

Dovey took her hand. "I understand. And I won't tell a soul. Mercer doesn't need to know about Clifford, or anything else we don't choose to tell him. Right, Sophronia?"

Josephine clung to Sophronia's arm, desperate as a child. "Oh, please keep my secret. I *had* to get away from Lowell—from Clifford! Mercer . . . Seattle . . . the expedition was my last hope! Clifford would have killed me sooner or later if I hadn't fled."

Sophronia tapped her lips with a meditative air. "But you *are* living a falsehood, and to lie is a sin. Nor do I approve overmuch of running away from one's husband."

"*I* approve," Dovey said stoutly. "Especially from a husband like that. And if you tell Mercer Jo's secret, and get her kicked out of the party, I'll never let you rest. I'll haunt you, Sophronia Brandt. I'll be a plague to you all the rest of your days!"

Sophronia frowned at the girl. "I believe you."

"You heard what Clifford said," Josephine pleaded. "You heard him call me his . . . his *wife*. So why did you do it? Why did you assault him, if you believed me a fallen woman and a liar?"

Sophronia sniffed, lifting her fine, pointed chin. "I could smell the liquor on him. And I believe immoderation is an even worse sin than leaving one's husband."

Josephine goggled at her, but Sophronia's stern mask suddenly broke in a smile. She pulled Josephine close, holding her about the shoulders as they found the boardinghouse steps in the dark. "I'll keep your secret," she promised. "I owe you that much, for the care you showed me while I was ill. But Josephine, you *must* do what's right by the Lord. You can't live with Clifford as a wife—that much is clear. But unless he grants you a divorce, neither can you remarry. You'll have to find some plausible excuse to give Mr. Mercer—and all the men of Seattle, too. You must remain true to your marriage vows unless Clifford agrees to set you free."

"I swear it," Josephine said at once. She had no interest in marriage; the very last thing she desired was another husband to batter and bruise her. All she wanted was an escape—a new beginning. She had that now, and she would do whatever she must to hold on to her freedom.

They returned to the large, shared room at the boardinghouse. It was warm, glowing with lamplight, and sweet with the voices of their friends, all of whom rushed to embrace Dovey and to hail Josephine and Sophronia as heroes.

"Mr. Mercer returned while you were out," Sarah Gallagher said. "And wouldn't you know it? He's found a ship to carry us to Seattle! We leave on the morning tide."

Josephine sank onto her bed, numb with relief. "Thank God," she muttered. "We can't get to Seattle fast enough for my liking."

Sophronia smiled at the news, but the look she doled out to Josephine was flat with warning. *Remain true, unless Clifford agrees to set you free,* that cool, pale-blue stare reminded her.

Josephine sagged against her pillow. Seattle was only days away now. All she had to do to get there—and maintain her place in the haven of that vast, green wilderness—was keep her word.

CHAPTER THIRTEEN
A FINE HELLO

The water was black as pitch, and its low, sinister voice chuckled beneath the planks of the dock. Broken shards of light, cast from the *Torrent*'s lamps, scattered and slid over the water's surface, flaring and dimming as the harbor stirred with its small, lazy waves. The darkness was perfectly appalling—according to Mr. Mercer they had reached Seattle at last, but there was no city in sight, only a dense shelf of black swallowing the end of the narrow gray dock. Sophronia could make out no building, no street, and the small, yellow points of light hanging high but distant—houses on a hill, she assumed, their windows still glowing against the night—were the only signs of civilization.

Despite the stillness, the eerie shroud of dark, Sophronia was first down the ramp to the dock below. Her boot heels made a hollow racket as she strode away from the *Torrent*. The slap and whisper of unseen water below sent a shiver up her spine, but she marched on, determined to be in Seattle at last, to actually stand upon its soil—to put the *Torrent* behind her forever.

As she pressed on toward the shore, the hard edges and long, low bulk of buildings resolved out of the darkness. A strip of cobbles, ash gray, barely lighter than the night, gave the suggestion of a new-laid road. The dock seemed to roll slightly beneath Sophronia's feet—a memory of the *Torrent*'s ceaseless rocking—but she ignored the disorienting heave of her own footsteps and concentrated on the shore.

Sophronia reached the dock's final plank. She opened her mouth to offer up a hasty prayer of gratitude, but instead of praises to the Lord, she let loose a gasp of shock. Her boot sank nearly to the ankle in thick, sucking mud. She snatched up her skirt and petticoats, lifting them as high as she dared, hoping she could clear the muck. Its thick, salty odor rose all around her, together with the sharp bite of fresh sawdust and the deep, cold smell of rain-soaked woodlands.

Sophronia tottered on. The mud resisted, holding obstinately to her boots, then sliding under her feet when she managed to wrench her way free. She could hear the other women behind her, uttering little cries of dismay as they, too, stepped onto land only to find it was barely more solid than the sea.

It doesn't matter, Sophronia told herself. *I'll walk a mile through knee-deep mud and never complain, if it means I'll never spend another moment on the* Torrent.

She had thought no vessel on all the world's oceans could be worse than the *America*. The *Torrent* had proved her wrong. It was a timber freighter—long, lean, and prone to rolling—and though it might have been perfectly made for the speedy transport of logs, the *Torrent* was woefully unsuited to the hauling of people, ladies especially. The journey from San Francisco to Seattle had been a misery of jolting waves, of creaking timbers and cramped quarters, and the damp chill inside the *Torrent*'s few small cabins had made Sophronia long for the homey comforts of the *America*. But at least, thank God, no one had fallen ill on this voyage; one small but distinct mercy.

Sophronia slid and stumbled across the muddy yard until her boots scraped against the cobbles of the road. She stood huffing against her corset, waiting for her breath to slow while she still held her skirts aloft. She had no idea how far up her legs the thick mud had splattered, and standing there with the vast night stretching all around her, she could not begin to guess when or where she might wash her clothes if they became too soiled. *A fine picture I must be,* she thought peevishly. *It's a good thing there is no one here to greet us.*

In fact, the *Torrent* had arrived well after ten o'clock at night. The residents of Seattle seemed to be abed. The waterfront was quiet, the black monoliths of its warehouses and shops perfectly still. She watched the women make their careful way across the great span of mud, their exposed petticoats pale against the night, the swaying of their laces and ruffles the only movement in the darkness. As each woman reached the firm cobblestone, they clustered together, exchanging fearful whispers.

"I heard the sailors talking this morning," Annie said, pressing close to Sophronia's side. "There are Indians in the hills. They're violent and full of hate."

Sophronia turned, peering over her shoulder at the dim suggestion of hills to the east. She could sense in the cold depths of the woods— between the tiny islands of candlelight—the steady, dark gaze of countless unseen eyes. The wilderness seemed to tower overhead, leaning, curving the great, tangled mass of its body to peer down at Sophronia and her friends.

Indians. A tremor of dread wracked her. *Uncivilized heathens, knowing nothing of the Lord.* What terrible fate might wait for her here, crouching in the dark forest? With a pang that nearly wrenched a cry from her throat, Sophronia longed for Boston, for Lowell—its ordered streets, its predictable citizens, its *streetlights.* But in the next moment, she pushed fears and longings both aside. She had committed herself to God's work. By His grace, she had reached her destination—her mission—and she would not fail the Lord. Not now, when she had come so close to her reward: the love she craved. Here she stood, in Seattle's dense, clinging muck. She was more than halfway to a husband already. Not even the threat of violent Indians would drive her from her object now.

Asa Mercer was the last to cross from the *Torrent* to the road. He tiptoed over the mud with surprising alacrity, as cheery and practiced as a schoolboy.

He grinned at them when he stepped into their huddled midst. "Well, ladies, we've made it at last. Here it is!" His arm swept wide, taking in the silent dockyard, the empty, unlit street, and the bleak, towering, black-shouldered hills with a grand gesture. "Seattle!"

"It sure is bully." Dovey's voice came drily from the crowd.

"The sailors are already unloading your goods," Mercer continued, "and will bring your baggage to the hotel. But now, I'm sure you could all use a good night's sleep. We've rooms waiting at the hotel." He clapped his hands, a gesture of brisk readiness. "Follow me!"

The women fell in behind Mr. Mercer, hurrying in his wake like ducklings after their mother, fearful of being left behind. The party rounded one especially large warehouse, revealing the cheerful glow of a tall, whitewashed building with wooden cornices, carved in the ornate curls of flowering vines. The building was grandly high, rising to an ambitious height of four stories, which seemed to Sophronia rather too hopeful for a place as empty and untamed as this city.

"The Occidental Hotel," Mercer announced.

Two streets crossed in front of the Occidental at an acute angle, squeezing the building's frontal facade to a point. Sophronia, used to the well-planned grids of East Coast cities, hesitated for a few steps. The odd proportions of the Occidental rising above that strange intersection produced an effect altogether disorienting.

She tore her eyes from the Occidental and found Josephine walking calmly at her side. "I would have expected some fanfare," the older woman said. "One would think the men of Seattle would be eager to see their new brides . . . few though we are."

"Something seems odd here," Sophronia agreed, "and it's not just the shape of that hotel. But we're all tired; perhaps we're making too much of this. I'm sure the lack of a welcome is only due to the late hour."

"According to the sailors' talk, Seattle is a bawdy town," Josephine said. "I don't think late hours ever held any man *here* back from celebrating."

A doorman emerged from the Occidental and exchanged a few words of greeting with Mr. Mercer. Then he stood back, holding the gleaming oak door wide, and doffed his cap with a smile that bristled his thick mustache. "Ladies, Seattle is most pleased to welcome you!"

The women filed into the warm, well-lit lobby, and as Sophronia edged past the doorman she heard him mutter, "Most pleased—no matter what some might say."

Jo nudged Sophronia in the ribs. "Did you hear that?" she whispered.

Sophronia was about to reply, but a shrill bluster from farther in the lobby froze the words on her tongue.

"So you've gone through with your mad plan after all, Asa Mercer," a woman's voice cried. "We'd heard about your telegram from San Francisco, but none of us could quite believe you would truly go through with this."

The weary girls of Mercer's party had stopped just inside the Occidental's door. They milled about rather helplessly, glancing between Mr. Mercer and whomever was speaking. Each girl, Sophronia noted, looked pale and shaken, and some seemed on the verge of tears. Sophronia shared a dark look with Josephine. Together, they pushed to the fore of the crowd.

The Occidental's lobby was well appointed, its shining wood floors covered with fine carpets, the seating area boasting several carved couches upholstered in deep-green velvet. A broad, mahogany staircase rose from the bellman's desk to the railed landing above, and several quality portraits adorned the large room's walls. Gas lamps glowed in sconces along the wall, their light playing merrily through cut-glass shades. The effect was altogether rich, and doubly welcome after weeks of living in cramped boardinghouses and the cabins of stinking, slime-cold boats. The Occidental's beautiful interior gave Sophronia her first glimmer of hope that Seattle was not all mud and darkness.

But the women who stood waiting in the lobby, straight-backed and high-headed, made an image somewhat less than lovely. There were seven of them, all middle-aged or close to it. Bedecked in stiff, watered silks and sober velvets with hats as generously plumed as any bird, they glared at the new arrivals with sharp, suspicious eyes.

Mr. Mercer gave a little wave of his hand, a placating gesture. "Mrs. Garfield. How pleasant to see you again, after all these weeks."

"Pleasant, my foot, Asa Mercer! There is nothing pleasant about this business." Mrs. Garfield, tall for a woman and ample in her figure, stood at the head of her compatriots, quivering with outrage. Her steel-gray hair gave the appearance of advanced age, yet her face was still quite smooth, if heavy in the cheeks. She met Mercer's eye with a forbidding glower. "This is a protest, sir—a protest! The upstanding women of Seattle do not approve of your carting in a load of wagtails to unsettle the already dubious morals of our unmarried men."

A collective gasp went up from the travelers.

Wagtails! Sophronia cut a nervous glance toward Mr. Mercer, who stood pale-faced beside the bellman's desk. Was his wide-eyed shock due to outrage at Mrs. Garfield's unjust accusations—or was he startled that a woman had guessed his true intentions? Sophronia's early apprehensions came crowding back into her mind. Perhaps, after all, she had sold herself into danger and shame. *But I am no loose woman,* she thought fiercely, leveling her icy stare at Mrs. Garfield and her friends.

"Please, ladies!" Mercer moved toward the protesters, but Mrs. Garfield hissed a wordless warning, and he stopped short. "These young women are of the finest quality. They haven't come all this way to unsettle any man's morals, I assure you. They've come full of hope for good marriages—to make proper homes and contribute to our youthful city."

The bellman, with a rather regretful expression, tapped Mr. Mercer's arm, then spoke a few low words into his ear.

"You must excuse me for a moment," Mercer said to the Seattle women. "My business with the hotel compels me . . . but I shall return, and . . ." He glanced around his party of women, caught Josephine's eye, and cast her a look of agonized pleading.

Josephine, as the eldest traveler, was evidently expected to take on a role of shepherdess. She drew an uneasy breath, shrinking into herself as Mrs. Garfield advanced on the girls.

"I won't tolerate this," Mrs. Garfield said, shaking her head like a mother scolding a pack of naughty children. "It is, in its very essence, *intolerable*."

Her friends murmured their assent.

"My husband is a powerful man in Seattle," Mrs. Garfield said, "a well-respected member of our community. And these women, too"— she gestured at the other protesters—"are well connected."

"Three cheers for you," Dovey muttered under her breath.

"We don't approve of you Mercer girls," one of the protesters said.

Catherine, tears shining in her eyes but still unshed, sputtered, "But whyever not?"

"Importing women like cattle!" Mrs. Garfield's already ample chest puffed to an even greater circumference. "Shuttling girls about like goods for the trading! No woman of virtue—of true morals—would ever consent to such a thing."

"And believe me," one of her friends added, "Seattle has enough women already who lack for morals."

"But you don't understand what it's like in Massachusetts," Josephine said. "The rebellion has made such an impact, you see, that the prospects for husbands are so terribly slim. What are these girls to do, if they can't find good men to marry at home?"

"Marriage!" Mrs. Garfield sputtered. "Look at the lot of you! None of you is fit for marriage. I'll tell you the type of young lady who's fit for marriage: a bright-eyed, bouncing lass, who can darn a stocking, mend trousers, sew her own frock, command a regiment of pots and kettles, milk a cow, and still be a lady at the end of the day. You lot, pining and lolling, fashion addled, slipping off from your hometowns to chase men across the country—why, if I were a gambling woman, I'd place a wager that every last one of you reads novels! And East Coasters . . . you're probably mortgaged by consumption, to boot!"

Sophronia's outrage expanded in her chest with a sudden force that nearly choked off her breath. Who were these women, untroubled in their fancy hats and their fine, watered silks, to judge any of Mercer's party? And how dare they judge Sophronia herself, who had suffered long—and nearly died in the grip of fever—to do the Lord's bidding?

She brushed past Josephine, stepping boldly across the ornate carpet until she stood face-to-face with Mrs. Garfield.

"You're right," Sophronia said. "Only a certain type of woman would make such a journey, long and difficult as it's been. Shall I tell you what kind of woman travels with a man like Mercer? The kind who isn't afraid of sleeping five to a cabin on a cold, rocking ship. The kind who can live off of stale oatcakes and hard sausage for weeks at a time. The kind who will nurse her sisters when they fall ill with the fever. Women who can do all this, and who will never raise a word of complaint!"

She felt the Mercer girls rustle and gasp behind her, and felt, too, their approval and gratitude.

Mrs. Garfield raked Sophronia head to foot with a cool, judgmental stare, taking in her disheveled hair, her worn, rumpled dress, the thick mud that caked her boots and stained her petticoats' hem. "Yes, indeed," she finally said, her voice flat with dismissal. "I can see that it takes a special kind of woman to submit herself to such a trial."

Sophronia's face burned. "Jesus said, 'Judge not, lest ye be judged.' If I were you, I wouldn't—"

Mrs. Garfield broke in smoothly, turning her face away as if the very sight of Sophronia was a grave offense. "If *I* were *you*, Miss, I wouldn't presume to quote the Lord. Scripture does not sit pretty on a harlot's tongue."

The girls let out a collective gasp.

Sophronia gaped at Mrs. Garfield, struck mute by the blow. A roiling heat flared in her chest, sending a fury unlike any she had felt before racing along her veins. She held the woman's cool, distant eye—then, while her better sense shrieked at her to stop, to walk away, to maintain her dignity, she stepped forward deliberately, ducked her head, and spat on the hem of Mrs. Garfield's dress.

A chorus of shrieks erupted, from protesters and travelers alike. Mr. Mercer came running with the bellman, waving his hands and imploring the women to maintain order. Mrs. Garfield gathered her insulted skirt in her hands and made for the Occidental's door, cleaving a path straight through the flustered newcomers. She paused beside Mercer, her flushed cheeks puffing with outrage.

"Never in my life have I been so ill used—never, sir! You have brought a plague upon our city. I hope you are pleased with yourself!"

The protesters sailed out into the night, vanishing in the gloom beyond the Occidental's lamps.

Sophronia turned to Mr. Mercer, hot with shame. "I beg your pardon. I behaved poorly; I did no credit to your good name."

Dovey laughed aloud. "You behaved *magnificently*! Sophie, I never thought you had such gumption in you."

Mr. Mercer smiled wearily at the girl, then took Sophronia's arm. "Mrs. Garfield got what she deserved. Put it out of your mind, Miss Brandt. It has been a long and tiresome journey. None of us are quite ourselves, but we'll feel better for a good night's rest. I'm afraid Seattle has more than its fair share of Mrs. Garfields, but you'll soon find that all the city isn't so hostile to your presence. You'll see in the morning: we're to welcome you with a reception. To bed now, and put Mrs. Garfield out of your mind. You'll want to look your freshest tomorrow."

The girls' trunks and bags were already waiting beside their beds. Each room contained two beds—narrow but soft as clouds—piled with plush bedding and so many pillows that they seemed an absurdity.

Sophronia was quietly pleased to learn that she would room with Josephine. The older woman lost all her air of sensible self-possession at sight of the beds. She fell face-first onto one, luxuriating in the pillows.

"Down," Josephine sighed, in a tone that said, *There is balm in Gilead.* "Do you know how long it's been since I've laid my head on a down pillow?"

Sophronia inspected the small closet beside the washstand. A scented pomander hung inside, and she breathed in the sweet perfume of rose petals and lavender. "I can almost forget that I've got mud to my knees."

"Mrs. Garfield certainly noticed your mud," Jo said, a twinkle of mischief in her eyes.

"Mrs. Garfield, indeed! Well, she won't forget me in a hurry, for better or worse."

"And we're to have a reception tomorrow morning." Josephine rolled onto her back, staring up at the ceiling in thoughtful silence. Finally she said, "I'm troubled, Sophie. If this is what the women of Seattle think of us—wagtails and harlots!—then what are the men expecting?"

"It can't be as bad as that termagant made it seem."

"I hope you're right," Jo said. "Let us pray tomorrow's reception will be kinder than the welcome we found tonight."

PART 2
MAY–JUNE 1864

CHAPTER FOURTEEN
THE RECEPTION

Morning came too soon. Josephine lay in her bed, her still-weary body reluctant to wake, the aches of long travel seeping all too slowly out of her limbs and into the deep, soft mattress. Muffled through the solid door, drifting down the long hall outside, she could hear women chattering together, their words lost but their excitement plain in their high, eager voices.

A brisk tap sounded on the doorframe. Sophronia sat up in a rustle of bedding, but Josephine shut her eyes tighter, refusing to acknowledge the morning. She heard Sophronia pad across the rug, heard the door creak as it opened.

"Rise and shine," Dovey called, too loudly. "The sun is up, and it's time to get ready!"

Josephine groaned and rolled away. Just the thought of standing—of forsaking the first good bed she'd slept in for more than a decade—made her bones tremble.

"I've brought your breakfast." Dovey's voice came nearer as the girl bustled into the room. Josephine heard the soft thump of a tray landing on the little table at the foot of her bed. "It was left in the hall outside. I've already had mine. It's simply delicious! Come on, Jo—get up! We have an exciting day ahead! You haven't forgotten about the reception, have you?"

Josephine's eyes snapped open. The fleur-de-lis pattern of the wallpaper, inches from her face, seemed to spring at her with a sudden, predatory fury. *The reception.* No, she had not forgotten—how could she? Her intrinsic dread of the day to come had colored her dreams with unsettling shades. Guilt had assailed her even in her sleep, gnawing at her gut and tensing her body. Mr. Mercer, who had been so kind to her—and indeed, all the men of Seattle—expected something of Josephine that she simply could not provide. When they learned that she could wed no one—not until Clifford freed her, at least—would they turn their judgment upon her, pile on her head a crueler scorn than even Mrs. Garfield had shown?

Dovey noted Josephine's frantically alert state. She nodded vigorously, her loose curls dancing over her shoulders. "That's it; get up and take in the day!"

There was nothing for it. The reception would go on, whether or not Josephine willed it. And as one of the newcomers to the city—a *Mercer girl,* as Mrs. Garfield had disdainfully dubbed the travelers—she would be expected to attend.

Josephine sat up in her bed, frowning at the tray. Two bowls of porridge waited there, along with a pot of tea and an array of sliced apples and cheese. A perfectly lovely repast, yet her stomach turned at the sight of it. How could she eat at a time like this, when at any moment her shame might be revealed—paraded before the whole of Seattle?

She shook her head. "I'm not hungry."

"Well, I am." Sophronia sat and tucked into one of the bowls. "It seems behaving like a perfect hellion is good for the appetite."

"You," Dovey said slowly, toying with the neckline of her parrot-green wool, "spitting on one of the fine, upstanding ladies of Seattle—a pillar of the community. I'm still in awe."

"Don't go emulating me," Sophronia warned. "I don't care how much I awed you. It was the silliest thing any of us could have done, offending those well-connected women when their opinion of us was already poor. We must work all the harder now to make a good impression."

"I still say it was bully. And that pompous hen Mrs. Garfield got just what was coming to her." Dovey turned to Josephine. "If you're not hungry, can I have your porridge? I'm starved."

Dovey ate with youthful energy and enthusiasm, talking all the while. She had seen several of the other girls in the hall, or passed their open doors, and gave a ready description of what each was wearing to the reception, and how she'd fixed her hair. The girl's plucky spirits did keep Josephine from getting entirely lost in her fears.

"What about you?" Josephine asked when Dovey's chatter slowed. "What will you wear—the green dress, or the blue?"

"The blue, for certain. It's the better of my two dresses. But I'm afraid the hem might be all off now. I've made friends already with the girl who cleans the hotel rooms. She lives here all the time, you know, in a room just down the hall. She was happy to loan me this crinoline—her spare. But it's not quite the same as the one I left in Lowell. I'll need to tack up the hem of my dress."

"Bring it here, and I'll tack it for you," Josephine said. She would be glad of the needlework—a distraction from her anxiety.

"That's awfully nice of you, Jo. I'll go fetch it now."

It was the work of only a few minutes to place a few well-hidden stitches in Dovey's hem while the girl stood on a footstool before the room's mirror. Dovey examined her reflection with no small air of approval, turning her face this way and that to admire how the pearl-gray light of her first Seattle morning complemented her coloring and the cheerful tint of her dress. When Josephine rose from her knees with a needle still held between her lips, Dovey's satisfied smile turned into a pout of speculation.

"Let's make you up, Jo," the girl suggested.

"Make me up? Whatever do you mean?"

"Put some color into your cheeks," she said. "Liven up your complexion."

Josephine, who had pulled her hair tightly into a bun before her impromptu tailoring began, stepped away from Dovey as if the girl were a snake in the grass. "I'm made up plenty. Besides"—she dropped her voice, as if the other girls in their separate rooms might hear—"you know I'm not out to catch a man. I'll take a post as a teacher and live alone, and that will be that."

"I doubt *that will be that*," Sophronia said darkly. "There are at least two hundred men in Seattle, all of whom want a bride. And there are only fourteen of us. You'll be bombarded with flowers and poetry and all kinds of sweetness, Josephine. You'll be courted, all right—make no mistake. What will you tell those men? You'll have to give some plausible reason for putting them off, at least until you can convince Clifford to let you go."

Josephine sighed. "I know. I'll just have to pretend my suitors don't *suit* me. What other choice do I have?"

"You could find a man who does suit you," Dovey suggested. "What Clifford doesn't know won't hurt him."

"What the Lord knows *will* hurt *you*," Sophronia shot back as she smoothed the wrinkles from her own sapphire-blue silk. "And anyway, if Clifford was angry enough to follow you all the way to San Francisco, he might come to Seattle, too."

Josephine folded up her packet of needles and closed the lid of her sewing box, more energetically than she'd intended. The thought of Clifford's recent attack made her want to shiver, yet she would not allow one muscle to twitch or tremble. Clifford had spent their entire marriage working hard to intimidate Josephine. Now that she was away from him, she would not give in to fear. Not anymore.

"Don't give Clifford more reason for anger," Sophronia advised. "You'll have to write him letters, and work with him patiently until he sees the sense in granting you a divorce."

"I suppose you're right about that. I just hope it doesn't take him long to see sense."

"Well," Dovey said, "when Clifford does let you go, you'll be free to accept any suitor you please. And there's no better time to start attracting their attention than now." She pulled one of the high-backed chairs away from the table. "Sit down. I'm going to make you up proper."

Josephine turned to Sophronia with a silent, pleading stare. She was sure the woman must have a lecture against face paints and fripperies in her vast repertoire of disapprovals. But to Josephine's surprise, Sophronia joined in, consigning the contents of her own toilet case to the effort.

"You, Sophronia?" Josephine pressed against the chair's hard back, shrinking from the little vials and jars her friends brandished like weapons. "I never would have suspected that you would paint your face. Aren't cosmetics in the realm of fallen women?"

"Only if they're gaudily applied," Sophronia said. "Now close your eyes. I'm going to brush castor oil on your lashes."

The oil had a thick, cloying smell, and slowed every blink of Josephine's eyes with its unfamiliar cling. Sophronia drew a blackened hairpin from her toilet case, lit a candle on the nightstand, and stuck the pin into the flame until the acrid scent of burnt metal filled the room. Josephine flinched when the pin neared her eyes, but Sophronia's hand was steady, and in no time, Josephine's lashes were as thick and dark as a healthy young girl's.

They dusted her forehead and nose with pale rice powder, then dabbed a touch of carmine on her lips and cheeks. When Sophronia pronounced the effort a success, Josephine gazed into the mirror with no small amount of shock. Her face was as delicately white as fashion demanded, complemented by a subtle, petal-pink glow. Her eyes seemed to dance with a vibrant, intelligent light that pleased and flattered her.

"Why—I look perfectly pretty!"

"Don't sound so surprised," Dovey said, smiling. "I always knew there was a picture of enchantment hiding behind that dowdy bun and colorless face. Here, let us do up your hair, and then you can get dressed."

Dovey and Sophronia laughed and joked like sisters as they combed out Josephine's long, mouse-brown hair. She had never seen the two in such harmony before. What had drawn them together, Josephine wondered—their brush with danger the night of Clifford's attack? Or perhaps the shared burden of the secret they kept—Josephine's hidden shame? Perhaps it was simply their mutual annoyance with Mrs. Garfield. Whatever had made Dovey and Sophronia see eye to eye, Josephine prayed their newfound bond would hold. Their encounter with Mrs. Garfield and her contemptuous society had rattled Josephine to her core. The Mercer girls had been in Seattle only a handful of hours, but already the city was nothing like she had imagined. If they were to find their way in this new world—put down roots in this frontier— then every woman of their party would need friendship and sisterhood. Animosity was a luxury Dovey and Sophronia could no longer afford.

Dovey worked a mystery with her comb, teasing and coaxing Josephine's hair into a mound as high and soft as a cloud, then securing it with a twist and a few copper pins, judiciously placed. Josephine stared at herself in the mirror, wide-eyed. The style Dovey had chosen certainly did suit Josephine's face and stature. She blushed, astonished that she could look so lovely—and so young. She seemed nearly of an age with the other girls in Mercer's party, and she mused over Sophronia's prediction of endless suitors offering poetry and sweet words, vying for Josephine's hand.

I oughtn't to want any attention from the men, Josephine told herself firmly, *my situation being what it is.* But seeing herself anew, as a woman transformed into a fresh young bride, she found herself nursing the smallest hope that she would attract one or two hearts. Just for the novelty of the experience.

Sophronia helped Josephine into her embroidered dress—the lavender linen, the fanciest garment she owned, though its style had long since passed into the realm of the old and dusty. The only hat she owned was of plain, woven straw, without a plume or blossom to decorate it. Dovey secured it to Josephine's high-piled hair with a long pin, then stepped back, cupping her chin judiciously.

"It wants something," Dovey said. Then her brown eyes brightened with mischief. "I know just the thing. Wait here."

She scampered out of the room, but in a few minutes she returned with a handful of waxy white flowers. Their stems dripped water onto the rug.

"Where did you get those flowers?" Sophronia asked sharply.

Dovey shrugged. "Downstairs, in the lobby."

"You *stole* them?"

"Right out of a vase. Don't tie yourself in knots, Sophie! No one saw. And nobody will miss a few flowers."

Dovey snapped the stems short, then tucked a few choice blooms into the brown ribbon band of Josephine's hat. "There," she said. "Now you look properly styled. In fact, Jo, you look an absolute glory. It's a shame for the men of Seattle that you aren't available."

Josephine laughed. "I really feel like a 'Jo' now—all bright and fresh and free. Well—*almost* free."

"Soon enough," Dovey said confidently. "Clifford will see sense—he simply *has* to."

"Thank you, girls." Josephine embraced them both, and for a moment their warm proximity drove away the last shred of her anxiety.

But another tap sounded at their door—Catherine Stickney, who breathlessly announced that several carriages had arrived to take them to the reception. At the news, Josephine's stomach erupted in nervous flutters again.

"Carriages." Sophronia sighed in relief. "At least it's not beer wagons this time. Perhaps Seattle is more civilized than I thought."

The four smart carriages, shining like new-polished stones, stood waiting outside the Occidental. Asa Mercer waited, too, and gave Josephine a mannerly bow.

"You look fine this morning, Miss Carey. I trust you slept well?"

"Yes, thank you." Josephine knew Mr. Mercer was only offering common courtesy. She knew, too, that the young man was no suitor. Even so, she blushed at his words. The heat in her cheeks only discomfited her all the more. Blushing was a foreign thing to her—but then, casual compliments from men were foreign, too. And if Sophronia's grim prediction proved true, Josephine would face showers of praise and more very soon. *I must get my reactions under control. I must give none of Seattle's men any reason to hope for my hand. Not yet, at least.*

"I'm glad to hear it," Mercer went on. "The Occidental is the finest hotel in all of Seattle." His mouth slanted in a wry smile. "I'm afraid it's also the *only* hotel in Seattle, but we are fortunate to possess such a worthy establishment."

Mercer helped Josephine into the nearest carriage, followed by Sophronia and Dovey. The man himself climbed in after them.

"I hope you ladies don't mind my company on the ride to the reception."

"Of course not," Sophronia said. "We're glad of you, Mr. Mercer."

The driver clucked to his horses, and the carriage began to roll. Josephine pulled back the window's velvet curtain, the better to take in her first true sight of Seattle. The city in daylight was far friendlier than it had been under the shroud of night. But still it seemed a place of bewildering contradiction. Its buildings were so new and stylish they might have stood in the freshest, most up-and-coming Boston neighborhoods; yet every plot and acre was ringed by deep, black mud, and streets and sidewalks alike were strewn with the debris of construction. Seattle was mired in the grime of its earliest infancy, a town struggling to rise from the dust of the earth.

The carriage turned at another too-sharp corner. The sudden swing of gravity sent Dovey, feather light, sliding across the seat into Josephine's hip. The girl giggled with the fun of it, until a timberman's hoarse shout rang from the high, wet deep-green hill that towered over the city. A roll of grinding thunder seemed to rush down the hill toward them, louder than any freight train. Josephine's heart raced; she braced her hands against the interior of the carriage as if she might hold it together by sheer force of will—as if she could stave off whatever monstrous force roared so near, threatening to split the carriage in two. Then she saw the source of that terrible racket: several massive logs, each at least a dozen feet in circumference, came sliding into view. They flew like winter sleds down a steep, deep-rutted, impossibly muddy track, descending from the crest of the hill to a lumberyard and sawmill waiting at the waterfront below.

"We call it Skid Road," Mercer said, stifling a chuckle at the women's surprise. "A simple but effective means of transporting trees to the mill, don't you think?"

The rich, earthy scent of wet mud, stirred up by the logs' descent, filled the carriage, and as the huge trees came to rest in the trampled expanse of the lumberyard, Josephine could hear the smack and hiss of thick mud settling, even over the horses' hooves and the rumbling of the carriage wheels.

Mercer pointed out more notable sights as they rolled through the city's streets. A fine home nearby—a Gothic dream with tall, narrow gables and fretted eaves like the lacy icing of a gingerbread palace—belonged, so Mercer said, to Charles Terry, the wealthiest man in Seattle, whose network of bakeries and cracker factories kept the logging men and sailors well fed. They rolled down an avenue of shops, each fronted by a tall, square-topped, whitewashed facade. Even with a dense layer of cloud hanging low in the sky, the shops were still so clean and new that they reflected a healthy glare; Josephine squinted as the carriage passed. The horses' brisk trot flagged as the carriage began to climb one of the many slopes that soared over the town. Mr. Mercer named the owner of every fine house on the hill—and there were more than a few, decked out with Grecian elegance or regal in their austerity.

Josephine found the young man's conversation lively, and his gladness at returning home was evident in the sparkle of his blue eyes. But she could not ignore Mercer's nervous tension—subtle, well hidden, but plain enough to Jo once she'd noted the faint tremor of his fingers and the agitated bouncing of his heels against the carriage floor.

He must dread the reception almost as much as I do. No doubt Mercer expected the story of last night's encounter with Mrs. Garfield to have spread. Ladies of Mrs. Garfield's type were often quick to sow a rumor.

The carriage turned past a dark-wood home, built in the style of an old hunting chalet, and rolled along beside a vast, parklike swath of green. Gaps between the trees offered brief glimpses of the harbor below, shimmering gray-green like chips of polished jade. Then the horses turned again, and Josephine gasped at the sight that greeted her.

A single building of creamy limestone stood alone at the crest of the hill. Stolid and strong, its tall, blocky shape the very illustration of grandeur, it rose to the height of two generous stories, crowned by a narrow dome. Four massive columns fronted the building. Even in the weak morning sun, the columns gleamed like precious ivory.

"The Territorial University of Washington," Asa Mercer said proudly. "My own dear place—my pride and life's work. I've handed the school over to other stewards now, but it still holds a special place in my heart. Do you like it, Miss Carey?"

Josephine shook her head in helpless amazement. To have traveled so far . . . to have left the unthinking brutality of her former life behind . . . to have found herself in this wilderness of deep mud and black water, surrounded by the wet tangle of the forest . . . and after all her trials, to be confronted by this gracious monument to order, hope, and knowledge . . . ! Her heart welled, and she found herself unable to speak. The university called to Josephine, tugging at her soul with the promise of safety, like a beacon to a storm-tossed ship.

Here, at last, is my goal, she thought, warming with satisfaction. *Here my life begins anew—and here I stake out the new bounds of my future.* Let the men of Seattle do their worst; let them pepper her with poetry and haunt her for her hand. Josephine would not be distracted, nor would she be deterred. Hers would be the life of an educator—her mission a grand one, to shape and guide the youth of Washington Territory.

"You built it yourself?" she asked in amazement.

Mercer chuckled. "Well—not with my own two hands. I founded the university after my own dreams, though—that much is true. And I have entrusted its care to men better able to steer its course. I feel my duty calls me elsewhere. I have a vision for this territory, Miss Carey. It's rough now, I know. It's little better than a sucking bog, and I don't only refer to the mud. This is not a place of high morals, of grand achievements. Not yet. But it can be; I'm sure of it. Washington Territory is home to men of good minds and better hearts. And now, it's home to women who possess the same virtues: intelligent, hardworking, and honest. We can come together. We can tame this land—not only the land but the men who inhabit it. We can become a territory worthy of that beautiful building, and all the ideals it represents."

Josephine's scalp prickled. *It's a beautiful dream. But what part can I have in it? I'm not the honest woman he believes me to be.* She had let Mercer down—had used his kindness and the whole territory's need for her own selfish ends. *God grant that he never learn of my deception. It would break my heart, for a man of such lofty morals to think poorly of me—to judge me as I deserve to be judged.*

The reception was to be held under a great tent in the field beside the university. As Josephine took Mr. Mercer's hand and climbed down from the carriage, she could see a great crowd—some women, dressed conservatively in subdued shades of red and green, drifting gently through the milling mass of bodies—but mostly men. The men were a vast sea of tailed coats and derby hats, of rough flannel and bristling mustaches, spreading out across the university's green lawn. That ocean of masculinity seemed to toss and froth with an eagerness that made Josephine blanch.

The other carriages rolled up the hill, and one by one, the women of Mercer's party alighted on the grass. They clustered together like chicks in a brooding house, eyeing the tent and its restless crowd nervously.

"You cannot remain in the Occidental forever," Mercer told them all, "so I have arranged for respectable families to host each of you. Some families will be happy to welcome two or three of you ladies into their homes, until you've found men to your liking and married. The hotel simply won't do—not for the long term. I want no misunder-standings about the nature or morals of any of you. We'll allow the city to cultivate no more rumors of the sort Mrs. Garfield holds to."

"That's very kind of you," Josephine muttered. She wished for the privacy and comfort of her host family's home already. It seemed she could feel the expectations of the whole city bearing down upon her shoulders, and the weight of it made her shudder.

Mercer led the women across the lawn. A great cheer went up from the waiting crowd; Josephine reached out and seized the nearest hand, and was glad it was Sophronia's. The pale woman looked upon that sea of men with unflappable disdain, and Josephine squeezed her hand, hoping to draw a little of her friend's composure into her own soul. The group of women reached the edge of the reception crowd; a narrow way cleared through its depths, and Asa Mercer, like Moses parting the Red Sea, led the women onward, to a small, bunting-draped platform that stood waiting beneath the tent. Josephine followed Mercer up the steps on wooden legs. She breathed as deeply as her corset would allow, looking out over wave upon wave of expectant male faces.

"My good men and women of Seattle," Mercer called, "I thank you all for your support and your unwavering patience in my—in *our* endeavor to imbue our good, young city with culture and refinement. These courageous women have persevered in the face of many hard trials, and endured much to reach this fair, bountiful land. I have had the privilege of coming to know each of them as a friend. I can attest to their great moral quality, and know that they will bring much in the way of improvement to Seattle."

From somewhere in the crowd, a man shouted roughly, "Where's the rest of 'em?"

Mercer flushed. "The fourteen ladies you see before you are the brave souls who have made the journey from Massachusetts to—"

"What," someone else called, "that's *it*?"

The crowd erupted in a clamor. "Fourteen girls! Asa Mercer, you horse's ass!"

Mercer worried at his bow tie with one hand, paling before the anger of the crowd. Josephine felt a tremor of pity for the man. He was still quite young—not many years older than the students of the university—and the same maternal protectiveness she'd felt for Dovey at the Lowell train depot stirred within her heart. Before she knew just what she was doing, Josephine stepped to the edge of the platform and raised her hands for silence.

The tumult died away, replace by the stillness of surprise. No one was more startled than Josephine herself, but now that she had the crowd's attention, she felt she had no choice but to attempt a suitable address. *It's the least I can do for Asa Mercer, after tricking the poor man into carting me out of Lowell.*

"Please, my friends. Mr. Mercer has been kind and generous to all of us—not only we who have traveled so far in his company, but you, too, the citizens of the town he loves so well. Don't be so quick to insult him, I implore you. Mr. Mercer worked tirelessly in the eastern states on Seattle's behalf. He endured the harshest criticism with good grace, and persevered for the sake of you all, when another man would have given in to discouragement and abandoned the work.

"He's not to be blamed, nor criticized, in the matter of our number. So few were willing to believe that his motives were pure. But we who placed our trust in Mr. Mercer know him to be an admirable man, and ever a friend to Seattle.

"I, for one, am more pleased than I can say to stand before you, here in this promising city." She turned for a moment to gaze at the university building, and her heart brimmed with hope. "I am pleased to join in your work, to help you all build a city worthy of good, bold-hearted men like our dear Asa Mercer.

"I am sure this city has more men as worthy as Mr. Mercer. And I am proud that I may now call myself a woman of Seattle, too."

The crowd shouted out one great "Hurrah!" and the tent filled with the sound of applause. Josephine's cheeks flamed; she had stood before many a classroom, but she had never imagined herself a public speaker.

Mercer edged close and whispered, "My thanks, Miss Carey. What would I have done without you just now? It's a good thing you convinced me not to leave you behind in Lowell!"

When the applause died away, Mercer, his confidence restored, accepted a vote of thanks from the city, then asked the crowd to vote their thanks to the newly arrived women, too. The plump, scowling specter of Mrs. Garfield still haunted Josephine's memory, and so, when every person present raised a hand in gratitude, she felt a wave of unexpected relief wash across her mind. *Perhaps this ordeal won't be as trying as I'd feared,* she thought. *Perhaps the worst is over.*

Mercer invited the crowd to mingle with their new citizens, and from somewhere on the lawn, a small brass band struck up a jaunty tune. A long table was laid with nut cups and small porcelain plates topped with slices of cake. A huge crystal bowl held punch, and as she beheld it, Josephine's throat tingled. She was dry as a stone, and not only from her speech. Now that the need for poise had passed, her body shook with a desperate, nervous energy, and she felt rather light-headed. A sip of something to settle her nerves would be just the thing.

Jo stepped down from the platform, intending to stick close beside Dovey or Sophronia—or any of the other girls. But there were so many men—Seattle seemed a great, heaving pack of rough-jawed fellows, their jackets furred with sawdust, their paw-like hands quick and awkward—and all of them eager to greet her, to congratulate her on her fine speech. In moments, Josephine lost sight of the nearest woman. She bobbed on that thick, pressing sea of men, demurring to their praises, praying that their current carried her closer to the punch bowl.

As she drifted, Jo couldn't ward away an ironic laugh. Mercer had thought she'd be deemed too old! Why, there was certainly no shortage of men flocking to her now, and not all of them were of an age with her. Perhaps it was only the making-up her friends had given her, the rice powder and carmine lending her a deceptive air of youth. For the first few moments adrift among the men, Josephine was flattered by so much kind attention, so many eager smiles.

The attention, however, quickly overwhelmed her. She could do no more than sidle through the crowd, stepping quickly, turning this way and that to avoid colliding with the broad-shouldered, towering men. They called out greetings to her, praises for her speech on Mr. Mercer's behalf, and offered their hands to shake, which Josephine, dazed and disoriented, grasped and let go again like a sailor floundering through the flotsam of a shipwreck.

Through some merciful act of God, she finally made her way to the refreshment tables. She reached for a cup of punch to wet her throat, but before she could take one up, a dozen cups were thrust at her, each gripped in the hairy, calloused hand of a would-be suitor.

"Take mine, Miss Carey," one of them said. "It's sweeter than the others!"

Another man said, "I've never seen hair as lovely as yours. Your great-grandmother must have been Lady Godiva!"

Mercer was wrong—he couldn't have made do with a hundred women! Oh, I'll be buried alive by all these rough, impatient fellows!

"You boys give poor Miss Carey some room to breathe. You'll smother her in a moment." The voice was a woman's, melodious and low, speaking just at Josephine's back. She turned quickly to find a petite, dark-haired woman smiling up at her. She was close to Josephine's own age, and dressed in the same smart, high-class fashions Jo had seen in San Francisco. The woman offered a cup of punch balanced on a saucer.

"Thank you." Josephine took it and drank.

"They're well-meaning, good-tempered louts," the woman said, casting a broad, charming smile around the crowd of men, "but they're louts all the same. I'm Mary Terry."

She held out a hand clad in white satin, and Josephine clasped it gratefully.

"It's all right," Mary said, "you can smile at the rhyme. I know it's a rather silly name, but it's mine to wear proudly. My husband, Charles, and I are to host you. You're most welcome in our home, I'm sure."

Mary's smooth, aristocratic face was framed by two coils of black braid, pinned neatly over each ear. A pair of smart little pin curls lay, neat and obedient, at the peak of her hairline. Her jacket of watered silk was the lustrous, burnt-orange hue of a ripe pumpkin, perfectly matched to her full, pleated skirt, and a brooch of ivory and diamond nestled at her collar. She looked every bit as splendid as the fine ladies of San Francisco.

She must be well-heeled, Josephine thought, her gaze transfixed by the wink of Mary's brooch. *And I look a perfect milkmaid in my old-fashioned linen.*

Then she recalled where she had heard the name Terry before. "You live in that fine house with the peaked gables, down near the hotel."

"I do." Mary grinned, and Josephine could tell she took pride in her beautiful home, and in her high status, too. But Mary's warm welcome seemed genuine, and Jo resolved to accept the woman's kindness with an open heart, and think no more of her own unfashionable appearance. "Our home will be yours until you've found your feet in Seattle."

And found a husband. Jo heard the unspoken words loud and clear, and bit the inside of her cheek to chase away a blush of shame. *Everyone expects me to marry—even my hostess. Clifford, you had better relent and grant me a divorce. Otherwise, this whole city might run me out on a rail!*

The thought of the Terrys' home called to Jo insistently—not because it was beautiful, but because some semblance of privacy—of peace and calm—waited for her there. *The sooner I'm tucked away under one of those narrow gables, the better.*

"When might we—" she began, but one of the well-meaning louts offered his hand to shake, babbling about his prowess as a logger, and Mary gave an indulgent laugh.

"I'll let you get acquainted with the gentlemen," she said as she disappeared into the crowd.

Oh, please don't go, Josephine nearly shouted, *or at least take me with you!* But after the previous night's fiasco with Mrs. Garfield, she thought it wiser not to offend the men of Seattle.

There was nothing for it but to remain where she was, rooted to the spot, a pale and rather weak sun around which a bevy of men orbited. They passed her ceaseless compliments—charming, Jo admitted to herself—and slung so many questions her way, about Massachusetts, the journey to Seattle, and even her taste in flowers and ribbons for her hair, that it was all she could do to answer one out of ten. Everything about the men, from their broad, blocky, lumberjack bodies to their patched coats to their wide-eyed, hopeful faces, merged into one, blending in Josephine's weary head to a single, homogeneous, definitely masculine presence, all of them speaking with the same resonant, baritone voice, all of them smelling of saltwater and sawdust. The exhaustion of her long journey caught up with her; she swayed a little on her feet. Her answers to their queries turned silly and meaningless. *If I don't find a chair soon—or a bed, better yet—I'll fall over in a faint.*

Jo snapped out of her daze at the sound of one man's shout—wordless and harsh, full of anger, like the bark of a bristling dog. He shoved another man in the chest; they stumbled together, grappling at one another's shoulders and arms while their mouths twisted and their eyes flashed with fury.

"I asked her first," one of them snarled, and the other shot back, "Doesn't matter! You're too ugly for the lady to love!"

Good Lord—they're fighting over me!

Josephine edged away from the fight, hoping she might melt into the crowd while the men were distracted by the rumble. But she bumped into another potential suitor, and turned quickly to dodge his hopeful smile. How she wished for Sophronia's icy stare—that would have cleared a path through the men, and no mistake!

The fighting men shoved and cursed all the harder, and Josephine bit her lip, fearing they might come to blows. She looked around frantically, hoping she might catch Mr. Mercer's eye and implore him to restore the men to sanity, but she could see nothing but the chests, shoulders, and wide, bull-strong backs of men.

Mercy, Josephine prayed frantically. *Get me out of here in one piece, if there is a God in Heaven!*

"That's quite enough, I think." A tall, thin gentleman with an untidy thatch of black hair stepped smoothly between the grapplers. He laid a calloused hand on each man's chest and pushed them gently apart. "Come now, Jim . . . Henry! How often have I seen you two drinking together? What a shame to come to blows. That's no way to welcome a lady to our town."

"Buzz off, Bill Jakes," someone called from the crowd. "The fight was just getting good!"

"Killjoy Bill," another man chanted. "Count on him to ruin a good time!"

Jim and Henry spat a few more curses at each other, glaring over the barrier of Bill's shoulder. Then they tugged their coats straight, righted their upset hats, and stalked off into the crowd. The watching men groaned in disappointment. The spell Jo had inadvertently cast over them appeared broken, and the greater number wandered away. She sighed deeply, tingling with relief.

Bill Jakes, as long and lanky as a two-year-old colt, turned to Jo with a lopsided smile. For one moment of resigned despair, she thought he, too, would start in with a flurry of questions, or thrust a slice of cake under her nose and insist she eat it as a favor to him. She braced for a renewed onslaught. But he only tugged at his drooping mustache, then lifted his hat with a cursory "Ma'am," and turned away.

Impulsively, Josephine reached out and caught the man's elbow. Bill looked around, startled, with a pleased half smile.

"I . . . I'm sorry," Jo said. "I shouldn't have . . ."

"Well, that's all right," he said. His voice was slow and easy. "I'm Bill Jakes."

"I heard," she said, and blushed. "My name is Josephine Carey."

"Pleased to meet you, Miss Carey."

"Jo—you must call me Jo." She didn't know why she insisted on the name, but this man—this perfect stranger—made her feel as light and free as she had felt that morning, staring into the mirror at a woman utterly changed.

"Very well. Jo." His smile creased the corners of his eyes. There was no brutality in him, no darkness—no hint of Clifford at all.

"I'm glad to meet you, Mr. Jakes."

"If I'm to call you Jo, then you must call me Bill. And I'm real pleased to meet you, too, Miss. Real pleased for certain." His face colored, and he ducked his head, rubbing the back of his neck like a schoolboy tripped up by an awkward sum. "Do you think I . . . might perhaps maybe . . . call on you one day?"

Josephine shivered with sweet, glad anticipation. "I'd like that," she said quickly, before she could recall too thoroughly her vow to Sophronia. "I'll be staying with Mr. and Mrs. Terry."

"Well, then, I suppose I'll be seeing you . . . Jo." Bill tipped his hat again, and without another word he made off through the crowd.

As she watched him go—weaving in and out of the knots of men, each one surrounding one of Mercer's girls—she wondered how ever she would explain her strange predicament to Bill. She had made a solemn promise to remain true to her wedding vows, and back in San Francisco, with her fear of Clifford so close at hand, it had seemed so easy and natural to give her word. But now, as she watched Bill Jakes disappear in the crowd, she wondered morosely just what her promise would cost her.

CHAPTER FIFTEEN
AN AMBITION BORN

Dovey crept to the dormer window and hooked one finger into the lace curtain. Ever so slowly, she pulled the curtain aside—just enough to expose the slimmest crack of cloud-washed sunlight. She peeked through the opening, biting her lip, watching the drama unfold in the walkway of the Harris house below.

Mrs. Harris, bright, hardworking, and happy in her marriage, accepted a bouquet of scraggly wildflowers from the young man who stood at the foot of her porch steps, hat in hand. Her voice carried faintly up to the dormer window. "I'm sorry; Miss Mason isn't at home just now. I'll give her your flowers and tell her you stopped by."

The young man turned and went away, hanging his head, the very picture of dejection. Dovey breathed a sigh. He was the third suitor Mrs. Harris had turned away that day, and the eleventh of the week. Dovey watched him pass through the front gate and mash his hat resolutely back onto his head. Then he marched off down the hill toward the heart of the city.

When she was certain he was gone, Dovey slipped from the attic bedroom and crept downstairs. Her feet barely raised a squeak from the staircase. In the eight days since she'd arrived in Seattle, she had developed the habit of drifting soundlessly about the Harris home, fearful that if she made any noise on the stair, or caused a floorboard to give the slightest squeak, all the single men of Seattle would hear and come running like dogs to a whistle.

Mrs. Harris was in the kitchen setting out a tidy luncheon on her prized blue willowware plates. Dovey sank into the nearest chair and would have fallen face-first onto the table, fainting away from the sheer exhaustion of all this endless courting—except she didn't want to spoil Mrs. Harris's lunch.

"Thank you," Dovey said weakly.

"For what?" Mrs. Harris set an aspic of chicken and eggs on the table and cut a generous slice for Dovey.

"For fending off another would-be husband."

Mrs. Harris giggled, belying her dignity. She had long, soft, auburn hair, and wore it pinned up in a halo of braids that, together with her warm-rose complexion, gave her the air of an angel.

"I understand your predicament," Mrs. Harris said. "It's a blessing and a curse, to be a young woman in Seattle. Why, I was newly married to John when we moved to the city six years ago, but that didn't stop a few lonely gentlemen from hoping. There are so *many* boys, and all of them looking for a good wife—a mother to raise and nurture their children."

Dovey turned her attention to her aspic. Both the raising and the nurturing of children were as far from her thoughts as the Earth was from the stars. If the men of Seattle aspired to fill their mudhole wilderness with packs of children, that was all the more reason for Dovey to steer clear of their affections.

But she wouldn't say as much to Mrs. Harris. She knew her genial hostess had secret hopes of her own—she had seen the young woman sewing a baby dress just the night before.

"So you see," Mrs. Harris went on, "everyone in Seattle is terribly glad to have you all here—you courageous Mercer girls. There may not be quite enough of you to go around, but *some* eligible women are a great deal better than *none*."

"Not everyone is glad," Dovey said. "Mrs. Garfield and her society let us know just what they thought of us, the first night we arrived. She called us wagtails!"

"Those who judge simply don't understand. It's hard to be a woman in this world, Dovey. I may be only twenty-three, but I can swear to that truth already. Women are better off trying to understand one another—to be friends. We can't drive wedges between us or separate ourselves where no separation is warranted.

"Since I've lived in Seattle, where women are so few, I've come to believe that we're all alike—women, I mean—no matter our present circumstances. We were all little girls once, with the same dreams in our hearts. We all wish the same comforts, aspire to the same achievements."

"I'm not sure I agree," Dovey said. She lapsed into a gloomy funk, poking at her aspic with the tines of her fork. "I don't believe I *do* aspire to your goals, Mrs. Harris. There may be no other girl in all the world who wants the things I want."

Mrs. Harris folded her hands on the table. Her smile was all loving encouragement. "Why don't you tell me, and I'll let you know what I think?"

"Well . . ." Dovey faltered. Her kind, young hostess had found so much joy in marriage—in keeping house, and in hoping for children to fill it. *And isn't that the very role women were made for?* Dovey shifted uncomfortably on her chair. Not once since leaving Lowell had she questioned her desires, or even stopped to examine them. She had simply *felt*, and had accepted her own impulses as good, as right. Now, with this very picture of the feminine ideal beaming at her across the kitchen table, Dovey doubted her own heart. Mrs. Harris was warmly content with her lot in life—her place in the Lord's grand scheme. Why couldn't Dovey be just as glad to settle down and marry? What crucial element of womanhood did her spirit lack?

"Go on," Mrs. Harris prompted. "You can say anything to me, Dovey, and I promise you I'll be kind."

Dovey straightened her spine. "All right, then. If you insist. I want adventure, Mrs. Harris. I want to take in more sights, see more cities—I want to ride trains and wander alone down unfamiliar streets, until I'm lost and have to find my own way back to where I started. I even want to sail again—take to the open sea, though I know just how terrible it can be. I want freedom—to roam about and explore. To make my own way through the world, with nobody to tell me what I can and can't do."

"I don't think that's so unusual, Dovey."

"There's more. I don't want to settle down and be *anybody*'s wife. Not yet. Maybe not ever. I only just escaped that fate when I left my family in Lowell, and I don't intend to tie myself to a strange man just because I've arrived in Seattle."

Dovey paused and drew an unsteady breath. "So there you have it. Now you know how peculiar I am. Do you despise me? Tell me the truth, please. I couldn't stand to take your hospitality if you secretly despised me."

She laughed. "Land sakes, Dovey, I think more women share your dream than you realize. And I don't despise you. Every woman does what she can with whatever circumstances the Lord hands her. But we *all* want to live openly, to experience all the wonders Creation has to offer. We all want to be free to guide our own choices."

"But we can't be free, can we?"

Father's face rose up somberly in Dovey's mind, his deep scowl of disapproval, the stern command in his eyes. He had made plans for Dovey—sought to lay a tight, restricting future around her like cobblestones impinging the roots of a growing tree. That same expectation weighed on her here—marry, be a wife, tend to a man, and accept his tending in return, without complaint or rebellion.

"Don't look so bleak, dear Dovey. It will bring you more freedom than you realize, to become a wife—and someday, a mother."

Mrs. Harris's soft smile never wavered, but Dovey heard the faintest hesitation in her voice, a quick flutter of doubt. *Even she feels impinged. Even she, with her fine home and her pretty china and her baby's dress to sew.*

With a pang of regret, Dovey recalled a flash of rose pink—Orquídea's vibrant gown flitting through the streets of Aspinwall; the girl's painted cheeks and gaily sparkling eyes. *Those* girls—the kind everyone so despised—their freedom was real. Poor Mrs. Harris, with her talk of marriage setting a woman's spirit free—why, she was only swallowing a bromide, Dovey realized, and hoping it would turn to truth once she had downed enough of it. *Those* girls went where they pleased, did as they pleased, earned their own money. They even lay with more men than just one measly husband. Maybe it was shameful and an awful scandal, but *that* was the kind of freedom Dovey wanted: real liberation. A pure absence of fetters.

Dovey filled her mouth with the aspic to keep her scandalous thoughts from spilling out. Mrs. Harris had been so kind and good to her; Dovey had no desire to bring disgrace to her hostess's home.

When their lunch was through, Dovey helped with the washing up, then, still mired in her pensive gloom, said she'd like to go for a stroll.

"Do you want me to come along?" Mrs. Harris asked.

"I'd like to go alone, if it's all one to you."

"And your suitors?" Mrs. Harris asked with a mischievous smile.

"I feel I can face them, now that I've had a good meal and some tea. I'll be all right. If they become too much to bear, I'll just run home again."

"It's going to be all right, Dovey." Mrs. Harris brushed her cheek with a gentle, sisterly kiss. "By and by, everything will work out according to the Grand Design. You'll see."

Dovey went briskly down the porch steps and out the front gate, propelled by her guilt. If Mrs. Harris knew only half the thoughts running through Dovey's head, she wouldn't want to associate with Dovey, much less kiss her. And the sweet, angelic hostess would throw Dovey right out on her bustle if she suspected where this stroll would take her.

But there was no doubt in Dovey's mind where she ought to go.

The Harrises' home stood near the foot of the largest hill—the one that wore for its crown the shining white university building. Dovey headed down the slope, walking in the damp grass beside the ruts of the unpaved road. The hill was covered in a deep-green blanket of cedar and glossy-leafed salal, the clusters of delicate, heart-shaped white flowers swaying in the salty harbor breeze. Below, the hill leveled out into the mudflats. The wet, dark smoothness of the tidal plain was broken here and there by pale, ragged patches of sawdust, the refuse of Yesler's steam-powered sawmill. Just below the deep-cut scar of Skid Road, the mill itself spread along the flats, a vast, dark thing, still as a sleeping beast, its smokestacks exhaling a perpetual black breath.

And there, just to the north of Yesler's mill, snugged between the bayside docks and the taverns that lined the final, flat stretch of Skid Road, was Dovey's destination. She could make out the prostitutes' cribs from the knoll—tiny shacks of weatherworn wood, standing in a matter-of-fact row.

Dovey made her steady way toward the cribs. Now and then men would call out to her, but when she responded at all, it was only with a cursory wave of her hand.

Once a man stepped in her path, bringing Dovey up short.

"Miss Mason, may I call on you this evening?" There was grime on his knuckles and sawdust in his red mustache. There was a certain rough, boyish appeal about his confident swagger, his winking blue eyes.

But Dovey shook her head. "This shop is closed to suitors until tomorrow."

She went on her way. Her laughter mingled with his and buoyed her spirits. The sweet, compelling promise of unfettered freedom hung just before her, and she would not be deterred from her path by any man—no matter how charming.

She reached the back alleys of Skid Road some fifteen minutes later. It was a fine afternoon; the sun broke through the heavy gray clouds, revealing a patch of sky that looked all the bluer for its rarity. A dazzle of golden light fell across the mudflats. Dovey blinked in the welcome glare, reveling in the sudden warmth.

She stood across the wide, unpaved alley from the row of cribs, leaning casually against a wall, in just the way Orquídea had taught her. It was daylight, and there was always work to be done in a newborn city. There were no men visiting the cribs just now—or if the girls had a few callers, they were already engaged inside their dark, narrow shacks. Most of the young women lounged in the doorways of their cribs, exchanging jests or challenges in rough, bursting shouts, or simply turning their painted faces up to bask in the unexpected sun.

They noticed Dovey right away, of course, fixing her with long stares, approaching one another's cribs to whisper behind their hands. Working girls were always quick to spot any change to their routine. Dovey supposed they had to be observant and keen. There was no one to look after them, save for other girls of their kind. And after her brush with Clifford in San Francisco, Dovey understood all too well the dangers a city's dark streets might conceal.

Now and then, when a girl would cast her an especially potent glare, Dovey would offer a smile, a nod, a little wave of her hand. That only set them to whispering all the harder. But soon enough, three of them worked up the crust to cross the street and meet Dovey eye to eye.

All three girls were well fleshed, with enough natural color in their cheeks that they were obliged to powder their faces heavily to obtain the lily-white pallor so coveted among fashionable ladies. *Business must be excellent in Seattle*, Dovey thought as she assessed them with a quick flick of her eyes. In Lowell, the night flowers had been thin and sallow, with limp, dull hair. These girls had lined their eyes with plenty of dark powder, and their lips were as bright and plump as ripe berries, but even through heavy paint, their robust good health shone through.

One of them, her straw-yellow hair teased into an enormous, pillowy roll at the nape of her neck, took in Dovey's elegant blue dress and unmussed ringlets with a scowl. "You don't look like a working girl."

"I'm not," Dovey said.

"So what are you doing on this street, then—alone?" asked another.

"I'm new to Seattle. I only came out for a walk, to explore the city."

"Explore the city!" the blonde hooted. She elbowed one of the other night flowers in the ribs. "You've found where the action happens, all right. New to the city, you say. Are you one of those Mercer girls?"

Dovey nodded vigorously. Her curls bounced against her shoulders. "Yes, I am. I'm Dovey Mason. Pleased to meet you all."

"Came in on Mercer's cargo? Sure you're not a working girl, then?"

The sly insinuation would have set Sophronia's ears to steaming, but Dovey only shrugged. "That's what some people in Seattle say, isn't it? About Mercer's girls, I mean—that we're prostitutes."

The tallest of the three girls, with hair a shade of red unsupplied by nature, gave a loud snort. "All women are harlots, one way or another. Flop on your back for one man only, or for a hundred—it's all the same, and every girl does it for pay. Coins in your pocket or a fancy house up on the hill—makes no difference in the end."

"I don't believe what the town gossips say, though," the blonde girl said. "The Mercer girls didn't come to Seattle to set up in the cribs. That was never the idea."

"Oh, wasn't it?" the redhead said, cutting her black-rimmed eyes at Dovey. "I see a Mercer girl right here, loitering in the general vicinity. Don't be a dunderhead, Haypenny."

The blonde girl—Haypenny—tossed her head in disdain. "Ruby, you know Asa Mercer would have been a perfect rot head to go all the way to the East Coast for a boatload of rowdy girls. More trolleys come dinging into town all the time, and all of them ready to take on new customers. If Mercer had wanted to fill up a few more knocking shops, all he'd have to do is open the doors and let the local cats in."

"I didn't come to Seattle with the intent to work—that is, to work as you girls do," Dovey said. "I only came because it's so far from home."

"Getting away from your crab old dad?" Haypenny said. "I know how that goes."

Dovey shrugged. "Something like that. But now that I'm here—now that I've thought it all out—I do intend to make my own money, I think."

"So you *are* a working girl, after all." Ruby sniffed with an air of vindication.

"I thought to teach," Dovey said. "I can read well and do my figures, and I'm smart enough to educate young children, at least. But I've never worked as a teacher before, and it seems nearly all Mercer's other girls have. We've only been in the city a week, but already they've beaten me to the work."

"Only one other way for a girl to make money in Seattle," the third prostitute said.

"One *other* way?" Ruby gave a loud harrumph. "This is the *only* way, Lila, and you know it."

Haypenny nodded. "That's true enough. This is the best place in all the world to make a buck—Seattle, I mean; not the cribs. If you can get into a good establishment—something north of Skid Road, say, or one of the fancy places up in the hills—"

"You can make ten times more money in a house than you can down here in the cribs," Ruby confirmed.

"Still, I'd rather be in Seattle's cribs than in a fancy house in any other town." Haypenny swept her arm wide, taking in the whole city with a single, enthusiastic gesture, and stirring up a gust of her oversweet floral perfume. "This town is crawling with men. They're everywhere, like fleas on a dog, and all of them are ready to go. Not even San Francisco can put so much jingle in your pocket."

"Or so many johnsons in your hand."

Ten times more money in a fancy house, Dovey mused. *And the mistress of the house takes a cut of all her girls' earnings. If a house has a dozen girls . . . or two dozen . . .*

Even if her old ambition hadn't kindled anew, Dovey still would have befriended the three young prostitutes. They were jolly and bright, with devil-may-care tempers, which Dovey envied and admired. She found it simple enough to adopt their slangy speech and the confident, swaggering gait characteristic of dockside girls. And once they perceived that she had no intention of setting up in the cribs and competing for their business—once she made it plain that she aimed to open an establishment of her own, where they might hope to work someday— they were ready to accept her as one of their own. Even Ruby put her arm around Dovey's shoulders, and the redhead's brusque manner now seemed no more off-putting than a jab in the ribs.

Seattle's night flowers maintained their own brand of society—one that would surely send Mrs. Garfield's set into a moral panic, but which was ready to welcome a girl like Dovey into the fold, as long as she showed them consideration and their due respect. This Dovey offered naturally, for she found much in their freewheeling ways and coarse speech to enjoy. Loitering in their company gave her a delicious feeling of the contrary, a veneer of unexpected power that she quite appreciated. Sophronia's eyes would pop if she overheard the blasphemies on Dovey's tongue, the frank discussion of activities better left private and the particulars of men's hidden parts.

I don't care, Dovey thought stoutly, falling into step beside her new friends. *Let Sophronia's gogglers shoot right out of her skull. I've found my cronies, and I've found how to make my own way. That's all I need care about now.*

"I made some extra early this morning," Haypenny said, patting the pocket of her skirt. "Let's go up to that new candy shop by the dry goods store and have some taffy. I've got a sweet tooth that won't let me rest."

Dovey fell into step beside her. "Why are you called Haypenny? It's an awfully strange name."

"She once did it with an Englishman for 'arf a penny." Lila's attempt to replicate the accent sent all the girls into a fit of giggles. "Penny's is the cheapest crib in town."

"That's not true," Penny said loftily. "I know a few cheaper. But I'm not selective, unless the man looks diseased." She jingled the coins in her pocket again. "Frequent work pays off. I don't see you girls offering to buy the taffy."

"Dovey here will buy us more than taffy once she starts up her house," Ruby said. "Look at her: she's a girl with taste. I can just imagine it now—beds that don't squeak, fine Persian rugs on the floor, and acres of red velvet."

"Scrumptious," Lila agreed. "When can you start up your knocking shop, Dovey?"

"I don't know," Dovey said. "I still have to run the figures. But a house must have plenty of expenses—all those rooms to furnish and acres of red velvet to buy. And then there's the property itself. I must rent some place from a landlord, if not buy a house outright. I'll need capital, if I'm to set up a place for you girls."

Ruby narrowed her eyes. "You'll need what?"

"Starter money. My father was a big wheel in business, you see. Trust me when I say that I'll need capital. So it comes back to the damned jobs again. There's no schoolhouse within ten miles of the city that needs a teacher now. How am I to raise my starter cash?"

"Can you sew?" Penny asked.

"Not well enough to darn my own stockings."

"You might help out in the Terrys' bakeries," Ruby suggested.

"That's no good," Lila said. "I've heard they're only taking boys for that work. They can lift the flour sacks and load the carts for delivery. They won't want a slip of a thing like you, Dovey."

Dovey's brow pinched in a sour frown. "Damn it all, anyway. It was the same story back in Massachusetts. No jobs to be found anywhere—not for me, at least."

Ruby tossed her head. "I tell you, there's only one way for a girl to earn her keep in this town."

They crossed another street and passed the dry goods store. A bolt of silk was half unrolled in the shop's window, cascading over a wing-back chair on lavish display. The girls stopped to admire the fabric's blue-and-white stripes and its rich luster, but Dovey's eye was drawn to a display of another kind. Tacked to the shop's wall, just to the left of the window, was a printed bill. She glanced over the announcement quickly, then tore it from the wall and held it up for the others to see.

"Look, girls. What about this work?"

The prostitutes eyed the bill, then shared a wary look among themselves. Finally Penny said, "What does it say, exactly?"

Dovey flushed. She hadn't realized none of these young women could read. She had no desire to flaunt the skill, or to make them feel inferior—not when they had been so welcoming, so supportive of her dream. She read the announcement for them.

"Wanted: collectors for the Revenue Service. Apply in person at—"

"Tax collecting?" Ruby scoffed. "You can't do that sort of work."

"Why not?"

Penny waved a hand in dismissal. "It's a man's job. Even a big, tough woman couldn't do it—too dangerous—let alone a short, skinny little thing like you."

"I'm tougher than I look," Dovey said. "You had to be tough, believe me, to survive the trek to Seattle. And look here—the salary is seventy-five a month! It won't take long to save up for my own establishment on a salary that rich. I'm going to apply."

Penny laughed, but there was no mockery in her amusement. "You're a real whip-cracker, Dovey. If it's your fond desire to pry taxes from the hands of the old cranks up in the hills, then good luck to you. But mark my words, Miss: if you really want to make a buck for yourself, you'll have to do it on your back."

Dovey folded the bill in her hands, scuffing her feet restlessly on the sidewalk.

"Don't look so grim," Penny added cheerfully. "Knocking is the easiest work there is."

CHAPTER SIXTEEN
A SUITOR CALLS

Josephine couldn't help a girlish giggle as she wrestled the duvet toward the window. It puffed high above her head, flopping over to cover her face, enveloping her with the perfume of the bar soap that had been rubbed over the ticking to protect the valuable feathers within. The sharp, pine-like scent of goose down undercut the florals of rose and lavender. She breathed it in until her head felt dizzy. It smelled like home—like a true home, warm and happy and safe.

"Look out!" Mary laughed. "You'll miss the window."

She took Josephine by the elbow to redirect her blind path, then helped her beat the feather bed down until half of its bulk could be shoved out the window, into the fresh, late-springtime air. As they prodded and pounded, a few feathers escaped the bed from a rent that had gone unnoticed. They shot into the bedroom and drifted about in a slow-falling cloud.

"Drat!" Josephine said, scrambling to catch the escaped feathers. They skittered away from her hands on currents of air and went spinning and dancing across the room before she could collect them.

"It's all right," Mary said. "The Jamesons up the street keep geese; I can buy their next few pluckings if need be." She braced her hands in the small of her back and leaned, stretching with a contented sigh. "Airing the ticks is my least favorite chore, but it's a good deal more bearable when I've got a friend to help."

"You could hire out the work, I suppose."

Mary shrugged. "I *could*. But there aren't many young ladies in Seattle who I'd trust inside my home. I think the majority prefer earning their money down at the docks, if you'll pardon my indelicacy. Besides, I like to work. What would I do with myself all day, if I didn't wrangle feather ticks and ply a duster and broom?"

Josephine smiled sympathetically as she examined the hole in the feather bed. "I can stitch this up for you, if you like."

"I wish you would! I'm no use at all with a needle and thread. I'd probably rip another hole in it just by trying. But I don't want to make you work any more. You've been so generous already, lending a hand with my housekeeping—"

"Nonsense!" Josephine gave Mary a friendly tap on the shoulder. "You've taken me in—a perfect stranger from all the way across the continent. Helping with housework is the least I can do. And as for sewing, I adore it. Even if it's just patching holes in mattresses. I haven't had a chance to sew a stitch in more than a week, since I arrived."

Josephine left Mary Terry in the master bedroom to dust the gleaming mahogany of its imported four-poster bed. She ducked into the cozy spare room she would call home until she found some means of supporting herself in Seattle. Her sewing kit waited on the shelf inside the room's narrow closet; Josephine picked it up eagerly and cradled it to her chest as she hurried back down the hall.

"I'm sure I have just the right thread," she began but trailed off at the sight of Mary, leaning over the airing tick to peer out the window to the yard below. "What is it?"

"There's a gentleman outside," Mary said.

Josephine glanced at the clock on the fireplace mantel. "It's only one o'clock! Is he a salesman?"

Mary's laughter was so bright and joyful that Josephine had to grin. "No, darling. If he's peddling anything, it's his heart. I believe you're about to receive your first caller."

Josephine joined her hostess, leaning across the feather bed's bulk to stare down into the yard. There was indeed a man there, making his unhurried way up the Terrys' stone steps and long, cobble-paved walk. He was dressed in a dark suit—rather smart, for a rough-and-tumble Seattle fellow—and though she could not make out his face from this angle, eaved as it was by the brim of his bowler hat, his long, lanky, thin-boned shape gave her memory a twinge of familiarity. The man's hands were in his pockets. He certainly carried no salesman's case.

A caller—this is disastrous! Josephine thought frantically. She had kept well to herself since arriving in Seattle nine days before, hiding out in the Terry home, receiving only her female friends from the voyage for company. After the sensation she'd made at the reception, the men of Seattle seemed to have forgotten all about her—and for nine days Josephine had told herself she was pleased to be forgotten. But now, as she watched the tall, dark figure strolling toward the Terrys' porch, a little thrill of triumph raced along her veins. A caller posed a pickle, indeed—for she was determined to keep her word to Sophronia at all costs. But it did give her a tingle of satisfaction, to know that Mr. Mercer had been wrong after all. *I'm not too old to attract a man's eye. So there, Asa Mercer!*

Just before he climbed the steps, the gentleman pulled his hat from his head, revealing a wild array of black hair and a thick, downward-curved mustache.

"Why—it's Bill Jakes!"

"You know him?" Mary asked.

"I met him at the reception. Briefly. He said he'd like to call on me, but then he never did. I assumed he'd forgotten all about me."

Mary glanced down into the yard again, her eyes shining. "I guess he remembered. Let's hurry downstairs."

"Oh—I can't see him!"

"What?" Mary regarded her with hands on hips, wrinkling her fine, pointed nose in disbelief. "Don't be silly, Josephine. Of course you can!"

Mary marched Josephine downstairs, picking bits of down from her sensible navy-blue dress and tucking stray locks of hair back into her tight-woven bun. They reached the foyer just as Bill knocked, and Mary swung the door open immediately, beaming up at him.

"Hello, sir! Hello!"

The enthusiastic greeting seemed to take Bill aback. He scratched at the back of his neck, the same bashful gesture he'd displayed at the reception. "Good afternoon, Mrs. Terry. Is Miss Carey at home?" As he spoke, he gazed right over Mary's head at Josephine, who stood pale and stiff with panic in the foyer.

Mary turned to Josephine slowly. Her smile was impish and wide.

Josephine threw up her hands, sighing. "Well, here I am. There's no denying it."

"Here she is," Mary corroborated, bursting with glee.

Bill's dark eyes gleamed with hope. "Miss Carey—that is, Jo— would you care to come out for a stroll with me? It's an awful nice day, and we don't get a lot of nice days in Seattle."

The day was very pleasant. The sky was a crisp, cheerful shade of blue, a color Josephine hadn't seen since her arrival in Washington Territory. Small puffs of white cloud skimmed across the sky like lambs frolicking in a pasture, and the Puget Sound beyond the waterfront winked and sparkled brightly. The sun raised a bright glare from the town as it made its valiant attempts to dry up puddles on the cobblestone streets and shrink the acres of mud that lined the long black streak of Skid Road. The yard of the house was adorned with two newly planted plum tree saplings, and from their bronze-purple foliage, Josephine could hear a chickadee calling with a sweet, beckoning rapidity. It was a day meant for strolling, for walking side by side with a quiet, pleasant companion just like Bill Jakes. Josephine shuffled her feet; she wanted to accept his invitation, but caution stayed her.

"I . . . I'm afraid I've already promised to help Mrs. Terry with housework today," she finally said.

"Nonsense!" Mary hooked her by the arm and pulled her toward the door. "I've managed to keep this house on my own before you arrived, darling, and I'll get by for today. You go on and enjoy the afternoon."

"But I—"

"Don't keep Mr. Jakes waiting," Mary said in a theatrical whisper. "*Enjoy* the day, Josephine. This gentleman is right: we don't see many afternoons like this one, here in Seattle. If you're to live among us, you must learn how to relish a rare fine day when it comes along."

With that, Mary pinned Josephine's straw hat to her bun and sent her out onto the porch before she could raise another protest.

"Supper at five," Mary called brightly, then shut the front door firmly in Josephine's face.

Bill chuckled. "Is she so eager to send you off with all your gentleman callers?"

There had been no other callers, of course. Josephine bit her lip, searching for a suitable reply that wouldn't expose her as the leftover of Mercer's expedition. "Mrs. Terry is enthusiastic about a great many things."

"I confess I didn't have anything special planned for the day," Bill said as they headed down the walk toward the street. "I'm not terribly good at thinking up romance. But I was eager to see you, ever since the day of the reception."

"It's been nine days," Josephine said, startled. "I thought you'd forgotten about me."

"I'm not a fellow who forgets. Business took me out of town, that's all."

They strolled up the hill toward the university. Stately maples and cedars cast a green-dappled, rich-smelling shade over the road, and small birds and squirrels played in the high, thick grasses that fringed the hillside. As they walked, Bill told her all about his business. He was a builder. Though he did not design fine, fancy mansions like the Terrys' lovely home, he could raise a simple, sturdy house fit for the lumbermen and shopkeepers of the city, and do it faster and better than any other man in the Territory. He found demand for his skills increasing with each passing season—as more men settled in Seattle, hopeful of finding a good wife and raising a family, Bill's popularity spread.

"And so that's why I was so late calling on you," he said, fiddling with his hat in his hands. "I was building down in Tacoma. The folks down there are real set on making their town the end point of the Transcontinental Railroad. They're growing faster than Seattle is, and there's plenty of work for a builder like me."

Josephine plied him with questions about his trade and watched his face light up with pleasure as he spoke of lumber and masonry, of good roofs and sturdy walls and all the parts that came together, one nail and tenon at a time, to create a home. Bill gave himself over to a quiet rapture as they conversed; Josephine could see from the straight carriage of his back and the clarity of his gaze that the joy he took in his simple, straightforward work was real. Here was a man who found gratification in a good day's work, and pride in knowing he'd made something useful to others. His voice, gentle yet cheerful, mingled with the sound of their feet whisking through the roadside grasses, and stirred Josephine's heart with simple, untroubled happiness.

It hardly seems possible that such a man can exist.

Bill was certainly nothing like the sample of masculinity she had known for the past ten years of her life. But he was truly what he seemed to be: a perfectly pleasant, thoroughly respectable man. Josephine had grown used to pretense throughout the decade of her disastrous marriage. She knew just how to spot falseness in a person, how to find the dark truth of a man's soul hiding beneath a carefully constructed facade. She was ever wary for signs of shifting temper and brewing danger.

Anyone who hoped to survive Clifford's rages must be adept at spotting a change of mood coming, before it arrived.

But there was no vice, no anger, hiding behind Bill's soft, smiling eyes. There was no hint of pretense about him. He seemed utterly content with life, pleased with his humble place in the world, with Josephine's quiet company at his side, with the soaring, blue sky and the little birds chipping and darting in the trees.

Oh, to be so carefree—to have a life of peace and joy! It was an impossible dream, Josephine knew. But as she strolled with Bill Jakes in the warmth of late spring, it seemed a touch more attainable than she'd dared to hope.

They arrived at the hill's crest. The shaded green tunnel of the road gave way to the open sward of the university, and the sun dazzled on the newness of the building's white limestone walls.

"It's quite a place, Seattle." Bill gazed down the great length of the forested slope to the mud-brown streets and pale buildings clustered around the bay. "It's not much yet, but it will be. Some day, our town will be a real city—a grand place, where hopes and dreams can flourish."

Josephine watched the town in silence—the carriages and wagons, small as children's toys, bustling along its roads as if they already went about grand business, as if the town was unfolding itself even now, stretching and pressing against its own small boundaries, growing into the land of dreams Bill envisioned. For a moment, she felt as if she could glimpse the future—neighborhoods and avenues spreading north and south, lining the great, hopeful, blue-shimmering arc of Puget Sound. Far across the water, the clear day afforded a view of rounded islands and the hilly peninsula beyond, its flanks thick with a green-black covering of timber, an endless expanse of trees to be harvested and sold, to feed Seattle's progression from its infancy into a brilliant, hopeful maturation. The timbered hills were crowned by the rugged peaks of the Olympic Mountains, resting like a white-pointed crown on nature's majesty.

"I can see it," she said. "It's such a lovely place—once you look past the mud and the gambling and all the rough characters in its streets. Seattle . . . I'm glad I came here, Bill. Really glad."

"That beauty out there," he said, nodding across the Sound to the mountainous landscape, "makes you real happy to be alive, doesn't it?"

Happy to be alive—you have no idea, Josephine thought, remembering Clifford's choking grip on her collar, the stench of whiskey on his breath.

Impulsively, she took Bill's arm. She could feel the warmth of his body through the heavy linen of his jacket, and her fingers tightened on his solid presence, on the fact of him, as if she intended never to let go. "It makes me feel contented, right down to my soul. It's no wonder you're such a pleasant man, Bill. You call this place your home, and look at it! It just sings in my heart!"

"Kind of makes you feel optimistic, to look on that pretty little vista," he said quietly. But he wasn't looking at the mountains anymore, or the winking expanse of the water. He gazed at Josephine, and his smile was warm and steady.

Optimistic—yes.

Josephine swallowed hard and looked away. She could still feel Seattle unrolling itself below, reaching toward its bright array of possibility. But Josephine knew she must curb her own elation and keep her expectations in firm check. She had a secret to keep, she thought sadly as she clung more tightly still to her companion's arm. And until she was free from her past, she mustn't allow hope to plant itself in her heart.

CHAPTER SEVENTEEN
NOBODY'S WIFE

Dovey found the address for the revenue building at the northern edge of the city. In fact, she suspected she had gone somewhat beyond the bounds of Seattle, wherever those lay. The cobblestone street had turned to an unpaved lane some time ago, and more recently degenerated into a muddy track through a stand of cedars and maples. She had passed the last business at least ten minutes ago—the workshop of a carpenter, its yard redolent with the oily tang of fresh-planed wood—and the nearest home was hidden now behind a screen of trees.

But Dovey had found her destination, sure enough. A plank sign swinging over the paling fence read, **WASH. TERR. REVENUE SERVICE**—but she hesitated at the gate. She had expected the Revenue Service to operate out of a proper office building—stone or brick, with a suitably stately appearance. This, however, looked more like a home than a taxman's haunt. The single white house, of simple construction and unadorned appearance, stood beneath the arch of the cedar boughs. Beyond its muddy yard, Dovey could make out a split-rail fence corralling several horses, their heads bent to a tin trough, and in the distance, the long, low shape of a stable.

She glanced again at the sign. "All right," she said aloud, "this is it." She had come all this way to angle for the job, and she wasn't about to let the Territory's habit of shabby making-do put her off. She marched up to the house's porch and knocked on the door.

The door opened a cautious crack. She could make out a thin strip of humanity in the gap—shadowed clothing, a man's unshaven cheek, and above it, blinking in some surprise, one squinting, wary eye.

"Good day," Dovey said.

The man allowed the door to squeal slowly open. Tall and dark-haired, he had a face marked by a fresh pink scar that sliced from just below his ear to the middle of his cheek. But despite that roguish accessory, he had an air of youthfulness that surprised Dovey. She had expected a gray-haired old gent, not this tall, lanky boy. He stood puzzling down at Dovey from his beanpole height, waiting in silence for her to speak again.

"I'm here about the job," she said.

The young man raised his eyebrows but did not reply.

Dovey fished the bill from her pocket and unfolded it, held it up for the man to see. "The tax-collecting job. I'm here to apply."

Finally the man made a sound—a rough snort through his nose that stirred the bristles of his mustache. "You? Come now, Miss. I'm a busy fella. I don't have time for joking."

"I don't have time for joking, either. I'm dead serious, sir. I want that job."

He made to swing the door shut. Dovey moved quickly, jamming the pointed toe of her boot under the door's gap; it wedged there and held, and she folded her arms beneath her breasts. She shot him her very sternest glare.

"I walked an awful long way to get here," Dovey said. "I'm not turning around without a job."

The man held still for a moment, watching Dovey's face in silence, his dark eyes unreadable. Then he glanced down at her boot stuffed beneath his door. A slow smile lit his face, and he stepped back, jerking his head to indicate that she should enter.

Dovey hustled in, afraid that if she hesitated this thin, fragile opportunity might blow away on the next wind—that the door might slam in her face, and cut off her dream forever. The interior of the man's house was neat and tidy but arranged like no proper home. A great, carved-oak desk occupied what should have been the parlor, and the narrow hall that stretched back into a darkened room was lined with filing cabinets and labeled crates.

The man ushered her to a chair opposite the desk, then seated himself smoothly. A ledger of sorts lay open before him; he picked up a pencil, made a few quick marks on his paper, then looked up at Dovey, tapping the pencil on the desk with a loud, even tick-tick-tick.

"What's your name?" he asked. His voice was smooth but not especially deep, and carried a note of dire sobriety that gave Dovey pause. He took his ledger and his filing cabinets very seriously, she could see.

"Dovey Mason. What's yours?"

"Cooper. Virgil Cooper. I head up the revenue department for this end of Washington Territory."

Dovey leaned forward on her chair. "You collect on President Lincoln's new taxes—am I right?"

"That's correct, Miss Mason. I see you've kept up on the news in the papers. Girls your age don't usually care about such things."

You aren't much older than "girls my age," Mister, Dovey thought wryly. But she was careful to keep her dimpled smile on her face. "My father was a businessman back in Massachusetts. He was awful sore over the tax."

"He's not the only one." Virgil Cooper braced both hands behind his head and leaned well back in his work chair. His sober expression vanished in an instant, replaced by a smug grin. The chair's spring gave a loud squeak. "Just about every man out here in the Territory thinks he can evade the tax. I've seen every trick and heard every yellow fabrication you can imagine. But I get my money—every cent of it. I'm the president's man, through and through. I believe this war is righteous, and by God, Washington Territory will do its part to fund the effort, if I've got any say in the matter."

"I'm the president's friend, too, Mr. Cooper." Which was not, strictly speaking, true; Dovey had been only twelve years old when Lincoln was elected to his first term. In her purview, Lincoln's presidency was simply a fixture—a thing unchangeable, the natural state of the world. But she had read his address at Gettysburg when it had run in the papers. She thought his words very fine, his sentiments ideal. She certainly held no grudges against him, and if it meant she might get the collecting job, Dovey was willing to carry a flag that read "Hurrah for Lincoln!" everywhere she went.

"But the work isn't easy, Miss Mason. Tax collecting is . . . well, it can be dangerous." He gestured toward his scar. "Got that when a man pulled a knife on me. He didn't want to pay his share."

Dovey gazed at Virgil's scar, unruffled. "I'm quick enough to dodge knives. And anyway, who'd think to pull a knife on a girl like me?"

Virgil stroked his chin, scratching thoughtfully at his dark whiskers. "You don't seem too put off by the danger."

"I've faced danger before. I know I'm just a little slip of a thing, but believe me, Mr. Cooper, I've come through trials that would give a man as big as you pause."

Dovey remembered Clifford—how he had tossed her aside so casually, slamming her body against the alley's brick wall—and suppressed a shiver. She wouldn't have come through that particular trial at all, if not for Sophronia's sudden appearance. But what Virgil Cooper didn't know was better kept concealed.

The tax collector gave a rough chuckle. "You know, Miss Mason, I have a mind to try you out. The truth is, I haven't had a single man apply for the job, anyhow."

"You haven't?"

"Not a one." Virgil shrugged. "Income tax isn't the most popular way to spend a buck among the scoundrels of Seattle. No man wants to get in his friends' bad graces by knocking on their doors and demanding the collection. And there's enough logging work up in the hills that any fella who wants a respectable job can find one real easy. It's put me in a bind, I can tell you. I'm going to fall behind in my quotas if I don't get another collector on board soon."

Dovey bit her lip. It wouldn't do to put Virgil off now with an ill-timed grin of triumph.

"And," the man went on, "I think you may present some advantage."

"Advantage? What do you mean?"

"Like you said, who's going to pull a knife on you? An unassuming, pretty little angel like yourself—you come riding up, smiling that sweet smile while demanding the tax, and you might put a man so off his guard that he pays up before he even thinks to get ornery."

Dovey nearly jumped up out of her chair. "I'll do it! When can I start?"

"Not so fast." Virgil chuckled. "Can you fire a gun?"

Her stomach sank and she felt a prickle of heat creep up her neck. *A gun?* Dovey had never held a gun in her life, let alone fired one. But she couldn't let the money slip away now—*seventy-five a month!*

She nodded wordlessly. Virgil's chuckle flowered into gut-busting laughter.

"No, you can't, but never mind. It's a skill that can be learned. Come on."

He rose from the desk and led her through the long, dark hall with its ranks of file cabinets. She followed him through the dim adjoining room—a small table and a narrow cot stood against one wall, and

Dovey presumed the place served for Virgil's living quarters. He opened a door below a narrow band of transom windows that glowed golden in the afternoon light. Dovey followed him out onto the house's rear porch, overlooking the horses in their corral and the sunlit stretch of a clearing, half reclaimed by thin saplings.

Virgil headed out into the clearing. "Wait here," he told Dovey, then strode some dozen paces away, stooped toward the grass, and straightened with a rusty tin can. He set it carefully on a tree stump and made his way back to Dovey.

"Here." Virgil fiddled with something behind his back, then produced a gun, seemingly from nowhere.

Dovey's first instinct was to lean cautiously away from the thing. She hadn't seen it on Virgil's person, and reasoned that he must have kept it stuffed in the back of his trousers, under the tail of his plaid-flannel shirt. Might he have other weapons squirreled away in his clothes?

"Go on," he said, "take it."

A note of impatience had crept into his voice. Dovey didn't want to give the man any reason to rethink his plan now. She stepped up smartly and took the gun from Virgil's hand, wrapping her dainty fingers around its smooth wooden handle as if she knew exactly what she was doing. The gun was heavy. The long projection of its muzzle and the fat cylinder were a dull, coppery gray. The barrel was engraved with the image of a stagecoach, pulled by running horses.

"That's a Colt Pocket Navy," Virgil said proudly. "The latest and the greatest in firearms. Go ahead—shoot that can off the stump."

Dovey swallowed hard. The gun trembled in her hand; its handle was slick with sweat. She extended her arm, hoping she was aiming the thing more or less in the direction of the can, and braced herself for the thunder of its discharge. She squinted her eyes nearly shut, squeezed the trigger, and . . . nothing. The trigger did not so much as give beneath the pressure of Dovey's finger. In the corral, the horses went on placidly munching their grain. Sparrows twittered in the uninterrupted quiet of the clearing.

Virgil threw back his head, bellowing with laughter. "You've got a dead eye, Miss Mason!"

"Oh, I think you're a rat, Virgil Cooper! Don't be so damn mean!"

He reined in his mirth with real effort. The scar under his ear had flushed red with the force of his hilarity. Dovey glared at him in sullen silence.

"All right, all right," he gasped. "I'm sorry. Here; let me show you how it's done."

He stepped close, guiding her hand with his own as he showed her how to balance the gun's weight, how to peer through one eye down the barrel and line up the posts of its sights, just so. When he showed her how to pull back the hammer, his thumb brushed her own softly, and Dovey reveled in the secret current of heat that coursed along her veins.

"Now," he said softly, "fire."

The roar of the gun was louder than Dovey could have believed. It kicked violently, nearly tearing itself from her hand. Her arm flew up into the air with the force of the shot, but she snapped it down quickly, aiming toward the stump, ready to fire again. The can was gone. The bitter odor of sulfur and heat hung heavy in the air.

Virgil doffed his hat and applauded, just as if Dovey had given a grand show on an opera stage. "By golly, that'll do the trick!"

"It was a pure accident," Dovey said. "That I hit the can, I mean. I don't think I'm a very good shot yet."

"Not yet, but I guess you don't need to be. A cute little thing like you with a loud, bucking Colt—that'll bring in the revenue! And bring it in even faster if you can't quite manage to shoot straight. Tell me you can ride a horse astride, and you've got the job. At least for a few weeks, to see how it goes."

"I can ride," Dovey said. She couldn't—she hadn't sat a horse any more often than she'd fired a gun. But she could learn. For seventy-five dollars a month, she'd set her mind to learn any damn skill Virgil Cooper wanted.

Dovey's stomach was empty and grumbling by the time she returned to the cribs. The lowering sun was just beginning to cast its rosy tinge along the belly of the clouds, and the evening air nipped sharply. Dovey hoped she wasn't too late to catch her new friends and relay the news of her good fortune before they settled into their night's work.

She walked along the plank-sided warehouse that stood opposite the cribs, watching the bright-painted doors of the narrow shacks, hoping for a glimpse of a friendly face. Men had begun to arrive from the lumberyard and the docks, stinking with the sweat of their day's labor. A few of them approached Dovey and inquired after her price, but she only shook her head distractedly, and they wandered away again in disappointment.

Finally, a door painted as red as an apple swung open, and a man sauntered away. Haypenny stepped out after him, fussing with the drape of her skirt and patting her great, rounded crown of yellow hair.

"Penny!" Dovey called to her from across the street.

Penny hitched up her hem and hurried to Dovey's side.

"You'll never believe," Dovey said, breathless. "I've landed the job!"

"Collecting taxes? You must be joking."

"I'm all in truth," she promised. "The job is mine—for now, at any rate. He'll give me two weeks to see how I do, and if I—"

"Who'll give you two weeks?"

"Virgil." Dovey's blush was sudden and disconcerting—not an event she had prepared for. "That is to say, Mr. Cooper—the head collector. He . . . he runs the Revenue Service, and he showed me how to fire a gun."

Ruby had wandered over in the midst of Dovey's explanation. She assessed Dovey's flaming cheeks and the glint in her eye—a sparkle Dovey knew was surely there, even without a mirror to confirm it—and passed Haypenny a sly, teasing smile. "Looks like our Mercer girl has found a husband after all."

"Never," Dovey said—perhaps too forcefully. "I won't marry—not ever. Especially once I start up my fancy house. Whatever cut I take from you girls will be mine alone. I don't want any man meddling with my business." She paused, toying with the collar of her dress, remembering the feel of Virgil's hand on her own as he'd taught her the use of the gun. "Though Virgil is awfully handsome," she added quietly.

"I'm happy for you, Dovey," Haypenny said. "It's real sweet to have a dream, and to see it come together."

"I've a long way to go. It will take a few years, I suppose, to earn all the capital I'll need. But I'm excited, girls—really thrilled! For the first time in my life, I feel there's a future ahead of me—one that's worth dreaming about. Oh, girls, I can't wait to write my mother and tell her I have a job!"

"How is your mother doing?" Penny asked.

Despite the girl's rough exterior, she had a warm and tender heart. Dovey had learned the truth of that over the past few days of their camaraderie. Penny's own mother had died of consumption some years back, leaving her only daughter to fend for herself. Penny had sworn she would pray for Dovey's mother every night until she was well again. Dovey felt sure the Lord would listen to the petition of a prostitute just as surely as the prayers of a hoity-toity city lady; the offer had touched her deeply.

"I just had a letter from Mother this morning," Dovey said. "She says she's feeling just about as well as she did before the boys went off to war. She likes Boston, and her cousin is good company. She was cross that I'd gone off to Seattle, but she said she understands well enough.

There just weren't any prospects left in Massachusetts—and Marion Stilton didn't count. Besides, as practical as Mother is, she'd rather see me married for love than for money. But the war has taken so many young men. It seems no girl has hope of a good marriage in the eastern states—not anymore!"

"Do you think your mother will fancy you working?" Ruby asked. "And as a tax collector, to boot! Won't it be a miserable disgrace in her eyes?"

"Maybe," Dovey replied. "But she'll just have to reconcile herself. I'm my own woman now; I make my own way in the world. I'm the only one who ought to say what's a disgrace for Dovey Mason and what isn't, don't you think?"

Ruby smiled—a rare event—and opened her mouth to say something. But words and smile both died on her tongue. She stared beyond Dovey's shoulder. "Look out," she muttered, "here comes a storm."

Dovey turned. Gathering dusk shrouded the city in purple, deepening the shadows that crossed the warehouses and alleys with bars of indigo. A pale figure cut through that twilight landscape, her skirt swinging in a furious, staccato rhythm.

"Somebody's wife, no doubt," Penny said. "Or somebody's sweetheart. Looks like she's itching for a fight, too. Hope her man wasn't one of *my* gentleman callers."

Dovey stifled a groan. "That's nobody's wife."

When Sophronia recognized Dovey, standing at an alley corner in her blue pagoda dress, flanked by two trollops and displayed like a bonbon on a glass plate, her stride faltered. Even at a distance, Dovey could see Sophronia's quiver of outrage. Her gut clenched, and she made herself stand firm and resolute as Sophronia hurried forward again. When she reached the corner, her face was paler than usual, her lips trembling with the angry words she barely managed to check.

"You look mad as hell," Dovey told her sweetly.

"Mrs. Harris is beside herself with worry for you, Dovey—*beside herself!* I'd ask how you could be so inconsiderate, but you've shown yourself just as loathsome more times than I can count already."

Haypenny squinted at Sophronia, then turned a slow, disbelieving look on Dovey. "You *know* this bitch, Dovey?"

The insult caused Sophronia to inhale so forcefully that Dovey thought her hat might be sucked right off her head in the ensuing gale. "I know her, all right," she said.

Sophronia rounded on her. "Where were you? What on Earth were you doing, away so long?"

"I was out looking for work."

Sophronia's ice-blue eyes narrowed. She sized up Penny and Ruby with one cold, sweeping glare. "I'll just wager you *were* looking for work, too. But you can give up that idea right now, Dovey—do you hear me? Right now! You didn't come to Seattle to become one of *them*."

That final word, laden so thoroughly with all the dismissive scorn in Sophronia's heart, made Penny and Ruby bristle like cats squaring up for a fight.

Penny took one menacing step toward Sophronia. "You better watch what you say around me, you screwed-up, putty-faced sop."

Sophronia gaped at the girl, then twitched her skirt and huffed. Evidently she found it more prudent to ignore Haypenny than to lob one of her high-minded lectures on morality against the painted and perfumed bulwark of this fallen woman. "Come, Dovey. You're going home now. And you'll stay there, like a proper young lady."

She reached for Dovey's hand, but Dovey danced back. "Go on, Sophronia. *You* go home, and leave me be."

Sophronia's thin cheeks bloomed with angry red spots. "Mrs. Harris is waiting!"

"You heard the girl," Ruby said, wrapping a protective arm around Dovey's waist. "She doesn't want to go with you. Now tiff off and leave us all alone."

Sophronia lunged forward and hooked her arm through Dovey's, clamping a hand as hard as a carpenter's vise just above her elbow.

"Yow!" Dovey yelled. "Let me go, you muck sniper!"

"Oh, I most certainly will *not* let you go." Sophronia began hauling her up the street, away from Penny and Ruby, away from the line of cribs and the damp, echoing alleys. "If you won't have sense enough to save yourself from infamy, Dovey Mason, then I must do it for you."

Dovey made a halfhearted attempt to reason with Sophronia—though she knew from long, tedious experience that the attempt was likely to be futile. "You don't even know what I intend. It's not what you think—not what it seems." Instantly, she wished she had kept her peace. The tax collecting was only a temporary occupation, a means to a far more glorious end. And if Sophronia ever caught wind of just what Dovey planned for her future . . . She shuddered to think of the uproar that would surely result. Sophronia would see no moral difference between whoring and merely maintaining a fancy house in which *other* women whored. It was all the same egregious vexation to her.

Penny and Ruby scampered after them, catching at Dovey's hand, trying to halt the avalanche of Sophronia's rage. But she seemed propelled by the righteous wrath of Heaven itself, and Dovey's friends could neither stop Sophronia nor wrench Dovey from her grasp.

"You aren't my mother or my big sister," Dovey said, "and once I start my new occupation, you'll be sorry!"

"Your new occupation, indeed!" Sophronia kicked at Penny's ankle to dislodge the harlot's grip on the edge of her corset. Penny fell back, cursing, and Sophronia marched on. "You won't be with these filthy fallen women—nor any other unfortunates. I'll chain you to the pipes if need be!"

Dovey made one last, desperate effort, twisting and cursing, throwing all her slight weight against Sophronia's iron grip. But the coarse language and vigorous thrashing only seemed to lock Sophronia's fingers all the tighter on Dovey's flesh. She subsided and walked on calmly at Sophronia's side.

From somewhere behind them, in the wide, muddy street of the cribs, Haypenny's voice rose, angry and shrill, into the evening sky. "Don't you worry, Dovey. I'll get this creeper back. I'll make her regret speaking poorly of you—and of us all!"

CHAPTER EIGHTEEN
A FORCED HAND

The meeting of the Women's League concluded with an eloquent prayer, delivered in Mrs. Garfield's cultured warble. Sophronia clasped her hands tightly in her lap, gazing down at the folds of her sapphire-blue skirt, listening as Mrs. Garfield beseeched the Lord to lend His mercy to the sinners of Seattle, to deliver them from this pit of wretchedness and sin.

Sophronia couldn't help but feel that she was one of the very sinners Mrs. Garfield prayed for. In fact, she rather suspected that she held the place of honor at the top of the plump woman's list of the potentially damned. Neither Mrs. Garfield nor her friends had forgotten Sophronia's shameful display of temper the night the Mercer girls had arrived in Seattle. Sophronia had startled them all by walking into the lobby of the Occidental and taking her seat among the other League members as if she belonged there. But she hoped that one day she would belong in truth, and as Mrs. Garfield's prayer went on, Sophronia offered up one of her own.

Let them see that I've repented of my sinful and shocking ways, Lord. Grant me acceptance—a place in this strange new world.

Strange—that was the kindest thing Sophronia could say of the city she now must call her home. She had tried with all her heart, with the very best of her good intentions, to be grateful for the opportunity the Lord had provided. In Massachusetts she had frightened away so many men with her sharp, bitter tongue—all those potential husbands, gone for good.

And she was already off to a poor start in Seattle. She had accepted three men's calls already, but none of them would do. The first had strolled with her along the rocky beach north of town, but the coarse fellow had been unable to speak without swearing. His tongue was as filthy as a sailor's; foul words filled the spaces that a cultured man would have left to thoughtful pauses, and he seemed to curse as easily as he breathed. By the time they'd made it back to Sophronia's host home, her cheeks had been hot with mortification, and she had turned away frostily without a word when he asked if he might see her again.

The second man had hardly been an improvement. Though his vocabulary was sufficiently civil for a lady's ear, Sophronia had detected the faint scent of whiskey on him. He wasn't drunk—not that she could discern—but clearly he was a man familiar with vice. She had declined his request for another visit more politely than she had the first man's, but her disapproval had been clear. So clear, in fact, that the man had turned on his heel with an indignant huff and stalked away down the street without once glancing back at her.

And the third suitor—well! Vincent Tidworth had seemed charming and pleasant, with fine manners, cultured speech, and a neat, dignified appearance. Sophronia had taken a liking to him right away—a cautious liking, of course. She had learned better than to foster attachment to any man before he showed his true colors.

And show his colors, he did! Their first engagement had been a pure delight. They'd driven along the crest of the hills that overlooked the town—always with Sophronia riding beside Mr. Tidworth on the driver's seat; a lady could not conceal herself in a carriage when out with a suitor—and shared a box lunch on the university's lawn. That ideal afternoon left Sophronia with the smallest glow of hope that he'd call on her again. Mr. Tidworth did call on her the very next day, presenting a bouquet of lovely wildflowers and a little bag of saltwater taffy, which they'd enjoyed as they listened to the brass band play outside Yesler's Pavilion.

But that evening, when he walked her home, the cad had attempted to kiss her on the cheek. Sophronia's affronted gasp had stalled Mr. Tidworth as he advanced toward her, his lips puckered presumptuously beneath his bristling mustache. Her sharp slap had sent him packing, and though she was pleased not to hear him ask for a third call, the trail of curses he left in his wake had soured her stomach.

If there is but one good man in all of Seattle, I will find him—I hope.

Seattle offered her final chance at happiness. She ought to view it through a prism of hope and light, a vista kissed by a promising sun. But the truth was, the newborn town terrified her. It was as gray and oppressive as its perpetual cover of cloud suggested—a lawless, filthy place where a woman of decency must fear for her safety—and for her future. How could Sophronia hope to find a good, respectable man to wed in a city peopled by miscreants?

"Lord," Mrs. Garfield said, "we pray that you will send to our city, our community, a wholesome cargo. Amen."

A wholesome cargo. At the sound of those words, Sophronia fought the twisting of her mouth, fixing a mask of perfect calm to her face with a Herculean effort. She was well aware that Mrs. Garfield and her compatriots still thought the Mercer girls a cargo of whores.

There is nothing for it but to show *them the error of their assumptions.*

Sophronia was determined to be a very pattern of virtue, to prove to these women by example—by main force of her considerable will—that all of Mercer's imported women were of high mind and real quality.

Even Dovey hadn't yet fallen, though the tommish little beast seemed determined to do so. The rest of the young ladies from Massachusetts were good, respectable girls—hardworking, moral, and generous to the centers of their souls. Even Josephine, with her dark secret, was still a respectable woman. Jo had kept her promise to remain unattached until Clifford freed her from the snare of that abysmal marriage, and Sophronia could find no fault in the older woman's comportment.

If I can but make the Women's Society accept me as one of their own— then I'll have cleared the names of all of Mercer's girls. Then she would have done the true work of a missionary—redeeming the damned, saving the doomed from a dark, bitter fate. No matter that the only damnation the newcomers faced was the scorn of Mrs. Garfield's society. Their rebuke certainly felt sharp enough to carry the weight of divine judgment.

The meeting adjourned, and Sophronia made her way out of the Occidental as quickly as she could. She had no hope of clasping a friendly hand among the members of the League—not yet. She would win their acceptance with time, but for now, as her first meeting closed in a rustle of skirts and a murmur of restrained, feminine voices, she sensed instinctively that she was better off giving the Women's Society the Irish farewell.

She took her cloak from the doorman with a murmur of thanks and slipped out into the dark, windy chill of a Seattle night. The sky was a patchwork of silver and black. Low-slung, coal-dark rags of cloud, backlit by a hidden moon, scudded behind the hills that towered like mysterious obelisks over the city. Skid Road stood out against the nearest hill in sharp relief, a straight silver track like a knife's slash through the body of the night.

Sophronia bundled herself tightly in her cloak and set off up Second Avenue, walking quickly, making for the Jameson house where she was so kindly hosted. She kept her eyes downcast, unwilling to watch the dim, eerie shadows of wind-chased cloud writhe snakelike over cobbles and shuttered shops. She pressed on for a good fifteen minutes, and only then, when her feet had not found the rise of the hill that led up to the Jamesons' home, did she glance up to take in her surroundings.

She did not recognize the street. None of the buildings seemed in the least familiar. In fact, she saw nothing that could have passed for a merchant's store. Somehow, perhaps thanks to her distraction over Mrs. Garfield's rejection, Sophronia had taken a wrong turn.

Her heart pounded wildly, but she counseled herself to calm. She stared up over the square-topped roofs of the nearby buildings, searching for the pale, angular jut of the Occidental's facade, rising high above the rest of Seattle's architecture. She spotted it, watchful and still, mysterious as a pagan ziggurat in the thin, filtered moonlight. But the hotel was not where she'd thought to find it.

You've wandered far off course, you goose. Hurry home before the night grows any older.

Sophronia swallowed hard and looked about her, studying the empty streets until she was sure of her bearings. Little wonder she'd lost her way. All the roads in Seattle looked very much the same—muddy, rough, lined with slipshod buildings and peopled by gamblers, drunks, and whores. But at least this present district, wherever she'd found herself, was devoid of people. No doubt its usual cast of unsavories had trickled down to that bleak avenue between the docks and Skid Road, where the gamblers diced away their salvation and the whores kept house in their rickety, painted cribs.

She decided the wisest course was to return to the Occidental and pick out her route home from its front door. Now and then, as she passed side streets, she caught the distant sounds of rowdy drinking and smelled the stale whiff of cheap beer. A man called to her drunkenly from one narrow street, and Sophronia's breath froze in her chest. She gathered her skirt and petticoats in her hands and rushed away, leaving the man behind her to simmer in his filthy lusts.

When she had nearly reached the Occidental—the familiar angle of its strange, acute intersection lay just ahead—Sophronia heard footsteps on the sidewalk behind her. They fell rough and heavy, with a slight, drunken drag, but they approached quickly enough that she spun in fear to face whatever creature loomed in the darkness.

It was a man—thick and square as a butcher's block, with long, reaching arms; he rumbled with hoarse laughter as he closed the distance between them. For one heart-pounding moment, Sophronia was sure it was Clifford come again—Clifford, stalking his prey all the way from the alley where she'd felled him in San Francisco. Then the man spoke, and she was sure it was not Clifford. But his eye flashed in a stray glint of the Occidental's lamps, and Sophronia saw the danger in his bleary stare.

"Pretty little thing like you, out all alone."

Sophronia looked around desperately. There was no weapon to hand—no convenient paling to wield as a club, no knife, no shield. There was nothing to hand but the usual thick, salty muck that clotted Seattle's streets, and a few discarded chicken bones in the gutter.

The man leered down at her. "What a doll, what a doll. Wouldn't a man be lucky to have a little wife like you?"

The words were meant to be pretty, no doubt. They only turned Sophronia's stomach, as did the stench of liquor and old, stale sweat that drifted from his body. She turned and headed for the Occidental with all speed, but the man overtook her, stepping into her path with an agility and precision that seemed supernatural in one so deplorably drunk.

"Step away," she said coolly, "and let me pass."

The man laughed, an oily sound, wicked and slow.

"I'll scream," she warned him.

He inched closer. A gust of whiskey made her choke and turn her face away. "Go ahead," the man whispered. "I like it better when they scream."

A fierce fire rushed through Sophronia's limbs, so sudden, so hot with desperation, that she nearly yelled with the force of it. She planted both her hands in her assailant's chest and shoved as hard as she could. He was drunk enough that the push sent him off-kilter—only for a moment, but it was all the reprieve Sophronia needed to win her way past. She dodged around his great, stinking body, but his hand flashed out, reaching for her breast. He caught the edge of her bodice instead, grimy fingers locking into the delicate fabric, gripping with a strength that made Sophronia feel, for one terrible moment of blind, senseless panic, like a mouse in a hawk's talons. Then she wrenched, twisting her body and clawing at his wrist. The fabric of her dress tore—but she was free.

She ran up the road, splashing through a wide, cold puddle. In her fear, she swerved past the Occidental and pelted up the street. *Fool!* she chided herself. But she knew now where she was. Only a block away, she could see the windows of the Terry house glowing, narrow and tall in their high-peaked, Gothic gables.

Sophronia pounded up the steps and onto the Terrys' porch. The door flew open, spilling a great, warm shaft of light out into the darkness. Sophronia flung herself into the shelter of that glow as if it could offer divine sanctuary. She clutched at the porch's carved post, breathless and heaving.

"Sophronia! Mother of God, girl, what's happened to you?"

It was Josephine who stood in the doorway—Jo, sturdy and sensible, a shield against the terrors of the night. Sophronia loosed one pitiful sob and threw herself into Josephine's arms.

Jo dragged her inside, shutting the door securely and then dropping down the latch for good measure. She eased Sophronia into a parlor chair and bent over her, patting her hair, murmuring comforts as she turned her friend's face this way and that with her gentle hands, searching for signs of violence. When she saw the torn bodice of Sophronia's dress, she straightened in grim silence.

"Jo? What is it? Who was outside?"

To Sophronia's dull surprise, Dovey came bouncing into the parlor, swinging a basket of quilt patches on her arm. The girl saw Sophronia, tear-streaked and utterly beside herself, and dropped her basket on the floor. She stared at Sophronia, dark eyes huge in her round, angelic face.

"Whatever's happened to you, Sophie?" Dovey took a few halting steps forward but stopped short of touching Sophronia.

Am I such a fright to look upon, Sophronia wondered, *or does Dovey still hate me for my behavior three days ago, when I dragged her away from the docks?*

She pawed weakly at her torn dress and gave a mewling cry of despair.

Jo bent over her again. She looked soberly into her eyes. "Listen to me, Sophronia. Were you *hurt* in any way?"

Sophronia shook her head. She tried to speak, but could only manage a weak little sigh.

"Whoever attacked you, he didn't throw you down—didn't force—"

"No," Sophronia said, shuddering. "No, thank heavens, no."

Dovey sank to her knees beside the chair. She took Sophronia's hand, and her touch was gentle, forgiving. "What happened, then? Tell us, Sophie—please."

"It was just . . . just a man. He came out of the darkness." She squeezed her eyes shut, trying to push away the memory. But it was too fresh, too immediate. The man would not be ignored; his rough touch would not be denied, even now, after Sophronia had struggled free. "He tried to grab me, but I got away."

Jo sighed and brushed Sophronia's brow with a kiss. "You poor thing."

A lump of self-pity rose up in Sophronia's throat. She swallowed it down forcefully, refusing to allow her fear any further purchase. "I'm all right. Don't worry about me, you girls—and don't pity me, either."

"Don't be silly," Jo said. "You need time to recover from this attack. Charles and Mary have gone out of town for a few days; you'll stay here with me until you're quite well. Now, just sit back in that chair. Dovey, is the teakettle still warm?"

"I don't want tea," Sophronia insisted. "I'm all right. Tonight's . . . display . . . was no more than what I deserved."

A blunt, hard silence fell over the parlor. Sophronia could hear the distant pop and crackle of the fire in the kitchen stove.

"What?" Dovey finally said. Her voice was flat with disgust.

"You heard me."

"I heard you. I just didn't believe my ears were functioning quite right."

"The Lord only sends what trials we can bear," Sophronia said, "and what rebukes we deserve." She tried to keep her voice cool and righteous, but it managed an unruly quaver.

Dovey snorted. "That's nonsense. Don't say such doltish things. You aren't to blame if some ugly, drunken ox attacks you."

Sophronia's composure cracked. She covered her face with her hands and vented a long, high-pitched whine, an undignified squeal of fear and despair. *It was a chastisement,* she told herself, *a rebuke for my haughty ways, a lesson sent to humble me, to make me a better woman.*

The terrifying assault *had* to be a message from the Lord—it simply had to. A part of His inscrutable but ultimately Grand Design, a test Sophronia could face and overcome. If this night's fear and suffering weren't part of an ordered plan, then nothing made sense—not the heartbreaks she had suffered, nor her decision to leave home; not the quiet pain that throbbed every day deep in Sophronia's heart, and certainly not the whole damnable mudhole of sin and disorder that was Seattle.

It must be a rebuke because I nearly allowed Mr. Tidworth to kiss me, she told herself frantically. Her pulse raced in time with her thoughts. *If he'd managed to kiss me, God only knows what sin I may have been led into! I must guard myself even more carefully—and I must determine a man's true character before I get too close to him.*

But how exactly did one determine a man's true character? In a place like Seattle, where sin seemed to fall from the sky with the frequent, heavy rains, how could any woman hope to discover the truth of a man's soul before it was too late?

"Come now, Sophie," Jo said gently. "Pull yourself together. You're all right now. Dovey and I are here; we won't let any harm come to you."

With an effort that shivered her to her bones, Sophronia squared her shoulders and stood on shaking legs. A small, framed mirror hung on the parlor wall opposite. Sophronia walked to the glass and stared at her reflection. Her complexion was flushed pink and swollen, the delicate skin of her cheeks inflamed from the salt of her tears. Slowly, with controlled care, she tucked a mussed lock of hair back into the white-golden roll at the nape of her neck.

"I'm going to marry," Sophronia said steadily. "I must have a husband to protect me. It's not right for a woman to go about undefended, as I was tonight. I'll marry the first true Christian man I can find. But he must be a true Christian. There lies my only hope."

"Tiff me dead," Dovey burst out rudely. "We've only been here a week and a half! You can't just up and marry the next man who comes along, even if he is a Christian."

"It's why we came, isn't it?" Sophronia countered, refusing to look at Jo. "To become wives? Well, it's time I got on with my task." And she would just have to place all her trust in the Lord—to know, without a shred of sinful doubt, that He would match her with a good man. He would give her to a man she could find contentment with, if not love. Sophronia examined her flushed face in the mirror, the tracks of her tears, and she suspected very strongly that love was out of the question.

"I don't care why we came," Dovey said. "It's better to stay unattached, to remain free."

Because the pain had sunk deep into her chest, gnawing like a starved rat at her heart, Sophronia turned her tongue sharp and lashed Dovey with its edge. "Unattached? Free? You don't know the curse you wish on yourself, you foolish girl! *I* do. There's a divine reason why you were led to this work, Dovey—a purpose and a plan for you in Seattle. If you don't bend your will to the Lord's, he will punish you—*punish* you!" She gestured sharply at her torn dress, and Dovey flinched, screwing up her brown eyes.

"Woman needs Man," Sophronia went on. "Eve was made for Adam, and her purpose was to be his wife. Women were not made for freedom, for unattachment. Women were made to submit themselves to the headship of a husband. Women need protection. If my predicament tonight hasn't taught you that much, then I shudder to think what you must endure until the lesson is learned!"

"All right," Jo said soothingly. "You've had a difficult night, Sophronia. Let Dovey alone and come upstairs. You'll stay here with us tonight. Don't worry about the Jamesons; I'll get a message to them tonight and tell them you're safe. Don't think about the rest now—husbands and proposals and what women were made for. Just come upstairs and let us tuck you in."

In Josephine's little room under the pointed gable, Dovey and Jo stripped Sophronia down to her chemise. Jo found a fresh nightgown in her narrow armoire and urged Sophronia to put it on. But Sophronia could only stand in her underthings, covering her face with her hands, shivering as she wept. She felt Jo's arms encircle her, strong and unshakable. Then Dovey embraced her, too, and the girl's nearness was a comfort to Sophronia.

In time she controlled her weeping again and shook off their clinging arms. She pulled Jo's nightgown over her heard.

"It's time I married," Sophronia said firmly. "It was time before I even came here to Seattle. But . . . well, I was too stubborn, too proud to do as the Lord wished."

She went obediently to Jo's bed, allowed the older woman to tuck the covers up to her chin as if she were a child in a nursery.

"Those days are over," Sophronia promised. "I'll do exactly as God directs, from this day forward."

"I don't believe you've ever done anything *but* what God directs," Dovey muttered.

But Jo hushed the girl with a glance.

"Don't be in a hurry to wed," Jo advised Sophronia. "Not even a man you believe to be a good Christian. A marriage is nothing to be rushed into. Take my word on that account."

"A husband is nothing to be gotten *ever*," Dovey added.

"Marriage is Woman's purpose," Sophronia said sternly. "And I will do what I was made for."

Dovey tossed her curls. "Maybe *my* purpose is something other than yours."

"God gave Woman only one purpose—one path," Sophronia said. "The sooner you realize that, Dovey, and cleave to the righteous path, the better off you will be."

She nodded with finality. Jo ushered Dovey from the room, leaving a candle burning for Sophronia, to chase away the shadows of the night. But as Sophronia lay still in the bed, musing on the subject of divine purpose, she didn't feel better off. The time had come to marry, all right. There could be no doubt about it. Why, then, did she feel so lost, so afraid?

CHAPTER NINETEEN
WHAT PASSES FOR MOONLIGHT

Josephine sank down on the green velvet couch with a sigh. In the parlor, the pink hobnailed lamps still burned in their sconces, tingeing the air with the faint scent of coal gas. Lamplight glowed in cheerful circles along the room's length, setting the gilded accents in the wallpaper to sparkling. The parlor's air of gaiety only seemed to mock the silence, the grave acceptance of fate that had settled over the Terry house and its miserable sleeper upstairs. Sophronia's wretched state was all the more heartrending for her stoic determination to marry, her certainty that she was somehow to blame for the assault—that she could stave off future violence with a man.

The thought of it twisted Jo's gut into knots. She had rushed into marriage with Clifford because she had thought the union might confer on her protection of another kind—a shield against aspersion, acceptance as a worthy member of society. But the price had been too dear. Jo longed to talk sense into Sophronia, to make the woman see that she couldn't trust her safety to a stranger—even one she believed to be morally upright. But a voice whispered in Josephine's head, repeating in a sly, mocking echo, *Sophronia isn't wrong. What choice does a woman have but to trust her fate to a husband?* Perhaps it wasn't Sophronia who needed her senses restored.

Dovey entered, carrying an enameled tray that was laden with two slices of fruitcake and a pair of steaming teacups. "I found the cake in the Terrys' pantry," she said, setting the tray on the sideboard. "Hope it's all right if we nibble the crust."

"Mary won't mind."

Jo accepted a plate from Dovey. She stared at her slice of cake. The bright bits of fruit were set in the cake's dense crumb like jewels in a golden crown, but Jo found she had no appetite. She laid the plate aside and sipped at her tea instead.

"Do you think Sophie will sleep?" Dovey asked.

"I hope she will. She needs rest. She mustn't make any rash decisions." *I did, and look at the mess I've ended in.* "The world will look fresh and new to her in the morning, and she'll choose a wiser path."

Dovey took a bite of fruitcake, then leaned from her chair to peer out the window. "Jo, I think there's a man outside," she whispered. "Do you suppose it's Sophie's attacker?"

"No, I don't." Jo stood eagerly and drained the last of her tea in one long draft. Sophronia's distress still weighed on her heart, of course, but even through that haze of pity, Jo felt a prickle of sweet anticipation. She headed for the door.

Dovey set aside her teacup with a loud clink and leaped to her feet. "Where are you going? You can't leave the house tonight, with some beastly creeper on the prowl."

"Stay inside," Jo said. "And trust me. I'll be safe."

She stepped out onto the porch just as Bill Jakes climbed the final stone step that led from the road up to the Terry home. His lean, rangy shape was well known to her now, so that even silhouetted against the night she recognized Bill at once. The swinging rhythm of his arms—just a touch too long for his body—was as much a comfort as the beat of her own heart. Jo leaned against one of the porch's ornately carved posts and smiled.

"You look real pretty in moonlight," Bill said. "Or what passes for moonlight in Seattle."

"Keep your voice down," she whispered, glancing back toward the house. For all she knew, Dovey was pressing her ear to the other side of the door. But she smiled up at Bill's shadowed face. "Back again to see me?"

Of course Bill was back again. He had called on Jo every other night since their initial walk. At first, she had kept him firmly in his place, insisting that their encounters remain blandly civil, so that no one—especially Jo and Bill themselves—might mistake their interactions for courting. But little by little, his affable charm had worn her caution away. Soon Jo looked so forward to their evening strolls and chats in Mary Terry's garden that all the mundane events of her daily life blurred into long stretches of featureless time, devoid of any color. The moments she shared with Bill were the only moments when she truly lived.

And even as her heart leaped like a fish in a sunlit pond, Jo felt the familiar twist of guilt in her stomach, the tightening of shame in her chest. She was not free to love Bill—and she had made a promise to Sophronia.

"I have to call on you often," Bill said, grinning, "or your other suitors might get the jump on me."

"There are no other suitors."

Bill reached through the darkness and found her hand. "I find that hard to believe. A woman as fine and clever as you must have men clamoring to marry you."

There were times when Bill's flirtations cheered Jo, and times when his pretty words sent pain stabbing through her heart. Tonight, with Sophronia's distress so raw and near—with the thought of Clifford so recently haunting her mind—a gust of thwarted longing blew right through Josephine's soul. It scoured away all her careful defenses, tore off and tossed away her mask of quiet dignity. She hung her head, unable to meet Bill's eye.

I must tell him the truth, she told herself. *Even if it hurts him. Even if he judges me a fallen woman, or spurns me for allowing him to hope for what can never rightfully be.*

She opened her mouth and tried to make her confession. But her throat constricted and her heart seized; she could not make herself speak the words that would ruin their love forever.

Finally she managed, "I wouldn't accept any other suitors, even if they appeared. I won't see anyone else, Bill—only you."

"I suppose that makes me lucky." Gently, he squeezed her hand.

"I need to ask a favor of you," she said. "Can you carry a message to the Jameson house tonight? Dovey is here with me while the Terrys are away, and our friend Sophronia has . . . has decided to stay the night, as well. I don't want Mrs. Jameson to worry."

"Sure, I can pay the Jamesons a late visit," Bill said amiably. "But I hoped to spend a little time with you before I went on my way. I must speak to you of something, Jo—a matter very dear to me."

Something in his tone—its sudden sobriety, the thickening of his voice, as if his throat had gone tight with emotion—made Josephine look up in a panic. Bill was watching her with an earnestness so strong it almost looked like sorrow—his brows pulled together, his eyes deep and imploring in the dimness of the night.

Josephine's heart fluttered, a bird trapped cruelly in a pretty cage. "Oh no," she whispered.

"I've come tonight to ask you to marry me," Bill said. "I never had much interest in marrying any woman—not that I have anything against women, of course. I just never saw the point of marrying—until I met you. So strong and sure of yourself . . . so fearless and honest . . ."

Those words stung Jo so fiercely that she gasped. She was *not* fearless—not by a long way—and as for honesty . . . !

Tossed on the waves of her thwarted desire, Jo turned abruptly away from him. "Oh, Bill! I *can't* marry you—I can't!" She covered her face with her hands. Even under the cover of darkness, she was unwilling to show Bill her tears. Perhaps he would read in their crooked tracks the truth of her secret, and Jo couldn't bear for Bill to know how she had deceived him.

A silence fell over the porch, the yard—the whole darkened city. Jo breathed raggedly in that stillness, wishing the sun would rise now and put an end to this dreadful day.

Finally, though, Bill broke the silence. His voice was not demanding; it carried no hint of anger. "Why not?"

Jo hugged herself tightly. Now was the time to spill out her secret—her chance to unburden her conscience. "I . . . I have . . ."

Like the last damp patch of a puddle drying in the sun, Jo's courage failed her—not that she had much courage to begin with. "I simply *can't*," she said with brusque finality. The image of Dovey came suddenly to her mind—roguish Dovey tossing her curls, denying and defying the whole damned world. Jo blurted, "I don't want to marry anyone. I want freedom—my own life. I don't want to be bound to any man—no matter how I may care for him."

"Shucks," Bill said at once. His voice even lightened a note or two, buoyed by what sounded very much like relief. "That makes proper sense to me. I felt exactly the same way, until I met you." His angular shoulders lifted in a shrug. "Well, all right, then. We don't have to marry. If that suits *you* best, it suits me, too."

Jo gazed at him in astonishment. *Is he breaking off his suit?* And if he had chosen to walk away from her heart, should she feel relieved or devastated?

Bill stroked his mustache for a moment, bridled by some troubling thought. He watched Jo's face in long contemplation. At last he said,

"Only, I'm heading out to Whidbey Island to take up a building contract there. I'll be living on the island for a few years while the work's available."

A blow like a hammer struck deep in Jo's chest. Bill going away? Never to visit her again—to walk with her in the evenings, to soothe her anxieties with the soft, simple music of his conversation? She gaped at him, pained and dumbfounded.

"Will you come with me?" Bill's voice was barely louder than a whisper. "The island's in need of a teacher, and I have connections to an awful lot of the families out there. I could secure the position for you."

With effort, Josephine regained command of her tongue. "Come with you? But you said we shouldn't marry."

He laughed. "*You* said we shouldn't marry. I'm merely going along with your preference."

Bill paused and cast a cagey glance across the Terrys' yard. The streets of Seattle were quiet and still in the watered-down pall that passed for moonlight. But still he hesitated, as if fearing the whole city was even now straining to listen.

Finally he said, "I don't see why we can't continue enjoying one another's company, just the way we have been doing. That is, if you're willing to make the move to the island. I know it's been your great ambition to take up as a teacher, and it's not so unusual for a schoolmarm to live alone. On the island, far from the people of Seattle who've come to know you, you'll be just another teacher living on her own. But you won't be *entirely* on your own. See what I mean?"

Jo stared out over the town, feeling the pinch and flush of her previous torment draining, relaxing from her face. She was aware that her eyes popped, that her mouth hung as slack as an empty jute bag, but she could do nothing about her display of confoundment.

Was this man truly proposing that Jo run off with him? Scamper off to some clandestine location, and there commit adultery? Was he suggesting that she take up as his . . . *companion* on some isolated island?

The very thought was an outrage. Or at least, Jo knew it should have outraged her—would have set any proper, moral woman to scolding and beating Bill clean away from the Terrys' porch and out into the night. But Jo liked Bill. She might, she realized with a rush of possibility that made her feel both giddy and ashamed, *love* him.

And he was leaving Seattle.

Jo pressed her hands tight against her stomach, trying to quell the sick dread that surged up at the thought. To be separated from Bill might cause a greater pain than to be judged an adulterer.

"I must know," she finally said, "why you would wish to maintain a . . . a *friendship* with me if we are not to be married."

Bill didn't hesitate in his answer. "I'm comfortable with you, Jo. That's all that matters to me. I know it's deemed real scandalous for a man and a woman to do what I suggested, but I've never been too fazed by scandal. I don't care a whit for the opinions of Seattle society."

"And what of the judgment of God?"

Bill shrugged. "I haven't seen much in my life that I can attribute to God—not with real confidence. No good fortune or affliction that didn't just look like dumb luck, once I sat and really thought about it. I'm not afraid of the Lord's retribution, Jo—not nearly afraid enough to let you pass out of my life."

He took her hand again. It was both warm and rough, and his touch was so familiar that it struck an ache deep in Jo's chest. It was not the pain of loss, nor of thwarted longing. It rose up from a satisfaction so complete that it filled her heart to bursting. She trembled with the force of that agony and treasured the perfect beauty of the ache.

Softly, Bill kissed her hand. "I can love you whether there's a ring on your finger or not. Say you'll come to the island with me. I'll be sure you're never lonely."

The delicate, quivering ache would not let her speak. She breathed deeply, and finally whispered, "I couldn't live with you, if I agreed to go—*if*. I'd go as a teacher, and I couldn't risk my position with the school on accusations of ill conduct. If I agree to go, I must have a place of my own. We must live apart, and no one must suspect . . ."

"I'll build you a home with my own two hands," Bill said softly. "Nothing would bring me greater joy."

She nodded. "I need time to consider it all. I must think it all through before I can give you an answer."

Jo did have the best intentions to think the matter through. She knew it was not in a woman's best interest, to trot off into the wilderness and take up a life of sin without dedicating proper contemplation to the plan. But as she watched Bill stroll off in the direction of the Jameson house, Jo's cheeks burned with the suspicion that her mind was already made up.

CHAPTER TWENTY
A WIDE SHOT AND A BULL'S-EYE

Springtime's lush, knee-high grass was so rank and abundant that it all but concealed the rutted track from sight. But Dovey was alert and avid; she had been on the lookout for the hidden lane since leaving Seattle's town limits behind her.

She reined Blue to a stop and fumbled in her saddlebag for the little map Virgil had sketched on a scrap of paper. Blue dropped his head into the grass and began grazing with a focus Dovey knew she'd have a hard time breaking. But one glance at her map confirmed it. She had found the property of one Mr. George S. Whistler: fisherman, sailor, and evader of taxes.

It was Dovey's first morning working as a collector. She had spent the past two days going around and around Virgil's corral, gathering dust on her dress and in her hair as she accustomed herself to the saddle—and to the strange sensation of riding astride. It gave her a tingling thrill, a flush of exciting indecency, to spread her legs in that shameless fashion. True, the only thing that got between her thighs was an old, jouncy saddle—it issued a leathery croak with every step the horse took, like a frog that had long since given up on the absurdity of life—but it was the generals of the act that excited her, not the particulars.

Equally thrilling were the trousers she wore under her skirt. Virgil had found an old, patched pair to fit her, and he'd cut off their frayed cuffs with his knife. The first time she had donned them, sliding them over her knee-length bloomers, she had blushed at the way they'd clung to her body, their intimate insistence, their habit of holding every inch of her flesh from ankle to hip.

How did men stand to wear trousers every waking moment? They were so *distracting*, in a way that sent a not-unpleasant tickle sliding around in her belly. Dovey had known from the moment Virgil gave her the job that Seattle would be in for a shock, when they first witnessed the spectacle of a girl riding astride. She wondered, would it heighten the city's distress more to see her legs clad only in stockings from knee to boot? Or would they take it harder to see a woman in trousers—to know that she must feel the secretive brush of the stiff fabric all up and down her limbs?

The question of the trousers proved Dovey's only real difficulty. Riding was certainly not the tribulation she had expected it to be. She gave credit there to Blue, the fat, roan gelding Virgil had dedicated to Dovey's cause. Blue was a plodder who cared for nothing but grass, grain, and shade. He forgave Dovey all her ungracious bouncing, ignored most of her novice tugs on the reins. But he would patiently walk in whatever direction Dovey pointed his head, and stop when she said "whoa," and that was all Dovey required for an equitable partnership.

Yet even though she knew Blue was a horse of a humble caliber, Dovey enjoyed a delicious sense of power and authority mounted on his back. When she was in the saddle, it didn't matter one bit that she was small and dainty. It didn't even matter that she was female. She towered over just about everybody, and could move with speed when Blue could be convinced of the necessity.

She derived an even greater confidence from the Colt strapped to her right leg. Virgil had presented her with a holster made of tooled mahogany leather, with two slim buckles of jingling brass. He'd talked Dovey through the process of buckling it snugly to her thigh—it wouldn't have done for him to do the buckling himself, of course. That was a touch even more secret than the clinch of trouser legs, and Dovey wouldn't have allowed such an audacity even if Virgil had been cad enough to try. When she swung up into the saddle, her skirt rose above her knees, exposing her trousers to view but concealing the pistol under a pile of ladylike ruffles and weaves. It was easy to reach under her bunched petticoats and draw the gun. She'd practiced the motion a few times for Virgil to see, and when he'd declared the effect perfect as a plum, Dovey had grinned.

She tucked the map back into her saddlebag, then pulled on the reins with a few muttered curses until finally Blue raised his head.

"Time to get to work," she told the horse, and pointed his head down the rutted lane.

The narrow road ran past an overgrown ditch, then twisted through a stand of cedars toward the rocky bay. George Whistler's house was little more than a shack, small and squatting, with a gently sloped roof and cedar shakes tacked haphazardly to its sides. But a fine, canvas-topped barouche stood in the yard, its sleek sides and the rims of its wheels enameled in snappy blue.

It must have cost a pretty penny to ship that rig all the way to Seattle, Dovey thought, squinting across the yard at the carriage.

Whistler, a potbellied man of middle years with bushy mutton chops sprouting from his jowls, appeared in the door of his little cedar shack.

"Well, hel-*lo*," he called, grinning. "What brings you a-riding up to my place, little cabbage?" He hoisted the belt of his trousers, as if readying himself for some vigorous activity.

Dovey beamed at him from the height of Blue's back. "I've come to see about your taxes, George S. Whistler."

The man stared up at her, blank-faced, for one stunned moment. Then he slapped his belly with both hands and roared out a gust of appreciative laughter. "Now, that's a good joke—a little slip of a girl like you, coming after taxes! Who put you up to it? Was it Lawrence, from down at the docks? No, no—it must have been Charley Pierce from the Flatiron. Charley sure put one over on me! The next time I see him, I'll say—"

"No, sir," Dovey broke in, still smiling sweetly. "I'm afraid this is no joke. I'm here to take the twenty-three dollars and thirty-six cents you owe for two years' worth of income taxes. And if you don't hand it over, I'm afraid I'll have to shoot you."

This time, George Whistler didn't bother to stop and stare in astonishment. He launched straight into that bellowing laugh, his bulk sagging against the doorframe, going weak and useless like a chunk of leaf lard melting in the sun.

His laughter died in a wheeze when Dovey reached under her petticoats. She drew the Colt from its hidden holster and steadied it in her hand.

Whistler's face reddened. "Well, now, I'd say the joke's gone far enough! I don't know if that thing's loaded, but you just put it right away again, young lady!"

"No, sir, I won't. Not until you hand over the money you owe."

"I'm not playing, now!" Whistler took a few angry strides toward her. She could all but see the fumes of fury rising from his pate.

Dovey aimed at a barrel a few feet from Whistler's shack and fired. Blue hardly flinched when the pistol roared in his ear; the gun kicked Dovey's arm almost out of its socket.

Whistler's barrel spurted a thin stream of brine. It puddled in the yard with a small, embarrassed splashing sound, like a little boy pissing his trousers.

"You better pay up, Mister," Dovey said. "I'm not real good at aiming this thing, and I don't know where the next shot might go."

"God-a-mighty, you curly-headed hellbitch," George Whistler muttered. "Just wait there while I go get the cash. And for the love of all things holy, don't shoot that gun again!"

Dovey counted every cent of Whistler's payment and tucked it into her collection purse. The weight and jaunty jingle of it tickled her so well that she kicked Blue into a trot and went bouncing and grinning all the way back to the city.

She rode into Virgil's yard as pleased as a cat in the cream. Outside the corral, she swung down from Blue's saddle—groaning a little with the ache of her long ride—and drew the collection purse from her skirt's pocket.

Virgil dashed from the back porch to meet her, leaping across the yard with his long, energetic stride, his rough cheeks flushed with expectation. "How did it go?"

For answer, Dovey dropped the purse into his hands.

He tossed it up into the air and caught it again; the coins gave a chipper clank. "That's what I'm talking about! Let me count out your ten percent."

Grinning, Virgil sorted the coins in his palm, handed over Dovey's cut, and, with a warm glint in his eye that made Dovey want to giggle, he added a bonus of a nickel. "Just 'cause you're so pretty," he said. Then he leaned toward her and brushed her cheek with a kiss.

CHAPTER
TWENTY-ONE
AN HONEST WOMAN

Josephine climbed the steps to the university building and paused a moment to gaze up at its four soaring pillars, each one crowned by twin scrolls that curled like the horns of a ram. She reached out to touch the nearest, running her fingers across the deep channels that ran from top to bottom, scoring the firm, cool flesh of the limestone. They were as lofty as Asa Mercer's ideals—and their purity and strength seemed to stand in mockery of Josephine's failures.

She passed beneath the university's arched doorway and pushed open the heavy, carved-oak door. Inside, a wide, central hall waited quietly, floored in shining oak and set with a few large, heavy tables. There were no fine carpets on the floor, no works of art framed upon the walls. The interior was austere—spare, even—but its high, vaulted grandness and ample space spoke of Mercer's cherished hope, the seeds he had sown for the future.

A handful of young men gathered around one table, heads bowed over books. Another group of scholars made their way across the central hall, talking together in quiet but earnest tones as they hurried from one lecture to the next. A balcony encircled the interior, and through its white-painted, wrought-iron railings, Josephine could see more young men entering a second-story room, and could hear a man's voice—a professor—raised in welcome.

What I wouldn't give to teach here, she thought, gazing about her, heart torn by regret and wistful hope. But it had been so long since she'd led a classroom—so long since she'd pursued a dream of her own. A university was surely beyond her now.

But her prospects were still rosy enough to please any woman. The schoolmistress position on Whidbey Island beckoned—as did a life of quiet satisfaction at Bill Jakes's side. There remained only one task to finish before she accepted the appointment as Coupeville's new teacher—she must tell Asa Mercer that her plans had changed.

She stepped forward to intercept the pack of scholars as they crossed before her. "Excuse me, sirs. I understand Mr. Asa Mercer still keeps an office here. Can you tell me where I might find him?"

The college boys were cheerful and pointed out the founder's office while they bobbed polite bows. In moments, Josephine was walking alone across the inner hall, toward Mercer's shut door, which seemed to recede away from her with every step she took, taunting her with the impossibility of her errand.

But she did reach his office at last, and his familiar voice bade her come in when she tapped on the door. Mr. Mercer looked up from a stack of papers; when he saw it was Josephine, his eyes widened in startlement.

"Miss Carey!"

She smoothed her lavender-colored skirt and gave a small, self-conscious laugh. "How strange—this is exactly the way we first met, isn't it? I'm even wearing the same dress!"

He rose from his seat, just as he had done in his cramped, musty office in Lowell, and gestured for her to sit. "And I am as pleased to see you now as I was then. What brings you here?"

Josephine sank slowly onto the bench. Anxiety assailed her—that was nothing new; she had wrestled with Bill's unlikely proposition for days now. With all her might, she had fought her alarming desire to accept his scandalous plan. Within the walls of the university, surrounded by its scholarly peace, the palpable presence of its high ideals, Josephine was more certain than ever that she must return to teaching—must take up that occupation which had always been her life's calling.

But faced with Asa Mercer's expectant half smile, the orderly arrangement of his desk, the neatness and clarity of his expectations, she trembled inside, and wondered whether she was truly making the right decision. Certainly, Josephine felt a great affection for Bill Jakes. The depth of her feeling might even go beyond mere affection, as startling as that thought was. And more than her longing for Bill's companionship, Josephine burned to do something for herself—to define her life in her own terms, to make some bold gesture that set her apart, mentally and emotionally, from Clifford and her past. Yet the promise she'd made to Sophronia hung heavy on her soul. She knew, as she settled shakily before Mr. Mercer's gaze, that if she gave in to the desire of her heart, she would disappoint everyone—the friends she had made on the voyage from Massachusetts, and especially Asa Mercer.

If I choose to do this thing—and Josephine knew, in the deepest recesses of her heart, that she had already chosen—*I'll be a disappointment to all the people I love and respect. I had best get used to it, and let the first of my friends down.*

"Mr. Mercer, I've come to let you know"—she paused, chewing for a moment on her lip, twisting her hands tightly in her lap, then she finished in a rush—"that I've agreed to take a position as a schoolmarm in Coupeville."

Mercer leaned back in his chair, his face paling, looking white as a sheet between the dark mass of his beard and the three symmetrical crests of his black hair. "I see."

"I understand that may come as some shock to you," she said. "And perhaps even a . . . disappointment."

He recovered quickly from his dismay, resting his elbows on his desk with a jolly air. "I take it you've found a man to marry, then, and his business will take you up to the island?"

"Erm . . . no." *Not exactly.* "I'm going alone. Perhaps you were right after all, back in Lowell, and I'm just too old to attract the interest of any man. I suppose I must resign myself to the life of an old maid." Her face heated at the falsehood, and she hoped Mercer took the color for a flush of embarrassment. "But I'm quite content to apply myself to my work. I enjoy educating young people. I always have. And I'll work all the more diligently, knowing I can send some of them to this magnificent university someday."

She fell silent. They stared at one another across the breadth of the desk, and Mercer's bright-blue eyes were distant and pensive.

"You're not . . . too terribly sore with me, I hope," Josephine finally muttered.

"Sore?" He chuckled lightly. "No, Miss Carey—never. You've been a friend to me; I still don't know what I would have done without you, that day of the reception. You saved my skin!"

"Then you don't regret bringing me from Lowell? Even though I won't marry a Seattle man?"

"I must be content with your choice, for it is yours to make."

He attempted a game smile, but it looked rather sad and defeated. Josephine's gut pinched with guilt.

"I can see you feel some contrition, Miss Carey. You must put all thought of remorse aside. You know, I chose Lowell for my expedition most specifically."

She tilted her head, wondering. "Why? I always wondered, but I never did find the chance to ask you."

"Seattle is the very edge of the frontier, and somewhat isolated, I'll grant you. But we do still hear the news of the nation here—even if it arrives late. There was perhaps no town in all the Union struck harder by the great rebellion than Lowell. So many businesses closed with such terrible speed; the economy was in a shambles virtually overnight. And so many young women were forced to find work. I knew that in such sad circumstances I could find exactly the kind of women Seattle needs. Hardworking. Dedicated. Strong and uncomplaining, of true moral character—and most of all, utterly fearless. Only adversity breeds such traits in a woman—or in a man. Only real testing tempers a spirit, and makes a person worthy of a grand adventure like Seattle."

Josephine hung her head. She had come through adversity—she had faced trials and dangers Mr. Mercer could hardly imagine. But it seemed the testing she'd faced had spoiled her spirit, not tempered it. Here she was, eager to lower herself into iniquity. What did that say about the substance of her character?

"I fear I'm not worthy of Seattle after all," she said softly. "And I'm sorry to have let you down, Mr. Mercer. I know you needed brides for your city—two hundred, you said! But here I am, leaving the town, without a ring on my finger, when you can't afford to lose a single woman."

His smile was so broad, so pleased, that Josephine looked up from her lap, a cautious hope welling in her breast.

"Fear not," Mercer said. He patted his palm against the stack of papers on his desk. "Somewhere in this pile is a letter signed by the town's board of trustees. They've approved my plan for a second expedition to the eastern states, to bring back more women."

"Oh! Why, that's wonderful news."

And God send that you'll have better luck this time, Josephine added silently. A fresh influx of would-be brides, whether they numbered in the hundreds or only another dozen, would relieve much of the guilt Josephine felt at traipsing off to the island, leaving the town's bachelors in the lurch.

"I expect to leave next year, if the funding comes through," he said. "The following year at the latest. I learned much from my first attempt in Lowell; I'm certain I'll be able to locate many more women who are eager to take part in settling the West."

"That's a great relief," Josephine said. Mercer's grin was so pleased, so shining with the surety of success, that she couldn't help smiling in return. "I . . . I'm only sorry you didn't find the women of true character you'd hoped for, the first time around."

Mercer rose from his desk and bowed smoothly to Josephine. "Miss Carey, I certainly did find women of admirable strength and rectitude. You are true, honest women—every one."

Josephine stood and clasped his hand warmly, her eyes and heart welling. His admiration for her was sincere; she had no doubt of that. But as he escorted her from his office and back across the university's tranquil hall, Mercer's unfailing belief in her honesty only filled her with a hot ache of shame.

I'm not the woman you think I am, Asa Mercer. Not at all.

But Josephine was her own woman now, and she was determined to build her new life in this wild frontier to suit her own heart.

CHAPTER
TWENTY-TWO
SWEETS

The Terry family was still away from the city, and so Dovey returned once more to the Gothic manse to keep Jo company for the night. In the spare room where Dovey was to sleep, by the light of a thick, tallow candle, she knelt on the rug to fold her trousers. Carefully, so as not to undo the neat pleats of her folding, she slid the taboo garment under her mattress. Her hand lingered on the rough cloth. She remembered Virgil's smile when he'd called her pretty—remembered the sound of his laugh as he'd tossed the purse into the air. Her face flamed up so hot that she withdrew her hand from beneath the bed and pressed her cool fingers to her cheek, just in the spot where Virgil had kissed her.

Saints alive, that man is handsome.

Dovey stood, brushed her skirt where her knees had pressed it to the rug, and headed down to the kitchen. Jo had already brewed the tea; the floral bite of bergamot filled the room and mingled warmly with the glow of the coal-oil lamps, wrapping Dovey in a comforting blanket of orangey light and orangey fragrance.

Sophronia had come to share their supper. She sat at the table, contemplating a cup of tea, and Dovey paused at the foot of the stairwell, admiring the delicate burnishing of the light on Sophronia's pale hair. The woman seemed to have recovered somewhat from her frightening brush with the alleyway thug. A little of Sophronia's tender color had returned to her cheeks and lips, and her eyes looked more determined than haunted.

Dovey dropped into one of the cane-back kitchen chairs and smothered her yawn with one hand.

"Tired?" Sophronia asked, glancing up from her teacup.

Dovey nodded. "Busy day. But look—I got something nice for us to share, girls."

She took a parcel, wrapped in brown paper, from her pocket and set it on the table with a flourish.

Jo left the stove and sat, eyeing the parcel and the blue string that tied it. "That string is from the candy shop."

"It is." Dovey grinned. "I stopped in there today and picked out a few treats. I think we deserve it, after all the trying days we've suffered."

She picked the knot from the string and unwrapped the parcel, revealing the cache of molasses taffies wrapped in twists of waxed paper, red-and-white peppermint sticks, and a handful of roasted and iced hazelnuts, each one sunk in the pillowy depths of a hard meringue kiss.

Sophronia looked up sharply from the candies. "Where did you get the money for these things, Dovey?"

"Don't you worry about that. I didn't steal them, if that's what you're afraid of."

Jo took a peppermint and gave it an experimental lick. "I think you're a darling for sharing. I'm glad to have something sweet to brighten my mood. Lord knows, I've needed it."

"You were both so kind and generous to me on the voyage to Seattle—sharing your food and all. A few sweeties are the least I can manage toward paying you back."

"You don't owe any payment," Sophronia muttered, toying with the handle of her teacup. "I only showed you Christian charity—the same any person would have shown."

"Lay aside that missionary act for a moment and have a kiss."

Dovey flicked one of the hazelnuts across the table. It skittered in Sophronia's direction; she trapped it under her palm with a quick swat, like a cat batting at a moth. Then she picked the candy up, stared at it soberly for a moment, and placed it delicately on her tongue.

"It's good, isn't it?" Dovey asked.

Slowly, reluctantly, Sophronia smiled. Dovey grinned back at her, pleased that her money could induce such a miracle as this un-Sophie-like display of enjoyment. She was pleased, too, that it was *her* money— that she had earned it by her own sweat and cleverness, and owed no man thanks for the weight of it in her pocket.

"Well, girls," Dovey said, "we've been in Seattle two weeks, just about. What do you make of the place so far?"

"It's far dirtier than I thought it would be," Jo said. "The mud gets in everywhere. I try to help Mrs. Terry out by tidying up, but it seems I'm forever sweeping. I don't know how any woman manages to keep house and her sanity in this place. But I suppose one just gets used to it. Eventually."

"And you?" Dovey asked Sophronia. "Has Seattle lived up to your expectations of its filth?"

But Sophronia didn't rise to the bait. She sipped at her tea, eyes distant, and said, "I certainly have not met any man yet who can be called a true Christian. At least, no available bachelors. But I shall not give up the quest."

Dovey groaned. "You aren't still considering that mad idea, are you?"

"I am determined. I shall marry the next devout and worthy man who proposes."

"It's a terrible idea," Dovey said flatly. "Rather than waiting on a man to care for you, I think you ought to go into business for yourself. Be your own source of strength, Sophie. Lord knows you're tough enough to do it."

"Go into business for myself?" Sophronia narrowed her eyes at Dovey, scrunching up her nose as if Dovey had just suggested she sprout wings and fly circles around the Occidental. "What do you know about going into business, anyway?"

Dovey rested her elbows on the table and leaned in with a confidential air. "Plenty. I just took a job, you know. Today was my first day on the rolls."

"Teaching, you mean?" Jo asked.

"Never. Can you imagine any school letting me in to teach the children? No—I've taken a position as a tax collector."

"A tax collector!" Jo shook her head in amazement. "Dovey, isn't that work better suited to a man?"

She shrugged. "I can do it well enough, if today's rounds were any indication. And it's easy work to do from horseback. Oh, girls, don't look so scandalized! It's only temporary work."

Sophronia and Jo shared an uneasy look.

"I'm going to save up my wages and start a business of my own. Why not? I'm a Mason. Business runs in my blood."

Sophronia cocked one white eyebrow. "I hesitate to ask, but . . . exactly what kind of business are you planning, Dovey?"

"You'll have to wait and see." Dovey wasn't keen to let the cat out of the bag any time soon. Once Sophronia realized what Dovey planned, the haughty creature would set her mind to a thorough thwarting of her grand dream. Time would reveal all to Sophronia—to the whole of the city. Dovey could wait as patient as a stone until then.

And Seattle ought to be pleased when I've got my capital together and set my plan into motion. For all Mrs. Garfield protested so vehemently, the cribs kept filling with customers, and the whores' pockets jingled like sleigh bells. Seattle loved fancy women, and another fancy house would be welcome.

What do you think of that, Father? Dovey wondered, as she sipped her tea with a swell of satisfaction in her chest, whether her father would feel proud of his daughter—there could hardly be a more viable business plan for Seattle than this one—or whether he'd be horrified. Probably the latter, but Dovey didn't much care. She knew her plan was a solid one—or if not exactly solid, then at least it was a damn sight better than marrying Marion Stilton.

"Anyway," Dovey went on, "my mother will be pleased as punch when I have an income of my own. I just know it. I've been writing her, you know. Her health is much improved. I think I can convince her to come to Seattle, with time."

"So she can drop into a faint at the sight of you riding a horse?" Sophronia asked shrilly. "You'd be the death of her, Dovey!"

"I would not. Mother's tougher than that, besides. And anyway, I can't live my life in fear of what everybody else thinks."

"You certainly can," Sophronia muttered, "and you should."

Dovey looked to Jo for assistance, but Jo only chose another piece of taffy from the cache and chewed it slowly, gazing back with a glint of amusement in her eyes.

"I'll bring my whole family out to Seattle if I can," Dovey said stubbornly. "Both my brothers, too. My business idea is a good one, and I believe I can earn enough income that I can give them all a fresh start—a better life than we faced in Lowell, with the cotton trade dying and the mills closed."

"Do you really think you can?" Jo asked. She leaned forward, and all the twinkle was gone from her eye. She watched Dovey's face with earnest curiosity. "Start up a good business, I mean—enough to support your parents and give your brothers a way to start over after the war?"

Dovey grinned. It was a fine thing, to have a friend's confidence—or even just her interest. "I think I can, indeed."

Sophronia snorted, but Dovey shook her head in curt dismissal. "I *can*, and I'll tell you why. I see something more in this town than you do, Sophie. To you, it's nothing but filth and grime and sin. It's a wound that must be healed. But to me, Seattle is like a little acorn that's just on the verge of sprouting. I feel as if I can see right into that seed, to the fine, strong roots and straight trunk and all the branching of its limbs. This town is opportunity, spread wide. And all any man or woman has to do in order to carve out a fine life is take the chance Seattle offers."

"Well," Sophronia finally conceded, "whatever business you plan to start, at least it isn't working docks. I guess that's something to be thankful for. But can't you find some other way to get there? Tax collecting . . . ! It's shameful, Dovey, just *shameful* to sit on a horse's back in that . . . that *spraddle-limbed manner!*"

"The dock girls work hard, and ought to be respected for their gumption," Dovey said.

"They certainly should *not* be respected. What you call gumption, I call sinning—and encouraging others to sin." Sophronia cast an appealing glance at Jo. "Don't you agree?"

Jo opened her mouth as if to speak, but an unexpected blush stained her cheeks. She dropped her eyes and looked hastily away, as if Sophronia's stare burned her.

"They're not sinners," Dovey insisted. "They're girls just like you and me. And what's more, they're my friends."

"Your nonsense shocks me! Your *true* friends would never do such filthy acts. Isn't that right, Josephine?"

Jo pressed her lips tightly together and said nothing.

"I know exactly who my *true* friends are," Dovey said pointedly, "and who they are *not*. And you can just listen to me for once. You're too judgmental, Sophronia. If you don't loosen up your corset laces now and then, you're apt to snap that stiff back of yours in two."

"Come now, girls. Let's not quarrel." Jo reached for Dovey's hand and took Sophronia's, too, but the frosty woman pulled her fingers out of Jo's grasp.

"The battle of morality," Sophronia said with stiff composure, "for one's very soul, cannot be termed merely a quarrel." She shoved her chair back from the table and stood, chin tipped high, refusing to look at Dovey. "Now if you will excuse me, Josephine, I shall go up to my bed."

She stalked up the stairs, leaving Dovey to fume in her wake.

Jo sighed, a sound too big and desolate to be attributed to Sophronia's mood alone. Dovey studied her friend's face, the dark circles under her eyes, the paleness about her mouth. Something was troubling Jo severely.

"Jo?" Dovey began.

But the older woman shook her head and rose from the table, too. "Don't fret over me, Dovey. I'm well."

But she didn't sound well—nor did she look well as she paced to the kitchen window and stood gazing out at Mrs. Terry's garden in the twilight.

Dovey wrapped up the remainder of her candies, tying the blue string carefully around the paper. She drifted quietly to Jo's side and pressed the package into her hand.

"For you," she said. "Because the Lord knows you can use something sweet right now."

Jo smiled in response, but her eyes were sadder than a dirge.

All the pleasantness had gone from their evening. Dovey crept upstairs and slipped into the dark of the spare room. She found her candle by feel and struck a nearby match. The flame illuminated everything—the narrow bed; the small, round, rose-patterned rug; the oak table pressed against the wall. Just now her world was small enough to fall within the circle of one candle's light. But soon it would grow—day by day, coin by coin—until even the sun couldn't shine bright enough to encompass the wide, endless vistas of her ambition—her freedom.

Dovey slipped her hand under the mattress to check that her breeches were still there. It was a silly thought—there was nobody else in the Terry house save for Jo and Sophronia. But she needed the reassurance of that rough cloth beneath her fingers, needed to know that the day hadn't been some strange, fantastical dream. She stroked the coarse weave of the trousers and recalled her mother's jewelry, stashed away under the loose floorboard back in her bedroom in Lowell.

The truth is, Dovey admitted, *I've always regretted selling your things, Mother. If I'd had a little more time—just one more day to prepare—I might have thought up some other way to raise the fare.*

But I promise, Mother, I'll make enough money here in Seattle—at the tax-collecting game or another job altogether—and I'll send for you. I'll send clear to Boston, and bring you home to me. And then I'll buy you all the earrings and cameos and riches you could ever desire.

Of course, Dovey realized her mother might not approve of the intended venture—a luxurious cathouse draped in acres of red velvet. No, Mother wouldn't approve at all, any more than Sophronia would. But Dovey couldn't let that hold her back. Her future was waiting, somewhere out there beyond the circle of her candle's flame, in the mud and cold and wide, green, youthful burst of possibility that was Seattle. It was waiting. And Dovey was ready to grab it with both hands.

CHAPTER
TWENTY-THREE
THE HOUR OF REST

The first high notes of the morning's hymn sang out from the fiddle, filling the chapel's close, rough-boarded space, winging up to the bare rafters. That welcome, wavering lance of emotion sliced into Sophronia's heart with a clarity that made her tense and shiver. She rose smoothly from the hardwood pew and raised her voice with the rest of the small congregation.

> The day is past and gone,
> The woodman's axe lies free,
> And the reaper's work is done.
>
> Sweet is the hour of rest!
> Pleasant the wind's low sigh,
> And the gleaming of the West,
> And the turf whereon we lie.

Her tongue knew the words, the notes, and she sang as automatically as the cotton mills of Lowell spun thread. But her thoughts, finally loosed from their cramped confinement by the fiddle's wail, roamed far from the hymn's sentiment and strayed into acres of shadow.

In the days that followed her last confrontation with Dovey, Sophronia had felt as fragile and transparent as blown glass. Dovey's parting shot—*I know who my* true *friends are, and who they are* not—reverberated in Sophronia's mind, chasing away sleep as she tossed restlessly in her bed, haunting every moment of peace with its harsh echo.

Did Dovey's scorn hurt Sophronia so because they had been friends—and were no longer? She couldn't decide. She hadn't thought of the girl as her friend—only a wayward soul in need of saving—but in that moment, when Dovey's bright, sharp eyes had burned with a fire of derision, Sophronia had felt something snap and shatter in her heart. The voyage from Massachusetts to the West had forged a bond between them, one Sophronia hadn't even realized was present until it burst and dissipated. Hadn't that been the way with all Sophronia's ties? Broken before she had known they existed—delicate threads snapped before she'd even seen where the slash of her blade would fall.

Here is my only solace, Sophronia told herself, clutching her Bible to her chest. Its old, leather cover had worn as soft as butter. In her arms, it felt as safe and familiar as home. *The word of God—my only comfort.*

But as the hymn ended and Sophronia sat again, turning her face up to the pulpit to hear the Lord's word, she didn't feel comforted. Not exactly. There was an empty place inside her, a distinct, cold void that hung low in her chest. It had always been there, since she'd been a girl—a space waiting to be filled, aching to be filled. She pictured it as the hollow of a tree. Umber brown, damp, and unwelcoming, it was a home to nothing—not the smallest thing that crept, not a single sparrow that fell.

It was God who must fill that space, Sophronia knew. Her father, the best loved and most righteous minister in Massachusetts, had taught her as much, and Sophronia believed him. Day by day she worked to make the void inside her a home in which the Lord might dwell. But the voice of God, which she so yearned to hear speaking in her heart at last, was as silent now as ever. The only thing she heard within was the ring of scorn in Dovey's voice—the shocking pop and shatter of a friendship breaking.

At least in the chapel, small and rustic though it was, Sophronia found the trappings of religion. True, Seattle could offer only hewn beams and primitive benches, where Lowell's churches had boasted the gleaming warmth of carved oak, shining with the touch of generations of fellow worshipers, and pews cushioned with velvet and silk. Here there was but one small, crying fiddle, where Lowell's chapel had rang loud and triumphant with the chorus of the organ. Sophronia drank deeply of Seattle's cup of religion, and faintly, on the back of her tongue, she found the taste of home.

I can make this place my home, she thought. *I can come to love it as much as I loved Lowell. And if I am to have no husband, I can still fill my life with good and worthy works.*

Since she had decided to accept the very next proposal that fell from a man's lips, Sophronia had received no proposals at all—nor even calls from gentlemen. In her moments of dry, sensible thought, she wondered if it were the grief that must show now on her face—the outward sign of her inner hollow, the intrinsic emptiness besetting her eyes. In her times of wild grief and bitter cynicism—which outnumbered her moments of clarity by far—she simply told herself that the Lord had sent down a penance of loneliness, that she bore a just punishment for a sin she could not name.

I must be brave, she told herself. *I must accept my rebuke in humility, if I am to be found worthy of eternal life at the last judgment.*

If she had earned so terrible a penance, then she was determined to serve it. She would do whatever the Lord willed. Even if her heart broke.

Harmon Grigg, the minister, ascended to his pulpit. He was approaching his middle years—well past Sophronia's age, but still young for a man of his occupation—with neat, oiled hair of a ginger-red color, sprinkled at the temples with gray. He had a trim mustache and thick brows, and blue, kindly eyes that stared out beyond the walls of his little chapel as he preached, as if he could see, spread before him, all the vastness and bounty of God's creation.

His text was the twenty-fifth Psalm. Sophronia opened her Bible to the correct page and began to read along as the minister spoke. But some combination of the text itself and the minister's warm, resounding voice, so confident in the truth of God's word, soon raised tears to her eyes. The verses lost themselves in a hot blur, and Sophronia hung her head over the Bible in her lap.

"'Turn to me and be gracious to me,'" Harmon Grigg read.

Sophronia tried to hold back her unseemly emotion, but quite against her will, a loud sniffle escaped. It rang sharply through the congregation, and the minister paused.

Sophronia, flushing with shame, glanced from her lap to the pulpit. Mr. Grigg was staring down at her, and his eyes were wide with surprise—and something else, too. For one brief moment, one instinctive beat of her heart, Sophronia tried to understand and name the feeling she saw stirring in the minister's countenance. *Sympathy.* Then her mortification overcame her once more, and she broke his gaze, turning her head to watch the wind ruffle the maples outside the tall, arched window.

Mr. Grigg went on with his reading. "'. . . For I am lonely and afflicted. Relieve the troubles of my heart and free me from anguish. Look on my affliction and my distress and take away all my sins. See how numerous are my enemies and how fiercely they hate me!'"

A sob threatened deep inside her chest; Sophronia clenched her fists atop her Bible, pressing her nails hard into her palms. She would not show emotion again—would not disgrace herself, would not make of herself a fool, fodder for women's gossip. She shut out the sound of the minister's voice and pushed away the memory of his sympathetic gaze. She saw nothing of the world but the trees stirring gently outside, and heard nothing but the imagined sound of the wind. She did not even hear the words of God.

It took Sophronia some time to master her tranquility again. By the time she was sure of her self-control, the fiddler played the closing hymn, and the service came to its end. She was glad. The quiet of her small, spare bedroom waited at the Jameson house, the pleasant cool of its dim spaces, the solace of privacy, where she might shed her tears without fear of judgment. She shut her Bible and hurried out into the chapel's yard.

Summer had arrived—or what passed for summer in this persistently cloudy place—and most of the mud had dried. The grass was thick and high and whispered against Sophronia's skirt as she made her way toward the dirt road that would take her back into town. At first she did not hear the shout of "Miss!" over the murmur of the grasses and the sounds of the congregation heading home to their noonday meals. But the call came again, and Sophronia paused, wondering.

It was Harmon Grigg who had shouted after her. He raised a hand, beseeching her to wait, and Sophronia, stupefied and tired out by her week's welter of emotion, stood like a deer caught in torchlight and watched him come on.

Mr. Grigg panted a little as he stopped beside her. His face was flushed with the effort of catching up to her; she could see the faint trace of freckles across his nose, a boyish accessory in contrast to the sober mien of a proper minister.

Sophronia bit her lip, certain he'd come to chastise her for her rude interruption.

"I'm sorry," she said at once.

Mr. Grigg shook his head in confusion. "Miss?"

"I . . . I interrupted your service. It was wrong of me."

He grinned, showing deep laugh lines around his eyes and a gap between his front teeth that Sophronia found quite charming. Then he swept his wide-brimmed, clerical hat from his brow. "It's I who've wronged you, if I've made you think there's something amiss. I only wanted to introduce myself."

"You're Harmon Grigg," Sophronia said, more tersely than she'd intended.

"Yes. You've been attending my services for some time, and yet I haven't taken the time to meet you properly. That's a failing on my part." He fell silent, and his eyes flicked down to her hand, hanging limp at her side.

Too late, Sophronia recalled her manners. "Oh," she muttered, and offered her hand. In her flustered state, she presented it palm down, then heated with mortification when she realized she'd invited a kiss to her knuckles. But she would not turn her hand now. Harmon Grigg took her fingers gently in his own, then bowed to leave a brief, soft kiss on her hand.

Sophronia cleared her throat. "I'm Sophronia Brandt. Pleased to make your acquaintance."

"You've been coming to services since mid-May."

"Yes, sir." She found it difficult to remove her gaze from the gap in Mr. Grigg's teeth. Or perhaps it was his lips she stared at—those lips whose touch she could still feel on the back of her hand.

"Did you come to Seattle with Asa Mercer, then?"

"I . . . I did." She wondered just what opinion the minister held of the Mercer girls. Did he, like so many other residents of the city, think them a cargo of whores?

"I've noted, Miss Brandt, how piously you attend church. I fear piety is a rare quality in any citizen of Seattle. Modesty, too—yet you seem a very proper woman."

"Thank you."

Mr. Grigg shuffled his feet and glanced for a moment down into the grass, as if searching for the courage to say more. Finally he drew a deep breath and added, "I have also noticed, Miss Brandt, that you are very beautiful."

Sophronia felt her eyes widen in a most indecorous way, but she could not seem to stop herself.

"You know, I have no wife, Miss Brandt. And today when I saw you, so moved by the Lord's word . . . well, I wondered if I might call on you."

Now, when she needed her composure and poise more than ever before, Sophronia found she had no voice. She gaped for a moment at Harmon Grigg, and covered the right hand he had kissed with the fingers of her left. So—after resigning herself to loneliness in this mud-soaked Gomorrah, she had finally found a reason to hope, just when she thought all hope was gone. Truly, the Lord worked in mysterious ways!

But despite the anticipation welling in her breast, Sophronia hesitated. Any man of Seattle was sure to have some serious faults. They all did. There were no good men in this place—not left unmarried, at least. This city was peopled by unsavory toughs, rascals who lived for liquor and loose women.

But he is a minister, she scolded herself. *A man called by God, to do good and holy work. He isn't like the rest of them. He can't be.*

Sophronia swallowed her doubts and gave Harmon Grigg a hesitant smile. "Very well," she said. "I shall be glad to receive you. You may call for me at the Jameson home, Mr. Grigg."

They parted ways, Sophronia blushing, the minister grinning like a boy with a handful of peppermints. She waked in a haze of shock all the way down the hill, blind to the verdant, lush trappings of summer, hearing nothing of the birds' sweet clamor in the trees. But by the time she reached the level streets of the city, Sophronia fairly danced back to the Jamesons' on light feet, and even when a gust of wind swept up from the tidal flats, carrying the thick, sour odor of seaweed decaying in the sun, she breathed the air in as deeply as if it were perfumed with flowers.

The days that followed were the sweetest Sophronia had ever known. Harmon Grigg called on her Monday afternoon, and, blushing, she accepted his invitation to walk along a forest path. They shared stories of home as they strolled up the gentle rise, with the fragrant boughs of trees, clad so brightly in their gay robes of summer green, arching overhead.

Sophronia told him all about Lowell, its former glories and its slide into poverty as the great rebellion dragged on. She spoke, too, of her sisters, the golden-haired girls whom she had tended with such motherly care—and whose laughter and mischievous games she missed every day.

Harmon spoke of San Francisco. When he was only a boy, he had traveled to the city with his father, coming all the way from Ohio after his poor mother had succumbed to a fever—and shortly after their arrival, his father had perished, too, killed in the collision of two ships in the heavy harbor mist. Orphaned and too young to work, Harmon had taken the charity of a minister and learned his trade, scraping by into adulthood, watching the city grow as he did, until the seaside town had flourished into the glittering jewel it was today.

That serene walk with its intimate conversation had soothed away Sophronia's fears as nothing had before—not even study of the Bible. Harmon's willingness to expose his past to Sophronia—to lay bare the vulnerable places of his heart—touched her deeply, and sent a warm throb of quietude spreading through that terrible, echoing emptiness inside her. He trusted her, and even seemed to like her—though God knew they were barely more than strangers. And as she gazed into his eyes, listening to the music of his cultured speech, as she caught the flash of his gap-toothed smile, Sophronia felt for the first time in her life that she was a person worth liking.

Harmon called on her again on Tuesday, and on Wednesday—and, to her delight, on Thursday as well. Each hour they spent in one another's company was sweeter than the last, and day by day, Sophronia's thoughts filled with him, with the particular timbre of his voice, the rhythm of his walk, the feel of his lips against the back of her hand. It did not matter where they went—whether they strolled the city's sidewalks, or took in the recital of the brass band outside the Occidental, or simply stood watching the low, gentle waves of Puget Sound lap the pebbly shore—Sophronia felt happy in his company, and confident in her hope.

When the sun set Friday evening and they walked back to Sophronia's home, both of them dragging their feet to delay the inevitable parting, Harmon paused at the foot of the path that led up to the porch steps. He turned to Sophronia with silent intensity, gazing deep into her eyes, lifting her hand in his own to press it close to his heart.

"Oh—Harmon," Sophronia murmured. An instinctive rebuke was on her lips, as she sensed that he might intend to kiss her. But a strange, wild welling in her heart wouldn't allow her to speak.

"My darling," he whispered, "you were sent by the Lord into my life." His face deepened with a flush, and he seemed to wrestle with his thoughts—with his emotions. But he spoke no more, and his audible gulp sounded as loud as a thunderclap in the intimate space between them.

He is *going to kiss me,* Sophronia realized. And then, with a jolt of fear and frantic hope, she realized that she didn't want to rebuke him. There was nothing in the world she desired more than to feel his lips press against her cheek—or better still, her mouth! She wanted to surrender to his embrace, allow his arms to encircle her like a shield against all the sorrows of her past.

She leaned toward him. And then abruptly pulled away, blushing, as her better sense caught up to her. "Oh! I . . . I ought to go inside now."

Harmon cleared his throat. "I suppose that's so. I had a fine time with you this evening, darling."

Although her heart raced so frantically it made her stomach queasy, Sophronia smiled at him. "As did I."

But despite their warm parting, Sophronia climbed the steps to the Jameson house blinded by mortification. She shut herself in her room and sagged against the door, pressing her hands against her face.

Lord! What a hussy I am. Wishing for a beau to kiss her without even a promise of marriage—it was beyond shameful!

Again and again she scolded herself as she readied for bed. But by the time she stood before her small, framed mirror, clothed in a flannel nightgown, all the scold had gone out of her. She gazed at the color high in her cheeks, at the sparkle in her eye. And she smiled. This evening with Harmon had felt so good, so right, that even Sophronia couldn't imagine any sin into it. Perhaps the yearning she felt for Harmon's embrace wasn't sinful at all but a sign from God that at last, after her many long trials and disappointments, she had found true love.

"That's it," she whispered to her reflection. "You've found him—the man who will be your husband." She smiled—and Josephine had been right, those many weeks ago aboard the *Illinois*; Sophronia *was* pretty when she smiled. She drank in the beauty of her own contentment like a parched man at a desert well.

As long as she remained true to her ideals, Sophronia knew, she would have Harmon to wed.

Let him call on me tomorrow, Lord—and the next day, too.

CHAPTER
TWENTY-FOUR
CONFESSIONS

Sophronia left the Occidental Hotel with a spring in her step and a buoyant song in her heart, swinging her small, beaded purse from its drawstrings as she glided across the street and up the slope of Denny's Knoll toward her hostess's home. The day had started gray and foggy, as so many days in Seattle did, but on that warm Saturday afternoon the clouds had burned away before the insistent cheer of the sun. The streets and sidewalks bounced their toasted warmth up toward her face, and the dusty, comfortable odor of sunbaked mud filled the avenues and alleys. She squinted against the glare as she hummed her happy tune.

She had worked diligently, ever since her arrival in Seattle, to undo the miserable first impression she'd made on Mrs. Garfield and her friends of the Women's League. Sophronia felt instinctively that she shared the high standards of the League—indeed, there was no nook or cranny of Seattle society where she would fit so perfectly. But a simple apology, no matter how heartfelt, was never enough to recover a woman of Mrs. Garfield's caliber from the type of vexation Sophronia had visited upon her. Sophronia had attended every meeting and function of the League, enduring the women's stares and their suspicious whispers with good grace—after all, their judgment was her due, the harvest she'd reaped with her display of ill temper on the first night of their meeting.

Now, at last, she seemed to have won Mrs. Garfield's forgiveness and the confidence of the League. They had welcomed her to the afternoon's meeting readily, and a few of the women had even gone out of their way to converse with her sedately about topics of great interest: a recent engagement between one of the Mercer girls and a gentleman of society; a variety of outrages committed by the city's prostitutes; the shocking scandal of the suffrage movement that had so taken root in the eastern states.

I'm a part of their society now, Sophronia told herself joyfully as she made toward the Jameson place. *I've Harmon's calls to look forward to, I've been accepted into the Women's League . . . I can finally be pleased with my life, all thanks to the Lord!*

It certainly wasn't time to start sewing a wedding gown—not yet—but Sophronia's life had taken a turn toward rich and ample blessings. *I was right to be steadfast in my morals. Finally, my righteousness will be rewarded.* All she need do now was—

"Miss Priss!" A harsh, nasal voice called from behind her.

Sophronia's jubilant steps faltered, and she turned slowly to peer over her shoulder. A perfect fright of garish colors and thickly flounced skirts followed her up the sidewalk. Sophronia recognized the prostitute—the way those mocking eyes gazed at her beneath lazy, dark-painted lids; the heavy rouge on her cheeks; most of all, the high, untidy pile of straw-yellow hair that seemed to teeter on her head like a wagon about to tip its load into the street. It was the line girl known as Haypenny—the one who had befriended Dovey.

Sophronia halted and rounded on the girl, her smile melting into a pinched frown of disgust and bewilderment. "What do you want? Are you begging for coins now? You'll get none from me! I want nothing to do with you." She made a shooing motion with her hands, as one might do to frighten away a pestering alley cat.

Haypenny gave a jeering, feline hiss and leaned casually against the corner of the nearest building. "Where are you heading off to, Stuffy Sophie? Have a dinner date with Harmon Grigg?"

Sophronia blanched. Her throat tightened, and she croaked as she said, "What's that to you?"

The prostitute slitted her painted eyes. "I know you're sweet on the preacher. Everybody does."

"It's none of your business." Sophronia sniffed and turned away, but the sly, lascivious nature of Haypenny's laughter halted her in her tracks.

"You know, Sophie, you ought to have a little talk with Harmon Grigg."

Sophronia swallowed hard. Reluctantly, she turned to consider the prostitute again. The girl's arms were folded below the spilling lace and riotous bows that adorned her low neckline. She leaned her hip against the building's corner with an air of sly satisfaction—and with a knowing smirk that sent a chill deep into Sophronia's stomach.

"A talk? About what?"

Haypenny detached herself from the wall and sauntered up to Sophronia, then right past her, around the corner and into the cool blue shadow that hung across Second Avenue. "About the *past*," Haypenny said casually, over her shoulder. "Don't you think a girl ought to know everything about her beau's *habits* before she ties the knot?"

Sophronia watched the girl mince away down the avenue, her hem lifted distressingly high, never once turning to glance back at her. Dread settled thickly in her chest, but Sophronia pushed it away resolutely.

That shameful wag can't possibly know anything about Harmon. Sophronia remembered all too vividly the threat Haypenny had made when she'd dragged Dovey away from the gang of prostitutes. *She's only trying to get my goat, for Dovey's sake. There's no reason to be alarmed by the nattering of a fallen woman.*

Sophronia turned and continued calmly toward her home. She would certainly *not* allow Haypenny's petty attempt at vengeance to unseat her confidence, or to spoil her pleasure in the day. But the girl's words did stick in Sophronia's mind, despite her efforts to dislodge them. *A woman really ought to know everything about her suitor's past. Yes, it's time Harmon and I discussed our lives, our habits—and best to do it now, before he makes his proposal.*

As it happened, Harmon called on Sophronia that very evening. She had just helped Mrs. Jameson clear away the supper plates and was drying the last of the freshly washed pots when his familiar tap-tap-tap sounded at the front door. She answered the door herself, beaming at him, glad to fill her eyes and soul with the image of her love in the summer dusk, his red hair glowing in the fire of the sunset.

"I've come to ask you out for a stroll," Harmon said. "It's such a lovely evening, and there's no one I'd rather spend it with than you."

She accepted eagerly and wrapped herself in her shawl, then pressed herself snugly against his arm as they walked down to the waterfront and turned north, making for the unspoiled, pebble-strewn beaches beyond the shipping docks. The last brilliance of the sunset clung to the horizon in shades of flame and rose, touching long, thin tendrils of cloud with vermillion fire.

"Isn't it lovely." Sophronia sighed. "It's been a perfect day, Harmon, and it's all the better now that I've seen you."

He smiled at her warmly. "I know it's only been two days since my last visit, but I couldn't allow another evening to pass without looking on your lovely face. You do look so enchanting in the sunset."

Sophronia blushed and lowered her eyes to the rocky strand. They picked their way over a few pale logs of driftwood, then found one on which to sit, high and large enough to function as a bench. The sun's warmth was still trapped in its dry, salt-roughened surface; Sophronia could feel it seeping through her skirt and petticoats.

"I'm so glad you called on me tonight," she said, holding Harmon's hand. "Forgive my forward manners, but I feel we're reaching a turning point in our courtship." She could not bring herself to look at him as she spoke, but he squeezed her hand gently, and, encouraged, she went on. "I thought perhaps it would be wise if we . . . spoke."

"Spoke?" He kicked lightly at the gravel of the beach, a charmingly boyish gesture. "What's on your mind, darling?"

Haypenny's snide laughter slithered through her mind, twisting like a snake in the weeds. Sophronia pushed her doubts away. She was determined to let nothing destroy her happy mood—especially not the envious taunts of a woman of ill fame.

"I only thought," Sophronia said lightly, "we might tell each other about the past. Make our little confessions before we . . . before we progress any further."

"Very well," Harmon said. Had a touch of uneasiness entered his voice, or was that merely Sophronia's fretful imagination? "Shall you go first, or shall I?"

Sophronia cleared her throat. "Once, when I was ten years old, I stole an entire crock of strawberry preserves from my mother's pantry and ate the whole thing."

Harmon stared at her a moment, uncertain whether her confession was real. Then he burst out laughing, slapping his knee.

"It's not funny!" Sophronia protested, struggling to keep back her own giggles. "Theft is very wrong. And besides, I got a terrible stomachache. Now you must make a confession."

He stroked his beard, searching his memory as he grinned out at the fading sunset. "Very well. When I was a boy of about twelve, I was so bored in church service that I took out my pocketknife and carved a cuss word on the pew. I felt terrible about it later—I was dead certain the Lord was planning to strike me down. So the next Sunday I sneaked a little pot of my mother's floor wax into church and covered it up again. But that sin lay heavy on my soul for many months afterward, I can tell you that for certain."

Sophronia giggled. "Imagine, a little boy destined to be a minister, doing something so naughty!"

"I guess I've been forgiven for that particular sin," Harmon said. "Now you."

They went on trading their confessions as twilight crept over the beach, spreading its purple wings across the sky and coaxing the first of the stars into view. Laughter over youth's sweet follies joined with the whisper of waves and the crying of gulls. Finally, when the stars wove a web of silver across the darkening sky, Sophronia gazed steadily at Harmon and took his hand again.

"I do have another confession to make. And I fear it's a serious one."

He wiped a tear of mirth from the corner of his eye. "I can't imagine you've ever had a real sin in your heart, Sophronia."

She swallowed her fear, and her hand trembled in his. "You might think otherwise, once you've heard what I have to say. I'm afraid you might lose all respect for me, Harmon."

"Darling! You need never fear such a thing from me. Tell me what burdens your heart."

"The last time we were together . . ." Sophronia faltered and stared mutely at the waves, at their pale line of froth sketching and erasing itself against the dark, wet gravel of the shore. She took a deep, ragged breath. "When we were together, I thought you intended to kiss me. And I . . . I hoped you would, Harmon!"

He had gone very still and silent. Sophronia bit her lip, watching the waves advance and recede, certain she had lost his respect and his love forever. She risked a glance at his face. "Do you think me a harlot? I've thought so myself. The impulse shocked me, but I—"

"No, darling, no. I don't think poorly of you." His voice was thick with emotion. "We've all had shocking impulses from time to time. I think you a woman of admirable character, for you were able to control your longings."

Something in his voice—some thin strand of regret—caught at Sophronia's conscience. "But you," she said desperately, "you are just as able to control—"

He gave a rueful laugh, short and hard, and turned his face away.

"Harmon?" Sophronia's voice quavered, and she recalled Haypenny's sly smirk with a chill of fear. "Do you have some other confession to make?"

"I only tell you because I think it's important that you know," he said quietly. "Before we go any further."

But then he fell silent, and slowly withdrew his hand from hers.

"What is it, Harmon? Please, just tell me!"

"In the past, I, too, have felt . . . unseemly desires. But I fear I was not as strong as you, and didn't control myself."

A harsh, brassy sound clattered in Sophronia's ears, like the ringing of a cymbal. She realized with the too-calm clarity of despair that it was the sound of her own blood rushing, that her heart was racing, that her spirit was falling down a long, dark pit.

"In my moments of weakness," Harmon went on, "I have sought out the company of low women."

Sophronia gasped. "Harmon—how could you?"

"I've made repentance," he said, turning to her hopefully, his eyes pleading for her forgiveness, too. "And once the guilt of it caught up to me, I never did it again. It has been two years since—"

She cut him off relentlessly. "How many times have you lain with soiled women?"

"Not many," he answered at once. "Not many, though . . . I have done it a time or two. I'm a man made of flesh, after all. But, Sophronia, the guilt of it—I'll never do it again. You need not fear that. I want nothing now but you—to settle down to a proper life."

Harmon took both her hands in his own, meeting Sophronia's eye with an absurd spark of hope—as if he expected her absolution for this insult, this sin!

"You may certainly not expect me to marry you!" Sophronia burst out. "Of all the grave offenses! Find another woman to tolerate your sins, Harmon Grigg! I'll have none of you!"

She leaped up from the driftwood log and turned and rushed away, stumbling over the stony beach. She ignored his frantic calls to wait, to let him speak, to hear his confession and repentance. Under his painful protestations, she could not blot out the echo of Haypenny's gratified laughter. The whore had taken her revenge, and no mistake.

Sophronia ran through the violet night until her lungs burned, ran until her throat rasped with pain and tasted of blood. She passed the muddy stench and the deep blue-dark scar of Skid Road, its hard, decisive slash down the face of the wooded hill. Ahead, glowing through the veils of darkness as on that fearful night when the stranger had attacked her, Sophronia saw the Terry house, the prim, white lacing of its peaked roofs standing stark and sharp against the dimness of the hour. She hurried up the steps of its steep yard and pounded on the door, choking back her sobs.

It was Dovey who answered the door, and for a moment Sophronia thought her eyes had deceived her, that she had not come to the Terry mansion after all. In her haste to flee from Harmon's sin, and from the sting of betrayal, had she run even farther up the hill?

"Lord, Sophie, what's the matter with you?" Dovey caught at her hand, but Sophronia reeled back from her touch.

"Where's Josephine?"

"Tell me what the matter is," Dovey said, frowning in concern. "You haven't been attacked again, have you? Poor duck—"

Sophronia balled her fists and shouted into Dovey's face, "I want nothing to do with you any longer—nothing, do you hear? Not you, or your filthy, painted friends!"

Josephine stepped through the doorway, wrapping Sophronia in a comforting embrace. She felt one moment of embarrassment over her disheveled state—her hair must be tossed and ruffled from the wind at the beach, and her boots were covered with clinging sand—but she could do nothing for a long, terrible moment except weep piteously against Josephine's shoulder.

"Sophie," Dovey said gently, "just tell us what's the matter."

"I won't! Let go of me!" She reared back, breaking Jo's embrace, and whirled to face Dovey once more. The girl's pert confidence and bold stare seemed to mock her, as much as the whore Haypenny's laugh had done. "You can just . . . just go to Hell, Dovey!"

She heard Josephine's loud, startled gasp. Dovey blanched and wrinkled her nose, cutting a wary glance toward Josephine. Sophronia could just about read their thoughts: *This isn't like our Sophie. Something's gone wrong.*

But I'll never speak of it, Sophronia told them silently, pressing her lips together, shivering with the cold of the night and with the force of her determination. *No one will ever hear of my dashed hopes, of yet another beau driven away. No one will hear how the Lord taunted me, promising love and then snatching it away just as I felt brave enough to reach for it!* She would bear her penance with patient humility, because that was good and right. But she would never speak of Harmon Grigg, or the shame and loss that wracked her, for all the rest of her days.

"Sophronia," Jo said, "what has Dovey done? Surely she doesn't deserve such harsh words from you."

"Don't try to smooth this over, Josephine. There are some wrongs too deep and terrible for your clever words to put right."

"But Dovey only—"

"I will not make nice with that recalcitrant, foolish child. I will have nothing to do with anyone who associates with prostitutes." It was because of those blights on the city, those maids of Babylon, that Sophronia had lost her final chance at love—and Harmon's loss, just when Sophronia had allowed herself to be so happy and cheerful in her hope, hurt ten times more than any that had come before.

Sophronia brushed the sand from her skirt and turned to Dovey with cool composure. "I never want to speak to you again," she said calmly, with perfect composure. Then she turned away from the women who stood shocked and silent on the Terrys' porch and walked back out into the night, alone but with her head raised high.

CHAPTER TWENTY-FIVE
THE WEIGHT OF DUTY

"How do you like that?" Dovey said grimly, watching the pale streak of Sophronia's unbound hair fade into the rainy night.

Jo shook her head. A hard, cold stab of confusion struck her in the gut, and she heaved a tired sigh. There was something about this parting that made her feel panicked and small. Something precious was breaking apart, drifting away. The bond that had existed between the three of them had always been tenuous, perhaps, but it was real. It was a painful thing, to see that friendship rip into tatters.

"It's fine by me if I never see her again," Dovey said stoutly. "I've had more than enough of Sophie's arrogant ways. If I never have to hear one of her prunes-and-prisms speeches again, I'll keel over dead of happiness."

Jo clutched Dovey's hand in despair. "How can you say that, after all we've come through together?"

"What have we gone through? A couple of ship voyages and a few acres of mud in Seattle? What of it? That's not enough to hang a friendship on. *Obviously*—you heard what Sophronia said to me just now! *Imagine.*"

"Sophronia nursed you back to health aboard the *Illinois*, when you were so sick we thought you might die. And in San Francisco—she came out to find you in the streets, even though she was terrified."

"If she hadn't come out to find me, I might still be in San Francisco, making my own way in the world."

"Making your way on your back," Jo added drily.

"With gold in my pockets."

"Clifford would have taken every bit of coin from your pockets, and then ripped the dress right off your body. You saw how he handled me. I couldn't have stopped him. It was Sophronia who saved you—saved us both."

"What of it? That's all behind us now." She propped her fists on her hips and glared up at Josephine. "And I don't care *how* I make my money, so long as it's *mine*—so long as no one can take it from me or tell me how I ought to spend it. I've found where I'm happy, Jo—on the back of a horse, with a pistol in my hand, collecting the taxes.

"And that's just for now. I've got more plans for my future. None of them concern a husband *or* Miss Sophronia monitoring my morals. And mark my words, that's why she's so upset tonight. That's why she shot off her mouth that way, and cursed me to the Devil. She knows I'm beyond her reach, and she can't stand it."

"I truly don't think that was the reason for her outburst," Jo mused, staring into the rain again. But all trace of Sophronia had vanished.

"It is. I'd bet my own money on it. She can't stomach a woman who intends to make her own way in the world. But that's just what I'm doing, Jo. I won't stop—not for Sophronia or anybody else."

Jo hesitated, twisting a fold of her skirt between her fingers. The rain drummed on the porch roof, and from somewhere down in the city, the wind lifted and carried the faint sound of laughter, of men's voices raised in drunken song.

"I'm planning to make my own way, too," Jo finally admitted in a soft, startled voice. It was the first time she'd said it aloud—the first time she'd even settled on the thought in her own mind. But now that the words were out of her mouth, she knew she was committed. She wouldn't be coming back to Seattle again.

"Are you?" Dovey asked, snapping out of her grim mood and beaming up at Jo with real interest. "That's bully, Jo! What will you be doing?"

"I'll be going off to Whidbey Island, to teach at the new school there."

"An island! My—that sounds grand. And far away."

Jo smiled. "It's not so far away. Only a short boat ride from Seattle. But I'm glad to be going, Dovey, even if I'll be rather isolated there." Not entirely isolated—not with Bill close at hand. But Jo couldn't quite bring herself to speak of that. Not yet. "I've had such a hunger to teach again, ever since I met Mr. Mercer back in Lowell. It's time I took it up once more—my true life's calling."

"I'll come and visit you, then. I'm awfully excited for you, Jo. It sounds perfectly grand—living on an island, just like a character in a novel!"

In the face of her friend's innocent enthusiasm, Josephine's face heated with shame. "Don't be so sure it's perfectly grand." She hesitated again, then finally pushed out the words she'd been dreading to say in one frantic rush. "I'm going there as a fallen woman. I'm taking up with my beau as his companion. But we aren't to be married."

Dovey whistled, long and low. "You have a sweetheart, Jo? I never knew!"

"No one knows about Bill. You're the first I've told, and the only one I shall ever tell. And you'll keep the secret, won't you, Dovey?"

"It won't be the first secret I've kept for you."

"He's a good man, gentle and kind, and patient enough that he won't pressure me to marry. I'll keep trying to get Clifford to grant the divorce, but he hasn't responded to one of my letters so far. It makes me nervous, writing him. He knows I'm in Seattle now, you see, and I'm always afraid he'll reappear, just like he did in San Francisco."

"All the more reason to leave the city," Dovey said briskly.

"That was my line of thinking, too. And I love Bill—I do! I never thought I'd be able to say that about a man. I never thought to find one who would treat me sweetly, and never raise his hand in anger. But I'm married, Dovey—*married*! It's a terrible thing, what I've decided to do. The Lord may never forgive me for it. I know for a certainty the people of Seattle never would."

"I can see why you don't want the upright types to know," Dovey said. "The folks of Sophronia's style. But *I'm* happy for you, Jo, fallen woman or no. I can see your joy shining out of your eyes when you talk about this fellow of yours. *And* about teaching, getting a school of your own! As far as I'm concerned, there's no shame in joy. I don't care how you come by it, as long as the joy is real."

Jo pulled Dovey into an impulsive hug, pressing her face into the girl's thick brown curls. "I am happy. I oughtn't to be, it's all so sinful, so *wrong*. But I am. Maybe that makes me wicked—rotten to the core."

"Only the likes of Sophronia would ever think you wicked."

Jo loosed her hold on Dovey and stepped back, eyeing the girl soberly. "Sophronia *is* our friend, even if she did ruffle your feathers. We won't speak ill of her, you and I."

"Maybe *you* won't speak ill of her," Dovey grumbled.

Jo fixed Dovey with her best schoolmarm stare, and Dovey threw up her hands in defeat. "All *right*. But promise me you'll set aside all these worries about sin, and be glad for the turn your life is taking. Maybe some folks will judge you harshly. They'll judge me, too. Neither of us is exactly doing our part—living up to what's expected of us."

"What's expected?"

"By Seattle," Dovey clarified. "By Mr. Mercer, who brought us here for such a high and proper purpose. By the whole damned world. But who *cares*, Jo? We're not sheep, to be herded where our shepherd pleases. We can plot our own courses through this world."

Dovey's boldness was so admirable, her confidence so grand, that Jo wanted to agree. More than anything she'd ever craved before, Jo wished for a share of Dovey's surety, her unconcern with judgment in the hereafter and the here and now. But in her heart, Jo knew she *did* care—very much—what Mr. Mercer would think of her, and Mary Terry with her sweet, welcoming smile; what Mrs. Garfield and her friends would think, what Sophronia would think. Sophronia most of all. Jo had made up her mind to defy the world's expectations—to flout utterly a woman's proper place. She knew she would face condemnation for that decision.

Guilt gnawed at Jo's gut until she felt hollow and cold inside. Despite Mr. Mercer's words of support when she'd met him in his office, she couldn't forget that Mercer had expected her to marry—to bring morals and civility to this untamed, half-formed town. He had certainly expected her to remain in Seattle if she did choose to teach—no matter what he'd said of following her joy and putting remorse aside.

The day after their arrival in Seattle, when she'd spoken up on Mercer's behalf, he had told Josephine how grateful he was that he'd brought her along after all.

He won't be pleased with me when he finds out exactly why I've gone to Whidbey Island—when word reaches him, as it must someday, that I'm living there in sin.

Guilt assailed her, too, when she thought of all the men in Seattle who lacked wives to make them settle and behave less like beasts. Absurd, that thought—she knew it was ridiculous. Even if she'd been free to marry, Jo could not possibly wed and civilize every unmarried man. But still, the weight of that responsibility pressed down on her heart.

Most of all, she felt a great, rushing, baring shame before God. He saw into her heart—He knew that even if she never touched Bill Jakes, still she was committing adultery. She was planning this very moment to forsake her marriage vows. She was a sinner. And no sinner could be entirely happy—could she?

"Mercer brought us here to marry," Jo said sadly. "And neither of us will. Sophronia's in such a fluster, I doubt she will, either. I suppose we're failures as Mercer girls. Maybe Mrs. Garfield and her fellow protesters were right about us. Maybe we are women destined for sin and disappointment."

Dovey snorted and tossed her head. "I'll never believe such codswallop. And for Mrs. Garfield, if she were here right now I'd spit on her hem, just like Sophie did. I'm going to have the life I want, Jo—the life I deserve—no matter what any man or woman thinks of me. I don't live to make others happy anymore. I left that Dovey behind in Lowell. *This* Dovey lives for herself. Call me selfish if you must—I call it being true to my own heart."

Tears welled in Jo's eyes; she hugged Dovey close, and then closer still, wishing her own heart might drink in some small measure of the girl's plucky courage.

She would need it. Tomorrow, Jo would tell Bill she had made up her mind. She would leave with him for Whidbey Island and start a new life—a life she would live for herself, and for no one else.

Dovey, Jo said silently, *will I be as brave as you are when I go? Or will this guilt I feel only grow, until it weighs me down and holds me here in this sinkhole of despair and doubt?*

She couldn't bring herself to ask the question aloud, and so she heard no answer. The only way to learn what the future held was to go on forward.

PART 3
JULY 1871–APRIL 1872

CHAPTER
TWENTY-SIX
THE NEW NORTHWEST

Josephine woke in a sweat. A peaceful slant of afternoon light fell through the curtains of her little house, filtering weak and green through the forest outside. She sat up on her bed, dabbing the sweat from her brow with the handkerchief she kept on her night table. She breathed deeply to calm herself, watching the lace curtains stir in the faint breeze. The air smelled of pine sap and last year's leaves, of hay from the Andersons' field and salmon smoking over alderwood, earthy and sweet, drifting to her secluded home from some great distance.

She was groggy from the lateness of her nap and from restlessness of her sleep. She had dreamed again of Clifford—of his hard eyes and harder hands. Even after all this time—seven years since she'd come to Seattle, since she'd seen him last, lying in the muck and shadows of that alley in San Francisco—Jo still feared him. She might deny it in the light of day, and even into the twilight. But when the dark of night drew up around her lonely little house in the pines, every twig that snapped in the forest and every stray rustle of the brush was Clifford coming to find her, Clifford stalking through the dark with the unfinished business of their marriage on his mind.

Jo tucked her handkerchief into the drawer of her bed stand. Her fingers brushed the old letter from Dovey—its envelope had yellowed around the edges, and she had read it so many times she didn't need to look at it again. But the terrible dream still haunted her, so she withdrew it and opened the envelope.

Found this in a paper sent up from San Francisco by one of my lady friends, Dovey had written. *Maybe he'll expire in the calaboose.*

The note was dated August 8, 1864—the same year they'd arrived in Seattle, and only weeks after Jo had moved to Whidbey Island to take up her new life as teacher—and mistress to Bill Jakes. Dovey had begun correspondence around that time with several women who ran high-class establishments in the California city, hoping to learn the ins and outs of the business for herself.

The note was folded around a newspaper clipping. Jo unfolded the scrap and read its words with her lips pressed tightly together.

JAILED! The miscreant from Massachusetts who stabbed two men in a drunken brawl at Jonesey's Saloon this May, killing one, has faced his due justice. Clifford Stokes of Lowell, Mass., will not face the noose, as Hon. Robert Greaves deemed the crime aggravated and almost sympathetic. Still, this violent presence who has plagued our streets since April will be locked away for seven years. All of San Francisco hopes his time behind bars will mellow Mr. Stokes and return him as a fit member of society.

Jo carefully refolded the clipping and slipped it back into the envelope, then pressed the heels of her hands against her eyes until white sparks danced behind her eyelids.

The clipping had once filled her with relief—with the certainty that she was safe from Clifford's vengeance. But the seven years of his sentence were nearly at an end. Once Clifford was on the loose again, would he return to the hunt, pursuing his old quarry with a redoubled hatred?

God keep me safe, she prayed. *Remove Clifford's old rage from his heart, and change him for the better. Let him forget me—let him leave me in peace.*

That was the best she could hope for.

Jo stood, listening to the whisper of the wind through the pines, the singing of the birds, and the repetitive, midsummer churring of insects in the grass. The familiar sounds of home soothed away her anxieties. She had a new life now, she told herself stoutly—the career as a teacher she had always dreamed of. Her little island school was a success; she had earned the respect of her students and the community, and also earned a tidy salary that kept her roof up and her belly full. True, she had no children of her own—she had never conceived in her marriage with Clifford, and now she supposed she must be barren. But her duties as a teacher gave her all the pleasures of motherhood without any of its pains. She had autonomy, self-sufficiency, and even, still—after so many years—the love and loyalty of Bill Jakes, the gentlest and most worthy man she had ever known.

If God meant to visit some punishment upon me, he'd have done it by now. Why, then, did she still fear Clifford? Perhaps a person never could leave the past behind, no matter how far or how long she ran.

Jo washed the pink traces of sleep from her face in the little china basin that stood beside her window. She passed an embroidered towel over her dripping forehead and chin, then paused, gazing at her face in the mirror, counting the lines that traced across her forehead and bunched at the corners of her eyes. She was forty-two years old now—forty-two, and an old maid.

At least, she was a maid as far as Whidbey Island knew. No one on the island had learned of her marriage to Clifford—the lie she lived, the shame she still sometimes felt biting deep into her conscience. Even after she knew him to be safely in jail, not a single attempt she had made to reach Clifford by letter, to negotiate her own freedom, had yielded fruit. In the eyes of the law—and more troubling, in the eyes of God—she was still Clifford's wife. She couldn't decide whether the lines her face had collected were scribed by worry—a tally of every cringe of shame she'd made since her deceptions began—or laugh lines, commemorating the joy she took in her new life, the simple, quiet pleasure she found at Bill's side.

She found pleasure not only at his side, but also in his bed. The island may have believed their schoolmarm a trustworthy spinster, but outside the realm of the schoolyard, in the privacy of her house with its merciful screen of pines, Jo allowed herself a full range of delights. Such was the domain of a married woman, after all. True, she was married to another man—not the gentleman she tumbled with. Her moments of guilt over that fact still loomed large on occasion, but they had dwindled over time, and their sporadic appearances did not seem quite so momentous anymore.

Jo hastened to the little potbellied stove in the corner of her one-room house. She laid the kindling on and lit the fire; as soon as it was reliably blazing she ducked outdoors to the tiny, shingle-sided icehouse. She fetched a plucked chicken; it would make a lovely stew. If she started simmering it that very hour, it ought to be just about ready by the time Bill passed by.

Bill was due back that very evening from his trip to Oregon. He had gone to Portland often of late, securing supplies for his expanding business building homes in the hills and forests around Seattle. She hadn't seen her beau for more than a week; her heart leaped with anticipation at the thought of his smile, his fond jokes—and his kisses. She glanced at the wall clock in its round, mahogany case—a gift from Bill. The boat from Seattle would arrive at the Coupeville wharf in less than an hour.

It never took Bill long to stroll from the landing to Josephine's house. And of course he paid a call to Jo first thing whenever he returned from his frequent treks to Oregon.

Jo busied herself with the stew until finally the clock chimed the hour. Then she made herself as neat as she could, pulling her most effortlessly pretty calico dress from her simple pine armoire and freshening her hair inside its netted snood. At last, just as she fastened the clasp of the pearl-bead necklace Bill had given her for her birthday, she heard his familiar whistle as he came down the lane through the pines.

Jo restrained herself from running to the door like a schoolgirl. She leaned against the jamb, watching with a thrill of joy as he passed through a deep, low slant of dark-golden light that angled down through the trees, the insects and dust motes drifting about his lanky body. She loved to watch him walking down that lane. The sight of him in an easy stroll, the sound of his carefree whistle, was more a home to her than her little house with its sturdy bed and neat, sensible room. There, in Bill's face and form, was all the warmth and comfort of a proper, happy life.

When Bill reached the clearing that served as her yard, Jo gave her customary glance around the forest. Even after seven years, caution was a necessity, although the nearest neighbors were a quarter of a mile away. Still, Jo had lived for so long with her wariness and care—always fearful that her affection for Bill would be noted. She didn't know what might happen if her thoroughly unacceptable situation was found out. The sensible side of her mind told her that half the town of Coupeville had pieced together the mystery already, but in her less rational moments she feared a spectacular downfall, her school and career wrenched away, and an ignominious end in the dockside cribs of Seattle. For the sake of her career, Jo maintained the disguise of a prim old maid most studiously. Bill had long since grown used to her peculiar shyness about shows of affection, and chalked it up, Jo knew, to a woman's proper modesty and skittishness about all things indelicate. If Bill suspected the clandestine existence of a husband, he never spoke of it.

Bill sniffed the air as he sauntered across the clearing. "Smells good."

"Just one of the Andersons' old hens I'm stewing up. She wouldn't lay anymore, so they sold her to me cheaply. Their biggest boy even dispatched her for me so I wouldn't have to. I can't stand to see chickens twitch and flutter after their heads are offed. It gives me the cold creeps."

He kissed her, long and sweetly, with his hand firm and warm in the middle of her back. Then he pulled back with a little chuckle. "Here's something else to give you a thrill." He removed a newspaper from where it was tucked beneath his arm. "There were two ladies visiting Portland who'd set the whole territory to flapping their jaws. Made quite a stir. The tales that were told about them—"

"Low women?" Jo asked warily. Whenever she contemplated fallen women, she got a sick little knot in her middle, a queasy reminder that she was to be counted among their ranks.

"I wouldn't call them low," Bill said. "Though some thought them the most debased—the most scandalous daughters of Eve to be found anywhere, since Eden was shuttered. Funny enough, most who objected to these ladies were women themselves. You can read all about it. I thought their story might bring a twinkle to your eye, at least."

Jo examined the paper in the afternoon sunlight. A fancy, Gothic script was scrawled across the upper edge: THE NEW NORTHWEST—and below, the newspaper's adage: FREE SPEECH, FREE PRESS, FREE PEOPLE.

Jo scanned its several columns quickly.

WOMEN, THE CIRCUS, AND THE PAPERS

The daily press was jubilant during the past week over the performances of ladies in M'lle Jeal & Co's Circus. We were treated to graphic accounts

of equestrianism, acrobatic skill and "postur-
ing"—though we haven't the least idea what that
last is. Not one word have the papers said about
these "strong-minded women" being out of their
"sphere." They have sent forth no wail about
neglected husbands and suffering children and
deserted firesides. They have not complained that
those women are not "clinging vines"; they have
not likened them to "lost Pleiades"; neither has
their modesty received the slightest contusion. It
is only when woman arises in the conscientious
discharge of her duty to amend the loose morals of
society, and arouse the public to a higher sense of
woman's moral and legal responsibility, that men
are seized with spasmodic modesty.

She searched another column, frowning in concentration, mystified
but wholly intrigued.

PROSTITUTION AND PROFIT

A sad case was lately tried in the United States
District Court for Oregon, before his Honor, Judge
Deady. Nicholas Gregovich had obtained a divorce
last spring in San Francisco from his wife, and was
by the California courts awarded the custody of
his child, a little one aged five years. The mother
subsequently stole the child and removed to Portland, and the father, following, found her with the
child in a house of ill fame. The scene of separation

between the mother and child, as related by an eyewitness, was heartrending. Evidently, so long as times are so sadly out of joint under man-made rule that women can earn more money by one hour of prostitution than by a week or month, or even a year, of household drudgery under some lawful master, just so long will there be found frail "divinities" who cannot resist the golden temptation. When the weaker sex assert their power to make the laws that vitally concern their personal weal, these houses of ill fame, that flourish under the pay and patronage of men, will languish and die for want of support. Then we shall hear no more of women who desert their husbands for the emoluments of prostitution.

Jo shuddered to picture the scene—the weeping child, the mother screaming in her grief, the harsh light of a red lamp flashing over the father's shocked, angry face. She swallowed hard, and read another column:

OUR CHAMPIONS

Miss Anthony and Mrs. Stanton are making an immense sensation in San Francisco. We have just received a number of letters from San Francisco— too late for publication in this issue—in which the appearance and success of these eminent champions of the right are agreeably and graphically portrayed. The CALL and ALTA speak in glowing

terms of these ladies. We are impatient for the day
to come when we can announce the exact time of
their advent in Oregon. Ho, for progression!

"Who are they?" Jo wondered aloud.

Bill peeked over her shoulder and noted the direction of her gaze.
"Miss Anthony and Mrs. Stanton? The suffragists, of course. You must
have heard of them before now, darling. Every paper in the territory
has something to say about the suffragists—little of what they say is
good, I'm afraid."

Jo shrugged. "I suppose I have heard the names, now that I think
on it, but I've paid so little attention to the papers of late. I've been
wrapped up in my students' ABCs and haven't looked very far beyond
their slates."

"Well, as it happens, they're the very ladies who made such a stir in
Portland. At least, Miss Anthony did, and her friend, Mrs. Duniway.
You would like Mrs. Duniway, Jo. I had the privilege of hearing her
speak, and she is a firecracker if ever I saw one. A teacher like you—or
she was, until she founded the very paper you're holding."

"A woman running a newspaper?"

"There are all sorts of wonders in Oregon these days. The hul-
labaloo Miss Anthony raised when she finally made her anticipated
appearance was not the least." Bill's stomach gave a tremendous rumble.
"I rounded up as many issues of the *New Northwest* as I could lay my
hands on. I knew you'd be keen on their stories. I've got them here in
my bag; I'll trade you for a bowl of that stew."

All through the following day, as Jo held sway at the head of
her cozy schoolroom, she found her thoughts returning to the *New
Northwest*. Her spine tingled over the details of its stories of outrage and
injustice, and its brazen, fearless tone sent waves of inspiration cours-
ing through her mind. She mused almost constantly on the subjects of
Susan B. Anthony and Abigail Duniway, the audacious lady editor of

the *New Northwest*. She imagined every aspect of their persons, from their voices—certainly mellifluous—to the countenance of each lady. *They must be splendid and bold*, Jo decided, *shining in the finest silks, tall and strong and yet so flawlessly feminine*. By the end of the school day, the famed suffragists had taken the shape of goddesses in her mind, beings of stunning power who could reach out and shape the world to their whims.

She dismissed the children and stood for a moment on the schoolhouse steps, watching them bound like yearling deer down the lane. Then she locked the door and headed for her isolated house, itching all the while to put her hands on the stacks of paper Bill had left behind—all those fascinating issues of the *New Northwest*, laced with the tales of the suffragists and ringing with the battle cries of women.

The vote, she thought, awed and dazed, considering the subject with the same superstitious caution with which one examines fate or the will of God. Did she dare even to ponder it—what suffrage would mean to her personally? The vista of possibilities opened so wide before her that she stepped back giddily from its precipitous edge. *Don't be a fool*, she told herself. *The day might never come when you will obtain your own divorce. It's too much to wish for; you'll be disappointed*. Yet a voice deep inside her heart said that it was certainly not too much to wish for: that the particular freedom she craved, and a hundred others she had not yet thought to desire, would be hers for the asking—hers to demand—if she could only secure that ephemeral power.

Day after day, when Jo's work was through, she opened the *New Northwest* to reread its many passages, just as she had once done with the *New York Times*, in the days when she had pored over every word of Asa Mercer's rebuttal to his accusers. The accounts of the suffragists—not only in Oregon, but in San Francisco, and elsewhere, too, in the great cities of the eastern states—took on the sheen of gold, and Jo read every column of every issue like a beggar counting up some unbelievable windfall of coins.

Jo read the papers so many times that when she found a small notice in the most recent issue, corralled in a fancy, scrollwork box, she sat still for several moments, blinking in surprise and holding her breath. How was it possible that she had missed this notice on all her previous perusals?

PROGRESS MARCHES NORTH

Our fair editor, Mrs. Duniway, will accompany
OUR CHAMPION, Miss Anthony, to Washington
Territory this September, there to impress upon
the lawmaking men of the region the vital importance of woman to the legal process and sphere.
"Clinging vines" will soon twine most avidly
around Olympia and Seattle. Let us hope the
"strong oaks" of Washington Territory can
withstand the invasion.

Jo leaned back in her cane chair. An air of both sobriety and excitement descended on her, all in the same moment. The seed of an idea was sprouting in her mind—no, not an idea; an obsession. She knew she ought to resist the pull of the *New Northwest*, ought to shrug off the compulsion it instilled in her to burst upon Seattle waving a banner of strength for her fellow women to follow. If she were sensible, she told herself, she would stay hidden away on this quiet island, where progress never marched, but where anonymity shielded her.

But she had heard the clarion of the *New Northwest*. Its courageous call had stirred in her a deep, imperative duty. The cause for which these bold, tireless women fought was a worthy one—and would benefit Jo all the faster, if she could aid its progress.

The cause would not only benefit her. She would work for the sake of her female students, too—the girls in pigtails who bent over their slates, for whom the world was already fixing the rigid restrictions of their lives—for her students' mothers, who toiled at hot, never-changing hearths to keep their children whole and fed. She would work for all women who wished to be free—*freedom*, that desperate need, the grace and mercy Clifford never would grant to Jo of his own accord.

Once she held the power of the vote, Jo could seize freedom for herself. She knew her hands were strong enough to claim that golden prize, to clutch it tight once it was within her grasp, and never let it go.

Jo laid aside the *New Northwest* and went out into her yard. Through the swaying pines, south of the island, she could just make out the blue expanse of the Puget Sound, and the tiny brightness of ships moving on the water. All of them came and went from the port of Seattle.

Clifford followed me to San Francisco, Jo reminded herself, succumbing to a shiver. *He knew I was involved with the Mercer party. He isn't so dull that he can't piece the rest together. He knows to search for me in Seattle. He may be there already, hunting me, waiting for his chance to spring like a predator—as patient as a cougar in the crags.*

That hunter in the shadows was a risk Jo had to hazard if she was to claim her freedom—her fate.

She dusted her hands together, as if clearing away the last crumbs of her doubt. Jo took one last, lingering glance toward Seattle. Then she went back inside to pack her bags.

CHAPTER
TWENTY-SEVEN
STRONG CONVICTIONS

Sophronia hesitated only a moment as she rounded the corner of James and Second. She could already hear the clamor of the prostitutes gathered on the brightly painted porch of the brand-new cathouse a block away. Their high, harsh voices lifted into the noonday sky like a flock of crows taking to raucous flight. Were they calling to their customers, Sophronia wondered, or did they shout and carry on merely for the pleasure of hearing their own vexatious voices?

Fallen women, Sophronia mused darkly as she pressed on toward the cathouse. *Shakes—Jezebels.* They were the commonest creatures in all of Seattle, except for the men who prowled around their cribs and fancy houses.

Sophronia had dedicated the past seven years of her life to reforming the "seamstresses," as the whores liked to call themselves with a wink and an indecent chuckle. The women knew nothing of needle and thread, but they knew the way out of their dresses well, though. Those years had been one long trial, an uphill task of Sisyphean proportions. As Seattle grew, attracting ever more men to work the forested hills, the lumberyards and sawmills, the population of seamstresses expanded at an alarming rate. Sophronia, having no husband or children to whom she might devote her time and energies, had thrown herself into the Women's League and dedicated her every waking hour to the reform of the fallen, the salvation of their souls.

If one were to look only at the cathouses that had emerged like bright, poisonous toadstools all across the city, one might think Sophronia had gotten nowhere at all in those seven years of labor. But in fact she counted a few successes with justifiable pride. She had managed to open a reformatory of sorts, a home for fallen women who wished to leave their sinful occupations behind and take up, with time and education, as ladies worthy of respect. On occasion, Sophronia felt the dozen or so women she had guided out of sin were but a drop in the bucket of Seattle's reckless hedonism. But one woman reformed was one fewer walking the streets, one fewer haunting the cribs—and one woman who would no longer aspire to severing the bonds of love between two good, respectable individuals.

If only that detestable Haypenny would turn up at Sophronia's home for fallen women! She would show *that* beastly sop the meaning of reform.

Sophronia drew nearer the bawdy house. A few of its women lounged against the porch rails, calling to passing men, though the hour was still far too early for most regular customers. The choking odor of the women's cigarettes hung thickly in the humid air. Sophronia tried to wave the cloud of smoke away discreetly, but even that slight motion caught the prostitutes' attention, like cats twitching after insects in the grass.

"Here comes Sophie, prancing down the street on her high horse," one of the women jeered.

Sophronia studiously ignored the jibe.

"Your hem looks long," another girl called. "Have you come for . . . *alterations?*" She stuck her cigarette between her lips, grabbed her own backside with both hands, and swiveled in a suggestive manner. Sophronia's mouth tightened with distaste. "I'm the best seamstress in the whole town, and my rate's half for pretty women!"

The other girls roared with laughter.

If Sophronia had learned one thing from her past seven years of labor, it was this: one should never rise to a prostitute's taunts. She glided by, head up, and did not acknowledge their mockery.

Then one of the prostitutes cried, "Miss Priss! Look sharp!"

Something bright and flashing spun in the air, hanging in a high arc above the porch before it plunged down toward Sophronia. By instinct, she reached up her hands to catch the object before it could strike her on the shoulder. It was a silver dollar. Sophronia looked up at the women uneasily.

"A donation for the Women's League," said the girl who'd tossed the coin.

The others snickered, and one of them, wide-eyed, hid her mouth behind her hand. But Sophronia nodded a gracious thanks and placed the coin in her collection purse, then hurried away. As she departed, she heard the women's laughter swell. There was a sharp note of nastiness in the sound that made Sophronia uneasy, but she could only ponder helplessly over the event. Why would a fallen woman donate to the League? The seamstresses always opposed any efforts to moralize them—most strenuously.

Sophronia turned at the corner and headed up Front Street, toward the neighborhood on the hill, which she was slated to canvass this morning. It was one of the finer collections of homes in the city, and the wives who kept house there were usually pleased to donate to the League's cause. Sophronia allowed her thoughts to unfold pleasantly into the near future, leaving the jeers of the prostitutes and the mystery of the silver dollar behind. Still unwed at twenty-seven, Sophronia might be an old maid, but her good works with the Women's League had admitted her at last into Seattle's high society. Once the outcast, one of Mercer's scandalous cargo, she was now an upstanding member of the better class—by dint of her popularity with the city's wives, if not by virtue of actual wealth. She enjoyed making her collection rounds, sipping tea with fine ladies, engaging in genteel discussion of all the city's news.

She had only two more blocks to go before she reached the first house on her list. But as she passed the dry goods store, a familiar face seemed to leap at her from the small crowd gathered around the shop's display window. The jolt of recognition shook Sophronia out of her reverie of pleasant anticipation. She stopped dead on the sidewalk.

"Josephine Carey?"

Sophronia had exchanged many letters with Jo since the older woman had departed Seattle for the island town of Coupeville, but she had not set eyes on her friend for many years. Jo's face had grown sterner over time, and like any experienced schoolmarm, she exuded a definite lack of tolerance for nonsense. But there was something more in Jo's mannerisms that made Sophronia eye her with cautious appraisal—a hint of anxiety that glittered in her eyes and laced her movements with a tight, jerky energy. Yet despite the fact that they had been so long apart, Jo gazed at Sophronia with a familiar warmth that brought smiles to both their faces.

"Oh—Sophronia!" Jo clasped both Sophronia's hands in her own. "I'm so pleased to see you. I'd hoped I would bump into you today. It seems luck is on my side, for once."

"What brings you to Seattle, Jo? Are you back for good?"

"No—no, I could never leave my little school. I love it too much. But I've come for . . . oh, it's a long story. It's past dinnertime; have you eaten yet?"

Sophronia had not. She found it prudent to go canvassing for donations on an empty stomach, as the women she visited often plied her liberally with cookies and slices of pie.

"Come on, then," Jo said, taking Sophronia by the arm. "I passed a little coffee shop just up the street. Let's have something to eat, and I'll explain everything."

They dined on elegant sandwiches, washed down with very fine tea, and Jo shared a most fantastical tale. She spoke of an Oregon paper called the *New Northwest*, and the many articles she had read in its columns. Jo was so enthusiastic about the stories that she leaned over their café table like a tree about to fall, but Sophronia found the snappish tone and bold proclamations of the articles rather shocking.

"I've heard of these suffragists," Sophronia said. "We've discussed their agenda often at meetings of the Women's League."

"Aren't they grand?"

"No, Josephine!" Sophronia set her teacup down with a rattling clank. "I think they're terribly scandalous. Encouraging women to abandon their families and homes—a woman's true and only calling in life!"

"They're not as bad as *that*, Sophronia. Why, Abigail Duniway herself is a devoted mother to six children. I think the suffragists are intriguing."

"In the way a rumor is intriguing, perhaps."

"*We* were rumors once—we Mercer girls." Jo sipped her tea with raised brows and a triumphant flush. She had a decided air of having caught Sophronia in a very clever trap.

"That doesn't mean I wish to become a source of scandal again. You still haven't told me what these suffragists have to do with your visit to Seattle."

"I've learned that they're coming to Washington Territory," Jo said, tipping forward again in her eagerness. "Susan B. Anthony and Abigail Duniway, I mean. They're to go to Olympia this fall and speak to the legislature on behalf of all the women in the Territory."

"Speak to the legislature! That's disgraceful. A woman has no place in a lawmaking venue."

Jo tilted her head and smiled. Sophronia couldn't decide whether the expression was affectionate or chiding.

"I want to hear Anthony and Duniway speak," Jo said. "I'm sure they'll give some sort of public address in Olympia. I came into town today so that I could find out more—learn whether anybody in Seattle is planning to visit Olympia and see the suffragists speak."

"I wouldn't count on it," Sophronia said. "What female creature in this city would care for such an excursion? There are only two types of women in Seattle, Jo: respectable wives and mothers—and the *seamstresses*. The latter are too busy sinning to care for the likes of Susan Anthony and Abby Duniway. And the former are too sensible and refined to go chasing after something as silly and useless as a woman's vote."

Jo chuckled, as if Sophronia had just made some jolly joke. "Come with me to Olympia this fall," she said, tapping Sophronia chummily on the back of her hand. "Come along and hear Miss Anthony speak. I know you'll like what she has to say, Sophronia."

"I most certainly will *not* hear that woman speak. The vote is nothing for women to meddle with. If the Lord had wanted the fairer sex tangled up in politics, he would have made *us* the heads of our households, rather than men. I have no desire to go against the Lord's will. And you shouldn't, either, Josephine.

"Besides, I've read some of the articles and letters these suffragists write. They're pushing for women to *work*, Jo—to earn their own keep."

"We work already. I teach; you edit the Women's League circulars and give piano lessons to the children of Seattle. You know there's no sin in a woman working."

"No sin in that sort of work. But you know the type of work I mean. Think, Jo—what other task is a woman fit for, unless it's work inside the home? She can't toil in the sawmill or load ships at the docks. She can't keep a shop—not all day long; her constitution is too delicate."

"I think you sell short the constitutions of a good many women," Jo muttered.

"Outside of the nurturing fields—teaching, nursing—you'll find women engaged in only one other professional activity."

"Selling her flesh?" Jo said frankly.

Sophronia blushed. "That's the sort of world these suffragists are seeking to create, Jo! A place where women may run free and engage in any sin their hearts desire. One need only look around the streets of Seattle to see where that particular freedom leads."

Jo gave that unreadable smile again, and then pushed back her chair. "I see I can't convince you," she said lightly. "You've always been a woman of strong convictions, Sophronia." She clasped Sophronia's hand in farewell. "It was good to see you again. God willing, we'll meet again soon."

Josephine left the café and drifted off, lost in a moment among the city's noise and bustle. A curious, hollow sensation settled in Sophronia's middle as she gazed at the empty chair where Jo had so recently sat. Was it only her long years as a spinster that made Sophronia feel so empty and disheartened? Or was it the confident enthusiasm sparkling in Josephine's manner—the gumption that seemed to fire her up, lighting her from within to make her glow in a way Sophronia had never known her to glow before?

Sophronia, musing and discouraged, reached for the last cookie on Jo's abandoned plate. She noticed something small and pale peeking out from beneath the dish—a folded scrap of paper. Jo must have placed it there, sometime during their conversation. Sophronia hadn't seen her do it.

She picked it up the paper and examined it curiously.

It was a clipping torn carefully from a newspaper. Sophronia popped the cookie into her mouth and chewed slowly as she read.

The clipping recounted a sad tale—a child abducted by a desperate mother, then pulled from the very jaws of Gomorrah when his father found the woman working in a bawdy house with the child in tow. Sophronia was inclined to judge the woman a poor specimen of motherhood, but the lines that followed the story gave her pause.

> When the weaker sex assert their power to make
> the laws that vitally concern their personal weal,
> these houses of ill fame, that flourish under the
> pay and patronage of men, will languish and die
> for want of support.

Sophronia left the cookie's crumbs clinging to her lip. *Can it be true? Can this be the stance of the suffragists?* Guided by the longer experience and—she assumed—the *wisdom* of the elder members of the Women's League, Sophronia had listened attentively to their opinions on the suffragists. But she had never, until now, taken it upon herself to read the letters of the women who rallied for legal clout.

My friends in the League wouldn't steer me wrong, Sophronia told herself. *They* know *the suffragists to be supporters of hedonism.* Indeed, a swift erosion of morals was the only logical outcome of women voting, women working, women doing away with the walls of propriety that protected the world from sin.

But the words in the clipping tugged at Sophronia's conscience. *These houses of ill fame, that flourish under the pay and patronage of men . . .*

Perhaps, after all, the suffragists' ideals were not so far from alignment with Sophronia's own.

Don't listen to the banter of suffragists, she told herself firmly. *They are nearly as sinful as prostitutes—chipping away at the institutions of motherhood and wifery.*

But Sophronia was neither mother nor wife, and she could not fault her own morals. Perhaps society allowed for broader definitions of femininity than the Women's League deemed proper.

Act in wisdom, she counseled herself, *and at all times display womanly modesty.* That was ever a sound policy. It might—perhaps—be safe to inquire further into the writings of these suffragist champions whom Josephine so adored. But Sophronia most certainly would not watch them climb upon a soapbox and hear their immodest speeches.

Satisfied with her own resolve, she paid her share of the luncheon bill and left the café. But as she stepped out into the street, she tucked the newspaper clipping into her glove. It nestled against her palm, safely hidden from the eyes of all the women she would canvass. But Sophronia could feel its papery whisper against her skin, and all afternoon, as she sipped her tea and joined in the gossip of the League's supporters, she heard the words of the suffragists speaking in her soul.

CHAPTER TWENTY-EIGHT
A NEW MAN IN TOWN

Dovey slid from the saddle, her sharp-toed boots hitting the ground with a smart thump that raised a puff of dust from the corral. She patted Blue's flank as the old gelding slurped noisily at the water trough, then reached between his empty saddlebag and his sweaty flank to untie the secret knot that held her collection purse out of sight. The heavy oilcloth purse fell with a clank of coins into her hand. She tossed it, considering its weight with no small amount of pride. A very good haul: Virgil would be pleased.

The thought brought a quick, hot flush to her cheeks. After seven years, she was still as stupid as ever over Virgil's smile and his low, velvety voice—his way of walking; his slow-blinking, half-crooked smile. She was stupider still over the things he did to her between the bedsheets. Dovey still remained unmarried, officially unattached to any man. But Virgil was just as officially unattached—and therefore free for Dovey's love—and that was some comfort. If the man simply had no desire to tie himself down to a wife, Dovey couldn't blame him for that. Marriages were nothing but trouble, especially from a woman's perspective—and yet if Virgil had ever asked her to be his wife, she'd have said yes in the beat of a bug's wings.

But the situation being what it was, Dovey never bothered to lose any sleep over her unwedded state. Unlike the other high-minded women of Seattle, she didn't define herself by marriage.

Of course, she mused as she pulled cockleburs from Blue's tail, none of the other women of Seattle would call Dovey high-minded—but she knew the truth. It *was* high-minded to have ambitions of one's own, regardless of one's sex. It was high-minded to work for one's bread. Dovey saw no reason why women couldn't or shouldn't toil and earn, just like any able-bodied man. Work brought her satisfaction—a sense of deep fulfillment she knew she'd never find anywhere else, especially not bent over a stove or with a baby dragging on her bosom.

At the end of a long day of collecting, Dovey would bathe, washing the saddle ache from her body, and settle into her cozy bed in the spare room of the Harris house. Where she had once stayed as a guest, she now dwelt as a tenant, proudly paying her hard-earned rent to Mrs. Harris every week. The Harrises were happy for the extra income; they needed it now, with three children in the house. Dovey was content to keep to her rented room and leave the children to their mother. She saw plenty of what Mrs. Harris went through, wrangling three little ones, and Dovey couldn't imagine herself into that role, no matter how many times she tried. The working life was perfection, as far as Dovey was concerned. She simply couldn't have been any happier with the tax-collecting circuit.

And she certainly couldn't have been any happier with her savings. It had taken seven years, but Dovey had amassed a comfortable stash of bank notes and coins, all hidden in boxes and cushions in her rented room. She bounced the day's collection on her palm again, mentally figuring her cut.

I've almost met my goal, she realized with a thrill. Soon she would have enough squirreled away to lease one of the big houses down by Skid Road and decorate it in the style of a really appealing, high-class brothel. The girls on the docks would be eager to come and work for her, once she opened for business. She had the trust of the seamstresses and intended to offer excellent terms to her girls. Her dream was so close she could almost reach out and touch the red velvet, could almost smell the clouds of cigarette smoke and fancy perfume.

Dovey pulled Blue's saddle off his back and slung it over the fence's topmost rail. As she wiped down his sweaty back, the gelding turned his head to nip gently at her behind.

"You awful flirt," she said, swatting his big, soft muzzle. "Not you, too."

Dovey was twenty-three now and had grown out of the innocent-girl charm that so put her clients off their guard. But even now, as a confident woman with a strut in her step, she still possessed the dark curls and beguiling dimples that endeared her to men. Many of her clients supposed they could keep all their coin in their pockets if they only flirted hard enough with the collector.

But Dovey still possessed the Colt, too. She had spent so many Saturday afternoons shooting at tin cans that she was as crack with her pistol as any exhibition shooter. She could wield the heavy gun with ease now, too; her arms had grown strong and capable, and her eye steely and unforgiving.

Dovey's reputation had spread—tales of the tax-collecting vixen with an angelic face and a nasty surprise hidden in a holster beneath her petticoat preceded her, and she seldom had occasion to draw the Colt anymore. But she was glad of its presence all the same. Seattle seemed to have grown rougher around its edges as the years passed—or perhaps Dovey had simply grown wiser, more cautious. At any rate, she was all too familiar with the dangerous types who populated the city, who made up its tangled network of businessmen and scoundrels. It seemed every man had his fellow's back, especially among the hard-driving, enterprising, still-unmarried crowd—and few of those men would balk at using violence to defend their interests and keep more dollars in their coffers.

She pulled up her skirt and petticoat, unstrapped the holster from her thigh, and laid the gun on the smooth-worn cedar stump that stood beside the trough. Then she found a cigarette and a match in her saddle-bag. Dovey struck the match alight on the stump. The first long, savory inhalation rasped in her throat, but when the drag hit her blood, smoke seemed to fill her veins with a thick, soothing peace. Her tension and aches eased.

If the Women's League could see me now, she thought mischievously. The League viewed Dovey Mason as Threat to Morality Number Two, right in line behind the seamstresses who plied their questionable trade in the cribs and cathouses near Skid Road. Dovey was often seen riding through the streets of Seattle, spread legged and trouser clad, fit to stop the hearts of every proper lady in the Territory. Dovey never smoked while she was on the job—she never could say when she'd be forced to draw her Colt, and she always kept her right hand empty. Therefore, she had no idea whether the Women's League was aware of her objectionable smoking habit. *Once they find out, they're sure to promote me to the greatest menace to morality in all of Seattle.*

Virgil stepped out onto the back porch, carrying a wide leather-bound ledger under one arm. He gave the air an exaggerated sniff. "Does my nose detect the cutest little tax hustler in Washington Territory?" When he found Dovey puffing away beside the trough, his slow smile sent a delicious thrill up her back. "Where there's smoke, there's fire."

He dropped the ledger on the chunk of cedarwood that served for a porch table and sank into a ladder-back chair, fishing in the breast pocket of his flannel shirt for a cigarette of his own. Dovey sauntered toward the porch, swinging the oilcloth purse in one hand. Her eyes never left Virgil's face. Even after seven years of tax collecting—and of lying in his arms whenever the opportunity presented itself—she was wild about him, entranced by his weathered good looks and his cocky, devil-may-care demeanor. Years of riding the tax circuit in all kinds of weather—and of fretting over his ledgers—had deepened the lines around his eyes, and his sharp goatee was now bisected with a streak of early gray hairs. Those features only made him all the more fascinating, in Dovey's estimation. *He's like saltwater taffy for the eyes,* she thought, dragging on her cigarette. *And for the rest of a body, too.* Sweet, satisfying, and addictive.

She took the second ladder-back chair, on the other side of the makeshift table, and set her collection purse on the cedar stump with a smirk of satisfaction. "That's the last of it—for this month, anyway. We're all caught up on the quota, and we still have a few days left in September."

"You are the hardest-working little cuss I ever did see." Virgil shook his head in wonder and scooped the purse into his lap. "But I'm afraid we've got a new man on the rolls now, so we can't close out the month yet."

"Bother," Dovey said. "I was looking forward to taking a few days off."

"It's just one new fella. Shouldn't be too hard to manage. He just got into town a few weeks ago, but he's already setting up a sawmill of his own, well south of Yesler's."

"Seems like a fool's errand to try to compete with Yesler's sawmill. That big, hulking thing practically runs the whole town. Just think of all the men who depend on Yesler's mill for work, in one way or another—and all the boards and shingles it produces for export. I'd estimate that Yesler's money is in nearly every pocket in Seattle."

"You'd be right about that," Virgil said, exhaling smoke. "But a few other mills have managed to survive in Yesler's shadow. There are an awful lot of trees to go around, and Yesler can't saw 'em all himself, no matter how hard he tries.

"And it seems this new fella is no stranger to running mills. Ran one back on the East Coast, before he ventured out here."

"A sawmill?"

"Nope. Seems it was a cotton mill. But the idea's the same, isn't it? Turning raw material into exportable goods. And if it's exportable, it's taxable."

"He can't be exporting already. It takes time to set up a mill. There's no money for me to collect yet, is there?"

"I'd imagine not. But you ought to stop by and see him, I reckon. Make an impression, so he knows the Revenue Service has its eye on him. You know how these East Coast types are—think they can cheat the system, think we're all backwoods fools who don't know right from left or a dollar from a penny."

Dovey picked up the ledger and flipped its grid-lined pages to the most recent entry. "All right, I'll see the man, and smile at him and bat my eyes. But after that, I'm taking a few days off. I want to—"

The words froze on her tongue. She stared disbelieving at the entry in the ledger—at the impossible, the unfathomable, written in Virgil's neat, careful hand.

John Mason—Lowell, Mass.——prev. textile mill, to set up saw business south of Skid Road

"Is something wrong, Dove?" Virgil tapped the ash from his cigarette. "You look like you just swallowed a bug."

"My God, Virgil. This is my father."

He narrowed his eyes; one side of his mouth curved up uncertainly. "Stop joking."

"I'm not joking. John Mason from Lowell, former owner of a cotton mill—it's him! Land sakes, Virgil, I haven't seen my father in seven years. I haven't even written to him!" She slammed the ledger closed with a hollow thump. "What in blazes made him come all the way out here to Seattle?"

"I take it you and your pa didn't have a very gracious parting," Virgil drawled, halfway amused.

"You can say that again. And it's not funny. Of all the people who've thought they could control my life to suit their own whims, he was the very worst."

"Well, I'll pay him a visit if you like," Virgil offered. "You can stay well clear of him, and leave this client to me."

Dovey sucked on her cigarette, long and deep, but the smoke did nothing to soothe the new rash of jitters that jangled her nerves. She was on the point of accepting Virgil's proposal—she recalled with a pang of fear the lock clicking in her bedroom door and her father's calm insistence that an arranged marriage would be for her own good, and in that moment she wanted nothing more than to stay as far from John Mason as circumstances would allow.

But she sighed and then crushed out her cigarette on the cedar stump. "No, I'll go. I'm not afraid of him, Virgil. I'm not a girl any-more—he can't control me as he once did. I'll go, and I'll tell him face-to-face that I'm beyond his reach now."

As she reopened the ledger to memorize John Mason's new address, she prayed desperately that her words were more than just brave talk. *Please, God, let it all be true.*

CHAPTER
TWENTY-NINE
CAPITAL

Dovey ground-tied Blue outside a narrow, whitewashed boardinghouse on the northern edge of town. She hesitated for a moment, patting the roan's warm flank as he buried his muzzle in a thick patch of weeds to search for the choicest bits.

"This is it," she told Blue quietly, watching the boardinghouse's two stories of curtained windows with a suspicious squint. "I'd better get this dang business over and done with."

When she knocked on the door, the proprietress answered almost at once. She was a stout lady with a gray bun and eyes that shone with kindness behind the lenses of her spectacles.

"I've come to see John Mason," Dovey said.

"Is he expecting you, my dear? I make it clear to all my boarders that female visitors are not allowed on the premises."

The proprietress smiled warmly and gave no hint of disapproval, but Dovey felt the blood drain from her face. *Lord, she thinks I've come to do the unmentionable deed!*

Dovey shot a quick glance down at her dress. It was a drab blue-gray linen, unadorned with the usual frills and fripperies that the working girls favored, and Dovey certainly wore no eye paint or rouge. Perhaps any lone woman calling on a male boarder would be suspect, regardless of how plain or painted she looked. This was Seattle, after all, where entrepreneurial girls came to earn money by the fistful.

Dovey certainly felt no shame at being mistaken for a working girl—she of all Seattle women knew how hard the night flowers worked, and she admired them for their independence. But after all, John Mason was her own *father* . . . !

"I'm with the Revenue Service," she told the woman drily. "Here to set up Mr. Mason's accounts. I was told I could find him at this address."

"Oh, the Revenue Service," the proprietress said graciously. "Of course. You must be the girl I've heard tell of, who rides about and shoots!" She giggled, a sound like a tiny bell tinkling. "Do come in, dear. Do come in."

The silver-haired woman showed Dovey to the correct room, then drifted away again, still chuckling with delight over having Seattle's scandalous lady tax collector under her own roof. Dovey paused in the empty hall, shuffling her feet against the runner rug, staring at the handle of her father's door as if it were a serpent waiting to strike. Finally, though, she summoned the will to knock.

The door swung open, and Dovey's heart lurched at the sudden sight of her father. Seven years had changed him little. The fringe of hair around his bald crown had turned from deep brown to pale gray, and his neatly groomed mustache was sprinkled with white. But he still held himself with the tall, confident carriage of a man who knew his business well, and his eyes still shone with the keen, unflinching assessment Dovey remembered so well.

It took only a heartbeat for him to recognize his daughter. His eyes widened, and the doorknob rattled as his grip tightened in surprise. "Doreen!"

"Hello, Father. May I come in?"

Silently, with a slow, deliberate air that spoke of caution, he stepped back to allow Dovey admittance. The private room was small, and its window looked out on a pen full of brown mules, switching their tails in the last sunshine of autumn. But the accommodations seemed comfortable enough. The bed was tidily made. A simple maple-wood washstand held a drabware pitcher and bowl, and opposite, pressed against the room's far wall, was a small table and two chairs. Dovey pulled one away from the table and sat, gazing up at her father with an expression she hoped was calm and composed.

"I admit it's a surprise to me," her father said, joining her at the table, "to find you at my room's door. But after all, this is, in part, why I came to Seattle—to find you."

Dovey shook her head in confusion. "To find *me*?"

"It wasn't my sole motivation. The western frontier is growing fast. The newspapers back east are full of reports of these booming cities, flourishing and expanding as more gold is found in the mountains and rivers."

"But there's no gold in Seattle, Father." At least, none had yet been found, though God knew how many hopeful prospectors tried their luck every day in the hills above the town.

"Not here. Not yet, and maybe not ever. But in California—ah, gold has brought about a new age of prosperity! Lowell's glory days are long gone, but Seattle is well placed as a port, with plenty of resources for conversion and export to San Francisco. I believe Seattle is just as well placed to become the next center of our nation's prosperity. It's bursting with resources—"

"And no Confederate rebels can cut off the supply of trees, like they did the cotton."

"Exactly." He smiled, and Dovey's heart twinged with a funny little pang. She hadn't seen her father smile in so many years. Despite her worries about his presence and the bitterness of their parting, it was a sight for weary eyes.

"I've made a study of the sawmill business," Father went on. "Sawmills aren't terribly different from cotton mills, when one looks at the basics of the operation. I was able to scrape together just enough seed money that I can give it a good start—and in a few months, I hope to bring your mother out from Boston."

Dovey's heart pounded, and her throat constricted with a sudden, desperate longing. "Mother . . . It would be lovely to see her again."

"Here, I feel sure I can start anew—provide your mother with the kind of life she deserves. And you, Doreen."

Dovey leaned back warily in her chair. It gave a slow, protesting squeak. "What exactly do you mean by that, Father?"

"This journey to Seattle, to restart my life as a man of business, has filled me with new purpose." He rested one arm on the table, and for a moment Dovey saw him again as he once was—before the collapse of his cotton mills, when he had been the shining, untouchable Lord of Lowell, secure in his confidence and power. "Here, I can be the man I ought to be—a provider for my wife, the shepherd of my daughter."

"Now, wait a moment—"

He breezed on as if Dovey hadn't spoken. "Your mother has been so pleased to receive your letters, and has shared many of them with me. I'm glad you've kept yourself safe and occupied, Doreen, but this business you've written of—collecting taxes—it simply won't do."

She opened her mouth to protest, to launch some defense against his smooth, unassailable surety, but he held up a hand and continued. "I understand that you had little choice. I don't hold that against you. Your decision to run away from Lowell was rash, perhaps, but I can't hold *this* against you—this work you've entangled yourself in. A person must support himself somehow, after all, and at least you found honorable employment. I've noticed not many single women in this town have managed to do the same."

"How gracious of you," Dovey said flatly, "to not hold it against me."

"As you never wrote of a marriage, or even an engagement, your mother and I have concluded that you remain unwed. Is that so?"

Dovey folded her arms and frowned at him, unwilling to confirm what he'd already ferreted out regarding her private life. *Our last conversation about potential husbands didn't go so swimmingly, Father. I won't be led into another.*

"As you are unmarried, it is my duty as your father to see to your care," he said. His tone was not unkind, but she could detect an undeniable firmness to his words, like a building's stone foundation—unmovable, sunk deep. "You are in need of my protection and care, and I have come not only to enter the sawmill trade but to do my sacred duty as your father."

"That's hogwash," Dovey burst out. "I am in need of neither your protection nor your care. Nor do I want either, thank you very much!"

"Doreen, be sensible. Bart and Ewing have settled into their own lives, with farms in the countryside—I dare say you know as much, from correspondence with your mother. They are grown men, working on families of their own. They need nothing from me—"

"And I'm a grown woman," she broke in. "I have managed my affairs just fine for seven years, without the benefit of your meddling."

"A man needs to protect—to provide. It is my purpose to shelter you from the world's harsh influence. I've already fallen in that duty once, Doreen, by allowing you to scamper away from your family and your duty in Lowell."

"My *duty*?" Stunned, she nearly spat the word.

"It is a woman's work to marry and make a family, to raise children and be a comfort to her husband. For seven years, I've tolerated your wild ways—what choice did I have, separated from you as I was? But now that I am coming into my own once more, I will be on hand to give you the guidance you need—"

"I need no *guidance*! I declare, I've got a better head for business than you have, Father. You think your sawmill is the way to earn a place in Seattle? You're wrong. I've a business plan of my own—one that can't fail in this town's economy. And with another month or two of working, I'll have all the capital I need to make a strong start."

Pleased with the truth of her boast, she crossed one knee over the other, a shockingly impudent gesture. Father's face paled, and his eyes flashed down to her hem—to the cuffs of her riding trousers, now indecently exposed.

His lips pressed tightly together, and his mustache quivered with his barely suppressed disapproval.

"I had heard tales," he said quietly, "that a young woman worked for the Revenue Service and rode about town dressed like a perfect hoyden, in trousers of all things. I'd hoped the Revenue Service had some other girl in its employ—I'd all but convinced myself that my own daughter, my sweet Doreen, could not possibly stoop to such inappropriate behavior. But now I see the error of my judgment."

"Now you see your error, indeed," Dovey said. She felt a childish urge to pull her petticoats up higher, to show off more of her shocking trousers. But she kept her arms folded resolutely and met her father's eye, unflinching.

The color returned to his face, as did the sly, considering glint in his eye. "You say you've saved up capital?"

Dovey swallowed hard. "What's that to you?"

"Funding for a business is hard to come by."

"Not if one toils for seven years, and scrimps and saves."

"Join your money to mine, Doreen. The new sawmill will be all the more successful with a robust initial investment."

Her mouth fell open. For a moment she could not breathe, let alone speak. Finally she managed a small, offended sound, half gasp, half disbelieving laugh. "I most certainly will not join my capital to yours!"

Father smiled at her—not the warm expression she had seen only minutes before, the one she had looked upon with poignant welcome.

This smile was cold, considering—the grin of a savvy businessman who meets an opponent at the negotiation table, and knows that he has won.

"You don't have a choice," he said matter-of-factly. "You're an unmarried woman. It is my right, as your father, to take you in hand and find you a husband. And when you are properly wedded, whatever estate you possess will belong to your husband by law."

A cold void filled Dovey's chest. *Is it true? Can he possibly be right? No—no, Lord, it can't be so!* Her seven years of working for Virgil had provided her with an admirable knowledge of the Territory's tax laws. But she had no experience at all with this sort of law. For all Dovey knew, her father might have a legal claim to her fate—to her marriage, to her future and happiness. And what he said about her money might be just as horribly, depressingly accurate.

Dovey met his stare, willing her body not to tremble, her eyes not to fill with tears. *You are better at business than he,* she told herself. *It wasn't your mills that failed back in Lowell. And it's not you who thinks to compete with Henry Yesler in the sawmill game. Think, Dovey. Think, and negotiate. Don't cave to his tactics.*

What she needed at this moment was time—time to research the Territory's laws, to determine what precisely her legal situation was—and how she might thwart her father's scheme once and for all. *If I can just put off this idea of his—another blasted arranged marriage!—for a few months. Or even a few weeks.* Surely that would be enough time to arm herself with knowledge, to work out some legal evasion of her father's plan.

But how could she hope to satisfy his concerns over her "improper" behavior? She suspected that merely quitting the tax-collecting job would not be enough to satisfy him, to delay the marriage he must now be doubly keen to arrange.

Then a bolt of inspiration struck her, so hard and fast she lurched forward on her seat as if stung on the bottom by a bee.

"Father, perhaps you're right. I'm twenty-three, after all. Maybe it is time I married and settled down."

He stroked his mustache with a wary hand, but his words were eager enough, half convinced. "I am glad to see your good sense returning."

"But as you noted"—Dovey hung her head—"I've developed something of a reputation these past seven years. I don't think any man will have me."

"I wouldn't be so sure about that, Doreen. I know how men's minds work, especially when it comes to business affairs. Any sensible man will be happy to take you for a wife, if it means a robust share in a strong new sawmill venture."

It was an effort not to skewer her father with a look of daggers. *Traded off as an investment—just the sort of romance every girl dreams of.* But Dovey managed to keep her face demurely, even remorsefully, downcast.

"I do know Seattle somewhat better than you, Father, if you'll pardon my saying so."

He made no reply, and Dovey, encouraged, spoke on. "Women who have made a . . . a certain reputation for themselves don't find matches in this town—not under any circumstances, or for any inducement. There are two types of women in Seattle—the low and the high. No low woman is fit for marriage." She looked up at him suddenly, clasping her hands in a display of desperation. "I fear I erred terribly in working as I've done. I didn't think of my future—only of the present moment. But I don't think my reputation is gone entirely—not yet. There may be just enough time to save me, Father."

"Nonsense, Doreen. As I said, any man of business—"

"But just think: if my reputation were to be restored, and I were known in this town as a reformed woman, of true moral character, I could attract a much better husband."

He stroked his mustache again. "Go on."

"There are some men in this town who have grown quite wealthy. And a few of them are still unmarried. If we could attract the attention of that sort of man, think how your business could flourish!"

His answering smile was slow, but there was no mistaking the approving glint in his eye.

"Naturally, Doreen, I'd be thrilled to see my only daughter married into a wealthy family. But as you say, your reputation . . . How can we overcome it?'

"I do know a way. There's a certain house downtown—near Skid Road, on the southern end of Seattle. It's a reform home of sorts, for fallen women."

Father shook his head. "Certainly not! I cannot have anyone thinking you're in need of *that* kind of reform. If anyone were to suspect that you'd worked as a dock girl, Doreen, we would have no chance."

"We can make it clear that I'm there only in service—to work for the aid of fallen women. I know the proprietress of the home well." *Too well, Lord preserve me.* "She is a well-respected woman in Seattle society, known to have unfailing morals, the very highest possible character. If she tells the city that I'm working at her side, to tame my wild ways and gain the skills I'll need as a good wife, then everybody will believe her. Sophronia Brandt never lies."

He considered the idea in silence, gazing out the window at the penned mules while he went on slowly petting his graying whiskers. Finally he said, "And you're sure your reputation will be mended, if you take up work at this house for fallen women?"

"Certain," she said. "My reputation will be washed sparkling clean. My stock will rise. I'll look like the very wisest investment in all of Seattle, Father—and so will you."

"Very well," he finally said. "Get yourself into this place, and once you're recognized as a woman who has mended her ways, I'll set about finding a proper husband for you. Let us hope the process doesn't take long. The sooner I can start my sawmill, the better for all the Mason family."

"It shouldn't be a lengthy wait, I should think," Dovey said. *How long can it truly take to scour the lawbooks and find some way out of this pickle for once and for all?*

CHAPTER THIRTY
SILVER DOLLARS

Dovey disappeared through the kitchen door, balancing a tray laden with cold cuts of smoked ham, a roundel of cheese, and a tureen filled with steaming onion soup. Sophronia heard the girl speaking cheerily to the women at the dining table—the residents of the reformatory home—as she laid out their midday meal. In moments Dovey was back again, alert and focused as she turned her attention to washing the cutting board and tidying up the kitchen.

Sophronia and Dovey orbited each other as they set the kitchen in order, each woman maintaining a regular distance from the other, maintaining out of long habit their caution and mistrust. But as Sophronia watched the young woman's efficient work, she surprised herself with the stirrings, deep in the most inaccessible reaches of her heart, of a grudging respect for Dovey.

She had sheltered at Sophronia's home for fallen women for two weeks now. Sophronia had reluctantly extended an arm of protection over Dovey in her time of need, certain she would be more trouble than she was worth. However, Sophronia had quickly realized that she'd come to appreciate Dovey's presence in the house for fallen women. The former prostitutes who lived with Sophronia—poor creatures who had aged out of their line of work, or who had become so disfigured by illness or accidents that they could no longer attract business in the midst of the stiff competition along Skid Road—seemed to show greater respect for Sophronia because Dovey worked by her side. Dovey was well known as a friend to fallen women, and her residence at the house gave Sophronia some legitimacy—and certainly added hope for the future of her mission.

And Dovey herself had changed since Sophronia had spoken to her last. Seven years of work had apparently mellowed Dovey's character, tempering her wild ways and garnering her a bit more sense and forethought. Tax collecting was far too uncouth, and riding a horse entirely too vulgar an occupation for a lady. And Sophronia had her suspicions that Dovey's boss, the notorious tax man Virgil Cooper, might be slipping Dovey more than just a cut of the collections. Men of his rough, roguish type could never be trusted with a woman's virtue. But despite the vapor of scandal that seemed to follow Dovey wherever she went, Sophronia had to admit that the young woman seemed to have benefitted, on the whole, from her years of work. Far be it from Sophronia to withhold praise where it was due.

"How do things stand with your father?" Sophronia asked as she swept the kitchen floor.

Dovey, stacking clean saucers in the cupboard, tossed her head. "If Jo is right about suffrage and the law, then it won't matter one whit how things stand with my father."

"So, then, your father hasn't given up his plan?"

"To force me into a marriage so he can steal my money? He's still at it."

"No one can force you to marry against your will, Dovey."

Dovey laid the last saucer in its place and shut the cupboard with a sigh. "Common wisdom says so—"

"The *law* says so; women don't need the vote to gain protection."

Despite the fact that Jo's newspaper clipping had not ceased to haunt Sophronia's waking thoughts—and her nightly dreams, too— Sophronia still clung to her suspicion of the suffragists. Jo, for her part, delighted that Dovey was now living under Sophronia's roof, had come to visit several times. The woman was positively bursting with enthusiasm for the suffrage movement, and her certainty that women needed the vote had rubbed off on Dovey.

But Sophronia was not so easily convinced. She had spent her whole life yearning for what, she now understood, she could never obtain: a happy marriage, a home and hearth of her own—and a husband's love. Any woman who fought so assiduously against Sophronia's ideal of feminine occupation seemed untrustworthy—even dangerous.

"Common wisdom *and* the law may say so," Dovey went on, "but it's not as simple as that. Family is one great entanglement. Father is planning to bring Mother out to Seattle one of these days—just as soon as he can get a trade running smoothly and put a few dollars in the bank. I'm sure he'll convince my brothers to come to Seattle, too, if they're not too much in love with Massachusetts. I want to enjoy their company when they arrive. I want us all to get along. I can't make too many waves with Father; it would break Mother's heart. If I want to keep my money and my freedom, I've got to go about it delicately."

Sophronia held her silence and swept the floor more vigorously.

"If we could change the laws themselves, then Father couldn't blame the whole scenario on me. He wouldn't be able to get his hands on my money, but it wouldn't seem to be my doing—can't you understand? I'd be innocent of thwarting his plans, and I could enjoy my family in peace, without Father's ambitions plaguing me. If we could change the law, my money would remain my own no matter who I married—or *if* I married. And when Mother comes from Boston, we could all be happy together. That's all that matters to me now."

"Do you still plan to open your cathouse?" Sophronia sniffed.

Dovey drew herself up and squinted across the kitchen at Sophronia. "Darn right I do."

"I'll thank you not to use such coarse language in this house, Dovey."

Dovey shrugged and wrung the dishrag over the slop bucket. "I've saved up a good sum, and I'm going to put it to good use."

"I can think of better uses for your money," Sophronia countered. "I've collected respectable sums myself, in the name of the Women's League. We'll use the money to expand this operation—to open more homes for the rehabilitation of fallen women."

Dovey snorted in rough amusement. "Good luck with that. There are more women happily working in Seattle than you'll ever be able to save. It doesn't matter how many homes you open. Except for the few old girls who find their way here to this shelter, they don't *want* to be rehabilitated."

"Of course they do! Why, prostitutes make some of the largest and most regular contributions to the League!"

Dovey looked up from the slop bucket, her brow furrowed in surprise. "They do?"

"Certainly. Hardly a week goes by that I don't collect a handful of silver dollars from the women over at that ugly, bright-green bawdy house on First Avenue or from the Lily Mansion down by the docks. Why, it seems very fashionable indeed for the working girls to donate a silver dollar to the cause, whenever they're able."

Dovey dropped the rag in the bucket. The resulting splash left a splatter of greasy water on her skirt, but she seemed not to notice. She slapped her thigh and hooted with laughter. "Silver dollars!"

"It's very generous," Sophronia said defensively.

"Lord, Sophie—don't you know? The girls are only cocking their snoots at you—and how!"

Sophronia felt herself blanch. She laid aside her broom and said slowly, cautiously, "I don't know what you mean."

Dovey rolled her eyes. "They use those silver dollars to keep from getting pregnant."

Sophronia stared in silent, horrified consternation—and not only at Dovey's appallingly frank speech about the delicate matter of motherly expectation. A singularly ill feeling crept over her as sweat beaded on her back.

"Don't look so shocked," Dovey chided. "Didn't you know that's why the seamstresses always keep a dollar coin handy? They stuff those silver pieces right up into their boots!"

"Their *boots?*" Sophronia gripped the edge of the kitchen table, unaccountably dizzy.

"Their *monosyllables*," Dovey said with brutal emphasis, "their long eyes, their Irish fortunes, their pokehole prannies!"

Sophronia heard her own shriek of dismay before she even felt it in her throat. It echoed from the tiles of the kitchen, and in the dining hall the clinking of cutlery stilled for a moment as the residents of the house paused over their lunches to snicker at their hostess's distress.

So! The prostitutes' donations had been meant as insults all along— and Sophronia could scarcely conceive of a more shocking insult than to be handed a coin that had been so evilly contaminated. She pressed her hand to her fluttering heart as a swoon threatened to overtake her.

"I . . . I cannot countenance such talk," Sophronia said weakly. "And in any case, silver dollars used for such a . . . a *purpose*? What nonsense!"

"It isn't nonsense. I can attest to their usefulness myself."

The implications of Dovey's words hit Sophronia like a hammer's blow to the chest. "Dovey! You can't . . . You aren't . . . You never . . . !"

The girl showed her dimples in an infuriating smirk. "I can, I am, and I certainly have. How do you think I've kept my corset laced tight all these years? Though I know a few other tricks, beside the silver dollar."

"You're unmarried," Sophronia cried in a pleading tone.

"And if the Lord is good to me, I'll stay that way."

"I would have hoped you'd kept out of . . . *that sort of trouble* by avoiding sin!"

Dovey shrugged and wiped the splash of filthy water from her skirt with a clean cloth. "My business is God's business, not your own. In any case, you can see you'll have a rough time of it, if you aim to rehabilitate the women of Seattle. Why, they make enough scratch lying on their backs that they can cast off a dollar just to get your goat, whenever it tickles them to do so."

The threat of the swoon passed. Sophronia balled up her fists and advanced on Dovey. "You awful, filthy creature! Bringing such language and such . . . such *tales* into my home! I've a mind to kick you out on your bustle, Miss—into the streets for your father to do with as he pleases!"

Now it was Dovey's turn to go pale. "I'm sorry," she said at once, and to Sophronia's surprise, her contrition seemed real. "I shouldn't have laughed at you. It's true, what I said about the silver dollars—but I only wanted you to understand what the women mean by their 'donations.' I didn't intend to hurt you, Sophronia."

Sophronia said nothing, only looked Dovey up and down with dry assessment.

"We must stick together now," Dovey said. "We can't be each other's enemies—not you and I, nor any other woman in Washington. We must pull in the same direction now—we have a common goal."

Sophronia lifted her chin haughtily. "You're speaking of suffrage, I assume."

"You really don't approve of it, Sophie?"

"Of course not. It's not a woman's place, to vote—to meddle in politics and laws. God has decreed *that* place the realm of men, and we ought to have no use for it."

"But we *do* have use for it!" Dovey's voice quavered with the force of her plea. "Don't you see? We're helpless without the vote, Sophronia. Think of Jo, waiting on freedom her husband will never agree to. And me—all the money I've saved, ready to be swept off into some man's pocket the moment I marry. And you, Sophie—you work so hard to reform Seattle. Think of the changes you could affect if you had the power to make laws. Just think of it!"

Sophronia had thought of it—indeed, since reading Jo's stealthily deployed clipping, she had thought of little else. She saw the sense in Dovey's argument—and Jo's. But still, Sophronia told herself stubbornly, right was right, and wrong was wrong. Whatever else might be counted against her in the final judgment, at least the angels in Heaven would say that Sophronia Brandt knew righteousness from sin.

"Jo is going to Olympia the day after tomorrow, you know," Dovey continued. "Miss Susan B. Anthony will be there. She's a great heroine of the movement, and Jo and I want to hear her speak."

"What nonsense," Sophronia muttered. But even to herself, she sounded as though she wanted to be convinced to come along on the trip.

"It's not nonsense. Miss Anthony is dedicated to the betterment of the women of Seattle. That is your goal, too. You simply *have* to come and see her, Sophie!"

"My goal and Miss Anthony's are not the same. I aim to make the women of Seattle *more* ladylike, not less."

"But still and all, it can't hurt you any to see Miss Anthony speak—merely to hear her words."

The words from Jo's scrap of newspaper rattled about Sophronia's mind once more. *These houses of ill fame will languish and die for want of support.* Sophronia admitted to herself, so quietly she almost couldn't hear the thought, that it might be edifying to see this Miss Anthony speak after all. There was no harm in merely gazing at the woman, listening casually to her words.

"Very well," she finally said, blushing, wondering what on Earth she was getting herself into. "I'll go. But only because I'm curious what kind of devilry this Miss Anthony is trying to teach to our women. If I hear her speak, perhaps I'll know how best to fight against the suffragists' audacities."

"That's the spirit," Dovey said with a wry, crooked smile. "We leave in two days."

CHAPTER THIRTY-ONE
BREAK NEW GROUND

The *Wild Wood* cut through the white-capped swells of Puget Sound, speeding south toward Tacoma. Dovey flung her arms wide on the deck of the stylish boat, breathing deep the crisp air of a seaborne autumn. The morning was bright through a layer of misty cloud, and seemed to hint at a sunny, optimistic day ahead. The salt-laden breeze that cooled her face and tangled her hair felt like imminent freedom.

Astern, Seattle dwindled to a dot on the horizon, its hilltop houses, crowded docks, and banners of gray smoke from the sawmill fading into the deep, uniform green of the shore. The *Wild Wood*'s first stop was the railroad city of Tacoma. There, the boat would retrieve Miss Susan B. Anthony, who had ported up by train from Oregon Territory. Dovey had spent her weeks in Sophronia's care reading Jo's copies of the *New Northwest*. Miss Anthony was a great favorite of the paper's editor; her exploits in the name of suffrage had been thoroughly detailed in the columns of the *New Northwest*, and Dovey's heart leapt with anticipation. She felt as if she were about to meet a great hero of legend—Davy Crockett, perhaps, or Daniel Boone.

Jo and Sophronia emerged from the *Wild Wood*'s luxurious cabin, tugging their shawls close as they joined Dovey on the deck. The wind tossed Dovey's curls, and Jo clutched protectively at her hat, though it was pinned quite securely to her bun. The three women stood in silence for a long moment, watching Tacoma draw near. A haze of black smoke hung over the city, the permanent coal-dust smudge from its many rail lines.

Dovey turned to her friends with a cheery comment about the journey ready on her lips, but she fell silent at sight of Sophronia's face. The pale woman's scowl was deeper and more determined than usual.

"Whatever is the matter?" Dovey asked her. "Are you seasick?"

"I never get seasick. You of all people should know that." Sophronia thrust a newspaper into Dovey's hands. "I *told* you this Susan Anthony was a crude character. I found this paper in the cabin. Just look at what it has to say about her behavior!"

Dovey took the wind-ruffled paper from Sophronia's hands. Titled the *Regional Crier*, its front-and-center column featured a prominent headline in bold, forceful type:

WOMEN'S VOTE CAMPAIGN A PLAGUE OF IMMORALITY

Dovey scanned the column quickly. It told of Susan B. Anthony's recent eviction from the orchard town of Walla Walla, a day's stagecoach ride across the mountain passes from Seattle. It seemed Miss Anthony had been tossed out of Walla Walla on charges of drunkenness. "This virulent plague of the campaign for a woman's vote," the editor concluded, "may be properly summed up with but one description: worse than the smallpox and chills and fever combined."

Dovey raised her brows appreciatively. "Kicked out of Walla Walla for inebriation? I think I'll get on well with Miss Anthony."

"Don't be ridiculous!" Sophronia snatched the *Regional Crier* away from Dovey. "This column describes shameful behavior for a woman—utterly shameful! It curdles my blood to think of how many ladies have come to exalt this Susan Anthony. And you two, Dovey and Jo, are the worst idolaters of them all!"

Dovey laughed off Sophronia's caterwauling and clutched Jo's hand. She could feel Jo's excitement trembling in her palm, a perfect reflection of the quivery, hopeful anticipation Dovey felt bubbling in her chest.

At last, the *Wild Wood* pulled into port. As the sailors made off the lines and positioned the ramp for boarding, Dovey pulled Jo to the rail and gazed down at a small crowd gathered on the pier. The *Wild Wood* was to take on some dozen passengers, all bound for Olympia. They stood waiting with bags in hand, several smartly dressed women mixed among the gentlemen in their travel jackets and John Bull hats. Dovey eyed each woman carefully from her vantage. She felt the smallest flush of disappointment. None of the women on the pier had the countenance she had dreamed up for Susan B. Anthony—the queenly bearing, the forbidding stare. All the potential candidates for the famous suffragist looked quite ordinary, even approachable.

"We had best go down and greet Miss Anthony," Dovey told her friends.

Jo paled at the suggestion. "Now that the moment's come, I find I can't move! Oh, what if I make a fool of myself?"

"Come on," Dovey said, shaking her head fondly.

Jo seized Sophronia's elbow as if hoping she might anchor herself to the other woman and avoid the terror of confronting a celebrity.

"There's no getting out of it," Dovey said, and tugged her reluctant companions down the boat's ramp. She marched into the waiting crowd and said loudly, "Miss Susan Anthony?"

One of the women stepped forward with a thin, rather wry-looking smile. Dovey eyed her appraisingly. In age, she was near to Jo—perhaps ten years the senior—and similar, too, in her plain style, free of frills and fripperies. She was dressed in a very smart skirt and blouse of rich brown wool, though a modest cascade of lace did spill from her high neckline—her only adornment, and a rather small and tidy one, at that. She wasn't even wearing a hat; though her hair was rather thin, with a wide, pale part, it was still quite dark and free from silver threading. It slicked down tightly against her head to curl in two neat rolls over her ears. Her face showed ample signs of age, but combined with her long, thin nose and sharp chin, the years she wore only seemed to enhance her confident bearing. *Confident* was not to say *haughty*. She smiled at Dovey and her friends, her face beaming with a sudden homey comfort that made Dovey feel as easy in her presence as if she'd known Miss Anthony her whole life.

"You must be the women from Seattle," she said. "I received your letter."

"We are representatives of Seattle, yes," Dovey said. But after that, words failed her. The *New Northwest* had recounted so many tales of Anthony's heroics that Dovey's nerves caught up with her all at once. She felt a bit jelly-kneed. Confronted by a Susan B. Anthony, who seemed just another friend from years past, Dovey couldn't figure out what she ought to do. Her brains had fled.

Well, Dovey reasoned, *it's Jo's fault I'm standing here now. I ought to let her do all the talking.* She pulled Jo insistently forward. "This is our fearless leader, Miss Anthony: Josephine Carey."

Jo made a tiny gasping sound. Anthony took her hand.

"Pleased to meet you, Miss Carey. 'Fearless leader'—so, then, I am to understand that you have formed a suffrage league in Seattle?"

For a moment, Jo stared at Susan's eager, encouraging smile. Her eyes were as wide and blank as those of a dairy cow. Then she swallowed audibly and nodded. "Yes—yes, ma'am. A suffrage league . . . in Seattle . . . yes, certainly."

Sophronia shifted on her feet and cut her eyes sharply toward Jo. She looked as if she might expose the fib; Dovey drifted close and kicked her ankle sharply.

"Well," Susan said, "that's fine to hear."

She introduced her companion—none other than Abigail Scott Duniway, the editor of the *New Northwest*. Mrs. Duniway was a pattern of plucky cheer, with rosy cheeks and a robust, plump figure. Though she approached middle age, she had a charming light in her eye that struck Dovey as altogether girlish—as did Mrs. Duniway's great, thick braid, which she wore coiled atop her head like a glorious, dark crown. She insisted the ladies from Seattle call her Abigail, and smiled broadly when they obliged. Dovey had read Abigail's columns until she had all but memorized them; she could not entirely reconcile Abigail's writerly voice—biting, acerbic, and even saucy—with this vision of ready smiles and airy delight.

"Shall we go aboard the ship?" Susan Anthony said. "I'm eager to speak to your legislators down in Olympia."

Dovey led the way back up the ramp, and Jo settled Susan's and Abigail's fares with the purser. They found comfortable chairs around a small table inside the *Wild Wood*'s lush, mahogany- and velvet-clad cabin. A hostess brought them tea, which they sipped contentedly as the steamship left Tacoma's port.

"Do tell us about your woman's suffrage league, Josephine," Abigail prompted. "We hadn't yet heard that one existed in Seattle, but naturally, we are delighted."

"We . . ." Jo glanced toward Dovey, glowering a little, but Dovey beamed innocently back at her. "Well, we've only very recently formed our league."

Dovey busied herself with her teacup to disguise her mischievous smile. Recently, indeed. As Jo stammered her way through a genteel evasion of the two ladies' questions, Dovey noted the growing flicker of speculation in her friend's eye. The league might not exist yet, but Dovey could see clearly that it was only a matter of time.

Poor Jo was flushed and quivery; Dovey thought it best to spare her friend from further squirming. And, if truth be told, she yearned to needle Sophronia—not too hard, just enough to see some color rise to her pale cheeks.

"Miss Anthony," Dovey said, leaning across the table eagerly, "I read that you were evicted from Walla Walla!"

Abigail Duniway gave a loud but not unpleasant laugh. "That mess! Land sakes! You ought to tell them the story, Susan. I think they'd like to hear it."

Susan gave another of her warm, friendly smiles. "Well, all right. I suppose it can do no harm.

"Some weeks ago—oh, it must have been September fifth—Abigail and I traveled by boat from Portland to Umatilla. Umatilla is such a small, out-of-the-way place—all cattle range and apple trees. It's not the sort of town in which one expects to meet an old acquaintance from the schoolyard. Yet that is precisely what I found."

"Susan isn't from Portland, you know," Abigail added. "She hails all the way from New York State."

Susan nodded. "So you see, it was something of a shock to meet a man I'd known as a child, far on the other side of the continent.

"He called out to me—he recognized me, even though it had been decades since we'd seen one another last. I could tell he was drunk, the poor man. He sat on the step of a general store with a bottle in his hand. The thing was already half drained, and it wasn't yet evening. He'd given himself over entirely to liquor.

"Well, what could I do? One cannot turn one's back on the wretched. I sat down beside him, right there on the stoop, and discussed with him the turn his life had taken. It broke my heart to hear he hadn't spoken to his mother in many years. I remembered her well from my girlhood days. I knew she must be sick with worry for her son—mothers never cease caring for their children, even when they grow up and make their own way in the world.

"I sought his permission to write to his mother on his behalf—to tell her that her son was alive, at least, if not exactly well.

"He said he would only allow me to write back home if I'd seal the deal with a drink! Well—I was taken aback, I assure you. I am not for liquor or wine, not in the least—"

Sophronia, forgetting her manners, blurted out, "You're not?"

"Goodness, no," Susan said smoothly. "Temperance is, I believe, one of the keys to a healthy society. But I couldn't leave this old chum of mine to languish in the dust. For his own sake, I agreed to the drink: one sip only, which I took from his own bottle of angelica liquor."

"You should have hear Susan cough and sputter, all the way to that night's speaking engagement," Abigail said.

"But that very same night, I wrote the man's mother. I thought no more of it, until two weeks later, when Abigail and I went up to Walla Walla."

"No good deed goes unpunished," Abigail said with an air of grim foreshadowing.

"When we arrived in Walla Walla, we found a contingent of women waiting to chase our stagecoach back out of town, shaking their fists and shouting temperance slogans! Wouldn't you know it, the mother of my schoolyard friend had ended up in Walla Walla, and had received my letter there. She'd struck up a correspondence with her son, and he straightaway related to her the story of how he and I had shared a drink, toasting to old times and family! The woman was ready to spit nails at me, and was convinced that the suffragists only sought the vote so that we might flood the streets of every good city and town with liquor."

Abigail laughed uproariously. "Isn't that just the way of the world!"

Sophronia blushed, and Dovey caught her eye. "Not quite the simmering kettle of sin you expected her to be, is she?" she whispered.

Susan and Abigail shared more stories of their speaking tours while the *Wild Wood* churned on toward the Territory's capital. At last, the port of Olympia made itself known through the dispersing gray fog of the October noon.

Susan rose with ready grace from her chair. "My friends, it's almost time to set my hands and my heart to work. But work is always better when shared. How would you like to accompany Abigail and me in Olympia?"

"Accompany you?" Jo asked rather shakily. "Where?"

"To the Capitol building, of course—into the legislature meeting. Judge Daniel Bigelow, a friend to our cause, has secured for us a chance to address the legislature while their session is in progress."

"We'll break new ground," Abigail added. "Today will be the first day women have addressed lawmakers in session, in all the history of the United States. Or its territories."

"Oh!" Jo gasped. "I . . . I couldn't possibly . . ."

Susan laid her hand on Jo's shoulder. "You possibly could. I do hope you'll come along with us, Miss Carey. We are stronger together."

Jo seemed so knocked for the stars that she could only gape mutely at Miss Anthony. But Dovey pushed back her chair and stood at once. "We *will* come with you, Miss Anthony, and gladly. Won't we, girls?"

Jo stood shakily, nodding but still dumbstruck—and after a moment's hesitation, Sophronia also rose from her seat. Dovey took both their hands, and a current of warmth and excitement seemed to travel between them. She looked toward Olympia eagerly as the ship made its way to the pier.

CHAPTER
THIRTY-TWO
WORTH THE REWARD

Jo stared out the window of the carriage as it crossed the streets of Olympia, making its way steadily from the pier, up the long, shallow slope of a knoll toward the Territorial Legislative Building. She could see the structure clearly at the crest of the knoll—a tall, boxy, stern-looking construction, two stories high and far broader than any barn. Its peaked roof was crowned by an elegant dome surrounded by a widow's walk; Jo could just make out a small shadow moving under the dome's white, open arches. A moment later, the brassy call of a bell rang across the city.

"They've called the session," Abigail said. But she remained comfortably settled in the carriage seat, without the least sign of haste.

Josephine felt as if she were rolling through a dream—unsettling and almost eerie yet strangely thrilling. With each beat of her heart, her resolve shifted. First she knew she would not—*could* not possibly stand before the legislature, even with Susan B. Anthony and Abigail

Dunaway at her side. And then, with a rush of fierce longing, she knew she couldn't do anything *but* enter that chamber and speak with all the passion that burned in her soul—fight for the rights of the women and girls she loved.

She was so preoccupied that she noticed little of the city of Olympia. Its cobblestone streets and boardwalk promenades, its shops and warehouses and wagons rolling loud over the paving, even its dense, briny odor—all these were so like Seattle that Jo paid them no heed. Only the Legislative Building seemed real to her. There, Jo felt instinctively, in that vast, austere chamber, her fate awaited. She was cognizant only of her divided mind, and of Dovey and Sophronia sitting in the carriage beside her. And, of course, of Susan's presence, grounding and solid as the foundation of a well-built home.

All too soon, the carriage arrived at the crest of the hill. Josephine climbed down on numb legs and stood gazing up at the high roof of the Legislative Building. Its siding was as gray as the Puget Sound, its windows dark with heavy draperies. It appeared altogether forbidding. What went on inside was meant to be a mystery—to women, at least.

"Here we are," Abigail said cheerfully. "Let's go in."

Jo shared cautious glances with her friends, but they followed Abigail and Susan up the staircase to the building's broad porch. A man in a brown wool suit stood at the door, his hands clasped behind his back like a guard at attention. As Susan approached confidently, the man stepped toward her, barring her way with his body. "Legislative meeting in progress, ladies," he said politely. "I'm afraid I cannot allow you in."

"That is exactly why we must go in," Susan said. "We have been granted a hearing before the legislature. Speak with Judge Bigelow; he will confirm that I am expected."

"You're Susan B. Anthony, then." The man's face lit with a smile.

"And this is my colleague, Abigail Duniway, of the *New Northwest* in Oregon Territory. These ladies beside me are the leaders of Seattle's league of suffragists."

The man tipped his hat and bowed enthusiastically. "I'm in favor of all you do. The way I see it, it's only fair that women share in our government. A good woman is just as sensible as any man—*more* sensible than most!"

Jo couldn't help gasping in surprise. Abigail leaned in and said quietly, "We've found very encouraging support from men in every city, state, and territory we've visited. Has your league not encountered the same in Seattle?"

Before Jo could make up some plausible response, the man was ushering them on. The interior of the Legislative Building was not as spare and gray as its exterior aspect. Its inner halls and parlors were dressed in all the luxury that could be found in a territory as remote as Washington. Great carved tables of polished oak stood below towering bookcases, and the floors were richly covered in fine, soft rugs. Several large paintings, reminders of the land governed by those who worked there, adorned the walls: ships at sea; mountainous landscapes; rolling, golden farmland. The women were guided through the building by a polite, snappily dressed young boy, a page of sorts, who led them directly to the chamber where the legislature was conferring.

There, another man waited in attendance on a massive carved-oak door. Jo could hear masculine voices, their low, carrying tones, reaching through the solid, gleaming wood and out into the hall where she stood close beside her friends.

Susan sought entrance into the chamber, but this door guard was not as welcoming as the first. His scowl was freezing and disdainful; he made an insulting, shooing gesture with his hands, as if the great Susan B. Anthony and her companions were nothing more than a flock of straying chickens.

"No women in the chamber," he growled. "Cease these indecorous shenanigans and begone!"

"Sir," Abigail said coolly, "we are here at the arrangement of Justice Bigelow. I am sure you do not need a mere woman to point out to you that it is most unwise to cross the will of the man who holds the keys to the local jail."

"Bigelow?" he said skeptically. "When did he throw in his lot with you women's-rights harridans? Bigelow wouldn't like to be appointed to office again, I see."

Susan stood her ground, unmoved by his outburst. "As Judge Bigelow is still in office, however, you would be wise to humor him. As Mrs. Duniway pointed out, a judge is not a man I'd care to disobey."

The man raked them all with a peevish stare. Finally he said, "Only three of you are to be admitted. Five women in the chamber will only lead to mass faintings, and loud weepings, and other such hysterics."

Jo looked to Dovey and Sophronia, her face falling with dismay. "Who?" she whispered.

"You go with Susan and Abigail, Jo," Dovey replied. "You're the best speaker of us all. It must be you."

"I . . . I absolutely cannot do it." Now that she stood on the cusp of that decision, Jo knew clearly which way she would fall. To step into the legislative chamber would be to court grave danger. If Judge Bigelow had arranged for such a celebrity as Susan B. Anthony to appear before this session, then no doubt word had circulated throughout the city. Reporters from the papers must be already waiting within. An event as unusual as a pack of women waltzing into the legislative chamber would be breathlessly recounted in papers from Port Townsend to San Francisco. Jo's name and location would be exposed; it would be all the easier for Clifford to find her.

To her surprise, Susan took her hand. Her touch was warm and soft, and she squeezed with a firmness that steeled Jo's spine.

Susan said, "You can do it, Josephine. You can step forward and take hold of your fate."

"But . . ." How could she explain to this remarkable woman, who surely never feared anything in her life, what this exposure would mean to her?

"Ten years ago," Susan said, "when I worked for the Anti-Slavery Society, we could not hold a single meeting, nor could any of us see through a speech to its final lines. Every demonstration we held erupted into violence. I remember one mob in Syracuse—the crowd was so angry over the ideals we espoused that they broke up the furniture and shattered the hall's windows. Men were at knives, Jo—knives and guns. One drew a pistol and pointed it directly at me. I thought my heart had frozen in my chest."

"What did you do?" Jo whispered.

Susan smiled. "I didn't die, that's for certain. I evaded the danger of that day, somehow—and I've seen terrible times since then, too. It's always hardest the first time to stand up for what you know to be just and good."

"But it gets simpler every time," Abigail added.

"And the risk," Susan continued, "is worth the reward. If we stay cowed and conquered, shut away at our hearths, silent and complacent, then women will forever be disenfranchised. But once we have proven ourselves capable, Josephine—once we have demonstrated our inherent strength, our courage—then we can never be called weak or frail again."

Tears burned in Jo's eyes, and she had to swallow down the lump in her throat before she could speak. But at last she said, "Very well. I'll go in."

The door gave a soft groan as it swung open. Jo stared ahead, gazing coolly at the chamber's far wood-paneled wall as if she could see beyond it to the glittering Sound outside. She kept her eyes on the wall so she would not see the faces of the men who stared at her—some with expectation, some in frank, offended shock. They were anonymous blurs in her peripheral vision, alike in their shape and color, and as long as Jo did not look directly at any man, she could ignore the creeping sensation that each man wore Clifford's hard, leering face.

She moved down the chamber's broad, blue-carpeted aisle side by side with Susan and Abigail, as if she had always been their fellow. Two galleries of staring men fanned out to either side, and Jo could hear more men muttering in a balcony high above the floor.

A few men coughed and sputtered in annoyance, as if their work had been interrupted by a trio of untrained children. Jo broke her resolve and glanced around. Throughout the two wide galleries, men turned to one another with confused expressions, gesturing urgently toward the women. The muttering voices rose to a clamor, until one man, seated at a huge, bunting-draped desk at the far end of the room, rapped a gavel against a marble disc. Silence fell—silence but for the emphatic scratching of pens on paper, somewhere in the balcony above.

The reporters, Jo thought grimly.

The man at the desk gestured; Susan and Abigail stepped confidently toward him, Jo hurrying to keep up.

"Susan B. Anthony, Abigail Scott Dunaway, and—er—their associate," the man at the desk pronounced, "to speak on the issue of women's suffrage—the bill introduced by Judge Bigelow."

A tumult of objection erupted from the galleries, but soon shouts rose to quiet them. Jo did her best not to tremble as Susan turned to address the chamber.

"Honored gentlemen," she began, "today marks not only my first appearance before a legislature, but the first time in American history that a woman has been allowed to speak before lawmakers in session."

A thrill raced up Jo's spine. Abigail had mentioned Territorial history, which was intimidating enough. But now Jo found herself standing hip deep in American history, too! She breathed deeply, struggling to keep the flush of fear and excitement from her face as she listened to Susan's speech.

Her words were both eloquent and logical, although Jo—to her shame, as an educator—understood precious little of the intricacies. Susan cited fine points of the Constitution with as much aplomb as any legislator might; she held forth at length on the subject of taxation without representation—that bugaboo of all patriotic Americans—and pointed out the crass injustice of collecting taxes from the female population when Woman was without her vote. Jo had already found deep admiration for Susan Anthony in the columns of the *New Northwest*. But as she listened to the woman speak so confidently, with such surety of victory—as she, Jo, actually stood there beside Miss Anthony, before the eyes of the legislature!—that admiration turned to awe.

Abigail addressed the chamber next, and her friendly cheer fell away, replaced by a cool, no-nonsense tone that made even Jo quake a little in her boots. She employed not only the strength and confidence Jo had always found evident in the columns of her newspaper, but she also used words themselves as deftly as any craftsman, painting in the minds of her listeners beautiful vistas of hope and carving ramparts of certitude.

At last, though, Abigail concluded her rousing support of Bigelow's bill, and both she and Susan turned to look at Jo.

"Josephine Carey," Susan announced, "leader of Seattle's suffragist league, now wishes to address the legislature."

Jo's tongue went, all in an instant, as numb as a deadened limb. She opened her mouth and drew a ragged breath; which, in the expectant silence of the chamber, echoed faintly from the paneled walls.

"Our strength," Susan whispered, so softly Jo almost could have imagined the words, "our courage."

But soft though they sounded, still Susan's words rang in Jo's heart. She planted her feet firmly on the blue aisle runner, bunched her fists in her skirt, and lifted her chin to face all the eyes of the room.

"Gentlemen, I am not an experienced speaker, not a woman of accomplishments like Miss Anthony and Mrs. Duniway. I am a schoolmistress; I live a simple life and work hard on my own to keep my living.

"I am not the only woman in the Seattle league who works hard. We all strive with our backs and our hearts—not only for what is just and good but simply to put food on our tables. No one I know works harder than my good friend, a young woman of twenty-three years.

Her name is Dovey Mason, and I have known her since she was a girl of sixteen, when we traveled together from Massachusetts to Seattle."

As quickly as she could, and in language that seemed dull as tarnished copper beside Abigail's deft wordplay, Jo recounted the tale of Dovey's predicament. She explained how Dovey had toiled in a dangerous field—one typically dominated by men—so that she might pursue her ambitions and fund a business. And that business would bring revenue to Seattle and taxes to Olympia, as surely as any man's enterprise.

"Yet now my friend stands to lose all her estate—everything she has worked so hard and honestly to obtain—to a law which no woman of our territory ever approved. This is a law which *every* woman would strike down for its injustice and archaic sensibility, were it only in our power to do so."

Jo fell silent. She could think of no lovely or moving words to conclude her impassioned speech. She clasped her hands at her waist and pressed her lips together, and listened to the mad hammering of her heart in her ears.

"Thank you, ladies," the man with the gavel said shortly. "You may exit the chamber."

That's all? Jo glanced at the man in disbelief, but he was absorbed in a stack of papers, already prepared to move along to the next item on his agenda.

With the twinge of minor indignation that always follows an anticlimax, Jo shuffled after Susan and Abigail as they glided from the chamber. The two suffragists moved with a confident grace that was entirely at odds with the lump in Jo's chest, the sense of sudden defeat she was feeling.

When the chamber door closed at their backs and Jo stood in the outer hall once more, she felt her nervous energy drain from her body, replaced by a deep, steady calm. Mingled with that calm was no small dose of disappointment.

Dovey and Sophronia leapt up from the bench where they'd waited.

"Oh, we could hear your voices," Dovey whispered excitedly, "but not your words. What happened? What did you say?"

"I hardly think it matters what we said," Jo replied. "They seemed to dismiss our words out of hand."

Abigail laughed under her breath. "No, no—that is just the way a legislature meeting functions. Susan and I spoke to our friend Bigelow at great length before we agreed to make this trip, to address the chamber. It went exactly as we expected—exactly as we'd hoped."

"That man with the gavel . . . he didn't seem to hear us at all."

"He did, Jo. All the men heard, believe me."

Susan nodded, and her smile shone with pride. "How could they help but hear you, and take your words to heart? You spoke very well, Josephine Carey, fearless leader of the Seattle league. Very well indeed."

On the carriage ride back to the pier, where the *Wild Wood* waited to return them all to Seattle, Jo finally allowed a certain glow to rise in her chest, to spread through her belly and her limbs. Finally it found its way to her face, where she wore it as a beaming smile. She *had* spoken well—she could feel it. Perhaps her words had even moved a man or two. That was how equality was won—wasn't it?—by moving a single heart, a single mind, one and then another, then another. She had struck a firm, steady blow against injustice today—she had achieved something worth the risk.

CHAPTER THIRTY-THREE

A CHANGED WOMAN

Word of the triumph in the legislative chamber flew from Olympia to Seattle, darting across the telegraph wires faster than the *Wild Wood* could sail. By the time Sophronia and her friends arrived at the pier, a crowd of women—and no small number of men—was waiting at the waterfront to greet them.

The crowd set up a great "Hurrah!" as the suffragists and their Seattle companions emerged from the ship's cabin. Sophronia hesitated, unused to the adulation of crowds, but Susan and Abigail led the way down the ramp as if the cheers and salutes of welcoming parties were all in a day's business.

Henry Yesler, owner of the massive waterfront mill, and his wife, Sarah, were the first to greet the women. Mr. Yesler's beard and gray-streaked hair were somewhat less than neat—whether from the waterfront breeze, or from hygienic laxity, Sophronia could not tell. He certainly did not resemble the man of great wealth and influence he was. One might have been more inclined to take him for an itinerant logger than Seattle's powerful millionaire. Sarah looked the part of the rich man's wife; her well-fed figure was draped in layers of green velvet, a pearl choker encircled her neck, and her auburn hair was tucked away in the bejeweled net of a sumptuous snood.

Sarah Yesler clasped Sophronia's hand in warm congratulations, but Sophronia could not help shrinking back from the woman. Talk among the members of the Women's League had painted a shocking picture of the Yeslers, adherents to the Spiritualism movement. Their unconventional views had led down a crooked path to even greater eccentricities—and not the least troubling of these was their enthusiasm for so-called free love.

But as Sarah showered praises on her head, Sophronia banished the scandalized voices of the Women's League from her mind. Sarah Yesler might be eccentric, but here she was on the dock, proving herself a kind and generous woman—and a person greatly interested in suffrage.

With her belief in scattershot and temporary love, she may not be the type of suffragist who will vote to rid the city of prostitution. But if Jo's account of the unconcerned legislature is any stick to measure by, we will need every ally we can find.

Sophronia returned Sarah's handshake with a solemn nod, and only in that moment realized that she had committed herself to the cause. She had joined the fight for women's voices; for better or worse, the cause had planted itself deep in her heart and, against all odds, taken root. It seemed Sophronia was a suffragist.

"We are so proud of your efforts at the legislature," Sarah said. "Look how you've inspired all of Seattle!"

Sophronia smiled a little shyly. "Mrs. Yesler, this small crowd can hardly be called 'all of Seattle.' I don't see one member of the Women's League."

Sarah offered a saucy wink. "All of Seattle that matters. Listen, dear—Henry and I would be honored to host you ladies of the local suffrage association—and Miss Anthony and Mrs. Duniway, of course—at our home tonight for supper. Do say you'll come!"

Sophronia concealed her surprise with real effort. The Yeslers were the wealthiest couple in the city; it was no small honor to receive an invitation to their home. "Of course we would all be delighted," she said.

"Good," Sarah replied, grinning. "I had no idea our fair city boasted a suffrage association. I must hear all about it—and join, of course."

Mr. Yesler sent for carriages to bear them back to his house—a rather strange, flat-topped, plain-sided building not far from his mill, looking more like a general store than the home of the city's most successful businessman. As they waited for their carriages, Sophronia was lauded and congratulated by more men and women than she could count, and her wrist developed a tingle from all the handshaking. Both women and men pressed around, inquiring about the suffrage association, thanking her for her work on the city's behalf. For once, and quite in contrast to her interactions with the Women's League, Sophronia felt as if the kindness she received was heartfelt, the enthusiasm real. She glowed amid the praise.

"How may we join the suffrage association?" one of the women asked.

Sophronia exchanged a wry glance with Josephine, half fearful, half amused. There was no association—not yet, at least. But Sophronia told herself boldly, *There's no time to start quite like the present.* She announced, "All are welcome! The next meeting of the Washington Women's Suffrage Association will be at my Northwest Reform Home for Fallen Women, a week from today!"

Despite the strange, stark exterior of the Yesler home, the inside was glittering and grand. It was laid out like a long hall, or like the ballrooms of the East Coast, full of soaring spaces and shadowed heights, and warm, polished woods and bright draperies that made Sophronia feel dizzy with luxury. She sat at a mahogany table, in a carved chair that by itself would have cost her minister father three months' salary, and spooned up her soup from a delicate bowl that likely cost more than all the workaday ironstone dishes in her home for fallen women put together. Sophronia gazed about her calmly, affecting the air of one who is used to a millionaire's luxury, while she discussed the Suffrage Association with the enthusiastic Sarah Yesler.

At last, the celebration wore to its end. Sophronia said her farewells to the Yeslers—and bade an especially warm good-bye to Susan and Abigail, who had accepted the hospitality of the Yeslers for the night.

"It has been such a long day," Sophronia said to them all, "and I have so much to do in the morning. One's hands are always full with a reform house to run."

"But dear," Sarah said, "how are you getting home?"

Sophronia shrugged. "I'll walk, I suppose. It's not a terribly long way."

"Are you well to walk?" Dovey asked cautiously. "Remember—"

Sophronia was not likely to forget that long-ago night, the strange man who had grabbed at her breast and torn her bodice. But she brushed away Dovey's concerns. "I will be perfectly well."

Mr. Yesler stood, setting aside his small crystal cup of digestif. "Nonsense, my good lady! I've carriages aplenty here. Let me send for one to drive you home."

It would have been ungracious to turn away Mr. Yesler's offer—and Sophronia truly did not relish the idea of walking through Seattle alone, after dark. When her carriage came rolling around the corner of the Yesler home, she climbed in and settled into the tufted-velvet seat with a sigh of satisfaction. True, her route would take her from the wealthiest home in the city to the blighted neighborhood at the edge of Skid Road, the place she called home. But Sophronia wasn't ashamed. Tonight, her house for fallen women had become something more, taken on a shine of future greatness. Now it was the meeting place of the Suffrage Association. It was a place to make great things happen.

As the wheels rattled over the cobbles, Sophronia wondered at the change that had come over her. It had stolen over her spirit so suddenly that she couldn't tell the exact hour of its arrival. What had made her embrace suffrage so thoroughly? Why did she no longer consider it a sin? Perhaps it was the womanly ways of the suffragists—strong and bold yet still modest, and respectable through and through. Perhaps it was the sense of awe she'd experienced in the legislative building, her desire to be a part of the great monument of government. Perhaps it was simply God, whispering a new mission into her heart—her truest and most direct path, the reason He had brought her to Seattle. Whatever it was, Sophronia suspected she was a woman changed for all time. And she was glad of the change—truly glad.

The carriage halted outside her home. She stepped out into the street and froze, staring toward her small porch with a sudden tremor of fear. The night was chilly, heavy with the scent of thick mud from nearby Skid Road. The silence, save for the blowing of the cart horse and the creaking of the driver's seat springs, was absolute. She peered hard at the porch—there was someone standing there, shrouded in darkness. The figure was tall and square-shouldered—male.

Her heart pounded, and she recalled the whiskey stink on the breath and body of the man who had attacked her. She could see again the wicked flash of his eyes, hear his grating laughter as he'd reached for her. She nearly climbed back in the carriage and demanded the driver take her back to the Yesler home.

But then the man came down the porch steps, stepping into the faint wash of lamplight from a window above—and Sophronia's fear turned to a great leap of hope—a joy so fierce and poignant that it filled her chest with a throb of pain.

Sophronia hurried across the cobblestones, staring in disbelief. "Harmon! Harmon Grigg!"

Harmon's face was pink from the October night; he sniffled in the cold. He held a bouquet of flowers, the late blooms of autumn—scraggly asters and a few wilted sunflowers, their leaves limp and hanging.

"I have no right to come to you again," Harmon said quietly. "Yet here I am, all the same."

He held out the flowers, and Sophronia took them in silence.

"Not a day has passed since we last parted that I haven't thought of you with regret—and love."

"Harmon . . . it has been seven years."

"I know. Seven years, and I have met no other woman as good and worthy as you. Seven years, and you have haunted my heart each day and night." He hesitated, shuffling his feet. "Seven years, and I have not so much as looked upon a fallen woman, Sophronia—except with Christian pity."

"I . . . I'm glad to hear it." Gently, she brushed the petals of a sunflower with trembling fingers.

"Miss?" the carriage's driver called.

"I'm all right," Sophronia told him. "You may go."

The carriage rattled off into the night. When they were alone, Harmon raised his eyes to hers, and Sophronia could see the pain in his eyes—seven years of regret, of loss. She had felt that pain, too.

"Won't you please—" Harmon began, but Sophronia took his hand in her own, and he fell silent.

"I was wrong, Harmon. I've always regretted driving you away. I don't know just what motivated me to do it. Fear? Insecurity? I'm afraid it may even have been something simpler, and more difficult to excuse: pride." She swallowed a lump of shame in her throat. "I've been straying my entire life, chasing such a strange dream—a vision of womanhood I could never attain. No woman could attain it. I know that now."

"Then you'll reconsider your decision?" Harmon asked. "I don't believe you were unjust, to cut me off. But I'm a different man now,

Sophronia, and nothing would make me happier than to keep you tenderly for all my days."

"A different man?" She gave him a quavering smile, and tears blurred her eyes. "I am a different woman, too. Different—and better."

And then, to show him just how far she had changed, Sophronia stepped deliberately into his arms and kissed him. The feel of his lips against her own, the nearness of his body, sent a hot thrill racing along her veins.

Sophronia *was* a changed woman—that was certain, and no mistake. No one was gladder of the alteration than she.

CHAPTER
THIRTY-FOUR
HER OWN DETERMINATION

Autumn still clung to Seattle with a weak, chilly hand. The day's ration of rain had finally let up, and the clouds skated away to the south just long enough to admit the brief glow of the early sunset. Dovey leaned on the rail of the Yeslers' porch and watched the sky fill with ruddy light. It touched the tips of the evergreen trees that covered the hills, and laced the long black slash of Skid Road with a flush of fire.

The beauty of the moment seemed all the more precious for its fleeting nature. Now she stood alone, a woman free to do as she pleased, without the watchful guardianship—the *ownership*—of a husband. But in the six weeks since she'd gone to live at Sophronia's house for fallen women, Dovey's father had only tightened the squeeze of his fist. As winter came on, John Mason grew more desperate for a livelihood of his own. His impatience to see Dovey "reformed" and properly mar-ried—and his greed for her money in his pocket—increased by the day.

Dovey's self-determination seemed as evanescent as the sunset—glorious and bright but already brooding on the edge of a long, cold night.

A carriage arrived from the direction of the waterfront, the horses lifting their feet high as they splashed through the great, dark puddles that reached across the road. The carriage rolled to a stop in front of the Yesler house; the footman stepped quickly to open the door, and offered his hand to the ladies inside.

Despite her dark mood, Dovey couldn't help grinning when Susan Anthony and Abigail Duniway stepped down onto the cobbles. It had been all of a month since their last meeting, and all that time, as she'd worked tirelessly with the Suffrage Association, Dovey hadn't forgotten a moment of their excursion to the Legislative Building.

Despite two long days in Olympia, working to see Judge Bigelow's bill transformed into law, both ladies looked as fresh and smart as if they'd just emerged from their boudoir.

Dovey shook their hands warmly. "It's so good to see you again, ladies. We've worked so hard since your last visit to Seattle—the Washington Women's Suffrage Association, I mean. You simply won't believe the successes we've found. We've made a great case with the men as well as the women of the city—more contributions are made every day, and we've begun to venture out of the city to rally support for the vote in other towns, as well."

"That's fine, Dovey," Abigail said. "Very fine."

"I'm so pleased to hear it," Susan added. But her mask of serene composure slipped for a moment, and Dovey saw a hint of weariness in her eyes, the briefest sag of defeat in her posture.

In a heartbeat, Susan was herself again. But Dovey could not unsee that startling vision. "Susan," she said, taking her by the arm, "what's the matter?"

She shared a slow, cautious look with Abigail—then Susan drew a deep breath and squared her shoulders, as if steeling herself for a particularly unpleasant task. "We have encountered a . . . a setback in our efforts. With the bill."

Dovey's gut filled with all the cold of the autumn night. "What do you mean?"

Abigail took Dovey's hand, as if trying to impart courage and perseverance right through her palm. "We only just learned today that the Territorial legislature has enacted a certain law. It restricts women from attaining the vote unless suffrage is made a Federal law first."

"But . . . what exactly does that mean?" Dovey asked tremulously.

"I'm afraid the vote must be granted to *all* the women of the United States before women in this territory enjoy the privilege."

"We shall continue to fight," Susan added. "Lawmaking is a veritable labyrinth, full of intricate twists and turns. There are still options open to us, and with the support of powerful men like Judge Bigelow and your own Mr. Yesler, the way is not closed entirely to us. Not yet."

"We've worked so hard . . ." Dovey trailed off miserably.

"I know." Susan wrapped her arm around Dovey's shoulder, and for a moment held her close. "You should be proud of your labors, Dovey—you and all the members of your association. This is only a setback, not an all-out vanquishment. We have lost this single battle, but the war goes on."

"And elsewhere, we are winning the battles," Abigail said. "Support for the women's vote continues to grow. Leagues are forming in surprising places. Even while we suffer setbacks like this one, still our strength increases." Gently, Abigail lifted Dovey's chin. "Don't hang your head, dear. We have so much reason to be glad."

"That's why we're here, isn't it?" Susan said, with a forced note of cheer. "The Yeslers were kind enough to invite us up for a celebration, and for goodness' sake, we will celebrate! A single setback is nothing to mourn. We must view it as motivation to fight all the harder. And we will fight—harder every day, until at last our victory is won."

So they wouldn't get the vote—not any time soon, and certainly not quick enough for Dovey's liking. Not quickly enough to protect her ambitions . . . or the money she had saved. Not quickly enough to stave off her greedy, grasping father.

Susan and Abigail excused themselves and went inside, out of the advancing twilight, away from the encroaching dark. The vast, wood-warm hall the Yeslers called home was lively with the chatter of guests and bright with optimism. But though Dovey tried to put on a convincing show of hope—sipping her punch with a smile, applauding with the rest when Mr. Yesler formally welcomed Susan and Abigail—the effort of forcing gaiety was more than she could bear. Long before the soup was served, Dovey felt wrung out and shaky with exhaustion. She could maintain her pretense of hope no longer.

Mr. Yesler called for attention. He ran a hand through the thick gray nest of his hair, an attempt to neaten it that only caused it to stand up at more alarming angles.

"A toast," he called, "to Miss Anthony and Mrs. Duniway, true champions of a worthy cause!"

All eyes turned to Mr. Yesler, to his raised cup of punch. *Now is my chance,* Dovey thought frantically. *I must slip away, now or never.*

She didn't even know where she would go or what she sought, other than privacy, a chance to be alone with her dreary thoughts. She only knew that to leave the party now would be a terrible breach of etiquette—an offense to her hosts and the guests of honor. She had to escape without anyone seeing. She edged to the rear of the toasting crowd and slipped down the length of the Yeslers' hall while Susan addressed the crowd.

She found a mahogany door, hidden behind the great, feathery globe of a potted fern. A scent of spice and onions came to her faintly through the wall. *The kitchen.* There was sure to be some outer portal, some conveniently hidden egress, somewhere in that kitchen. She opened the door just enough to fit her small body through and slipped into the steamy room.

The staff looked up from their work, then raked her with dubious scowls. But she ignored their questions and walked on boldly through their midst as if she knew just where she was going and had every right to be there.

Sure enough, an outer door stood beside the range stove. Dovey marched directly to it and swept out of the kitchen, into the deep-gray dimness of night. The November air bit sharply, even through her thick, velvet sleeves. She looked around quickly, seeking some sheltered place to huddle with her thoughts.

She stood in a small courtyard of sorts at the rear of the Yesler house. Its flat, grassy plain was crossed by the ruts of carriages. Water, reflecting the house's lamplit windows, shone in some of those long, thin tracks like threads of copper and gold. Across the darkened yard, she could see the low black line of a building and could hear the sleepy night rustlings of horses.

A stable.

All at once, Dovey knew exactly where she had to go—and exactly what she had to do. The plan formed in her mind with such force that she stood stunned for a moment by its brilliance, gazing unseeing into the night as its pieces fit together with elegant simplicity. If it worked, she would be free—or at least, as free as any woman could hope to be.

Dovey crossed the yard quickly, hoisting the hem of her velvet dress as she splashed through the muddy cart tracks. A cheer went up from the party behind her, muffled by the walls of the house. She found the door of the stable and walked the line of the stalls in the darkness. She could make out little of any horse's merits in the darkness, but still she considered each in turn, holding their eager, curious faces in her hands, stroking their necks as if to sense their pluck and vigor through their warm hides.

Finally she settled on a small, stocky mount who seemed both gentle and alert. Dovey searched the side of the building until she found the tack shed, and found a head collar, lead rope, and saddle. She also found there, through sheer luck, a heavy wool cape, discarded on a hook by one of Yesler's servants.

Dovey let herself into the horse's stall, patting and soothing the little mare to quiet her whickers. The mare allowed Dovey to ease the saddle onto her back without any fuss, and did not throw up her head when Dovey slipped the collar over her nose. Quickly, Dovey led the mare out into the yard.

There was no mounting block in sight. Perhaps the Yeslers were rich enough that Henry employed a special groom to leg him up into the saddle. Dovey sighed with frustration; she would have to clamber aboard by any means she could. She jumped several times, one hand knotted in the horse's mane and the other pulling hard at the pommel of the saddle, until she finally was able to sling herself like a sack of potatoes over the hard leather seat.

The mare thought Dovey properly mounted and began to walk at once, her hooves sliding and clopping through the puddles. Dovey tried to halt her with a commanding "Whoa," but in this graceless position the stays of her corset were shoved into her ribs, and she could manage no more than a timid wheeze. Dovey clawed at the pommel for purchase, kicking her legs against the air; finally she managed to rotate slowly over the horse's back and haul one leg over the saddle.

Her skirt and petticoat were in disarray, and probably torn into the bargain, but Dovey didn't care. Somehow she had kept hold of the lead rope, that one ragged lifeline that served as a rein. That accomplishment could be counted a miracle. Now Dovey only needed to pray that the mare would respond without a bit in her mouth.

I'd best find out, she told herself, *and hope for the best.*

She kicked the mare into a trot. As she splashed away from Yesler's home, the sounds of forced cheer and dutiful optimism faded into the darkness. Dovey would no longer impose false glee upon herself where it did not by nature exist. If she were to have no vote—no power over the law, no protection for her interests—then she would at least work with what little she had been given. It wasn't too late to take control of her fate—not yet. That knowledge gave her real happiness—a very small measure, to be sure, but it was a satisfaction she had no need to falsify.

It took Dovey half an hour to reach Virgil's place on the northern edge of town. Before she could make out the house itself, its white siding grayed by the dark, squatting beneath the pines, she could see the red-orange ember of a lit cigarette glowing against the pitch-black of night. She called out over the muddy clop of her horse's hooves.

"Virgil!"

Dovey saw the ember rise suddenly as he leaped to his feet. Then it danced a little jig as Virgil came rushing down the porch steps and out into the lane. Now she could make him out, a faint shape against the dimness, comforting and solid, real—and waiting for her.

She pulled the mare to a halt. Virgil stared up at her in surprise, his face shadowed by night, but the gladness in his eyes sent a wave of gratitude and relief through Dovey's stomach, so strong and sudden that it raised tears to her eyes.

"I haven't seen you for weeks," he said wonderingly. "Or heard from you, either. Where did you run off to?"

"The home for fallen women. I've been staying there."

He laughed shakily. "Why, Dove? Why would you go there?"

"Why not? It's what I am now—a fallen woman." The tears broke, and Dovey wiped them away quickly with the edge of her borrowed cloak, ashamed of her weakness. "Virgil, why did you never ask me to marry you?"

"Why . . . ?" The question seemed to utterly confound him. He took a long pull on his cigarette and glanced away, out into the night-dark forest, and would not meet Dovey's eye.

"Don't you love me any?" she asked. Her voice sounded so small, so fragile, that she wanted to scream—to roar like a lion and show him how strong she really was. To show *herself*. But she could manage nothing more than that sad little squeak. "Even a little? After all the work I did for you—"

"You're worth more to me than the tax collecting," Virgil said quietly, and there was an intensity in his voice that pulled at Dovey's heart.

"And after everything we've done together . . . why, I went right into your bed without any fuss. Sophronia would call me a 'fallen woman' for that—a sinner. I sinned for you, Virgil, and it never meant a thing to you."

"That's not true," he said. "It's not true that it never meant a thing to me. It did—does. *You* do, Dovey. You mean the world to me."

"But you never would think of marrying me. And I'm a fool to ask about it. Why would you buy the cow when you could get her milk for free?"

He laughed and shrugged, clearly as uncomfortable with her accusations as he was with her tears. "It's not like that. Marriage just . . . never crossed my mind, I guess. A man in Seattle gets used to being a bachelor—there are so few women around. At least, few women who are worth taking to wife."

"That's why I'm here," Dovey said, bracing herself, praying silently that God would show mercy on her heart and her fortune.

She slid from the saddle and landed heavily in the mud, staggering a little. Virgil reached out and caught her, held her firmly by the shoulders. She could feel his hands trembling through the thick wool of her cape.

"Marry me," Dovey said.

"What?" He spoke so suddenly that the cigarette fell from his lips.

"You heard me. I'm here to convince you to marry me. Take me as your wife. It's the only way."

"What are you talking about, Dovey?"

"My rights. My money—that's what I'm talking about. It's why my father locked me up, and why he's still trying to arrange a marriage. By the law of Washington Territory, when I marry, everything I own will become the property of my husband. My father is only trying to find a man willing to negotiate a favorable split of all the money I've saved."

"But you've been saving that money up to start your own business."

"That doesn't matter to Father—and it doesn't matter to the law, either." The tears came again, but this time they were accompanied by a storm of helpless, hopeless sobs. Dovey's face burned with humiliation as she wept, and she was glad for the concealment of night so that Virgil couldn't see the twist of her mouth, the redness of her cheeks. But he pulled her close, held her tenderly against his chest, and smoothed her dark curls as she cried.

"If we'd only won the vote," Dovey wailed. "It could all be different then. But I've just spoken to Susan Anthony, and it's all been reversed— all our hopes ruined! I have no right to my own money, Virgil. There's nothing I can do!"

"Nothing except marry."

Dovey reined in her emotion with a strong hand. "And if I must marry—" She pulled away from his embrace, welcome as it was, and stared up into his night-darkened face. "If I must marry, there's no one I want other than you."

Virgil let go of her body; he stuffed his hands into the pockets of his trousers, paced a few feet away, and stood rocking on his heels, contemplating the silent, dark forest. Finally he turned back to Dovey and nodded. "All right. I'll do it, if it means so much to you."

Dovey knew she ought to be glad. An arrangement of marriage was supposed to be a time of joy—and she did love Virgil, loved him so wildly that sometimes she thought her heart would crack open from the force of it. But the law had compelled her to accept a fate she never wanted for herself—and a life Virgil didn't want, either.

"You seem awful sad, for a woman about to be wedded," he gently teased.

"I want to be able to stand on my own, Virgil. I want to be strong. You know I'm a strong woman."

He cupped her cheek with one warm hand, brushing away her tears with his thumb. "You're the very strongest woman I ever met."

"But here I am, selling myself off in marriage. Beholden to a man—kept like a horse or a dog. That's the last thing I ever wanted for myself."

"It's not as bad as that," he assured her. "I'll let you do what you please with your money. I won't interfere with your plans."

"But that's just it," she said, and fury rose within her, so strong that she stepped back, out of his embrace. "*Let* me do what I please . . . with *my* money! Virgil, it's not right!"

He nodded slowly. "I guess you're right about that. It doesn't seem right, after all, a girl as smart and capable as you, and the law won't trust you to mind your own business." He held out his hand, an offer of support in the empty space between them. After a moment, Dovey took it. "I'll help, Dovey—any way I can. With the fight for suffrage, I mean. I'm not much, but I've got your back—yours, and all the women of Seattle. And we'll keep fighting—you and me, together. The fight for the vote can't be over and done yet. We'll win yet—you'll see. We'll keep on swinging our fists, for you and all the women of the territory."

Dovey threw her arms around Virgil's neck. Then she kissed him, long and hard, saying with her passion all the words of gratitude and hope that her voice could not manage.

When she finally broke away, Virgil said, "Well—when's the happy date?"

"Now," she replied. "Tonight. It has to be now—time's running out, and Father might turn up with his hand-selected bridegroom in the morning, for all I know."

Virgil toed the end of his cigarette in the mud. "Wasn't expecting to get married tonight. It's a bit sudden, is all."

"But it has to be now, Virgil, or everything's lost."

He shrugged, and gave her one of his crooked smiles. "Well, all right. Let me get my hat and coat. Ought to look dandy for my wedding, after all."

They rode back into the city together. The whole long, night-dark way, relief warred with anxiety in Dovey's gut. *Could* she manage a wedding at so late an hour? Finding a minister would be tricky. But the urgency of her errand lashed at her, driving her on. It seemed she could sense her father looming in the darkness all around, and his sly, contented smile seemed to leer at her from the shadows between the trees. Dovey knew her time had all but run out. She must marry Virgil tonight, or lose everything.

But before they could find a minister, Dovey resolved to return Henry Yesler's mare to his stable. Dovey might have a reputation for scandalous ways, but she had no desire to add horse thievery to her repertoire of daring acts. At the Yesler home, all the lights of the party were still burning bright against the darkness, but the sound of forced merriment had died away. As they approached the rear yard, Dovey could detect the tension of fear in the voices of the people who clustered near the kitchen door and ranged along the side of the house, peering into the night.

As Dovey rode into the muddy yard, she heard Jo's voice calling, "There she is!"

Several people hurried forward, Henry Yesler among them. He laid hold of the mare's head collar, and Dovey felt ready to melt with shame. She dropped from the saddle rather sheepishly.

"I was obliged to borrow your horse," she told Mr. Yesler. "I'm awful sorry."

"It's no matter, Miss Mason," Yesler said, and smiled. "Your friends were terribly worried, though, when they realized you'd gone missing."

Jo and Sophronia rushed up to embrace her—and the way Sophronia clung to Dovey with real relief took her aback.

Dovey hugged them tightly in return. "I've settled the matter of my father," she told them. "It will all be put to rest tonight."

"What do you mean?" Jo cast a wary glance up at Virgil, who still sat his horse in calm silence. He tipped his hat soberly.

"There'll be a wedding tonight," Dovey said. "But I'm to marry a man of my choosing, not my father's."

Susan and Abigail drew up to the little crowd.

"You're well," Abigail said with obvious relief. "You gave us a shock, dear."

"I'm about to give you another. All I need is a minister. But I don't know where we might find one at so late an hour."

Sophronia smiled and took Dovey's arm. "I know just the man. I'll take you to him, if we can get a carriage."

"Leave the carriage to me." Susan winked rather impishly. "The Yeslers have been kind enough to put their entire household at my disposal—and Abigail's, too. If we find we have a sudden craving for a late-night tour of the city, we'll be most graciously accommodated. That is—if you'll have us as guests at the blessed event."

Dovey grinned. "There's nothing I'd like better, Miss Anthony. Now let's get a move on."

In short order, the carriage came rolling smartly out from the Yeslers' stable, with two cheerful lanterns swinging from the corners of its footboard. Sophronia gave the driver her instructions, and they all crowded in, cheeks flushed and eyes shining with the mischief of their adventure.

When they reached the small whitewashed chapel on the hill, the minister came stumbling and yawning from the modest manse nearby, still tugging at his hastily donned trousers and coat. Dovey expected the man to light up in a fluster of indignation when he realized why the party had come, and at so ungodly an hour, too. But when he saw

Sophronia step down from the carriage, her pale-golden beauty shining against the night, he greeted her with a kiss so long and lingering that it made Dovey's eyebrows climb.

"Harmon Grigg." Sophronia introduced him in an uncharacteristically shy voice. "He's the minister here—and . . . and my beau."

"Well," Dovey said, properly startled. "All this time I lived with you, and I never knew it."

"Jo isn't the only one who can keep a secret," Sophronia returned with a touch of her old loft and primness. Then she turned to her beau. "There's to be a wedding, Harmon. And it must be tonight. Can you help us?"

Harmon gave a joyous laugh, and clapped Virgil heartily on the shoulder. "Why, of course! Come in. There's no better time than the present."

Virgil helped the minister light the chapel's lamps. Little by little, the warm wood interior of the church revealed itself as the pools of light spread. The lively glow illuminated Dovey's friends, too. The hems of their dresses were mud-stained from their search of the Yeslers' property, their hair and hats in disarray. But for all their ruffled state, Dovey thought she'd never seen a lovelier group of bridesmaids.

"There's no one I'd rather have stand with me at my wedding than you," she told Jo and Sophronia, taking their hands. "And you, Susan and Abigail. I can't tell you just what it means to me, that you ladies should be here with me."

Susan brushed a speck of dust from Dovey's shoulder—a futile gesture, as Dovey was the most bedraggled figure present, thanks to her late-night ride. "We're pleased to be here," Susan said. "And pleased to count you a friend."

When the lamps were lit, Sophronia's minister took his place at the altar. The Bible lay open before him. Virgil stepped up beside him, wearing a game smile of jocular disbelief. And as Dovey stepped toward her bridegroom, with Jo and Sophronia a half step behind, she found that she was glad of this wedding after all—truly contented after all. She had taken her fate into her own hands. She was strong and clever, a woman of her own determination, even when all the laws of the Territory sought to hem her in.

She reached the altar and glanced back down the length of the chapel. Susan and Abigail waited in the pews, their eyes steady and encouraging, their demeanors unshakable, like two bulwarks against the lashing wind of injustice. *I am as strong as you,* Dovey told them silently just as the minister began the sacred words. *We will keep fighting, all of us together. And one day—God send it's soon—we'll win.*

CHAPTER
THIRTY-FIVE
VICE OR PREFERENCE

The gala's final attendee offered her gracious thanks to Sophronia, then swept from the Occidental's lobby in a rustle of silk and a cloud of orange-blossom perfume. Sophronia turned to the long table, strewn with flower petals and half-empty bowls of hazelnut comfits. The pretty, spangled singer imported from Portland and billed as the night's great attraction was only a lure, an enticement meant to funnel donors through the doors of the Occidental. At the table's center, amid the nuts and empty punch cups and the detritus of celebration, stood the gala's real star: the wooden collection safe, artfully painted with the words **Washington Women's Suffrage Association**.

Sophronia gave the box a brisk pat. She had spent most of the singer's performance hovering in the vicinity of the collection safe, and she had heard many a satisfying clink throughout the evening as the enchanted audience dropped their donations in. The night had surely been a rousing success, and as pleased as Sophronia was with the donations, she was more delighted still to see that nearly as many men had attended the event as women. The men had made contributions to the collection box, too. Enthusiasm for the cause was growing among all the residents of Seattle, male and female.

Funny, Sophronia mused. *Asa Mercer went to Massachusetts eight years ago seeking women who could influence the men of Seattle toward a positive change.* Certainly suffrage had not been what Mercer had had in mind; but here they were, gentlemen and ladies working together to reverse the legislature's November ruling, or at least to present a new bill promoting suffrage, with terms more acceptable to the Territorial government. *We've changed the men for the better, and no mistake. You couldn't have predicted it, Mr. Mercer, when you stood in Lowell's town square so long ago. But we press on for justice, and work together now, hand in hand.*

Sophronia had seen Mr. Mercer himself at several of the Suffrage Association's fund-raisers. He had always been a man of far-thinking habits and was enthusiastic about the cause. That knowledge suffused Sophronia with a glow of gladness. She had never befriended Asa Mercer, but she thought him an upstanding man and was grateful to him every day for providing her with the opportunity of Seattle itself—the chance to start her life anew. Now, at last, Sophronia was just what she had always aspired to be: a missionary for the greater good.

She swept the wilted flower petals into a box, shaking her head and smiling at her own past follies. To think she had ever thought the vote would be detrimental to women! She saw the world more clearly now. She perceived that suffrage could be just the thing—perhaps the *only* thing—that might save Seattle from its stew of sin. And so she strove toward the vote with all her might, and felt a righteousness in her work, a satisfaction she had never known before.

Sophronia cherished that same sense of righteousness and joy with Harmon, too. Their engagement brought a flush of pleasure to her cheeks whenever she thought of it. Harmon was as kind and loving as he had been in their days of courtship, and his dedication to the Lord's work had only deepened over the years. Best of all, he seemed determined never to err with loose women again, no matter what temptations might cross his path. And God knew, Seattle's roads were strewn with temptation. It wasn't always easy for Sophronia to trust Harmon, but she gave him her best effort, her most honest faith—and he gave Sophronia his best in return.

The Occidental's door swung open, and a woman in a showy gown glided into the lobby. Her silk was of the deepest wine-dark purple, trimmed with cut-glass beads that glittered in the light of the oil lamps. Cuffs of white rabbit fur turned up at the ends of her sleeves.

"Oh, I'm so sorry," Sophronia said, straightening from the cleanup. "I'm afraid you've missed the gala."

"No matter. I didn't come to hear some Oregon canary twitter."

Sophronia blinked in surprise. She had been so distracted with her task—and her thoughts of Harmon—that she hadn't recognized Dovey. And no wonder; rather than her usual tumble of curls falling to her shoulders, Dovey had swept her hair up in an elaborate nest of twists and braids. She looked altogether elegant and mature.

"Why, don't you look fine," Sophronia said. "Married life agrees with you, I suppose."

Dovey shrugged. She crossed the room to the collection box, opened her beaded purse, and dropped such a steady stream of coins inside that Sophronia stared in frank amazement. It was a very generous donation.

Sophronia raised her brows, a mute inquiry.

"I'm still working," Dovey said.

"Not collecting taxes still? It was shocking enough when you did that work as a freewheeling spitfire, but you know it's terribly improper for a married woman to work at such a job."

"I like the work," Dovey said nonchalantly.

"But you have a husband now! It would be proper to leave the work to Virgil."

"Well, it's a good thing I *do* continue to work," Dovey rejoined, even as she dropped her purse on the table and began gathering up the empty punch cups. "That was a large donation I just made, and you're welcome, by the way. Now that my father has finally decided to skitter back to the East Coast to fetch Mother, it's full steam ahead with the old ambition. He leaves for Boston as soon as his loose ends in Seattle are tied up, and I'm just about ready to start my business. When I get my cathouse going, I may donate even more to the Association."

"Oh," Sophronia groaned. "You can't be serious about that! A brothel would only bring shame on your husband, and after all he's done for you . . . !"

"I help out with the Association however I can, Sophronia. You know that."

"As do I, but—"

"This business I intend to start—and soon, too—is in the best interest of our cause."

Sophronia began stacking the comfit bowls on a silver tray. She nested each one with a louder clink than was strictly necessary. "How can you make such a claim? You know all the suffragists are opposed to prostitution."

"Not all of them," Dovey said. "Just most. And anyway, the 'seam-stresses' of this city are very much in favor of winning the vote. Why not? Their houses are taxed like those of any businessman, and as much money as they earn—well, their contributions to the city's coffers are considerable. You remember the incident of the silver dollars."

"If only I could forget it," Sophronia muttered, resisting the urge to wipe her hands on the tablecloth.

"The ladies who are really good at their work make more money than half the men of the city. *I'm* an ally to those ladies, Sophie—an influence for the cause, planted conveniently among some of the city's richest taxpayers. I'm a bridge between the fine ladies of Seattle and the seamstresses. I can convince those rowdy girls to make substantial contributions to our cause—and once I've got a position of real standing among them, as the owner of a good establishment, my influence will go even farther."

"We don't need any more of their foul contributions. As you say, I recall the silver dollars all too well. Besides, the seamstresses certainly will not contribute once they understand the direction I intend for our Association."

Dovey, who had been gathering up the bright paper-flower decorations from the lobby's end tables, straightened slowly and turned to Sophronia with a wary squint. "What are you talking about?"

"I intend to use the vote to put an end to vice in Seattle—and in the rest of Washington Territory, too."

Sophronia braced herself for a storm of anger. Dovey loved vice too well, and was ever prepared to embrace sin.

But after a moment of shocked silence, the young woman threw back her head and gave a loud hoot of laughter. When she had recovered herself enough to speak, she said, still chuckling, "If you want to do away with vice, Sophie, you'll need to secure the men's support—not only the women's. But it'll never work, your crazy plan—you're looking at this all wrong! A woman is a woman, whether she's a seamstress or a fine lady up in the heights. Either we'll *all* have the vote, or *none* of us will; once we win suffrage, you can't exclude a woman from casting her ballot just because you don't like how she earns her keep. You think you'll convince all the working women of Seattle to do away with vice—that very same vice that puts the jingle in their purses? You'd have more luck convincing the stars to turn off at night.

"Besides," Dovey added, more soberly now, "I strenuously object to the very idea of 'vice.' There's no such thing—there's only *preference*."

"Sin is sin," Sophronia said stiffly. "It's in the Bible, the very word of God, as plain as day. The Lord has destroyed cities before, for being too far gone to sin. He won't hesitate to do the same to Seattle, I'm sure."

"And you think that's why He led you to Seattle—is that it? So you could stop the fire from the sky with a wave of your righteous little hand?"

Sophronia stifled a gasp. She willed herself to calm so she would not betray her shock to Dovey. That was *precisely* what Sophronia felt, deep in her heart—though she certainly did not picture the event as such a melodramatic caricature. But her mission was, she now knew, to save Seattle from its own morass of sin. And all of Dovey's mischievous affinity for vice wouldn't convince Sophronia that sin was a force to be tolerated in the world.

"We've been allies in recent days," Sophronia said coolly, "and I'm sure I appreciate your contributions to the Suffrage Association. But you're asking me to turn a blind eye to immorality—to chuck degradation under its chin."

"I'm not asking you," Dovey said. "I'm telling you. You can't change the face of Seattle, Sophronia. It's a losing proposition."

"Still, I shall try. For the good of the city and all its people, I shall try."

"You don't *know* what's good for the city and all its people. I told you once, long ago, that the seamstresses are hardworking girls, worthy of your respect. You propose to do away with their sole occupation. How is that good for *them*, Sophronia?"

Sophronia sighed in exasperation.

"I'll tell you why you can't alter this city's character," Dovey said, gathering up her purse and taking the folds of her fine skirt in one hand. "Because I won't allow it. We've been allies—that's just as you say. But

I won't be your ally in this. When women have the vote, you'll see just how the chips fall, Sophie. You'll see."

Dovey turned and floated out the Occidental's door, her elegant gown sparkling, carrying her head as high as did any fine lady in the hills. Sophronia watched her go. Bitterness turned her mouth in a frown so firm and vehement that her cheeks and chin ached. She was fully prepared, despite the recent goodwill that had bloomed between, to return to the days when she and Dovey had been enemies. The girl was simply no good—trouble, through and through. It was up to Dovey whether she made right with God before the fire rained from the sky. Sophronia could do nothing to save that spitfire from sin, and she was tired of trying.

CHAPTER
THIRTY-SIX
SANCTUARY LOST

Jo woke to a soft spill of morning light gleaming through white lace curtains. She sat up slowly in the soft bed, stretching her arms and back, taking in the quiet peace of birdsong in the dense woods outside. She had stayed the night at Dovey and Virgil's modest white house on the north end of town—not for the first time. Jo had come to Seattle often this spring, busy with obligations for the Suffrage Association. Dovey was ever a welcoming hostess, and had put Jo up in the spare room yet again after Sophronia's fund-raising gala. Jo had slept as well as she always did at Dovey's place. But the woodland sounds outside the window made her long for her own quiet, one-room house in Coupeville and the gentle peace of Whidbey Island. It was time to return home— and there remain for as long as Jo could arrange it, drinking in the springtime tranquility, enjoying her easy days with Bill.

She rose, splashed her face with water, and dressed in the soft morning light. Then she made her way out into the cozy, white kitchen, where Dovey sat glaring at her Staffordshire teapot. A banner of steam lifted thinly from the pot's spout.

"Good morning," Jo said.

Dovey seemed not to hear, gloomily absorbed in the steeping of her tea.

Jo fetched her own china cup and sat at the table opposite Dovey. "I didn't hear you come in last night. Were you out late after Sophronia's gala?"

"I went riding after," Dovey said. "Sophronia streaked me, all right, and I was a regular storm of anger. I still am."

"I can tell. Did you heat the water for the tea with the blaze in your eyes?"

Dovey yielded to Jo's cheer with a reluctant smile.

"Now tell me just what happened between you and Sophronia," Jo said.

Dovey obliged, regaling Jo with a tale she'd heard more times than she could count, ever since their first meeting at the Lowell train depot. When Dovey had finished her complaints, Jo sighed, truly vexed at the persistent hardheadedness of both her good friends. "You and Sophronia could get along just fine, if you'd only make up your minds to do so."

"But she's wrong, Jo—she's just plain wrong about the vote, and the working women of the city, and . . . well . . . about everything!"

"I suspect she feels the same about you."

"It doesn't matter what she feels about me," Dovey said stoutly. "I won't let her ruin the livelihood of so many women. If Sophronia has her way, the vote will mean poverty and destruction for women all across Seattle. That's not what I've been working for—nor you!"

"If the two of you would only discuss your points of view civilly, without riling one another—"

"It's impossible *not* to rile Sophronia! She was made to be riled. No—if she persists in this mad idea to vote out vice, then I'll withdraw my support from the Suffrage Association."

Jo set aside her tea with an uneasy frown. "That's a strong measure, Dovey. Your contributions have been so helpful—they've allowed us to accomplish so much."

"Oh, that's not the half of it. I'll influence the city's prostitutes to work against the Association, too."

"Dovey—you wouldn't!" With their good friend Dovey supporting the Association so wholeheartedly, the seamstresses had begun to donate a respectable sum each month, too. A withdrawal of their support would spell a major setback for the cause—perhaps an outright disaster.

"Sophronia won't listen to sense, Jo. And I can't sit by in silence while she stampedes over the rights and well-being of so many women!"

Jo shook her head sadly. "I hate to see the two of you at odds—I always have. But it's simply intolerable to watch you and Sophronia quarrel with the Association between you, like a couple of dogs tussling over a bone. It isn't dignified, that's what."

Dovey shrugged and sipped at her tea. "I've never been terribly concerned with dignity."

"I do hope you and Sophronia find some cause to mend the rent between you. And soon, too—before you topple the Association with your squabbling." She stood and smoothed her skirt with cool poise. "Now I must go, Dovey. The boat leaves soon for Whidbey Island. Thank you for your hospitality; write me, if I don't see you again soon, and tell me how things stand with the Association."

Jo brooded at the ship's rail, all the way back to the island, paying no heed to the bright spring day. Even on the walk from the pier to her house in the woods, she remained indifferent to the charms of the fresh, new season. The crocuses blooming beneath the evergreens and the apple trees, fragrant with their clouds of blossoms, made no impression on her mind or her heart. All that existed for her was the gloomy distraction of the Suffrage Association's imminent danger—its treacherous balance between Dovey and Sophronia, those irascible girls who had never learned the meaning of forgiveness.

Jo forgot all her dark intensity the moment she stepped inside her house. Her fretful rumination vanished in a sudden chill of terror. Every shelf in her home was empty, all her books and knick-knacks strewn about and broken on the floor. Large, heavy boot-prints, outlined in dried mud, tracked about the room, showing where some invading brute had trampled as he'd rummaged through Jo's belongings. The quilt and sheets had been dragged from her bed and lay crumpled in one corner as if carelessly thrown; Jo saw with a shudder of dread that the mattress had been slashed with a knife, and spilled its feathers onto the floor. Her night table was overturned, the porcelain pitcher that held her water smashed on the floor below.

"My God," Jo gasped.

The smell of lamp oil was acrid and thick in the air. Jo stared about her at the terrible disarray, dulled by the force of her panic. A great puddle of oil lay on the floor near the crumpled bedsheets. She approached it cautiously and bent over the mess. In the center of the puddle, the end of a cigarette lay, sodden and unburning. *Thank God,* Jo thought, shivering with relief. The butt had snuffed out before it could light the fuel.

Jo reached down slowly and picked up the cigarette. The paper was soaked in oil, its whiteness discolored. But still she recognized the peculiar way its end had been twisted and crimped—recognized it at once, even after eight long years.

Clifford had found her. He had come to her home—stood in her own room, defiled her blessed sanctuary. He had found her. Josephine's long, dreadful nightmare had finally come true.

Jo dropped the cigarette on the floor and straightened quickly, spinning as if she might catch sight of Clifford at the door. But he was not present now—at least, not that Jo could see. She staggered toward the door, then froze halfway across the room. Her immediate instinct was to give in to blind panic, to run screeching outside. But only the Lord knew whether Clifford was lurking outside, waiting in the woods to ambush her.

Bill, Jo thought frantically. *I'll tell Bill. He'll take me in—protect me. He'll stop Clifford.*

But no—she discarded that thought with a desperate shake of her head. Bill had gone down to Portland and wasn't due to return to the island until late that night. His boat from Olympia to Seattle might have landed in Seattle by now, for all Jo knew—but the distance between them seemed impossibly wide, and for all the aid or comfort he could grant her, Bill might as well have been at the North Pole or locked in the Tower of London.

I must rely on my own wits, she told herself sternly, trying to force some sense into her jolted brain. She had no way to reach Bill now. She must seek the aid of whomever was close to hand.

Jo turned and walked briskly out her door, flinching at the sight of the forest, all the shadows and concealments that leaned and crouched beneath its boughs. She returned to the lane and moved as quickly as she could—without giving in to panic and running like a frightened rabbit—down the narrow dirt road. Her nearest neighbor was a quarter-mile away. As she bore steadily on toward the Andersons' property, Jo imagined she could feel Clifford's hate-filled glare watching her from the trees, sliding through the pines to keep pace with her flight.

She reached the Andersons' fence line and found the family's eldest son working in the garden.

Jo called to him. "James! James, come here, please!"

The boy, fifteen years old and strong as an ox, looked around, noticed Jo's frantic wave, and dropped his hoe. He hurried to the fence with a greeting for his teacher, but when he saw the fear in Jo's eyes, the words died on his lips.

"Where is your father?" Jo asked.

"Gone to Seattle, Miss Carey—and my mother with him. They've taken all the children, too. It's just me at home."

Jo gritted her teeth. There was nothing for it; she must trust her safety to the neighbor boy.

"I have a task for you," she told him, struggling to remain calm. "I'm afraid it's terribly important, but I'll pay you—or my friend will, at least. Run inside and fetch me two pieces of paper and a pencil."

James did as she asked, and quickly, thank God. Jo used the square top of a fence post as a writing table, and quickly scribbled out one note to Dovey and Virgil. They, at least, had guns, and knew how to use them. They had also had no small experience with confronting angry men. Perhaps, if James could reach one of them in time, they might prove useful to Jo.

The other note she jotted to the local sheriff, begging for his aid. But Jo had heard from many a resident of Coupeville that the man was often difficult to find—the island was a big place, after all—and she hung little hope on that weak thread.

Quickly, Jo gave the boy instructions on where to find Dovey, and thrust a few coins into his hand for the boat fare to Seattle.

"Dovey will pay you very well for this service," she told him. "Only please, don't allow yourself to become distracted. Find her or her husband as quickly as you can."

"I will, Miss Carey," James said. "I promise!"

She watched James sprint off toward town, heading for the piers and their rank of southbound steamers.

I'm not foolish enough to board a boat to Seattle myself, Clifford, Jo thought resolutely. He had not leapt out of the forest between her home and the Anderson place, and so she felt certain that he had retired to the docks to skulk about the boats. There Clifford assuredly waited, at Jo's most obvious point of egress, grinning his hate-filled leer, watching for Jo to come flying from the woods, scatterbrained and shrieking like a chicken fleeing a fox in the coop.

I've evaded you all this time. I'll avoid your clutches still. Just see if I don't.

Jo watched James sprint down the road until he was merely a speck among the distant homes and shops of Coupeville. Then she returned to the road and set off for her schoolhouse. It waited in a peaceful patch of sunshine at the top of a small rise, less than a quarter mile from the Anderson home. There, Jo would shut herself in and wait, calm and patient, for help to arrive.

CHAPTER
THIRTY-SEVEN
AN URGENT MESSAGE

Dovey splashed an armload of linens into the dolly tub and cursed as the breeze shifted, pushing the fire's smoke directly into her eyes. She lifted the peggy stick with a grunt and plunged it into the steaming water; the odor of hot lye rose up to strike her in the face.

Laundry, she grumbled to herself as she worked the peggy stick up and down, beating the clean back into her linens. *Truly the most disagreeable aspect of married life.*

The wind shifted again, buffeting Dovey's eyes with the sting of smoke and lye. She stepped away from the fire, hissing as she wiped the reflexive tears on her sleeve. When her vision had cleared, she saw a lone figure hurrying down the lane toward her gate.

It was a man, and for a moment Dovey wondered whether it was some cranky old shipwright or lumberman come to seek his vengeance for years of taxes collected. But then she blinked away the last of her tears and saw that it was only a boy, lanky as a colt, his face screwed up with an urgency that made Dovey's heart go still.

"You Mrs. Cooper?" the boy panted.

"Yes, sir," she said cautiously. "What's the panic?"

He approached and held out a folded piece of paper. Dovey took it and read the note through once—then again, this time with a quiver of increasing anxiety.

"Lord," she breathed.

"Mrs. Cooper? Are you all right?"

"Yes, yes. Wait here." She ran into the house and found two silver dollars—more than enough to pay the boy's return fare to Whidbey Island and compensate him for his service, which Jo's note begged her to do. Then she sent the boy on his way and stared at the note again, Jo's handwriting blurring into dark, indecipherable lines as Dovey's head turned to a mush of fear. She stuffed the note into the pocket of her work dress. Not knowing just what in God's name she should do, or even in which direction she ought to step first, Dovey turned in a helpless circle in her yard, staring up at the trees that arched overhead.

Virgil was off collecting, and although Dovey knew that Jo's Bill was due back at the nearby docks to catch the next steamer to Coupeville, she couldn't be certain of finding him. The docks were always a tangle of men and horses and cargo. Even if Bill's boat were on schedule, the docks would be a labyrinth to navigate, and that would only waste precious time.

The police. Dovey discarded that idea instantly. If there was any vice to be found in Seattle, it was among the men who wore the silver stars of law enforcement. That corrupt gang of rowdies was in sweet with every businessman in the city, and no man of money liked those tax-grubbing Coopers one bit. Dovey knew she would find no help for Josephine there.

She ran to the end of the lane and stared down the hill, out at the small square of Puget Sound she could see from this vantage. A steamer was arriving, a low black slash creeping slowly down from the horizon. Dovey knew from many years of watching the boats come and go that it was the *Townsend*, which made regular runs between Seattle and Coupeville. She had an hour at most until it arrived—maybe, if she were lucky—offloaded its cargo, and then returned to the island.

But what help could Dovey rally in that single fragile hour? She had no idea when Virgil might return from his collecting circuit. Nor did she know just where he had gone today. Dovey ran through her short list of allies, flipping her thoughts as fast as one riffles through the pages of a book. She came up only with prostitutes and ruffians, and knew she couldn't convince any of those women to come away just now. Most of the seamstresses were sleeping, preparing for their nightly shift. They wouldn't be inclined to travel so far to aid a woman they didn't know—not even for Dovey's sake.

The only other friend she could name—the only help she could think of at all—was Sophronia.

"Hellfire," Dovey growled.

She stalked away from the laundry kettle—*let it boil itself dry!*—and went to the corral to saddle Virgil's fastest horse.

Dovey rode breakneck through the streets of Seattle, as fast as if the Devil himself were on her heels. She reined in hard outside Sophronia's house for fallen women; the horse tossed its head high and gave a groan of displeasure as it skidded on the cobbles. Dovey threw herself from the saddle and careered up the steps, shouting as she pounded at the door.

Sophronia answered it at once, face flushed, eyes wide with anger at the rude intrusion. When she saw it was Dovey howling like an alley cat on her doorstep, Sophronia's cheeks burned all the redder.

"What are you doing here?" she whispered, as if fearful the whole city might overhear and know that she was associating with the uncouth Dovey Cooper.

"Jo's in danger," Dovey blurted. "Clifford's back. He's tossed her place and nearly burned it down. She needs our help, Sophie. Come on! There's a steamer heading up to Coupeville, but it leaves soon. We've got to go—now!"

Sophronia shook her head in befuddlement. "Clifford . . . But what can we do to help?"

"I don't know, but there must be *something*!"

"We must contact the police!"

"You know they won't stir a finger. Especially not if the trouble's up on the island. It's us or no one, Sophie. I know you don't like me any, and the feeling might be mutual. But we have to help Jo. She has no one else to rely on!"

Sophronia hesitated, going even paler than was usual. Finally she pulled a letter from her pocket. "Dovey, I've just received this correspondence from Susan Anthony. It seems she has secured an opportunity to speak before the legislature again—one last time to make our case, to convince them to revoke the November decision and give us the vote. But our only chance to speak is tomorrow morning. We must be there—all the way down in Olympia. We can't leave it all to Susan, who isn't from Washington. We must represent our case! And . . . if we go all the way up to Coupeville, how can we make it to Olympia on time?"

Dovey growled in frustration. "Jo is more important than anything, Sophie—even more important than the vote!"

Sophronia swallowed hard. For a moment, Dovey thought she'd argue again. Anger and disbelief bubbled in her gut, wringing her with helpless nausea.

But then Sophronia's eyes seemed to clear, the veil of shock and indecision falling away. "You're right," she said. "I'll just have to trust in the Lord to provide a way. Let's go, Dovey. We can't leave Jo on her own with Clifford lurking about."

"Good old Sophie! I could kiss you, do you know that?" Dovey took Sophronia's hand and pulled her down the porch steps, into the street. Virgil's horse stood waiting, watching Dovey with a dark, rolling eye.

"I'll mount up first, and then I'll pull you up behind me," Dovey said.

"A horse? *Riding?*" Sophronia covered her mouth with her hand, and Dovey feared she might faint.

"It's not as hard as it looks."

"But—"

"*Jo*, Sophie! There's no time to argue."

Dovey hoisted her foot into the stirrup and, with a hop and an elaborate curse, wrangled herself aboard. She reached down to grasp Sophronia by the forearm. The prim, proper lady had never attempted to mount a horse before; Dovey had to lean and pull and haul at her until finally she was more or less astride, squeaking in fear at the height and the unfamiliar movement of the animal beneath her.

"Hold to me tightly," Dovey said.

Sophronia obliged, with a grip so tight Dovey feared she would be squeezed right in half. She kicked the horse's ribs, and he sprang forward in an eager lope.

"Dov-eey!" Sophronia shrieked and plunged her face into Dovey's curls, hiding herself from the men on the boardwalks who turned to point and stare at the spectacle of two women bumbling astride down the street.

The horse tossed its head and grumbled at the way Sophronia jounced and jostled on its back. Dovey feared that it might take to bucking if she couldn't get Sophronia to relax.

"Let up your grip a little," she said. "Loosen up your hips; let your body go all wiggly, so you can move with the horse's stride."

"I . . . I can't!"

"Sure you can," Dovey said. "Just pretend you're a seamstress looking for a nice man to take back to your crib."

"Dovey Cooper! You are simply an outrage!"

Outrage she might be, but Dovey's advice was good. Sophronia relaxed, after a fashion, moving with the horse just enough that it pinned its ears and snorted but decided not to throw both women from the saddle. Soon Dovey and Sophronia were leaning and shifting together, flowing in time to the horse's rhythmic stride.

They made it to the dock just before the *Townsend* cast off its lines. Dovey thrust the horse's reins into a dock boy's hand, followed by a few coins to stable him until she returned. Then she helped the mortified Sophronia down from the saddle and hauled her up the *Townsend*'s ramp.

"My," Dovey breathed, watching as the ramp was pulled away from the steamer just moments after their boot heels hit the deck.

"Dovey . . ." Sophronia muttered.

Dovey turned to look at her, bracing for the tongue-lashing she knew must be coming, the lecture on proper behavior, the scolding in the name of the Lord. But Sophronia said nothing. She only threw herself into Dovey's arms, and they clung to one another, shaking with fear and excitement, as the *Townsend* pulled away from Seattle and turned its great black nose to the north.

CHAPTER
THIRTY-EIGHT
SILK RIBBONS

The sun had fallen below the horizon by the time Dovey and Sophronia hurried across the little town of Coupeville and gained the wide, rutted dirt road that led up into the pines. On a distant rise, a whitewashed building, tiny across the expanse of farmers' fields, stood out sharply against a backdrop of forest—Jo's schoolhouse, the narrow tower of its belfry held up like a signal of distress against the oncoming night.

"There it is," Dovey panted. "She said in her note that she'd take shelter in the school."

"We're almost there, thank God." Sophronia seemed to find a fresh burst of energy; she rushed past Dovey, holding her petticoats high, showing far more of her ankle than she ever had before.

They were both flushed and out of breath by the time they made it to the schoolyard. Dusk was descending, pulling a shroud of violet shadows across the fields, dimming the small school's whitewashed siding to gray.

Dovey and Sophronia hesitated at the paling fence that marked out the schoolyard's boundary. They watched the building in silence, wary for any sound, any sign of movement. Its small, covered porch was empty and dark. There was no sound save for the intermittent drip-drip of water falling from the schoolhouse roof, onto the lid of a fat rain barrel squatting at the porch's side.

"Should we—" Sophronia began, but Dovey stilled her with a hand on her arm.

Something in Dovey's gut told her not to call out, to keep as silent as a mouse under a cat's nose until she knew for certain that the coast was clear. Without taking her eyes from the schoolhouse, she grabbed Sophronia's hand, and together they made their way stealthily up to the porch.

They weren't more than a few feet away when Dovey knew her instinct had been keen—and possibly sent by a merciful God. All at once, a man's harsh voice boomed inside the schoolhouse. Dovey could make out no words—perhaps he wasn't speaking any words but only hollering in a thick, hoarse rage—and then, so loud and clear that the sound seemed to impact deep in Dovey's stomach, the smack of a fist hitting flesh. Jo's voice cried out wordlessly in pain. Then, clear as an alarm bell, she screamed for help. Her sobs came stifled through the schoolhouse's walls.

"Oh Lord," Sophronia whispered, gripping Dovey's hand so hard that her nails bit like teeth. "It's Clifford in there. Jo! What can we do? Dovey, we must do something!"

"Stay calm," she murmured. "I've dealt with angry men before. This is nothing new to me."

But it was something new—new and terrible, to know that one's dearest friend was trapped in the dark with a ravening beast. Dovey pulled her Colt from the holster on her thigh. This time, when she raised her petticoats to reveal the length of her stockings and the shape of her limb, Sophronia didn't bother with a sniff of distaste.

Dovey crept up the porch steps on her toes and tried the door's handle. It was locked from the inside. She returned to Sophronia's side as another round of shouts and pitiful cries erupted inside the schoolhouse.

"All right," Dovey said. "I have an idea."

"You can't shoot him," Sophronia said, cupping her horrified face with her hands.

"Oh yes, I can!"

"You'll go to jail, Dovey! No one will believe it was self-defense; he's not attacking *you.*"

Dovey paused, her fingers locked tight around the Colt's handle. Sophronia's argument made good sense. She quickly scanned the school-yard, squinting into the dusk. The building had no window on this side, but the roof of the little porch was so gently sloped that it was almost flat. That offered some possibilities. In the grass beside the schoolhouse, Dovey spotted a few gardening tools, evidently used to keep the yard: a small hand trowel and a rake with a long handle and thick iron tines.

"Get up there on the roof, over the door," Dovey whispered.

"Me?"

"Yes, you! You've taken Clifford down once before. It's time you gave him an encore."

Sophronia seemed about to protest, until she heard Jo scream for help again—and the low, cruel thunder of Clifford's laughter. She tugged at her skirt as if settling her bloomers into a more comfort-able arrangement, then strode toward the porch. With Dovey's help, Sophronia clambered up onto a rain barrel, then, gasping and grunting with the effort, pulled herself up to the flat roof as silently as she could.

Dovey passed her the heavy rake. Sophronia bunched up her skirt around her knees and perched above the door like a gargoyle, tense and snarling with a ferocity Dovey had never seen the woman display before—not even when railing against the evils of prostitution. Sophronia held the rake poised over one shoulder, ready to swing it with brutal force. She gave Dovey a single grim nod.

Dovey sucked in a deep breath and shouted, "The sheriff is here— and a whole posse! You'd better come on out, Clifford. There's no escape."

The clamor inside the schoolhouse cut off abruptly. There was the clatter of fast, heavy footsteps, then Clifford's voice called out, close beside the door.

"Ha! A posse? You don't sound much like a sheriff, little girl."

"I'm not a sheriff," Dovey said. "I'm a tax collector. And don't you think the Revenue Service knows where to scare up a posse now and then?"

Clifford roared with laughter. "You can't fool me, girl. I've spent years tracking down this thieving bitch I am obliged to call my wife. I'm not letting her go as easily as that. She owes me—with interest. I'm here to extract my due."

Jo gave a faint whimper from the depths of the schoolhouse. Dovey gripped the Colt so hard her wrist ached.

"I advise you to come out peacefully," Dovey shouted. "The sheriff is ready to shoot, and the least display of funny business might set him off."

"Cops! Prove it, girl, or shut up and stop wasting my time."

Coolly, Dovey aimed her Colt into the air and fired off a shot. The gun kicked hard in her hand, as it always did, but the roar of its discharge sent a surge of power through her body. When its echo had died away, rolling in waves down the fields and out across the Sound, there was silence inside the schoolhouse.

Then the door creaked open.

Clifford revealed himself in the doorway, and Dovey's stomach clenched at the sight of him. Seven years in prison had changed him little. His face was still handsome enough to set any girl's heart racing, but his broad shoulders hunched and shivered—with fear of the gun, Dovey wondered, or with the force of his own dark cruelty? When he saw no one in the yard but Dovey, small and slim, delicate as a china cup in the pale plaid of her work dress, a grin of hateful amusement twisted his mouth. He glanced dismissively at the pistol still smoking in her hand.

"Well, look at you," he said, advancing one step, then another. "Don't I know you from somewhere, pretty little thing that you are? Put that gun down and come over here."

Dovey snorted. She turned the gun on Clifford. Sophronia, huddled on her rooftop perch, shot a pleading glance down at Dovey. The rake trembled in her arms.

"Do you think I'm an idiot?" Dovey said. "I'd never go near a brute like you."

"Come on, you little tart. Ease that gun to the ground. I'll give you something else to hold." He took another step and then paused, eyeing Dovey with more doubt, more caution.

"Don't come any closer." Dovey allowed her voice to quiver with fear. She shuffled backward, clutching the gun with both hands, for all the world as if her sense had fled and she no longer had any idea how to use the thing.

The display of feminine fear seemed to bolster Clifford's predatory confidence. He chuckled deep in his throat and took another step across the porch—then another.

Sophronia swung her bludgeon with so much force that the rake whistled as it sliced through the air. It cracked against Clifford's head as loud as a rifle shot. Clifford toppled sideways and fell in a heap off the end of the porch, too stunned even to cry out.

Jo staggered to the door, clinging to its frame. She was shaking violently; her face was puffy from Clifford's blows, and blood from her nose and split lip dripped onto the collar of her dress. But when she met Dovey's eye, Jo's weeping turned to tears of gratitude and relief. Her smile was bloodied, but it was wide and amazed.

"You," Jo said thickly.

"Me, all right," Dovey replied. She holstered her gun and came forward to guide Sophronia down from the roof. "And her," she added as Sophronia, back on solid ground once more, twitched her skirt into place.

Dovey stared down at the unmoving bulk of Clifford, sprawled in the grass. "We need to tie him up, good and tight. Is there any rope inside the schoolhouse, Jo?"

She shook her head, dazed. "None."

Sophronia instantly hiked up her skirt and her petticoats.

Wonders never cease, Dovey thought wryly.

"Here," Sophronia said. "Dovey, pick the ribbons out of my bloomer cuffs. They're silk—silk is very strong. It ought to hold him well enough."

Dovey did as she was told, pulling two wide, pink silk ribbons free of Sophronia's drawers. Then she removed her own bloomer ribbons and clutched the whole bundle in her teeth. Together, she and Sophronia dragged the unresisting Clifford to the edge of the porch. They pushed and prodded him into a more-or-less seated position, pulled his hands behind his back, and knotted the silk ribbons tightly around his hairy wrists, binding him to the porch railing.

When the work was done, Dovey straightened and admired her handiwork. Clifford sat slumped and unconscious, anchored to the schoolhouse as firmly as a ship to a pier.

"What do we do now?" Jo asked. She wobbled on her feet; Sophronia hurried to her aid and eased her down on the porch step, dabbing with a handkerchief at her tender, bloody face.

Full night had come. The stars were a bright scatter where they showed through patchy cloud. From somewhere in the forest, an owl called, fell silent, then called again, from a point far away. Dovey saw that there was nothing to do now but wait. *For what?* she asked herself. For someone to come along who might be able to summon the sheriff, she supposed. She felt rather dull and used up, at the end of her resources and cleverness. Her only clear thought was that she must not leave Clifford alone. He might come around and break the silk ribbons. In that case, he might need shooting after all.

"You can't walk any distance, Jo," Dovey said practically. "Not all roughed up as you are. Stay put here on the step; we'll wait until some farmer or cart driver happens by, and send them for help."

"You're right, I suppose," Jo said.

Then she leaned her head against Sophronia's shoulder and wept with a pain Dovey felt throbbing in her own heart. Dovey settled on Jo's other side and took her hand, stroking it, kissing the cool, slender fingers.

"I'm sorry, Sophie," Dovey said quietly. "I don't think we'll make it to Olympia tomorrow morning."

They waited on the porch for at least three hours. The excitement of their evening had long since drained away into despair. Dovey knew that they could catch a boat back to Seattle in the morning—providing Jo was in any shape at all to limp down the hill and through the town of Coupeville—but morning was still some long way off. She'd found a few quilts in a cedar trunk in the schoolhouse—Jo used them to bundle up the children on winter mornings, when the stove was too stubborn to light. Dovey tucked the quilts gently around her friends and settled down to wait out the night in watchful silence, always with one wary eye on Clifford, who drifted in and out of consciousness as the night wore on.

Finally, though, when Dovey had begun to nod with exhaustion, she saw the dim flicker of a lantern on the road, bobbing steadily up from the town of Coupeville.

"Look," she muttered, elbowing Jo in the ribs. "Look—somebody's coming!"

Dovey stumbled to her feet. The quilt fell away, and the chill of night hit her with its full force, making her teeth chatter and her skin prickle. She hurried across the schoolyard, waving her arms, calling out to whomever carried the light.

The lantern paused its swinging as the bearer halted. Then it came on quicker than before. As it drew near, Dovey could make out not one figure, but three—a trio of men pressing toward her from the darkness.

Dovey's breath caught in her throat, and her eyes stung with joyful tears. Even under the cloak of night, she recognized Virgil's stride, his stature, the alert turn of his head. Dovey ran across the road to meet him.

"Virgil! Oh, you found us! But how?"

Grinning, he handed the lantern to one of the other men, swept Dovey into his arms for a kiss, and then produced a crumpled piece of paper from his pocket. "Found this on the ground outside the corral, and my fastest horse missing."

Dovey examined the paper in the lantern's light. It was the note Jo had sent her.

"I knew exactly where you'd gone the moment I read it," Virgil explained. "You'd never leave Miss Carey in the lurch."

Dovey turned to the other two men. One, she recognized straightaway. "Harmon Grigg! You're here, too? I can't seem to believe it."

Virgil nodded. "When I hustled down to the docks to find a boat bound for Whidbey, I encountered Mr. Grigg there, beside himself with worry. It seems a few of the ladies at the house for fallen women spotted Miss Brandt climbing onto the back of a horse, riding double with another girl. I knew Miss Brandt must have gone with you."

Dovey laughed in delight. "What a stroke of luck." She peered at the third man—very tall and thinly built, with a neat black mustache and a cheerful face. But she did not recognize him. "And you—"

"Bill." Jo's voice cut across the darkness, laden with the weights of fear and regret—and rich with the timbre of love.

Jo limped into the circle of lantern light, leaning heavily on Sophronia's arm. Bill reached to embrace her; she buried her bruised face against his chest, shaking with silent sobs.

"There, there," Bill muttered. "Poor, sweet Jo. It's all over now. It's all over."

Sophronia shared a secretive glance with Dovey, raising one pale eyebrow in surprise.

Dovey took Virgil by the hand. "But how did you get to the island, and so late at night?"

"That was easy enough. I'd been collecting this very afternoon on one of the local shippers. When I realized I had the need to get to the island as quick as could be, I just returned to the man and gave him back all his taxes in exchange for a ride."

"Virgil! That's mighty bad of you."

"I'd say it was worth the risk," he chuckled. "And you keep your lips sealed, my huckleberry. What the Revenue Service doesn't know won't hurt me."

"Come back to the school and see what we've caught," Dovey said. "We don't quite know what to do with him."

When they returned to the porch with the men in tow, Clifford seemed to sense their presence through his daze. He groaned and stirred, then tested the bonds on his hands with a few experimental jerks. When he realized that he could not break free, he grunted in half-aware rage, then sagged back against the porch step.

Virgil bent with his lantern, examining the bright silk ribbons that bound Clifford's hands, the purple goose egg on the side of his head.

"You did a number on him, all right," Virgil said. "All by yourselves?"

"I don't see any men about, other than you," Dovey said.

Virgil landed a quick swat on her bottom, and heat flooded Dovey's cheeks. "I knew you were a tough one."

"Don't you forget it."

It didn't take long for Harmon and Virgil to locate the sheriff—it seemed the man became quite easy to find in the middle of the night, when he took to his bed. A police wagon arrived, its back high-walled and set with iron bars, and Virgil helped the yawning sheriff load Clifford in like a sack of growling potatoes.

The sheriff tipped his hat to Dovey and Sophronia. "Resourceful ladies, you two are. We'll handle this brute from here. He won't give you trouble again." Then he turned to Jo. "Miss Carey, I'll need to speak with you—to understand what all this fellow has put you through. It will help your case, when he faces a judge for sentencing."

Jo nodded and said meekly, "I understand." She could not meet Bill's eye, and Dovey squinted at the pair of them in the lantern light— Bill's concern obvious and tender, Jo shyly deflecting his touch, his gentle words. *She never told Bill that she's a married woman,* Dovey realized. *I wonder what he'll do when he sees how it all stands.*

Sophronia had been whispering apart with her minister, but she broke off and approached Virgil, twisting her hands nervously in the folds of her skirt. "Mr. Cooper, do you think the captain of your borrowed boat will be up for another journey tonight?"

"To where?" Virgil asked.

"To Olympia. I believe we can get there by the morning."

Dovey glanced down at her own rumpled and soiled dress, and patted her wild tangle of hair. "Just as we are? Sophie, you're mad!"

"Yes," Sophronia insisted. "This may be our last chance to convince the legislature to debate the bill again and reverse their decision of last November. We have to take the chance. If it means standing before the legislature just as we are, then so be it."

Still Dovey hesitated. She knew Sophronia had not given up her plan to deploy suffrage like a weapon, to strip Seattle's working women of their livelihoods. But as Dovey stood shuffling in the grass, Jo came forward and took Sophronia's hand.

"Let's do it," Jo said. "If suffrage has any hope left, this is it. The vote could change everything for us." She glanced toward the wagon, its iron bars gleaming dully in the starlight. "Everything."

Poor Jo—just look at her. Dovey bit her lip as she stared at Jo's blood-crusted lip, her shiner eye. *The vote might be the only thing that can get her out of this mess with Clifford and Bill.*

"All right," Dovey said. "I'll do it for you, Jo. Only let's get moving. Olympia is a long way off."

CHAPTER THIRTY-NINE
PROPER

It was Sophronia who led the way up the steps to the entrance of the Territorial Legislature Building. The man who guarded the door was not the same friendly fellow who had welcomed the suffragists with such enthusiasm months before. This man scowled at their bedraggled appearance, and huffed a short laugh of disbelief.

"We are expected," she said loftily.

The women had done their level best to put themselves to rights aboard the *Folly*, a small, rickety little steamer with one Spartan cabin that had let in the wind and damp the whole long way from Whidbey Island to Olympia. They had helped one another brush the dried mud from their dresses, but ample evidence of rough use still clung to their skirts and sleeves. They had smoothed one another's hair using only their fingers and a canteen of fresh water, and Sophronia and Dovey tenderly cleaned the blood from Jo's face. But there was nothing to be done about her bruises, which had grown more livid overnight.

When the *Folly* had docked in Olympia, two hours after sunrise, they'd helped Jo hobble down the ramp to the dock, and Bill gave her his arm to lean on as they made their way on foot toward the capitol building. But Jo and Bill had exchanged no words, as far as Sophronia could tell. She was tense with anxiety on Jo's part, and fearful they would miss their chance to speak despite all they'd done to reach Olympia on time.

The man on the door folded his arms and gave a grunt of skepticism. Sophronia was not inclined to be intimidated. She knew she belonged in that building—in the legislative chamber itself. With the deep, soul-soothing conviction of absolute righteousness, Sophronia knew she had come to the point of her mission at last. She would not be turned away now.

"Ms. Anthony is already presenting," the man told her. "You can't go into the chamber; you'll have to wait in the hall outside."

"Our presence is vital inside the chamber," Sophronia replied. "We must be admitted."

"Well, you won't be," the guard snarled. "The hall outside—and nowhere else."

He opened the door, and Sophronia swept inside, casting a dark glare over her shoulder at the guard. She led the way to the legislative chamber with the others trailing in her wake. She gestured for them to stay close, and found the door to the chamber guarded, as it was before.

"Good day," she muttered to the man on the door.

He tipped his hat, but as he took in the mud-stained, tattered women and their contingent of rough-looking men, his eyes turned wary.

"I wonder if you might tell me—" Sophronia began, but she did not finish her question. She leapt toward the man with sudden burst of energy, reaching for the handle of the door.

The man squawked in alarm and managed to catch hold of the door handle; he and Sophronia scrabbled madly for its mastery, both with teeth gritted and flashing eyes. Then Sophronia aimed a hard bump of her hip to the man's leg, sending him staggering to the side.

She shoved the chamber door open and, together with her companions, nearly tumbled inside. The Territory's lawmaking men sent up a collective mutter at the intrusion, and when they noted the women's obvious disarray—and Jo's sorry state—the mutter swelled to a clamor. Sophronia feared after all that she had erred—that their bedraggled look would turn the legislature off from their cause and spoil all the Suffrage Association's efforts.

But Susan Anthony and Abigail Duniway turned from their place at the chamber's head, where they had been addressing the assembly moments before. Susan gave Sophronia a smile of encouragement— subtle but warm—and Sophronia, her courage bolstered, glided down the aisle to join them.

Susan gestured toward Sophronia and her friends. "Here are three women from Seattle now. I shall yield the floor to them, gentlemen."

One of the men in the gallery scoffed. "Madam, it is an insult for your . . . *associates* to present themselves before the legislature in such a sorry state."

Sophronia felt Jo wither beside her, and even Dovey seemed to shrink from the venom in the man's voice. *My time has come to be as strong and brave as my friends. Lord, don't let me fail.* Sophronia stepped forward and lifted her chin before the assembly.

"I know our appearance is shocking," she said in a carrying, confident voice, "but we are better spokeswomen for the plight of females in Washington Territory as we are, stained and ragged, than we could ever be in the finest silks and velvets.

"Gentlemen, our hard-used state makes us fitting symbols of the trials women must endure when they haven't the shield of suffrage. We work and are taxed but must yield all our representation to our husbands—if we have any husband at all—and hope our interests are respected. Our property is not our own; we are left to choose between loneliness or destitution."

Sophronia reached for Jo's hand and tugged her gently forward. The chamber filled with murmurs of sympathy over her injuries.

"Without the vote," Sophronia said, "we suffer at the hands of those we cannot easily escape, because we lack autonomy under the law.

"And I assure you, gentlemen, that the men of the Territory also support suffrage—at least in Seattle, where they have joined us in our fight for the liberty of Woman."

Harmon, his hat clutched in his hands, raised his voice in agreement, and Sophronia's chest warmed with pride.

"Therefore, since men and women together work for a common goal, and believe in a common good, let there be no further delay. Bigelow's bill must be reconsidered; let us give all citizens of our territory the representation they deserve."

"You were marvelous," Susan said warmly as they exited the chamber together. "You are a natural leader, Sophronia. You should be pleased with your presentation today, no matter the outcome."

"And when will we know the outcome?"

They stepped outside the chamber; the guard Sophronia had so boorishly shoved aside gave her an injured stare, but she returned it with a smile as sweet as honey and breezed past him to the building's outer hall.

"I pray we'll have our answer by the end of the day," Susan said, "but laws have a nasty habit of taking their time with their making. We must hope for the best. Just now, that's all we can do."

Abigail Duniway drew close to Sophronia. "Your speech was lovely. I couldn't have done better myself. I watched the chamber as you spoke, and I saw many men nodding in agreement, and more who looked musing and thoughtful. You changed their hearts, I think."

"I?"

"Oh yes. It was certainly your words that swayed them."

Sophronia blushed. "Never. I am no great speaker—not like you and Susan."

"Oh, I disagree. You have a future in politics, I think, if we can only secure suffrage, and carve you a pathway in."

A future in politics. It was the least womanly occupation Sophronia could think of. She grinned at the thought. Certainly, speaking before the legislature was not a feminine pursuit—it was a thing entirely unsuited to a lady.

Yet it had felt good—*right*.

Sophronia gave Abigail a grateful smile. She pulled Jo and Dovey close, reveling in their nearness, in the sisterhood she could feel flowing between them, a strong, steady current, a warm rush of pride.

"Today I learned how to be a proper lady, in truth," she said.

Dovey wrinkled her nose, that familiar expression of curiosity. "The stuffy atmosphere in that chamber has gone to your head. What are you talking about, Sophie?"

But Sophronia only laughed and hugged Dovey all the tighter. Strength, solidarity, and loyalty—those were the traits of a proper woman. Dovey and Jo had taught her as much. The Lord knew it had taken Sophronia a long and weary time to learn the lesson, but she had puzzled it out at last.

CHAPTER FORTY
IF IT SUITS

The chapel bell made a joyful clamor, ringing among the treetops. Startled by the sound, a flock of pigeons burst into the sky. The birds scattered against a low bank of clouds and turned, soaring in a great arc down from the hill, toward the streets and alleys of Seattle far below. Jo closed her eyes and breathed deeply, reveling in the fresh bite of cedar in the crisp springtime air, the secretive green scent of wet foliage, the familiar sourness of seaweed rising on a wind from the tideflats. It was a beautiful day for a wedding. Jo could hear the promise of happiness in every toll of the church bell, could taste the salt of joyous tears on the Puget Sound breeze.

Sophronia, richly dressed in a gown of purple silk that shimmered in the diffuse glare of the overcast day, stepped carefully down the chapel's steps, one arm linked with Harmon's, the other cradling a bouquet of white roses. As custom demanded, the bride and groom stared straight ahead, refusing to make eye contact with their guests, who now whistled and hooted as if trying to drown out the ringing of the bell.

But Jo could see the happy flush on Sophronia's cheeks, the smile she tried in vain to hide. When Sophronia gave in and laughed with joy, Jo cheered as loudly as the rest of the wedding guests and tossed her handful of rice into the air.

She pulled a handkerchief from her sleeve and dabbed away a tear as Harmon helped Sophronia into their waiting carriage. Sophronia turned as the carriage pulled away from the church, waving gaily, and tossed her bouquet into the air. A few young women shrieked in delight and scampered into the lane, playfully tugging at one another, each hoping to tear off a white rose of her own, to gather in some of the bride's good fortune.

"What, now you won't run after the bouquet?"

Jo turned, tucking her kerchief away again. "Dovey! I didn't see you at the wedding ceremony."

She blinked in surprise at the sight of her friend, decked in a deep-red satin nearly as sumptuous as the bride's gown. Her dark curls were piled high on her head and topped with a stylish felt hat, pinned at a saucy angle. Dovey's black-gloved hand was laced lightly through her father's arm.

Wonders never cease, Jo thought. *Who ever would have suspected Dovey Mason to reconcile with her father?*

"Mr. Mason," Jo stammered hurriedly. "How good of you to come to the wedding."

He gave a short, huffing laugh. He seemed nearly as surprised to be here with his wild daughter as Jo was to see the two together. "It was a lovely ceremony," Mr. Mason said. "Full of feeling. I confess, it took me back to my own wedding day, so many years ago."

"You'll be seeing your blushing bride again soon," Dovey told him, giving his arm a little squeeze.

Jo raised her brows. "Will you?"

"Father and I are heading back to Boston in a few days. We'll bring Mother home to Seattle. And wouldn't you know, Jo, both my brothers have agreed to come to Seattle, too, with their wives and children! Oh, it will be lovely to have the family together again."

"That's grand, Dovey!" She leaned close to her friend and whispered, "And your . . . *venture?* Do you still plan to open your own establishment?"

Dovey winked. Her dimples flashed in a quick, mischievous grin. "You'll just have to wait and see, Josephine Carey. Don't be shocked if I take Seattle by storm one of these days. But first things first: Mother is waiting. And I'm so glad to see her again."

She let go of her father's arm and retrieved the little beaded purse that hung from her waistband. "Look here," she said, reaching inside and withdrawing a handful of glittering things. She picked delicately at chains of gold and teardrop earrings, holding each one up for Jo to admire. "I've bought Mother some new jewels—ten times better than the ones I took from her all those years before. Do you think she'll like them, Jo?"

Jo wrapped her arm around Dovey's waist and squeezed, resting her head for a moment on the girl's shoulder. "I'm sure she'll love them, you dear, funny thing."

"Darling," Mr. Mason said to his daughter, "we really ought to pack for the journey. Let's get home to that husband of yours and see that he has everything in order."

"Virgil *does* know how to run a business, Father," Dovey scolded. "The taxes will all be collected *and* your sawmill will run like clockwork while we're in Boston. Don't fret." Dovey snapped her purse shut and grabbed Jo in a hug so sudden that Jo gave a little cry of surprise. "Dear Jo, I'm so happy. Remember the day we first met?"

"I certainly do," Jo said. "You were a skinny, bedraggled runaway with a ripped-up dress and a pillowcase slung over your shoulder. Look how far you've come: you're an admirable woman now, Dovey—confident and strong. And I'm so proud to call you my friend."

Dovey planted an enthusiastic kiss on Jo's cheek. She reached surreptitiously for her kerchief again, afraid that in a moment she'd well with fresh tears.

"Three Mercer girls, tossed out into the wild, cruel wilderness," Dovey said. "Who would have thought our stories would turn out like this?"

"Like what?"

Dovey grinned. "Happily ever after." She hooked her arm with her father's once more. "We really must be off now. But, Jo, we'll see you when we return from Boston. You'll come meet my mother, won't you?"

"Of course. Travel safely, Dovey—Mr. Mason."

Jo watched them stroll down the hill toward Seattle, arm in arm. The glow of warmth she felt at seeing Dovey and her father reconciled slowly gave way to a pang of sadness. *Happily ever after.* Jo sighed. *Not quite.* She had received a telegram the night before from the suffrage association in Olympia. The bill had failed again, despite the efforts of all the suffrage groups in the territory—and in spite of the continued support of Susan Anthony and Abigail Duniway.

And yet, Jo could not feel entirely despondent over the setback. Each time they faced the lawmakers in Olympia—each voting man they reached with their message, every penny they collected to fund the effort—brought them closer to victory.

We will have it, Jo told herself stoutly. *We'll have victory—equality—freedom.* It was only a matter of time before the tide turned, and until it did, Jo would continue the fight.

She walked slowly down the hill toward town, arms folded, eyes turned down, entirely lost in her thoughts. In her mind, Jo ordered fresh plans for the Suffrage Association, prepared for the next bout with the legislature, and braced herself for another long battle. She was so tangled in her musings that at first she did not notice the feet stepping along beside hers, covering the ground with a long, easy stride. But once she became aware of that familiar, easy gait, the swing of his long arms, Jo looked up at him and smiled.

"Bill Jakes. Where did you come from?"

"I tried to make it up for the wedding, but my boat was delayed. I only caught the tail end of the fight over the bride's bouquet." He gave a low whistle. "Ladies sure do fight mean when there's something at stake."

"We're *persistent*, not mean," Jo chided gently, still wrapped in concerns over suffrage.

"I don't know. I'm pretty sure I witnessed some hair pulling back there on the chapel lawn, and maybe some scratching and kicking, too. That counts as mean by my reckoning."

Jo laughed. "I'm glad you found me. I have good news." She pulled a letter from her pocket and waved it under Bill's nose. "Clifford's trial is over, and he'll be in jail for a *very* long time. I don't think he'll get out before he faces the final judgment."

Bill's eyes lit eagerly. "That is good news."

"That's not the best of it. He wrote me, Bill—and he's agreed to the divorce. He's willing to let me go."

Bill's whoop of glee rang across the hillside. He wrapped his long arms around Jo's waist and twirled her around and around in the middle of the road, until the green tunnel of trees spun dizzily around her and she was breathless with laughter.

"Put me down, you brute!"

"Jo, I've never had such welcome news! You're free now—free to live however your heart directs."

She gazed into Bill's eyes—his dear, familiar eyes, as full of love and hope as they had ever been.

Bill lifted her hands and kissed each one, his lips lingering against her skin until her heart beat hard and fast.

"My love," he said, gazing up from where he bent over her hand, "if I ask you one more time to marry me, will you say yes?"

A current of joy rose within her heart, lifting her soul on madly, gladly beating wings. She gave Bill a little laugh, wordless in the warmth of her bliss.

"Will you?" Bill pressed, and kissed her hand again.

Jo shook her head until the tears spilled from the corners of her eyes. "No," she finally managed, still chuckling. "No, darling!"

Bill straightened with an uncertain smile. "You won't?"

"I won't!" She wrapped her arms around his neck and pulled him close, pressing her cheek to his, content for a moment just to feel his heart beating against her breast. "I like my life just the way it is, Bill— *our* life. I don't want to change a thing about it. Not one single thing. I don't care who thinks less of me, or who judges me a fallen women. I'm *happy* with you—just the way we are."

Bill shrugged, and pulled Jo closer still. His lips found her cheek, and he pressed a kiss to her, so long and reverent that it stole her breath away.

"Well, shucks," he whispered in her ear. "That makes proper sense to me. And if it suits you best, it suits me, too."

Jo eased out of his embrace. The cedar boughs arching overhead blurred with her joyful tears, but when she blinked them away, the sun broke through the blanket of clouds in a golden stream. Bright, warm light spilled down over Seattle, over the great, blue-gray expanse of the bay, the rich emerald green of the hills, and the high mountains beyond.

"Happily ever after," Jo whispered, and slipped her hand into Bill's.

HISTORICAL NOTE AND
AUTHOR'S REMARKS

Seattle has a more entertaining and shocking history than most American cities can boast of. My interest in Seattle's rowdy, Wild West origins began with the enthusiasm of my husband, Paul. Like me, Paul is a great fan of history, and his particular area of interest is the founding and early decades of his hometown (and the city where we happily lived together for the first five years of our relationship).

When we lived in Seattle, Paul would organize regular outings, which he called Seattle Days. He would lead a group of friends on a walking tour of the city's historic neighborhoods, pointing out locations where exciting and obscure bits of history had played out in the distant past. Seattle Days always included a visit to the top of the Smith Tower (once the tallest building west of the Mississippi; now dizzyingly dwarfed by modern skyscrapers), and Paul would gleefully inform all attendees of his tour that the plaque outside the entrance to the beautiful white Art Deco building was incorrect: the Smith Tower was not named for one of the founders of the Smith & Wesson firearm company, as the monument asserts, but for the founder of the Smith Premier Typewriter Company.

Paul's trek through Seattle's history always concluded with his favorite attraction: an *official* tour of the Underground, a collection of subterranean streets and sidewalks beneath the Pioneer Square neighborhood—an eerie, damp warren of bricked-up shop fronts, disused bank vaults, and abandoned bars, all cast in the smoky-violet light of weak sun filtering through the purple, magnesium-glass skylights that patchwork Seattle's sidewalks. The Underground represents the last remains of the original city (version 1.0 was destroyed in a spectacular fire in 1889; Paul will fill you in on every last detail of the event if you're curious).

On every Seattle Day, I would walk the increasingly familiar route of the Underground, listening to the tour guide speak about the city's early days. I'd listen just as much to Paul as he whispered plenty of supplemental history into my ear, expounding on the guide's speech, which was always rather truncated for time—or edited in the name of family friendliness.

One of my favorite parts of the Underground/Paul tour was the story of Asa Shinn Mercer's initial expedition to the eastern states.

In 1864, Mercer noted that the newborn city of Seattle was home to ten men for every woman—and most of those women were prostitutes, who capitalized on the unbalanced demographics to earn their fortunes far faster than they could in more established localities. Mercer hoped that brides of "true character" would appease the overwhelmingly masculine population of young Seattle, tempt the men into domestic life, and bring some much-needed order and civility to this rowdy frontier town.

He did manage to bring back a boatload of women—though far fewer than he'd hoped. And those intrepid, plucky Mercer girls, trying to make their way in the pit of mud and vice that was early Seattle, stuck in my imagination. For years I intended to write a novel about them—*someday*. But neither Victorian-era American society nor the western frontier were my fortes, so I continued to work with settings and themes that felt more natural to me: ancient history and American Indian cultures.

Then, in April of 2015, I went out to lunch with Jodi Warshaw, my editor at Lake Union Publishing. We had just finished the rather strenuous edits on my novel about Empress Zenobia, *Daughter of Sand and Stone*. It was time to discuss my next project for Lake Union, but Jodi didn't seem terribly keen on any of the ancient history or Indian stories I pitched.

Finally she said, "You know what I'd really love to find—from you or from any of my authors? A story about really plucky, pioneering women going out into a rowdy, western frontier town and just making it theirs—really coming to *own* it."

All at once, I remembered the Mercer girls. I was so excited that I nearly jumped out of my seat, and as I filled Jodi in on some of Seattle's earliest history—and the fascinating part women played in the city's founding—I could tell that we had finally found an idea that appealed to us both. That weekend, I wrote the official proposal and outline for *Mercer Girls* and sent it off to Lake Union.

It was during the writing of the proposal that I experienced a rare and very welcome stroke of *insanely* good luck. Via a chain of twisty Google searches, I found myself with the contact information of Peri Muhich, a historian from Camas, Washington, whose exhaustive knowledge of Asa Mercer's two expeditions to New England—and of the women who chose to come with him to Seattle—was nothing short of astounding.

Peri enthusiastically agreed to meet with Paul and me for lunch, so that I could ply her with questions about the Mercer girls and about the cultural and political climate of Seattle during the 1860s and 1870s. Paul and I trekked down to Vancouver, Washington, just across the Oregon border, where we met Peri and then proceeded to gleefully spread Mercer girl photos and documents over more square footage of the local Applebee's than our dining table occupied. Over the years, Peri had assembled a stunning array of artifacts and documents pertaining to the Mercer girls, including all of the novels that had previously been written on the subject (none of them published more recently than the early 1990s, and all of which she very kindly loaned to me).

Three history buffs going into full geek-out mode apparently make for a real spectacle; other diners and several of the restaurant's staff wandered over to look at Peri's beautiful mounted portraits of many of the Mercer girls, and to listen as she answered my questions about the expedition and about the character and motives of Asa Mercer and the women he accompanied to the West.

Peri advised me to use caution in my depiction of the expedition and its participants. From the mid-twentieth century through the 1980s, the Mercer girls were a fairly popular source for historical fiction and historical romance (and inspired the 1968 to 1970 television series *Here Come the Brides*), but they were not always depicted in the most flattering light. Many of the girls and Asa Mercer still have relatives living in and around Seattle, and they take their affiliation with history quite seriously, even holding regular reunions. The descendants of the Mercer girls take exception to seeing their foremothers depicted as prostitutes or women of otherwise questionable morals—and rightfully so. My discussions with Peri and perusal of her documents convinced me that the women who joined Mercer's two expeditions were in no way "fallen women." I certainly had no intention of portraying them as anything but moral, upstanding people, because that's exactly what I believe all the Mercer girls were. After all, the one thing Seattle did not lack for in those days was prostitutes. As one of my characters in this novel says, if Asa Mercer had been seeking to fill the brothels, he wouldn't have had to go all the way to New England to do so!

My original plan for this novel was to feature one real-life Mercer girl in particular, but after considering Peri's advice and her experience with Mercer descendants, I decided instead to invent three fictional women as my main characters. Josephine and Dovey are based heavily on a few real women from both of Mercer's expeditions, but Sophronia is a whole-cloth invention. However, her rigid ideals and dedication to "moralizing" the city were typical attitudes shared by many upstanding women of Seattle, whether they came to the city already married to the town's founding fathers, or whether they arrived in one of Mercer's two expeditions.

Although I pulled interesting facts about various Mercer girls to create Jo's and Dovey's stories, no reader should interpret either Jo or Dovey as attempts to depict any real, historical woman. Jo and Dovey are ultimately just as fictitious as Sophronia: truly inventions of my imagination, with only a few biographical details lifted from the life stories of real women, simply because those details are fascinating and fun.

Jo's creation was most heavily influenced by the biography of Lizzie Ordway—the woman I'd originally intended to be the central figure of this novel. Ordway had an amazing life. She was the oldest woman who traveled with Asa Mercer—thirty-five years old at the time of the first expedition. Highly educated and an accomplished teacher of languages (and many other subjects, one assumes), she seems to have come to Seattle with professional rather than matrimonial motives.

Ordway quickly settled into her new life, first taking up as a teacher at Coupeville on Whidbey Island, then moving to Kitsap County on Washington's peninsula, where she opened and established new schools to meet the needs of a rapidly growing population. Ordway gained true fame among the teachers of Washington Territory when she managed to settle and reform the notoriously rowdy Port Gamble student body. Port Gamble's children, about whom she had been thoroughly warned, left her "agreeably disappointed" when she found that they came "readily under discipline." She wrote of her hopes to "arouse ambition in them to redeem themselves, and to feel a love for and an interest in their studies."

Later in her life, in 1881, Ordway successfully ran for Kitsap County's superintendent position. She continued to win elections to the post for the next eight years, and was highly regarded throughout her career, and long after her death in 1897.

The same drive and confidence that gave Ordway the ability to reform the Port Gamble school made her a success in the women's suffrage movement. She dedicated a significant portion of her working hours to the cause and developed a close and trusting relationship with Susan B. Anthony. In fact, Ordway joined Anthony on her speaking tour of western cities and even appeared at her side during a key 1871 speech in Seattle. She also accompanied Anthony and Abigail Duniway to Olympia on October 19, 1871. On that fateful date, Susan B. Anthony became the first woman in American history to address lawmakers in session.

Although only Anthony spoke on that occasion, the chamber was so crowded with male and female observers that the crowd spilled over into the lobby outside. I'm afraid the scene was very different from the way I depicted it in this novel—but I wanted to stress the underdog status of the suffragists by painting a very particular, metaphorical picture: a small handful of women standing up against a vast chamber full of men, those lawmakers imbued with the power of ceremony that ensured the females present remained outsiders.

Of all the women who came to Seattle with Asa Mercer, Lizzie Ordway was the only one who never married. Her reasons for remaining single were apparently not recorded. Perhaps she was wholly committed to her career in education—and to her activism as a suffragist—and had no time or attention for a husband. Perhaps she was considered already "too old" to marry when she arrived in Seattle at the age of thirty-five, and so had no suitors. Perhaps she preferred the company of women, and turned all male suitors away. Whatever her reasons, she remained single but active in the school systems and in various women's leagues until her old age.

Lizzie Ordway's work with Anthony and Duniway was key in the suffrage movement. Ordway was a major force in making Washington the third territory to grant women the vote, just after Utah and Wyoming. None of the states had yet seen the sense of suffrage, but in 1883, after many attempts to pass the bill, Washington Territory's legislature finally enacted full suffrage for women. (Black men had received the right to vote in Washington in 1869; with the passage of the 1883 bill, Washington Territory became the first place in America where black women cast their ballots.)

Washington Territory revoked women's suffrage just five years later. Sophronia may be a fictional character, but she had many real-life counterparts—and once they'd gained the vote, Washington's upstanding women, including many of the Mercer girls, quickly used their newfound political power to outlaw prostitution, gambling, and liquor.

Unfortunately for the women who worked so hard to gain a political voice, the practical ramifications of obliterating vice were more than Seattle could handle. Although the lumber mills were booming, it is no exaggeration to say that the city's economy truly hinged on prostitution, gambling, and liquor. Once vice became illegal, the economy of the largest city in the Territory crashed, and the men who ran Olympia panicked. They revoked the female vote in 1888, instead upholding their 1871 decree that Washington women would not achieve the vote until and unless it became a Federal mandate.

And that's how Dovey found her way into this book.

Despite my conviction that the Mercer girls were certainly *not* prostitutes, I wanted to include in this novel a discussion of how relevant prostitution was to this developing city—and the conflicted place it held in the minds of American women in the nineteenth century. If the elimination of that particular vice was enough to send lawmakers into a vote-revoking panic, then clearly the oldest profession couldn't be left out of this story.

But prostitution in the West was much more than just an economic issue. The profession didn't just generate funds for growing cities and territories; it also represented one of the very few viable (if frowned upon) means for a woman to support herself. Women who wanted to earn their own keep—or who had no choice but to do so—had a very small handful of options. They might teach, midwife, care for others' homes and children, operate a laundry, or work in a restaurant. A very small number of them might break into jobs usually reserved for men, but only if the stars aligned just so.

By far the easiest line of work to enter and keep was the world's oldest profession. It was also the most lucrative work available to women, particularly in a town of early Seattle's demographics. Sure, the work demanded that a woman live with heavy stigmatization, but for many of them, the pros far outweighed the cons. Men in Seattle were so plentiful and so starved for female affection that throughout the city's early history, many of its most well-off citizens were prostitutes, or the female owners of brothels.

In Seattle, prostitution provided women with autonomy and power as well as a steady income. In the nineteenth century, when women were fighting for equal citizenship, the freedom that came from earning a good living of one's own was a precious thing. I realized that I couldn't tell the story of women's history in early Seattle without delving into the prostitution issue, so I gave one of my fictional Mercer girls an aspiration to run her own brothel, with the hope that it didn't tread too close to an accusation that any *real* Mercer girl was involved with such sordid affairs. In those days, operating an "establishment" was a viable career choice for an enterprising woman, and it would have opened the door to wealth, political power, and social clout.

But of course, no upstanding citizen of Seattle approved of the night flowers, in brothels or outside of them. Newspapers of the time printed vociferous oppositions to Asa Mercer's first expedition; many who objected did so on the grounds that the only sort of single woman who would come to Seattle must be one of *those* types, and the town already had plenty of fallen women, thank you very much!

I wanted Dovey in this book so that she could represent the other side of the Seattle story. The upstanding, highly moral women who fought for suffrage were fascinating and admirable, but their ends were ultimately at odds with the interests of many female citizens. After all, as Dovey points out in this novel, Seattle's prostitutes were women, too, and their livelihoods depended on a maintenance of vice. I felt I couldn't tell the story of historic Seattle women without giving equal representation to the "seamstresses" who made its economy run.

But again, I must stress that Dovey is pure fiction. I colored her character with the intriguing tints and shades of two real-life Mercer girls, but nothing about her—especially her interest in prostitution—is representative of any real woman.

Annie May Adams was a girl of sixteen when she boarded the *Illinois* in New York City, intending to travel to San Francisco. But once she got to know Asa Mercer and the women who traveled with him, she decided to continue on to Seattle. I took Annie's age, adventuresome spirit, self-determination, and interest in San Francisco and applied them to Dovey, but they are, of course, only surface features.

The other Mercer girl who added some of her gloss to Dovey's facade was Anna Peebles.

Anna and her sister, Libbie (whom I especially admire for her ability to spell her name correctly), were members of Asa Mercer's second expedition, which left New York City in January of 1866, arriving in Seattle on May 28.

The second expedition was a success in some respects and a failure in others. Mercer did manage to find more women willing to accompany him to Seattle—he returned with thirty-four single women, more than triple his 1864 cargo of eleven. But he was still far short of his goal.

This time around, he'd hoped to bring home a whopping *seven hundred women*.

How could he dare to hope for such an extravagant success? On this second expedition, Mercer's hopes hinged on convincing the United States government to fund the expedition itself, as well as a sort of promotional campaign to encourage single young women to set out for the West. He might have been able to achieve that lofty goal, too. Apparently he'd befriended Abraham Lincoln, and was scheduled to meet with the president on April 16, 1865, to discuss the importance of the expedition and how best to fund it. But of course, the president was assassinated on the night of April 15.

Mercer remained in the East for several months, scraping together as many women as he could. As with his first expedition, at least a few of them saw themselves as career girls, not brides-to-be. Anna and Libbie Peebles were tempted by the promised salary of seventy-five dollars per month for teachers, and had no interest in marriage. Anna wrote snappishly in her diary that Mercer "wanted to arrange plans for us."

Anna did not consider herself to be a Mercer girl. Dead set on working rather than finding a husband, she dissociated herself from the Mercer party and wrote of how one Mrs. Garfield "occupied herself in making slighting remarks about the Mercer party before me, believing me to be one of them." (One can see here the inspiration for Mrs. Garfield's unfriendly reception of my Mercer girls.)

Somehow, Anna Peebles was unable to land a position as a teacher. Instead, her host family helped her find work as a deputy collector for the Revenue Service, which paid the monthly seventy-five dollars she sought. It was an unusual job for a woman. Anna rode about the Territory on horseback, collecting taxes and debts for two years, before finally ending up in both the teaching position she'd originally wanted and in the marriage she'd avoided. She and her sister, Libbie, both worked for the suffrage cause, and Anna hosted Susan Anthony for dinner in November of 1871, when the first campaign for the suffrage bill was afoot. Anna remained involved with Anthony's campaigns, and appeared to have a friendly relationship with the famous suffragist.

One can see shades of Dovey in Anna's biography.

As I researched the real women who would inform the development of my fictional characters, I was struck by one repeating theme in historic papers and journals. So many of Seattle's upstanding women were vehemently opposed to both of Mercer's expeditions. Exactly *why* was never made clear—at least, not as far as I could discern. It was obvious that some of Seattle's citizens thought the Mercer girls to be prostitutes, or at least woman of low moral character who might take to prostitution at the first opportunity. But some detractors seemed to be motivated by envy. This anonymous diatribe was published in the *Seattle Gazette* on May 17, 1864—the day the Mercer girls arrived.

> THE BEST SORT—The buxom, bright-eyed, full-breasted, bouncing lass, who can darn a stocking, mend trowsers, make her own frock, command a regiment of pots and kettles, feed the pigs, milk the cows, and be a lady withal, in company, is just the sort of a girl for a young man to marry; but you, ye pining, lolling, screwed-up, wasp-waisted, putty-faced, consumption-mortgaged and novel-devouring daughters of fashion and idleness, you are no more fit for matrimony than a pullet is to look after a family of fifteen chickens.

Although this colorful rant was not directed at the Mercer girls specifically, there is little doubt as to its intended target. It illustrates the vitriol these women faced as they attempted to settle into a divided society, and paints a clear picture of the state of Seattle's social mind in the mid-nineteenth century.

It's also rather amusing. My editor Jodi encouraged me to work it into the novel, as bits of ephemera like this one always bring color and flavor to historical fiction. I borrowed some of its inventive language for the scene where Mrs. Garfield "welcomes" the ladies to Seattle.

The presumption that the Mercer girls were women of poor character has clung to them over the decades—and a tarnish has fallen over Asa Shinn Mercer, too. Some accounts of his day were unfavorable, and painted him as a layabout or worse, though I think it's worth noting that all negative depictions of Mercer date from his second expedition, when he was surely reeling from the death of his friend Abraham Lincoln as much as from the catastrophic financial failure of his mission. History has been unkind to this bright, hardworking young man, remembering him as a depressed drunkard with shifty morality. He may have been depressed in early 1866, but there is no good evidence that he ever comported himself poorly, and the mere fact that he went to great effort and expense to seek "true women" for Washington Territory speaks highly of his moral character. I would prefer that history remember Asa Mercer for the man he really was. He was a forward thinker, self-motivated and altruistic, willing to look for creative solutions to the serious social problems that faced the town he loved. He founded the college that eventually became the University of Washington, which is consistently rated in the top twenty universities in the world. His legacy is an admirable one.

The forty-five women Asa Mercer guided to Seattle were of equal character—intrepid, high-minded, and dedicated to the cause of suffrage. Each of them came to Seattle for reasons of her own, but each of them made significant and fascinating contributions to the history of Washington and the United States.

I hope this novel has done justice to their legacy.

My key research sources were as follows: personal interviews with Washington State historian Peri Muhich; the Washington State Historical Society's Women's History Consortium and Women in

Washington collections; the research website of the Mercer Girls chapter of the Daughters of the American Revolution (SeattleMercerGirls. com); the secretary of state's Legacy Washington website, which provided access to the historic newspaper *Seattle Gazette*; and the University of Oregon's Historic Oregon Newspapers collection, which provided access to the *New Northwest* and an abundance of information about the suffrage movement in the region. Details of historic homes in Seattle, and the families who lived in them, were provided by the website of Seattle historian and author Paul Dorpat (PaulDorpat.com). To gain general knowledge of historic Seattle, I turned to the nonfiction books *Skid Road: An Informal Portrait of Seattle* by Murray Morgan; *Doc Maynard: The Man Who Invented Seattle* by William C. Speidel; *Sons of the Profits* by William C. Speidel; and *Boren's Block One: A Sinking Ship* by Sidney S. Andrews.

For readers wishing to learn more about the real Mercer girls, I confidently direct you to Peri Muhich's website, MercerGirls.com. There, Peri has shared a truly amazing wealth of information about Asa Mercer and the women who traveled with him. You'll also find a list of several other novels, written in decades past, each giving a different take on the Mercer girls.

My sincere thanks are due to my acquisitions editor at Lake Union, Jodi Warshaw, who lit the fire under my seat to write this book. Thanks as well to Dorothy Zemach, my developmental editor, whose input made this book much stronger and more exciting. Thanks to Michelle Hope Anderson, my copy editor at Lake Union, who soldiered through all the em dashes. Thanks to the readers who have supported my career, and who expressed such excitement to read *Mercer Girls* whenever I mentioned the book on social media throughout its development and writing.

Thank you to the excellent guides of Bill Speidel's Underground Tour, who bring history so vividly to life. If you are ever in Seattle, reader, I encourage you to take the Underground Tour and immerse yourself in Seattle's unique and wonderful history. Remember to tip your tour guide.

My ultimate thanks and bottomless love to Paul Harnden, my husband. Every word I write is for him.

—*L. H.*

Friday Harbor, WA, 2015

ABOUT THE AUTHOR

Photo Credit © Paul Harnden 2014

Libbie Hawker writes historical and literary fiction featuring complex characters, with rich details of time and place. She is the author of eleven novels and lives in the beautiful San Juan Islands with her husband. Find more information about this author at LibbieHawker.com.